ARMY BLUE

Also by Lucian K. Truscott IV
Dress Gray

ARMY BLUE

Lucian K. Truscott IV

Crown Publishers, Inc.
New York

Grateful acknowledgment is given for the following: On page 3, lyrics from "All Along the Watchtower," by Bob Dylan. Copyright 1968 by Dwarf Music. All rights reserved. International copyright secured. Reprinted by permission. On page 13, lyrics from "Purple Haze," by Jimi Hendrix. Copyright 1967 Bella Godiva Music, Inc. Worldwide administration Don Williams Music Group. Used by permission. On page 81, lyrics from "Do You Love Me?" by Berry Gordy. Copyright © June 1962 by Jobete Music Co., Inc. Used by permission. On page 88, lyrics from "Tighten Up," by Archie Bell and Billy Buttier. Copyright © 1968 by Cotillion Music, Inc. and Orellia Publishing Co. All rights reserved. Used by permission. On page 91, lyrics from "The Letter," by Wayne Carson. Copyright © 1967 by Sebanine Music, Inc. All rights administered by Warner-Tamerlane Publishing Corp. All rights reserved. Used by permission.

Published by Crown Publishers, Inc., 201 East 50th Street New York, New York 10022

CROWN is a trademark of Crown Publishers, Inc.
Manufactured in the United States of America
Library of Congress Cataloging-in-Publication Data
Truscott, Lucian K.,
    Army blue / Lucian K. Truscott.
       p.   cm.
    1. Vietnamese Conflict, 1961–1975—Fiction. I. Title.
PS3570.R86A76   1989   89-1245
813′.54—dc19   CIP

ISBN 0-517-57384-9
10 9 8 7 6 5 4 3 2 1
First Edition

For Carolyn Stephens Truscott

And for
Anne Harloe Truscott
Col. Lucian K. Truscott III, U.S.A. (Ret.)

In memory of
Sarah Randolph Truscott
Gen. Lucian K. Truscott, Jr., U.S.A.

The truth is in motion.
The truth is emotion.
J.L.

The truth is sometimes found not in what was,
but rather in what might have been.
D.H.V.

With pipe and song we'll jog along,
Till this short time is through,
And all among our jovial throng,
Have donned the Army Blue.

"Army Blue"

O N E

"Whatchew Gonna Dew, Eltee?"

Firebase Zulu-Foxtrot
Day One

He flipped a switch in the dark and next to him a transistor radio crackled and an announcer's voice muled enthusiastically and noise shattered the dim red air of the M-113 armored personnel carrier.

Tall trees crashed to the ground somewhere deep in the woods, crushing one another like God's dominoes.

A thousand tank treads crunched through gravel, chewing rocks into wet dust and spitting it sideways.

Three two-barrel carburetors blew flutter valves wide open and screamed in the night, sucking wind and gasoline in second gear.

Bald tires tore into wet blacktop, burning, screeching, blowing smoke, yowling in the dark.

It was Jimi Hendrix, but it sounded like the war.

> *"There must be some way out of here,*
> *Said the joker to the thief,*
> *There's too much confusion, I can't get no relief."*

Somehow, it all had to mean something. The music had to mean something. The war had to mean something. He could feel it, the war snapping at his tired bones. He could hear it barking out there beyond the perimeter. It was their country, Vietnam was. It was their war. They all knew something he didn't know. They all believed in something he didn't believe in. They were fighting a war neither he nor his men wanted to fight. What was left to him crackled through the transistor speaker and asked him questions he couldn't answer and told him things he couldn't understand. Rock and roll spat the jerky electronic language of war. It organized the senseless noise of the killing. In red bursts of brush-made electrons and pealing protons, it told you secrets furtively in the dark. It banged on your head and it screeched in your ears: They're out there waiting for you, the cries of the living and the songs of the dead. They are waiting on your fear. They know it's coming. They are waiting for you to fuck up and they won't leave you alone. Not now.

Never.

Lieutenant Matthew Nelson Blue IV was stretched out on an air mattress laid on a layer of sandbags that covered the aluminum floor of his M-113 armored personnel carrier. He was studying the 113's ceiling, a bewildering maze of electrical conduits and hydraulic piping that converged on the firewall behind his head. The firewall was a half-inch sheet of welded aluminum that separated the troop-carrying compartment of the 113 from its engine and driver's compartment. Overhead, a twelve-watt red lightbulb shone dimly inside of a rattrap wire cage, bathing the dusty interior of the 113 with an eerie rosy glow.

The Lieutenant was lying there on his back, fingers laced behind his head, staring at the ceiling of the 113 and listening to the radio and thinking about the war. He couldn't remember how or why he got where he was right this minute. One day he applied for admission to West Point, and the next day he was on his way to war. It was a logical progression, but it didn't make sense. He wasn't "for" the war, exactly, but neither was he "against" the war. His brother had fought in Vietnam and so had his father and now he was holding down his own little piece of Vietnamese real estate, and while your own flesh and blood was at risk, you had better "believe the bullshit" about the war, as they said at West Point, or you were lost.

That was the weird thing. He hadn't "believed the bullshit" they fed you at West Point about the war in Vietnam. The domino theory. The war against "communist aggression." "Making the world safe for democracy." All of the bullshit West Point put out about the war hung around your shoulders and fell from your waist like an ill-fitting uniform. He wasn't even sure they actually expected you to believe the bullshit. It was as if the Academy—no, not just the Academy, the whole nation—was going through the motions one last time, the final throes of trying to come together before everything splintered apart, before the world, in essence, sounded like Jimi Hendrix.

So he was lying there on his back listening to Hendrix wring the sounds of havoc from his guitar and wondering if he should change the end of the letter he'd just written to his girlfriend back home in Virginia. He hadn't been in the best of moods when he wrote the letter. Just that morning the platoon had been ordered to pack up and deploy to a new location, thirty kliks due south of Bong Mieu. It had taken all day to make the move, and the platoon had only two hours of light before it got dark to dig in a new night defensive perimeter. It was the third such move they'd made in a week, every one of them no less than twenty miles down unsecured dirt roads and jungle paths with no air cover and only token artillery support. The Lieutenant didn't want to frighten his girlfriend unnecessarily, and he was afraid the last page of his letter, railing and screeching about the three extraneous redeployments they'd made, would do exactly that.

Lieutenant Blue was twenty-three years old. He stood five feet ten inches. He had brown hair and the features of a high school quarterback, an intense, eager look that had nothing to do with enthusiasm and everything to do with fear and loneliness. He was the platoon leader, and there was only one of them. He was always worried about something: about the letter, about the enemy, about the redeployments, about the dark. He didn't want to sound as afraid as he felt. Usually the letters he wrote her consisted of long, windy lists of what they were going to do together when his tour of duty in Vietnam was up, exactly 131 days from now. But tonight he had complained about the redeployments and complained at length about the recent arrival of the new battalion commander, a Lieutenant Colonel Henson W. Halleck, an individual with whom the Lieutenant was only too well acquainted.

Lieutenant Blue and Halleck, who was then a major, had taken an immediate and total disliking to each other the day they met, about a year ago, when the Lieutenant was a student in Halleck's class at the Infantry School at Fort Benning, Georgia. Halleck was teaching a class about the so-called rules of engagement in Vietnam, the code that dictated what you could and could not do in combat over there. He had finished describing the concepts of the "free-fire zone" and the "limited-fire zone," expressing his disgust with the fact that nowhere but in a free-fire zone could you call in artillery fire on a hamlet or village, even if you were taking fire from the village, even if that fire had wounded or killed one of your men.

Then he had chuckled and said, "Yeah, but we all know what bullshit the rules of engagement are, don't we?" and he had proceeded to instruct the class of impressionable young lieutenants on how you could get artillery fire anytime you wanted it, on any village you wanted it rained down on. All you had to do was drop off a couple of cases of beer and maybe a bottle of Scotch or three to the fire direction control sergeant in the artillery battery that was supporting you. The sergeant would then conveniently forget the map grid coordinates of any and all villages in the vicinity, and you could call in artillery fire on a village anytime you wanted.

Lieutenant Blue raised his hand.

"Sir, what you're telling us . . . are we supposed to ignore the rules of engagement? And if we do, sir, won't we be, in effect, breaking the law?"

Major Halleck chuckled and said, "You figure it out."

After class that day, he stopped Lieutenant Blue and ordered him to get a burr haircut, a head-shaving not called for by Army regulations. He told him to get his head shaved or he didn't want to see the Lieutenant in his class again. Lieutenant Blue, opting not to shave his head, had taken the order quite literally and had simply stopped attending Major Halleck's classes. When Halleck realized that the Lieutenant had, in effect, disobeyed his order, he threatened him with a formal charge of insubordination. Lieutenant Blue ignored the threat and continued to cut his class. Only Halleck's unexpected reassignment to the Army's Tropical Warfare School in Panama had saved the Lieutenant from further confrontation with Major Halleck over the heart-stopping issue of the length of his hair.

This night, however, Lieutenant Blue was again firmly within the grasp of Halleck, now a Lieutenant Colonel, who had materialized as the new battalion CO a week ago and who seemed to spend at least half his waking hours dreaming up stupid, meaningless daylight redeployments and night missions for the weapons platoon, Lieutenant Blue's platoon. The last page of the Lieutenant's letter had been a vituperative indictment of Lieutenant Colonel Halleck for everything from his chronic bad breath to the fact that he had a hooch girl spit-shine his boots and starch his fatigues every night, so he'd look good for combat duty the next day, presumably.

The Lieutenant wasn't looking forward to the next 131 days under the watchful gaze of Lieutenant Colonel Halleck. Hell, he hadn't been looking forward to those 131 days before the arrival of Lieutenant Colonel Halleck. Now he positively dreaded each successive day he spent waiting for the radio to spit out another one of Halleck's brilliant maneuvers. Judging by the CO's performance after a week, it was only a matter of days before one of his extracurricular missions for the weapons platoon ended up with dead and wounded, possibly in double digits.

That was what he had to take out of the letter. It would only drive his girlfriend crazy. He resolved to rip up the last page of the letter first thing in the morning, before he put it on the resupply chopper from Battalion. Yeah, the good old resupply chopper. The Lieutenant leaned back on the air mattress and blessed the day he got the weapons platoon. One of the advantages of having five 113s, four of which contained 4.2-inch mortars, was the fact that the weapons platoon was always base-camped apart from the rest of the Battalion, off by itself in the far boonies, where only one helicopter a day paused long enough to bother him—the morning resupply chopper.

Rare was the morning that the stillness of his little clearing in the jungle would be broken by the *thwap-thwap-thwap* of the battalion commander's C&C—command and control—ship. Rarer still was the arrival of anyone outranking the battalion CO, say the brigade or division commander. And rarer to the point of nonexistence was the arrival of a battalion staffer like the S-3, or the S-1 or the S-2. No, those little base-camp hooch-rats with desk jobs liked to stay right there, behind their desks, as far away as possible from the fearsome boonies that surrounded the weapons platoon. It was a lonely existence out there in a tiny, platoon-sized base camp thirty kliks from civilization. It was lonely, but where others feared to tread, Lieutenant Blue was king.

Yes.

King of every last dust-covered, olive drab inch of it, every dirty, smelly track, every gleaming weapon, every swinging dick wearing the green.

Yes.

It was lonely most of the time, but it sure beat the hell out of cozying up to Halleck inside the battalion base camp, where Halleck was king.

Lieutenant Blue unlaced his fingers and turned over on his side and closed his eyes. He felt better now that he'd decided what to do about the letter to his girlfriend. Now he could get some serious rack and prepare himself for whatever surprises the next wonderful day in Vietnam held for him.

He was just drifting off to sleep when he felt a hand on his shoulder.

"Eltee. Eltee. Wake yo'self up, sir." The hand and voice belonged to Dirtball Magee, his RTO, the skinny little guy who carried the platoon radio.

The Lieutenant rolled over and squinted into the red overhead light. Dirtball's face was only a foot from his, and he could see the hairs up Dirtball's nostrils and the brown chewing-tobacco stains on his teeth, and he could smell Dirtball, who was aptly named for his inadequate attention to personal hygiene.

"What's up, Dirtball?" the Lieutenant asked with a yawn.

"It's that new battalion CO, sir. He's on the horn and beatin' the bush for yo' ass again."

"What does he want now?"

"I don't know fo' sure, sir, but I heared somethin' from one of the S-3-shop clerks this mornin', when I choppered back to Battalion to get us some batteries, sir. You know him, black dude calls himself Rufus Thomas, from New Orleans."

"Yeah, yeah, I remember Thomas. He was in the platoon before he got wounded on that damn sweep they called . . . what did they call it?"

"Sledgehammer Three," said Dirtball.

"That's right. What a name. About the only thing we pounded accurately on that operation was the ground."

"Anyways, sir, Rufus was sayin' somethin' 'bout us goin' out to that trail intersection agin tonight, sir, and settin' up and checkin' fuckin' IDs, sir. You know. Where we was at two nights ago, at 367428 grid coordinates, 'tween here and Son Ha."

"That's what Thomas said?"

"Sho' 'nuff," said Dirtball. He stuck his head out the cupola atop the 113 and spat tobacco juice through his front teeth and dipped quickly back inside.

"Not that bullshit act again," said the Lieutenant. "What does this guy figure? Some VC is going to come down the trail tonight and we're going to check his papers, and he's going to be carrying a little card says 'Me VC'? He's got to be out of his mind. Checking IDs in the boonies thirty kliks from nowhere. Jesus."

"Whatchew gonna dew, Eltee?"

"Where's the radio?"

"Right here, sir."

"Give it to me, Dirtball."

Dirtball reached outside the ramp of the 113 and grabbed the platoon PRC-25 radio, commonly referred to as the "prick-25." He pushed the whip antenna out the cupola and picked up the mike.

"Rattlesnake Six, this here's Rattlesnake Two, over," said Dirtball in his distinctive Arkansas drawl.

The radio crackled with static for an instant, then stopped.

"This is Six, over." It was Halleck. The Lieutenant recognized his voice, not to mention his call sign. The guy had been battalion CO for over a week now, and he'd been radioing missions to the weapons platoon two or three times a day, but the Lieutenant had yet to lay eyes on him in person. Halleck did everything over the radio, from inside the air-conditioned comfort of his hooch or up in a goddamned command-and-control chopper. No sense in messing up your spit-shine or getting your starched fatigues all sweaty and dirty. No sir. Just pick up the radio and fight the war from a seated position. The modern electronic battlefield suited Halleck just fine.

"I gotchew, Six. Wait one, over," said Dirtball. He handed the mike to the Lieutenant.

The Lieutenant hesitated for an instant before he pushed the button on the mike. He knew Halleck was going to send him and his platoon out on another bogus mission, and this time somebody might get killed. For what? For nothing, that's what.

What would Dad do? he wondered.

Shit, what was he doing wondering what his father would do? He could hear the old man's voice, calm and reasonable and level and utterly certain of the rightness of it all:

Do exactly what you're told, son. Don't talk back. Don't ask questions. Don't speak unless spoken to. There are elements to the mission that you're not privy to. Buckle down and grit your teeth and just do it and ask questions later. That's the way the Army works, son. And that's the way young men learn the lessons of command.

What utter bullshit. All his life he'd listened to his old man intone the lessons of command, the way of true manhood. You never talked back. You did what you were told *now*. You asked questions fucking *later*. Always fucking *later*. Never *now*, when you actually needed the answers.

He shook the old man's voice from his ears and tried hard to find the voice of his grandfather. Down deep in his gut he didn't really like blowing off twenty-three years of his father's teaching, but he reasoned that it was okay, as long as he kept it in the family.

What would Grandpa do?

Would he grit his teeth and take the call from this bloody nincompoop again and run his troops all over hell's half-acre . . . for no reason at all? Would he risk twenty-four lives just because some guy's got a hard-on for him from back at the goddamned Basic Course? Would he?

What would Grandpa do?

He'd figure out a way to fix Halleck's wagon without fucking up any of his guys or himself, that's what he'd do. He'd use his noggin. He'd slip one past that fucking colonel so fast he wouldn't even feel the breeze. He could hear his grandfather's growl:

This is one of those times when you rear back and treat a son of a bitch like he's a son of a bitch, boy. You out-son-of-a-bitch him, that's what you do. You finesse him with a fast shuffle and sit back and wait for the son of a bitch to try and out-son-of-a-bitch you. There's always a way around a dumb son of a bitch: the way of the smart son of a bitch. Use your noggin, boy. That's what God gave it to you for.

The Lieutenant took the mike.

"Rattlesnake Six, this is Two, over."

"This is Six, Two. Ops order follows, over."

The Lieutenant depressed the button on the side of the mike, pursed his lips, and made a staticlike gritty noise with his tongue against his teeth—*cccccchhriiic-cccccchhriiic*—then he released the button.

"This is Six, say again last transmission, over," said Halleck.

"*Cccccchhriiic* . . . you're breaking up, Six . . . *cccccchhriiic*. Can't read you," the Lieutenant said into the mike, interspersing his words with static noise. He released the button.

"This . . . is . . . Rattle . . . snake . . . Six," came the answering transmission, one word at a time, an attempt to get words through clearly.

"Ops . . . order . . . follows," said the new battalion CO.

The Lieutenant rolled his eyes and listened.

"Grid . . . coordinates . . . three . . . six . . . seven . . ." There was a pause, as Halleck waited to see if the Lieutenant received his transmission.

"*Cccccchhriiic* . . . *cccccchhriiic*," said the Lieutenant.

"Four . . . two . . . eight . . . do . . . you . . . read . . . me . . . over," said Halleck.

"*Cccccchhriiic* . . . *cccccchhriiic* . . . *sssssppppppttttt*," said the Lieutenant. "*Sssspppt* . . . breaking . . . *sssspppt* . . . up, Six."

"Ops . . . order . . . grid," came Halleck again, still trying to get through.

The Lieutenant depressed the button again, sputtering into the mike for ten seconds, imitating static. Then he reached over to the

PRC-25 and hit the radio's power switch, turning it off. He tossed the mike aside and reclined on his air mattress.

"That takes care of Lieutenant Colonel Halleck, Dirtball. We're not going on any wild-goose chase in those boonies tonight and get mortared for three hours like the last time. Fuck him if he can't take a joke. Give me a shake around 0530, will you? I want to see Sergeant Davis and Repatch before first light. I'm sure Halleck's going to be out here sweating and puffing and strutting. I'd better make sure everyone's got a haircut and a shave and has a shirt to wear."

"Damn. You put a bad stick in his shit, huh, Eltee?" said Dirtball. "I'll see you in the mornin', sir."

Dirtball crawled out the back of the 113 and the Lieutenant went back to staring at the red light again, his eyes drifting shut. Halleck might chopper his starched ass out to the boonies in the morning, but he wasn't going to get any of the Lieutenant's twenty-four resident olive-drab-clad asses shot off tonight.

Lieutenant Blue rolled over on his side. He could hear Dirtball rustling around in the dark at the back of the track. The wind picked up, and red dust whipped through the red light inside the track like smoke from a fire in hell. He pulled his poncho liner around his shoulders to shield himself from the dust and the dark and the penetrating chill of the night air.

That was the thing about Vietnam.

It could get so damn hot during the day your skin would grow scales like a rattlesnake and your blood would run reptile-cold and you'd start looking around for rocks to sun yourself on, because that's what rattlesnakes did with the heat, they dug it, they reveled in it, they coiled around and stilled their rattles and said Bring it on, motherfucker, I'm an icy-ass rattlesnake, don't you know it? Your sun ain't gonna melt my frosty soul. . . .

Then at night you'd shed your scales and turn into a kid hiding alone under a tent-fort on a rainy night in the dark and damned if it didn't cool off so much you'd need PJs and a quilt and a mama to hold you tight.

And all you had was your fucking poncho liner.

Vietnam.

The thing about Halleck was, he was Vietnam in a nutshell. He didn't know what he was doing, and he didn't know why he was doing it, he just showed up every day to get his fucking ticket punched. And if the VC didn't get him, somebody else sure as hell would. Aw, hell, he'd probably end up getting a heatstroke on the Division tennis courts and rotating home on a goddamned stretcher with a nurse holding his hand.

"Good night, Dirtball," said the Lieutenant, who needed to hear another voice in the dark.

"G'night, Eltee. Sleep tight, man," said Dirtball in muffled tones from the back end of the track.

He was under his poncho liner, too.

One hundred and thirty-one . . . No! One hundred and *thirty* more days of this shit with Halleck breathing down your neck and Charlie looking down your shorts and twenty-four pairs of eyes and twenty-four pairs of ears watching you and listening to you all day and all night expecting more wisdom and needing more courage from your twenty-three years than you knew was in there . . .

Jesus.

He switched on the transistor radio again, and it crackled and Jimi Hendrix spat sparks into the dark:

> *"Purple haze all in my brain,*
> *Baby please, you don't seem the same,*
> *I'm acting funny and I don't know why,*
> *'Scuse me while I kiss the sky."*

The lyrics flickered through his mind like radio static in the dark . . .

The wind whistled through ventilation holes on the barrel of the .50-caliber up on top of the track, in tune with Hendrix. The red dust blew, and Hendrix wailed, and the Lieutenant pulled the poncho liner over his head and waited.

Then the song faded and the red dust blew through the holes in the barrel of the fifty, whistling the songs of the war and the dark.

He fell asleep on the downbeat.

1

The day he got the phone call that would change his life forever began the same way nearly every other day of his life had begun. It was five-thirty in the morning, and Colonel Matthew Nelson Blue III was driving to work at the Infantry School.

Five-thirty in the morning on Monday was not many people's favorite time of day or day of the week, but it was Colonel Blue's. He was driving down Victory Boulevard, the main drag outside the gate of Fort Benning, Georgia, and with the sun low on the horizon out the left window of his 1955 Ford sedan, he had a view of familiar surroundings uncluttered by outsiders, nonbelievers, or civilians. He was alone on the road, driving to his battalion headquarters, and nothing was in his way.

He stopped for a red light. Used-car lots occupied three of the four corners of the intersection. They were festooned with yellow and blue and green and red triangular flags hanging from lines crisscrossing the dusty clay fields of cars. Many of the cars, the Colonel knew, had been repossessed from the families of GIs who had missed payments because Dad was a corporal ten thousand miles away in Vietnam, and the family was having a hard time making ends meet on $245 a month, $135 of which was the base amount paid to an Army corporal, and $110 of which was "hazardous duty pay," a sum set by Congress to compensate a soldier for his services overseas under fire during time of war.

Next to each of the used-car lots, a row of trailers stood below signs advertising automobile and life insurance. Car insurance sold on the strip outside Fort Benning was twice the cost of insurance available just a mile away, in downtown Columbus, Georgia, and life insurance policies offered to GIs inside the trailers did not cover death in combat. The Colonel shook his head. He wondered when the communities that sat outside the gates of Army posts around the country would start backing up their conservative voting habits with attitudes that treated GIs as people instead of prey.

Colonel Blue drove by the barrackslike Camellia Apartments and passed through the stone gates of Fort Benning. The commercial strip came to an abrupt halt and was replaced by a road of pastoral tranquility. He took a deep breath and exhaled slowly. He wished that it weren't so, but every morning he reacted the same way to the long drive down the Benning strip. Lately, the topless go-go bars and tattoo parlors were being joined by bevies of fast-food joints, all-night convenience stores, and miniature-golf courses, but these latest additions to the landscape did little to soften the overall tawdriness of the scene. When he got to the headquarters of his unit, he knew the pile of paper on his desk would contain at least one repossession order against one of his men, and a half-dozen notices of arrest from the local gendarmerie, who seemed to consider arresting GIs for minor infractions of the law as much a sport as a duty. This kind of crap didn't go on during World War II, the Colonel remembered. In those days the Army uniform had commanded respect, not derision. What was it about the war in a little country so far away that permitted people back home the illusion that nothing had changed, that everything was normal, that no allowances need be made for the fact that young men were losing their lives every single day of the week in defense of democracy and liberty? Had the nation gone stark raving mad?

The Colonel shook his head and whistled through his teeth. Ahead, the brick buildings and manicured lawns of the main post beckoned reassuringly. At least here the madness had not yet intruded. At least here the blue Fort Benning stickers on the front and rear bumpers of the Ford drew a salute instead of unwanted extra attention from the traffic cops downtown. At least here on Fort Benning, Army life was comfortably predictable, the rocks were painted white, the picket fences ran straight and true, the cigarette butts were policed up every morning at reveille, the fatigues were starched olive drab, the boots sported spit-shines, the haircuts showed white sidewalls above the ears, and the phones were answered with a crisp "Yes, sir."

And here beneath the branches of the great live oaks, under lawns trimmed as short and neat as a recruit's hair, the dead were laid to rest with a twenty-one-gun salute and the mournful bugle call of taps, and the war was not ten thousand miles away, it was right here among us: in the eyes of the boys fresh off the farm and green from the ghetto, who snapped salutes with uncallused hands; in faces glowing so young and new they were kissable; in the chanted cadence of a platoon passing on a reveille run; in the neat rows of jeeps and three-quarters and deuce-and-a-halfs in the motor pool, in the sweet scent of gun oil in the weapons room, in the cough of the Sergeant Major's "Mornin', sir," affectionate and knowing and assertive and tired, in the smell of bacon and coffee wafting down from the mess hall through the battalion area. The war was the Army and the Army was the war, and forever the twain would meet amid the dust and the dirt and the clay and the sand under the pines and elms and oaks of Fort Benning, Georgia, as the Colonel trained yet more young men to go to war.

"Mornin', sir," said Sergeant Major Armstrong Clinton as the Colonel eased open the orderly room door. Sergeant Major Clinton thrust a mug of coffee at the Colonel without looking up. With his other hand he was filling another cup. He blew into the cup and peered at the Colonel beneath eyebrows the size and color of small rats. His face had the ruddy complexion of one who had spent half his life outside in the hot sun and the other half inside the cool, dark recesses of the NCO Club. He had a bulbous nose and a cleft chin, he stood five feet four inches tall and was just about as wide at the shoulders. He reminded those who liked him of Jimmy Cagney and those who didn't of Joe Stalin. In truth, he had a little of both of them packed somewhere on his stubby frame. But the thing that set him apart was the fact that Sergeant Major Clinton was probably the only man on Fort Benning who had bribed his way into the Army, having slipped a five-dollar bill to the man who measured his height at the recruiting station on Whitehall Street in New York City the day after Pearl Harbor. The recruiter measured five-four, but he wrote down five feet six inches, and Sergeant Major Clinton signed up for the Infantry, where, he reasoned, anybody stupid enough to pay for the dubious privilege of humping a pack and a rifle as a dogface would be excused for having volunteered for it.

He was right, of course. Sergeant Major Clinton was right about a lot of things. He was right, for example, about the Colonel.

Colonel Matthew Nelson Blue was considered by many too nice to be a Colonel, too considerate to be a commander. It was right there in his face, at forty-five "as smooth as a baby's ass," as Sergeant Major Clinton once described it to an old Army buddy over one too many beers at the NCO Club.

"You should see the old man, Zeke," said Sergeant Major Clinton. Sergeants major have called their colonels "the old man" since Attila the Hun swept across the plains of Asia.

"Born with a silver spoon in his teeth and a golf club in his mitt, he was. Got a fine howdy-do and a smile for every swingin' dick diddly-boppin' his ass through the battalion area. He was any happier in this man's Army, you'd think there was somethin' wrong with the *Army,* stead'a him. Makes you wonder, the old man does. Even knowin' he comes from a fine old Army family and a fine old *Virginia* family at that, what on God's green earth keeps a man so *up* as him in a damn outfit so *down* as this one? You'd think he'd be sick of grinnin', the way shit is goin' these days. But not the Colonel. Old man Blue's about as blue as a damn Kansas sunflower growin' in grade-A pigshit. I seen some sunny dispositions in my day, Zeke, but this one ain't sunny, it's *nuclear.*"

There were those who would quarrel with Sergeant Major

Clinton's description of his Colonel, but you'd find few of them in the 196th Infantry Brigade, the One-Nine-Six as the troops called it. The Colonel wasn't exactly a giant at five feet ten inches, but his slender build made him appear taller than he was. He wore a set of fatigues the way some men wear a Savile Row suit, as if baggy trousers and a roomy shirt had been designed and tailored for him and him alone. His face was unlined, but it wasn't undistinguished. He had a hockey scar over one eyebrow, and a kick from a polo pony when he was a boy had curved a shiny depression in his left cheekbone. The scars hadn't left him with boyish good looks, but neither had they given his face the grim cast of a wounded and angry man, which is what he was. You had to look in his eyes to glimpse the darkness within. You had to get to know the Colonel even to guess at what lay beneath his calm surface, and he was not an easy man to get to know. The countenance of the good-looking, easygoing Colonel was pure camouflage. He may have followed in his father's footsteps, but he looked just like his mother, a patrician Virginia lady of fine-boned breeding and demure stature who charmed everyone she came in contact with, even as she plotted how to have her way with them. The Colonel's was a handsome ease that concealed a steely resolve, which, in his case, had survived four decades of angry battle with a father who resembled him not at all in appearance, demeanor, or rank.

His father was General Matthew Nelson Blue, Jr., a bulldog of a man the size of Sergeant Major Clinton, who had the temper of a mule skinner, the ambition and drive of a rat on steroids, and an enviable political appointment as the nation's only ambassador-at-large. Neither man had asked for the other, not the father for the son, or the son for the father, and perhaps that was the point. They were stuck with each other, stuck in the same family, in the same Army, in the same country. They had hated each other for forty years. The Colonel had bitterly resented growing up in the long shadow cast by his father. His career in the Army had been eclipsed from its beginning by that of his father, a commander of divisions, corps, and armies, and a hero of monumental proportions during World War II. And the General had resented from the day his son was born the competition for his wife's affections that the boy represented. They had fought savagely until ten years ago, when the two men had simply stopped communicating. It seemed as if the planet wasn't big enough for the two of them, so they ignored the existence of one another. It was a battle fought not with words but from within a terrible conspiracy of silence that had taken its toll on both men. The son had twice developed a bleeding ulcer during their cold war. His father had in turn suffered a heart attack. They had watched each other's suffering from afar, but neither man had wavered. Such was the depth of their resentment and the strength of their hatred for one another.

Colonel Blue took the mug of coffee from Sergeant Major Clinton and stood in the orderly room watching the men line up for reveille through the open door.

"Going to be a nice day, Sarenmajor," said the Colonel. Colonels had called sergeants major "Sarenmajor" since Hannibal's day.

"You got that right, sir," said Sergeant Major Clinton. "Not too hot. Only gonna be eighty-five today, sir."

"Is that right? That what the weather says?"

"S'what *I* say, sir," said Sergeant Major Clinton. He sipped his coffee and glanced at the Colonel over the lip of his cup. The old man was smiling up a storm.

The Colonel picked up the newspaper and walked into his office at the end of the orderly room. The brigade was located in the last area of World War II temporary barracks still standing at Fort Benning, and the headquarters was a long, single-story building in the middle of four clusters of barracks, one for each company in the brigade. They weren't the finest accommodations a nation had ever erected for an Army, but Colonel Blue had specifically requested the aging clapboard structures, preferring them over the dormitory-like brick barracks that had gone up during the 1950s. He thought the older barracks were, well, more intimate. They were two-story wooden buildings painted a sickly pale green color, one platoon to a building, one bay to a floor. In the middle of each company area there was a small one-story building that served as company headquarters and weapons room. Next to it was a similar building that housed the company mess hall. The way the old World War II wooden barracks were arranged gave each company a sense of identity. You could look out a window in any of the barracks and see the rest of the Battalion gathered around you. You weren't just in the Army, you were in *C Company,* or *A Company,* or *B Company,* or *Headquarters Company,* and those men you could see through the windows next door weren't just another bunch of swingin' dicks, they were *your* swingin' dicks. They weren't just a gaggle of young men in funny green outfits, they were a *unit.*

You woke them up in the morning and you fed them and you gave them a rifle and you marched them off somewhere and you pointed them in the right direction and they would kill for you. Then you fed them again and you put them to bed and the next morning they would do it all over again. Once a month you paid them about what workers in fast-food restaurants made, and occasionally you went downtown and collected them from some dingy jail. You helped some of them balance their checkbooks, and for others you wrote letters home and read the replies when they came in the mail. You taught them to clean and polish and to fire their weapons. You learned their names, and the names of their wives and their children if they had any, and you remembered that which made each man an individual—this one was an all-state football player, that one a champion pool hustler, that one over there an assistant professor of English at Columbia, and the shy one with the yellow hair and perpetually dirty hands was a pig farmer back in Tennessee.

You did these seemingly minor, basic things for them, and when you asked them, they would go forth and kill for you. It was amazing, just plain amazing, when you actually sat down and thought about it, which the Colonel had done many times and at great length. No explanation accounted for the behavior of men in the Infantry. Ironically, the best line the Colonel had ever heard about the Army was one delivered by his father. Another man, a General under whom the Colonel had once served, had been there when his father delivered it, and told the Colonel the story years later.

The two men were in London, just before the United States declared war and became involved in the land war in Europe. They were at a dinner party at 10 Downing Street, and Clare Boothe Luce, who had invaded Europe as a correspondent for her husband's magazine, *Life,* had somehow wangled herself an invitation. In fact, she was the only woman at a table that included General Blue, Field Marshal Montgomery, and several other, lesser generals.

Near the end of the meal, Mrs. Luce tapped the edge of her water goblet with her knife and, having secured the attention of every man at the table, engaged them in a kind of parlor game. She posed a question: What did the gentlemen think was the most perfect thing in the world? They went around the table, each man expounding at length on why he thought a Rolls-Royce, or a Gainsborough, or a custom-made shotgun, or a trout stream in Scotland was the most perfect thing in the world. Finally the question was posed by Mrs. Luce to General Blue. He took a drag on his cigarette and looked her in the eye.

"An Infantry Battalion."

"And why is that, General Blue?" Mrs. Luce asked with a thin smile.

"Because an Infantry Battalion will do any goddamned thing you tell it to do," said the General. The rest of the military men at the table broke into applause.

"I'm surprised no one championed a woman as the most perfect thing in the world," said Mrs. Luce. "Especially you, General Blue. I thought you might be the one to make a case for us."

"What for?" asked the General, studying the glowing tip of his cigarette. "I've never met a woman who would do anything you told her to do."

The officers at the table laughed. Clare Boothe Luce smiled. The parlor game ended right there.

The Colonel had always thought the story about his father would have been the perfect Army tale, were it not for the fact that Clare Boothe Luce spent the rest of her life bragging to anyone who would listen about her wartime affair with General Matthew Nelson Blue, Jr. His father never mentioned Mrs. Luce, either to acknowledge or deny the rumors she caused, but the Colonel had always known they were true. He'd always hoped his mother would never hear the rumors, but he knew she had. What broke his heart was not their truth, but the fact that his father did nothing either to shut her up or to dispel them. He relished the rumors and cared not about their effect on his wife.

There was a knock on his door.

"What do you have for me this morning?" asked the Colonel. "More of the same?"

Sergeant Beshear, the brigade personnel sergeant, stood in the door, a sheaf of papers in his hand. He was what they called a "college boy," a recent graduate of Penn State who got drafted and found his way into the NCO school, which had graduated him nine weeks later an Army sergeant with a specialty in personnel. Sergeants who came from the NCO school were also known as "shake-and-bakes," after a television commercial for a product that promised something equally, improbably instantaneous, like fried chicken from the oven.

"We've got a problem, sir," said Sergeant Beshear.

The Colonel signaled with a nod of his head, and Sergeant Beshear entered.

"One of the officers lost his weapon last night."

"Which officer and which weapon?" the Colonel asked.

"Lieutenant Hatcher lost his .45, sir."

"How in hell did he manage that, Sarge?"

"They were in the field as aggressors for Infantry Officer Basic Course last night, and he says it just disappeared." Sergeant Beshear handed the Colonel a manila folder. The Colonel opened the folder and studied its contents for a moment and looked up.

"Where is Hatcher now, Beshear?"

"He's downrange looking for the weapon, sir."

"When's he due back here?"

"I'm not sure, sir."

"Has he got a radio with him?"

"Yes, sir. He took the C Company jeep. We ought to be able to raise him on the second battalion net."

The Colonel stood up and headed for the radio out in the orderly room. He met Sergeant Major Clinton coming through the door.

" 'Fore you get on the horn to Hatcher, sir, there's somethin' I got to tell you." He closed the door to the Colonel's office behind him. They were alone.

The Colonel sat down.

"Shoot, Sarenmajor," he said.

"I been talkin' to the brigade's supply sergeants this mornin', sir, and we're thinkin' that maybe it ain't really necessary for that weapon to be reported lost, sir. If you know what I mean."

"I'm not sure that I do, Sarenmajor. Why don't you be more specific?"

"Well," said Sergeant Major Clinton, shuffling his boots on the linoleum floor, "it's like this, sir. Your average supply sergeant in this man's Army has a habit of kinda puttin' stuff away for a rainy day, sir. You know, excess stuff that mighta come in a shipment of parts, maybe an extra sleepin' bag that turned up, maybe a box of ammunition magazines, maybe some extra spare parts to the .45-caliber pistol."

"What are you getting at, Sergeant Major?" said the Colonel, sounding exercised.

"It's lookin' like this, sir. Between the brigade's supply sergeants, I'm thinkin' we could build us a .45-caliber pistol, sir, and I know a man down in B Company's got a set of tools—used to be a machinist, he did—who can stamp us out a new serial number, same as Lieutenant Hatcher's, pretty as you please. That way, you wouldn't have to report the missin' weapon to division HQ, sir, with all the shit-suckin' that's bound to bring on."

"What you're talking about is strictly illegal, you know that, don't you, Sergeant Major? A violation of about three or four Army regulations."

"Well, sir, there's better laws been broken for worse reasons, I know that for sure."

"I appreciate your motives, but not your methods. You knew that would be my answer when you came in here, didn't you?"

"Yes, sir, I figured you wouldn't be too keen on the idea, but I figured it was my job to give you the opportunity, if you know what I mean, sir."

"Well, thanks but no thanks, Sarenmajor," said the Colonel. "And why don't you tell those supply sergeants the same thing while you're giving them the word from me that no extra weapons had better materialize in this brigade as long as I'm its commander. You got that?"

"Yes, sir. Got it."

"And why don't you radio Hatcher and tell him to get his ass out of the boonies and back here ASAP. I want a word with him."

"Will do, sir."

"Tell Beshear to bring me proper forms to file a missing-weapon report while you're at it."

"Will do, sir."

Sergeant Major Clinton opened the Colonel's door and ambled into the orderly room. The Colonel shook his head slowly from side to side. They broke the mold when they made Sergeant Major Clinton, the Colonel thought. Truly they did.

He took a sip of coffee and checked his watch. Six-thirty. He picked up the phone and dialed.

"Martine?" he said. His wife sounded half asleep.

"One second, dear. Let me turn down the television."

"Martine? Are the kids up?" Two out of four were still at home and didn't exactly take after their father when it came to getting up in the morning.

"They're vertical, but I'm not sure I'd call that *up*," said Martine. She was tall—as tall as the Colonel—and blond and notable for her sense of humor in the face of the thousand and one trials and tribulations of the Army wife. She hadn't been born into the Army, but looking at her, you'd never know it. In twenty-five years of married life in the Army, she had moved the family eighteen times, with hardly a chipped plate or a skinned knee. This was the Blues' third assignment to Fort Benning, and she had demanded that they live off-post for the first time, to "get out of that damned substandard Army housing," as she explained to the Colonel. He acquiesced to her wish, and now they were happily settled in an old farmhouse on the outskirts of Columbus.

"What's on the agenda today, honey?" the Colonel asked. He had left the house before anyone else was awake, and it was his habit every morning to check in with his wife when she had awakened.

"Bill's got football practice after school, and Debbie's got her piano lesson. I'm going antiquing with Zelda Lipscomb this afternoon, but I'll be back in time to pick up Debbie. Bill's got a ride with one of his friends. What time do you expect to get home, dear?"

"Seven, seven-thirty. It's Monday. We have that damn officers' call at brigade headquarters at six, and it usually goes about an hour."

"Can't they schedule that meeting during working hours?"

"Every hour is a working hour in the 196th Light Infantry Brigade, Mrs. Blue. Where've you been keeping yourself? I know. You've been civilianized since we moved off-post." He laughed and sipped his coffee.

"Listen, Colonel Blue. We both could stand a little civilianization, if you ask me. You're not going to be an Army officer forever, you know. It might do you some good to remind yourself what normal working hours are, every once in awhile."

"Yes, dear," the Colonel said in a tone of mock resignation.

"Well, try to get home earlier if you can."

"You know I will, Mrs. Blue," the Colonel said. "I've got to go. I've got another call."

" 'Bye, love."

" 'Bye."

Personnel Sergeant Beshear was standing in the door.

"I'm not sure you're ready for this one, sir," said Sergeant Beshear.

"What's up now, Beshear?"

"It's the MPs on line one, sir. Something about a demonstration at the main gate to the post."

"What does that have to do with us, Sarge? We're not on riot alert this month."

"It's not exactly a riot, sir. It's three women and two babies, standing outside the main gate holding antiwar signs."

"Yeah?"

"One of them is Lieutenant Sullivan's wife, sir. She's holding a sign that says 'Stop the War,' and she's pushing a baby carriage."

"Jesus. What next?" said the Colonel, picking up the phone. He intoned his customary greeting: "Colonel Blue."

The voice on the other end of the line was terse and clipped: "Colonel Blue? Colonel Ramsey, post provost marshal. Your sergeant fill you in?"

"He sure did, Colonel."

"Well?"

"Well what?" asked Colonel Blue.

"One of those women out there belongs to one of your lieutenants, Colonel. I've got orders to see this demonstration is stopped. I suggest you call that lieutenant in, and if need be, the two of you get down there and take care of the situation."

"I'm not sure that's the job of an Infantry brigade commander, sir." He called the provost marshal "sir" despite the fact that the provost was also a full colonel. Little nods to protocol, he knew from many years of experience, could go a long way in the Army.

"I don't care what you think your job is, Colonel Blue. I'm telling you the commanding general told me to stop that demonstration, and I want you to round up your lieutenant and tell him to get his goddamned wife out of there."

"Isn't this a job for the MPs, Colonel? My understanding is that there are only three of them. It hardly seems necessary—"

"They're outside the gate, Colonel," the provost marshal interrupted. "Under civilian control."

"Then it appears they are a concern of the Columbus authorities," the Colonel said.

"The sheriff and the chief of police are on the scene, but the women refuse to disperse," said Colonel Ramsey.

"Then what's the point, Colonel Ramsey?" said the Colonel, losing his patience.

"The point is this, Colonel. We've got a very difficult situation here. My hands are tied, because I don't have jurisdiction. The sheriff's and the chief's hands are tied, because they can't find any state or municipal statute they can enforce against the women. The women have refused to disperse, but I've got my orders, Colonel Blue, and now you've got yours."

"Yes, well, I'll see what I can do," the Colonel said without enthusiasm.

"I'll be hearing from you, then," said Colonel Ramsey.

"That you will, Colonel," said the Colonel. He hung up the phone and called to Sergeant Major Clinton.

"Sarenmajor?"

"Yes, sir. Right here, sir." Sergeant Major Clinton appeared in the door.

"What's happened to this man's Army, Sarenmajor? Can you tell me that?"

"No, sir. Cain't. Even if I could, wouldn't be my place, sir. No, sir."

"Did you hear what they want us to do, Sarenmajor?"

"Yes, sir. I was listenin'."

"It's a different Army, isn't it, Sarenmajor? Demonstrations at the front gate. Three women and a baby, for crying out loud, and they've got the whole damn post at a standstill."

"Been a different Army ever day I been in it, sir. That's all I can say for sure."

"Well, find out where Lieutenant Sullivan is this morning, and get him on in here."

"Yes, sir," came the reply from the orderly room.

The Colonel leaned back and laced his fingers behind his head. What next? he wondered. A gay cook having a nervous breakdown because his boyfriend left him? A whole squad on LSD, slithering about the squad bay on their bellies because they thought they were snakes? A transvestite sergeant arrested in a singles bar downtown when he tried to pick up the son of a local banker? All of this and more had happened to the 196th Infantry Brigade over the past year, so he shouldn't be surprised by the morning's developments. He glanced at the front page of the newspaper.

Of course! It was the morning of the Moratorium, the big antiwar march on Washington. But what in hell did the march on Washington have to do with Fort Benning, Georgia? Why here, why now, why me? The eternal puzzle, the endless, bottomless pit of bewilderment inhabited by every commander from top to bottom, from general to corporal, from division commander to fire team leader. Current tenant: Colonel Matthew Nelson Blue III.

There was a knock at the door, and a diminutive figure in ill-fitting fatigues appeared.

"Lieutenant Sullivan reporting as ordered, sir," said the figure, fairly vibrating with fear as he spoke. He was an OCS lieutenant who had successfully dodged the draft for several years after having graduated from college, and thus was at least twenty-five or twenty-six years old, yet he looked not a day over nineteen. The Colonel had given him the weapons platoon and not much else, on the theory that less harm could be done there. So far, the theory had worked out as planned.

"You have any idea why you're here, Lieutenant Sullivan?" the Colonel asked, with no particular malice in his voice. Just curiosity.

"No, sir, I don't," said Lieutenant Sullivan.

"Do you have any idea where your wife and child are this morning?" asked the Colonel.

"At home, I presume, sir."

"Well, they're not."

Sullivan looked momentarily confused, then alarmed.

"Has something happened that I don't know about, sir? Is there something I should know?"

"I'll say there is, Lieutenant," said the Colonel, standing behind his desk. "Your wife and child are presently standing outside the main gate to Fort Benning, and your wife is holding a sign that reads 'Stop the War.' Do you know anything about this?"

"No, sir, I don't." Sullivan looked directly at the Colonel without blinking, his fear suddenly in abeyance.

The Colonel studied Sullivan for a moment, then walked around his desk and threw his arm around the young man's shoulders.

"You and I have got something to do, Sullivan," said the Colonel. "And it ain't gonna be pleasant for either of us. Are you ready?"

"I'm afraid I'm not ready, sir. But I'm willing," said Lieutenant Sullivan.

"I've been told to clear your wife's demonstration from the post gate, Lieutenant Sullivan. I don't think it's my job to accomplish this task, and I'm not sure that what I've been asked to do is within the law. For all I know, your wife and her friends have every right in the world to be standing out there protesting or whatever else they want to do with themselves."

"They do, sir. I mean, they've got the right to be there."

"You sound pretty sure of yourself, Sullivan. Are you sure you didn't know something about this before it happened?"

Lieutenant Sullivan stopped in the middle of the orderly room and turned to face the Colonel.

"I knew about her feelings concerning the war, sir. And I knew she had something planned, but I didn't know what it was. I figured what she did was her business, sir. We're married, but I'm the one who's in the Army, sir. Not her. What she does on her own is her business, sir. If I'm not mistaken, that's why we're here—to fight for her right or anyone's right to speak freely about anything that they care to speak about, whether that speech takes the form of verbal communication or a poster held up outside an Army base gate."

"You sound like you've given this some thought, Lieutenant," said the Colonel.

"If you were my age and you had been recently drafted, I'm sure you would have given the same matter the same amount of thought," said Sullivan.

The Colonel directed him to the orderly room door and turned to Sergeant Major Clinton.

"You know where I'll be, Sarenmajor," he said.

"Yes, sir."

"Come on, Lieutenant," said the Colonel. "Let's take a ride in my new jeep."

The two officers climbed in the jeep, the Colonel up front, next to the driver, Lieutenant Sullivan straddling the jump seat in back, next to the battalion radio and its fifteen-foot-long whip antenna, looped forward and tied to the jeep's windshield. The drive to the main gate took about twenty minutes. Neither officer said anything. Once the radio crackled with a call from one of the company commanders who was in the field on a training exercise with one of the OCS classes. He wanted someone at brigade headquarters to call his wife and remind her to send a birthday card to his mother.

When the main gate first came into view as they rounded the last bend in the road leading off-post, it was almost unrecognizable. More than a dozen military police vehicles were parked in a semicircle inside the gate, blue lights flashing. Some fifty helmeted MPs stood in a line, nightsticks at the ready across their chests. On the other side of the gate, a huge cluster of police vehicles from every conceivable jurisdiction could be seen. Civilian police in blue, tan, black, and gray uniforms were standing around in no particular order. On the edge of the police cluster, a lunch truck had pulled up and opened the aluminum doors to its coffee and sandwich display box. Half of the civilian police had gathered around the lunch truck and were munching doughnuts and sipping coffee.

The Colonel told his driver to proceed through the gate and stop next to the lunch truck. As they passed the gate, both the Colonel and Lieutenant Sullivan looked around for the protestors. So many MPs and policemen were crowded into the grassy triangles on either side of the road that they couldn't see the women.

"Do you think they've gone home, Lieutenant?" the Colonel asked.

"I doubt it, sir. Melissa wouldn't miss this for the world."

The driver stopped the jeep next to the lunch truck. A rotund man wearing a tan shirt and pants and a cowboy hat and boots approached.

"I'm Sheriff Grady," the man said. He was wearing dark glasses, and a pair of black leather gloves were jammed through the epaulet atop his left shoulder. "You the Colonel they been tellin' us is comin'?"

"I'm Colonel Blue," said the Colonel, stepping out of the jeep. He held out his hand to the rotund sheriff, who shook it perfunctorily.

"You gonna do what they said you gonna do?" asked the sheriff.

"I don't know, Sheriff Grady. What did they say I was going to do?"

"Get rid a' them damn protestors over there," said the sheriff, pointing in the direction of a grove of trees to the right of the Fort Benning sign.

The Colonel looked where the sheriff was pointing, but he didn't see the protestors. What he saw was a huge gathering of policemen standing around drinking coffee and talking.

"Where are the protestors, Sheriff?" the Colonel asked.

"Right there," said the sheriff, pointing toward the sign. "We done confiscated their signs. Found a law said you gotta get zonin' approval for advertisin' signs. But they still standin' there, under the trees, where they been all mornin'. And I want 'em the fuck outta here, Colonel. Off my property."

The Colonel stepped on the jeep's bumper and peered over the heads of the policemen clustered under the trees. About fifty yards distant, up against the sign, he saw them. Three well-dressed young women, two in skirts and the third in an ankle-length dress, two with baby carriages. They were surrounded by policemen who didn't seem to be paying much attention to them. On the other side of the Fort Benning sign, the line of MPs stood at the ready. In all, there must have been at least thirty officers of the law for each protestor.

"It doesn't seem that you all are in too much danger here, Sheriff," said the Colonel, stepping down from the bumper. "If I were you, I'd go ahead and dismiss my men. My guess is the demonstration will break up as soon as those women can make their way back to their cars."

"I'm not much for your opinion, Colonel," said the sheriff. "They told me you were comin' down here to get rid a' them. Now get it done so we can be about our business."

"I don't take my orders from you, sir," said the Colonel. He turned to Lieutenant Sullivan, who was still in the jeep. He winked. He signaled the driver.

"Let's go," he said.

They drove back through the gate to the far side of the line of MPs, and the Colonel told the driver to stop. He turned to face Lieutenant Sullivan.

"Do you want a word with your wife?" he asked.

Sullivan nodded.

"Scoot around the far edge of the sign. She's standing right there."

Sullivan walked through the line of MPs and around the corner of the sign. His wife and two of their friends were standing in the midst of about fifty policemen, who by this time were ignoring them and talking among themselves.

"Melissa," he called. She turned.

"Johnny! Look at this! Can you believe it?" She was beaming, flushed from the excitement.

"I think you guys have given Fort Benning more of a Moratorium than they had counted on, don't you think?"

"You'd better believe it," said Melissa.

"Do you want to have some lunch later and tell me about it?" Lieutenant Sullivan asked.

"Sure," said his wife.

"Why don't we all meet at Lum's at noon," said Sullivan. He leaned closer to his wife and kissed her on the neck. "We can celebrate," he whispered.

All three women laughed, and his wife kissed his cheek.

"We'll be there," she said. She raised her right arm. Her hand was a fist. The others raised fists, too. Sullivan glanced at the policemen. None of them seem to have noticed. Sullivan walked to the corner of the Fort Benning sign and paused. The women had formed a line, strollers leading the way, and were pushing their way through the assembled policemen. The woman in front had one hand on her stroller and one fist in the air. It was his wife. Sullivan walked back to the jeep and vaulted into the backseat.

"It's over, sir," he reported.

The Colonel didn't envy Sullivan's position, caught between his wife and the Army, which was why he had purposely never given Sullivan an order to say anything specific to his wife. His confrontation with the sheriff had convinced the Colonel that there were better ways to handle civil unrest than that which was in evidence at the main gate to Fort Benning. While the nation's forefathers had foreseen the need for a right to assemble peacefully, he doubted they had foreseen the consequences of such a freedom being exercised at the gate to a major Army post in south Georgia in 1969.

It wasn't an easy equation. The Colonel was very much in favor of the war in Vietnam—he had served two tours there, after all: one before the Gulf of Tonkin Resolution, as an "adviser," and the second in '67–'68, commanding a Battalion in the Mekong Delta. And he was "bothered" by the antiwar sentiment in the country. That was the word he always used: "bothered." He didn't know quite what to make of it. In part, he suspected, antiwar sentiment was motivated by self-interest—the self-interest of those who didn't want to be drafted, those who were unwilling to risk their lives in combat anywhere, for whatever reason. But he also suspected that self-interest played no part whatsoever in the opposition of others to the war. He knew it was possible to see the war as something less than a noble crusade against communism, for democracy. It seemed as though everyone had come down with a kind of Asian flu, and temperatures were running very, very high. There were times when he wondered if either Vietnam or America could survive the war. When he had watched the Democratic National Convention in Chicago on television the year before, he had wondered if the cure would be worse than the disease, but this wasn't one of those times. Three women, two children, and a couple of handheld signs did not a riot make. Everyone on Fort Benning might be running a fever, but three women standing outside the main gate wasn't exactly Lincoln Park.

They were on their way back to the brigade area when the radio crackled again. This time the voice was recognizable as Sergeant Major Clinton's. This wasn't like him at all. He broke radio protocol, failing to identify the Colonel as "Six."

"Sir, sir," said Sergeant Major Clinton, clearly nervous. "You got to get back here. We got a call for you from Pentagon Switch. I told them you was on the way, and they're holdin', sir! Pentagon Switch is holdin' for you, sir!"

"Wait one," said the Colonel into the mike.

The Colonel considered the possibilities. Pentagon Switch was the communications center at the Pentagon that transferred all calls from within the Pentagon—as well as those from distant lands—to any telephone within the military telephone network. It might be news of a reassignment from Infantry Branch. It might be an old pal floating a call through the Army phone network during duty hours in order to save a buck or two—not unheard of among military men overburdened by the costs of raising and educating children, and unburdened by adequate pay and allowances. Who could know?

"Tell Pentagon Switch to place the call again in ten," said the Colonel.

"Yes, sir," said Sergeant Major Clinton, still clearly flustered. "Will do."

The Colonel turned to Lieutenant Sullivan.

"You don't think the Department of the Army has focused in on our situation already, do you?" He was joking, a big smile playing across his face.

"I couldn't tell you, sir," said Sullivan, looking nervous. This hadn't been the most wonderful morning of his life.

"Don't worry, Lieutenant Sullivan. I'll take whatever heat they can crank out. That's one of the advantages of being a lieutenant, didn't you know? *Not* being a colonel. Colonels are kind of like hot pads. They afford some protection from the heat of situations like the one you found yourself in this morning."

"I don't know what to say, sir," said Lieutenant Sullivan.

"When in doubt, don't say anything, Sullivan," said the Colonel. "Silence contains no clues. You've heard that one, haven't you?"

"No, sir."

"Neither had I, before this moment," said the Colonel.

The jeep pulled up outside brigade headquarters. Sergeant Major Clinton was standing on the gravel walk leading to the street.

"Colonel, sir, Pentagon Switch refused to hang up and call back. They're still holdin', sir. Bigger'n shit, sir."

"Okay, Sarenmajor. Let's see what Pentagon Switch has got for us. Nothing would surprise me at this point. *Nothing*."

The Colonel walked into his office and sat at his desk. Sergeant Major Clinton set a cup of hot coffee at his right hand. The Colonel picked up the phone.

"Colonel Blue," he said directly and clearly, as was his custom.

"Colonel, this is Pentagon Switch. We have a call waiting for you. Can you stand by, sir?"

The Colonel sipped his coffee and said, "Will do."

"Wait one, sir," said the voice calling itself Pentagon Switch.

There transpired a series of clicks and clacks and whistles and wheezes over the phone line leading to the brigade headquarters of the 196th. Finally the line cleared and a voice could be heard clearly.

"Pentagon Switch, sir. I've cleared you through."

The Colonel waited while another series of clicks and clacks and wheezes and whistles filled his ear. Then the sounds subsided for an instant, and he could hear.

"Dad . . . Dad . . . is that you?" he heard.

"Colonel Blue here," he said, hesitating.

"Dad. It's me. Matt. They've got me under arrest. I couldn't think of anyone else to call."

"Under arrest for what, son?" asked the Colonel, gripping the receiver so tightly his knuckles whitened.

"Desertion in the face of the enemy, Dad. But it's bogus, totally bogus. It's crap. I didn't desert anyone or anything. They're out to get me, Dad. You've got to understand. It's crazy over here. I've seen things you wouldn't believe . . ."

The phone crackled and wheezed and faded.

"Matt? Matt?" the Colonel called. He listened for several seconds on a dead line, then hung up.

He'd been cut off, and he didn't even know where his son was calling from, except that it was somewhere within the Republic of Vietnam.

2

The General, at age seventy-two, in more than fifty years of service to his country, had never been fired, but on the morning of October 15, 1969, the *Washington Post* said that was exactly what had recently happened to him. Two weeks previously, the paper said, the General had been called into the office of the White House Chief of Staff and asked to submit his resignation. The General walked into the Chief of Staff's secretary's office, plucked a sheet of typing paper from a pile on her desk, and hand-wrote:

Dear Mr. President. I resign.

He signed the letter as he usually did:

Matthew Nelson Blue, Jr., Gen., U.S. Army Retired.

Now he was sitting in the breakfast room of his Georgetown town house, reading the paper. The front-page story in the *Post* said the White House had waited thirteen days to announce the General's resignation, trying to figure out how to manage the story. But now it was official. General Matthew Nelson Blue, Jr., was no longer the United States of America's ambassador-at-large. The story printed the White House line that the resignation was part of a "house-cleaning," but hinted that there was more to it than that.

"Thirteen goddamned days it took them to work up the guts to announce my so-called goddamned resignation. If they'd stop trying to goddamn handle things and start standing up and taking responsibility for the crap they're responsible for, we'd be one hell of a lot better off," he bellowed to no one in particular, though he knew he'd get a response from his wife, who was one room away in the kitchen.

He spoke in a hoarse, gravelly growl starting somewhere down within his ample midsection and reaching a full-blown rumble by the time he barked, a result of scarred vocal cords from having taken a swig of carbolic acid as a child.

"They're not too bright, are they, Buddy?" asked his wife. That's what she called him: Buddy. He didn't know where she'd come up with the nickname, but that was it. Buddy.

"You'd think for once the bastards could tell the goddamned truth. Just once. For the thrill of it, just to experience the sensation one time, so they'd know what it felt like. Who do they think it's going to hurt, telling the world that their pet general has gone haywire? Christ! If they told the truth, all the fingers would be pointing at *me,* for crying out loud. *I'm* the one who left the reservation. *I'm* the goddamned oddball. Hell, I'm seventy-two years old! What in hell can I do to them in the time I've got left? What in hell are they afraid of? I'll tell you why they're afraid. If the world knew why they had to ask for my resignation, somebody would take a hard look at how they're fighting that goddamned war."

He paused for a moment, and removed his half-glasses. His hair was white, and his face deeply lined from years outdoors in the sun. He had a slightly bulbous nose that had been broken six times, twice in fights, the rest by horses' hooves and polo mallets while playing the sport he had loved and played better than any man alive in the 1920s and 1930s. He was not a tall man, only five feet nine inches in his stocking feet, and the years had broadened him considerably, so he was wide at the shoulders and thick equally in the chest and the waist. "Stocky" was the way the newspapers described him—generously, he'd always thought. Now the days of newspaper generosity were probably over for good. It wouldn't take the *Post* very long to figure out that he had left some overturned furniture behind him at the White House. Soon enough, the ultimate insider would become the terminal outsider. All he had to do was answer the phone a couple of times, take a few reporters' calls. Tell a few secrets out of school. It was just a matter of time. The old soldier was going to be hung out to dry. It had happened before. God willing that his health stayed good, he might be lucky enough to have it happen again.

When he finished breakfast and reading the paper, he liked to repair to his study upstairs and read, or work on designs for furniture he built in the garage downstairs. After a lunch at the Army-Navy Club downtown, the General would take a nap, then work in his garden. This was his new, post-resignation schedule, of course. Things had been mighty different over the past half-century, his years of public service in the Army and within the government in various capacities. But the General was used to change. He thrived on it. He had been born in a sharecropper's shack in southwest Oklahoma before the turn of the century, and he had lived through two world wars, the coming of the automobile, the airplane, television, and the computer. He had watched technology seep into virtually every crevice of humanity, and for a long time it had seemed that technology would win the struggle between man and machine, prevail in some unknowable way. But now he was watching technology get its great comeuppance in a war in a little country ten thousand miles away, where peasants carrying rifles and bags of rice on their backs were holding off the greatest military onslaught since World War II. More bombs and artillery landed on Vietnam in *one day* than had landed on Europe in all of World War II, and still the technological war was not being won.

He had been married, widowed, and married again. He had watched his children grow up to become people he hardly recognized. Change was the only constant the General had ever known. As a general in the Army, he had shaped events, fought battles, won wars. As Deputy Director of the CIA, he had helped reconstruct postwar Europe. But when it came to his own home, he had been at the mercy of events that in truth he had never really understood. If there was one thing he'd have changed, he often thought, he would have learned to love earlier, in order that so much of his life that now felt alien to him would instead be his own.

Getting fired hardly left the General a lonely and embittered man. In fact, it was pretty good. He felt about twenty years younger. About the age of his wife, to whom he had been married since 1948, the year after his first wife died. Belinda Blue was considered by many in Washington a dark and mysterious woman who had spent twenty years in Washington accumulating about forty years' worth of power. She had coal-black hair, and her twinkling green eyes darted from side to side as she spoke, giving the unintended and erroneous impression that she wasn't paying attention to the person with whom she was speaking. She looked ten years younger than her fifty-one years, and she had a petite figure frequently clad in an unusual mix of old skirts and pants she had saved over the years, and topped with bright, youthful blouses, jackets, and furs. She was one of the first women in Washington the *Post* described as "perfectly put-together," an approbation not frequently applied to the hostess class. In a town not exactly celebrated for its fashion-consciousness, Belinda Blue was a fresh breeze blowing through the endless procession of parties and receptions and teas that political life required of both husband and wife. She stayed trim by riding her horse on the trails of Rock Creek Park every morning and training her jumper two afternoons a week on a farm across the river in Great Falls, Virginia.

General and Mrs. Blue entertained frequently, giving dinner parties for which they were widely celebrated. Belinda Blue's parties differed from most Washington gatherings. They were less socially than politically oriented. She liked to say that she refused to entertain for entertainment's sake.

"There should be a *purpose* to every gathering in my house," she told the *Washington Post* "Style" section in a feature it did on her. "And that purpose should be political, though not in the conventional sense. The General and I aren't as interested in the politics of vote-getting as we are in the politics of ideas. I like to talk. I like to talk politics. I like people who like to talk politics. That's what we do. We eat and we drink and we talk politics."

That kind of blunt speech in social Washington had earned Belinda Blue a galaxy of critics and detractors, chiefly among the ranks of the uninvited. But those who populated her political salon were as numerous and devoted as her critics were vicious. Her devotion to the cause of civil rights and what she loosely referred to as "economic justice" had won her a strong following among predominantly liberal Democrats, as well. That, in turn, had landed her on the boards of such established liberal organizations as the National Association for the Advancement of Colored People and Americans for Democratic Action, even though Belinda Blue had been born to relative privilege in Great Britain and was still a resident alien in the homeland of her husband.

They had met in London in 1939. Lieutenant Colonel Matthew Nelson Blue, Jr., had been sent by Army Chief of Staff General George C. Marshall to England with the First Ranger Battalion for training at the British Commando School. A secondary mission for Lieutenant Colonel Blue was to establish liaison with the British military command, for Marshall was already anticipating a land war in Europe against Nazi Germany and wanted to know with whom he would be dealing. More precisely, he wanted to know who was strong, who was weak; who drank too much, who too little; who was loud and pushy, who was quiet but effective; in American terms, who was a Grant, and who was a Lee.

Once in England, Lieutenant Colonel Blue was quickly promoted to brigadier general, skipping the rank of colonel altogether. Under the protocols of wartime London, a general rated a vehicle and a driver. The vehicle was a London taxi painted olive drab. The driver was a young curator from the Royal Albert Museum who had volunteered for wartime duty in the service of her country. Because her specialty at the museum was London architecture, she was deemed to have special knowledge of the complicated maze of London streets and addresses, and was therefore drafted as a driver. Her first passenger was General Blue. Her name was Belinda Thomason. She had black hair and darting, curious green eyes that knew London like the city was her backyard.

The General spent a year in England before returning to the States to ready the 22nd Infantry Division for combat in North Africa. He and Corporal Thomason had a brief affair. When he left, neither heard from the other for the next two years. The war drifted and surged in the way wars do. Starting in 1942, the General returned to London periodically to participate in planning sessions by the Allied High Command. When he did, Ike's chief of staff made sure a certain driver met the General's plane. When the war ended, the next three years drifted by in a haze best described as Relief That It Was Over.

When the General's wife, Carey Randolph Blue, died in 1947 of kidney disease, the General waited an interval of six months and wrote his former driver. Belinda Thomason wasted no time writing back. Her job at the museum didn't mean as much to her as it had in the years before the war. The walls were stone, the faces were stone, half of the museum's art was chipped out of stone. The arrival of General Blue's letter lifted a fog from her life. She replied immediately. They were married nine months later.

And now she fussed in her kitchen, and he fussed over his newspaper. The kitchen was *hers*. She had made sure of that, making the General agree to move out of the southern Virginia farm he and his deceased wife had inhabited since the end of the war. The Georgetown house was entirely her creation—well, all of it anyway that he hadn't built himself, using the skills of carpentry and cabinetmaking he had honed in garages around the world over a thirty-year career in the Army. The kitchen was hers until he walked in, then it became theirs, for the General was a wonderful cook who liked nothing better than presiding over the preparation of the roots and greens he had grown in his garden. It was part of the magic of their dinner parties. Everyone came to the Blue house knowing that the first hour or two wouldn't be spent standing around the living room with a stale drink in your hand, wondering when dinner would be announced. No, at the Blues', you gathered in the huge kitchen, open on one end to the dining room and on the other to the den, and watched two creatures in white aprons drift from counter to stove to sink in a kind of elegant ballet. If you got lucky, one of them told you to peel the carrots, or go out in the garden and pick the lettuce. Best of all was cleaning up, the General's specialty. He stood over the sink, scraping dishes, loading the dishwasher, and dispensing brandy, old Army stories, and unconventional wisdom in equal measure. You had the feeling in the kitchen of General and Mrs. Blue that you were somewhere near the heart of the beast, somewhere in the vicinity of the soul of an America you'd suspected was there. It wasn't something you went home and described to your friends, not in 1969, and certainly not before then. But you knew that you'd been someplace special, and maybe, just maybe, life within that kitchen was magical, the way America had always been meant to be.

The Blues gave great parties; the Blues were great horsemen; the Blues knew their way through the cracks and crevices of Washington politics as well as most politicians and better than the rest of them; the Blues made the columns and in fact the Blues *wrote* quite a few of them; yet the Blues stood anxious and alone and frequently angry in a town that prized cooperation, coalition, and complacency above all else.

"In Washington, You Are Who Your Friends Are," announced one headline on a magazine piece that was meant to be a satire on the scene. Whatever satirical edge the piece started out with was dulled by the third paragraph, where the truth crept inexorably in. The headline was deadly accurate. The Blues commanded a lot of cooperation, were identified with numerous coalitions, and experienced their fair share of complacency. But the number of real friends they had was limited by the willingness of each of them to tell powerful people to go to hell. People in Washington were reluctant to be too closely identified with iconoclasts of the order of the Blues.

Perhaps because friendship in Washington was by nature so transitory, most of all the General missed the friendship that was logically due him as the father of a son and a daughter. But his daughter was a stranger, an expatriate living her twenty-fourth year in Rome with an Italian motion picture set designer. It was hard even to get her on the phone. His son, the Colonel, had been lost to him years before—so long ago, in fact, he couldn't recall where the hatred had come from, why it continued, what had gone so terribly wrong.

For a man who had once commanded two million men in combat,

loneliness was part of the price one paid for greatness. There was nothing lonelier than waking up in the morning and moving two stickpins on a map and knowing that by noon two hundred men would be dead—two hundred of *your* men, American boys. And that didn't count the four hundred who would be likely to die on the other side. They were men, too. They had been somebody's boys. By lunchtime, then, six hundred bodies would be out there somewhere, half-buried in the dirt of artillery explosions, cut in half by machine-gun fire, shredded by shrapnel. Dead.

What a man like the General needed was the safety of his family, but for the General, ever since the Army had taken him to its bosom, it had been the Army first, and all else had come second. He had never really been part of the America that fathered kids and looked after them and built a future for them and passed along a legacy that amounted to something more than what had come before. What the General had left was a litany of ground taken, armies defeated, nations conquered, surrenders accepted. Fatherhood had to do with the future, with a hunger for the unknown, even the unknowable, and in one sense the General had come well prepared. He had lusted after life ever since he first sensed that the barren prairies of southwest Oklahoma were but a wide gateway to a better world somewhere out there beyond the flatness of the horizon. But lust for life and a savage drive for success were no substitutes for the kind of failing downward that fatherhood entailed, where no decision was without grievous consequences for both father and child. Everything you did with and to your kids that seemed right at the time was bound to turn out wrong in the end. At your best as a father, you gambled. At your worst, you took potshots in the dark.

The trouble with General Blue was the trouble with most fathers of his generation. They were never there. Fathers were supposed to be immune from the details and duties of family life that stuffed up mothers like a bad cold. Families meant late nights and crying and sneezing and feeding and burping and wiping and changing, and fathers were supposed to *work,* while the rest of the rabble back at home, presumably, *familied.* Fatherhood for the General had meant presiding, not participating.

Well, now he was paying immunity's price. When Carey Randolph Blue died, he had been able to replace his wife, but not his family. He was one of the most influential, popular figures in Washington—at least until he had been fired, anyway—but when it came right down to it, apart from his second wife, he was alone. He didn't know his children, and they didn't know him. He had missed his chance to communicate his love to them. Moreover, his way of expressing affection and concern was clumsy at best, and downright stupid at worst.

Once when his son was ten years old, he had come home with a C in English on his report card from school. He should have taken the boy into the study and had a talk with him about the importance of studying hard at school, getting good grades so he could get into a good college. Instead, the General had taken the boy's recently acquired baseball mitt—half of which had been paid for out of his son's lawn-mowing and car-washing earnings—doused it with kerosene, and burned it to a cinder in the driveway.

He didn't even say to his son, "That'll teach you." He just walked by him on his way to bed. The next morning he told the boy to clean up the mess.

The boy cleaned up the mess, and he never forgot it.

Never.

"What's on the agenda today, sir?" Belinda teased the General, wrapping her arms around his neck from behind.

"You think that goddamned Hancock is going to call this morning?" he asked. His mind was somewhere else. He hadn't even heard her, which wasn't surprising, considering that there wasn't much left of his hearing in either ear.

"Why don't you stop worrying yourself about Hancock, Buddy. Our pet CIA Director hasn't turned out the way we thought, now, has he? But he'll get what's coming to him soon enough."

"You goddamned right he will," said the General. "That little bastard kissed my ass and every other ass in view for twenty goddamned years, and soon as he got to be Director, he forgot every goddamned phone number he ever knew. I curse the day I ever yanked his ass out of that stinking hole he dug for himself in Teheran and moved him to Berlin with me. If I had it to do over again, I'd tell Dulles to kick his ass all the way to Sri Lanka, issue him two ceiling fans, a washcloth, and a bar of brown soap, and misplace his personnel file. He'd still be there, you know that, Miss B? Rotting in a stinking sweathole so far out of the action you'd have to go all the way to goddamned Harvard to find someone who could locate the goddamned place on the map."

The General emitted a rasping, hacking guffaw that was the product of thirty years of three-packs-a-day cigarette smoking, a habit he had broken only when a heart attack nearly killed him in 1947, the year he became Director of European Operations for the newly minted CIA. In 1948 he had sent for William Hancock, the Yale-educated intellectual and former OSS man who would serve as his aide and right-hand man for twenty years. Together they oversaw all of Allied intelligence in postwar Europe until the General was promoted to Director of Operations of the CIA in 1953, the most senior deputy directorship in the Agency. President Eisenhower, who had just been elected, called the General back from Germany and told him he wanted one of his own men at the CIA, someone who could keep an eye on Allen Dulles, the headstrong former head of OSS in Europe during the war, now CIA Director.

"There's one too many of these Dulles fellows around here, Matt," said the President, referring to the fact that Allen's brother John Foster was Secretary of State, an arrangement that had been foisted upon Eisenhower in return for his backing for the Presidency by the Republican Party. "With you over at the CIA, I'll have to worry about only one of them."

The General stayed at the CIA until President Lyndon Johnson appointed him ambassador-at-large and promoted William Hancock to the directorship of the CIA.

"I wish you'd stop railing on about little Billy Hancock, dear. He really isn't worth the worry now, is he?" Belinda asked, still hugging the General's neck.

The General took a deep, wheezing breath and turned to face his wife. His eyes were full of fire, and the corner of his mouth twitched as he spoke.

"But he was like a goddamned *son* to me, don't you see? I brought him out of the wilderness. I taught him how to bury a hatchet in somebody's back so quietly, cleanly, so they wouldn't know it was there. He wouldn't be Director right now if I hadn't brought him along like a goddamned colt, watering him when he needed it, pointing him toward the tall grass, reining him in . . ." His words drifted off in a rasping stutter.

"I know it hurts, dear," said his wife, stroking his silver hair. "I know. I know."

"No, you don't," said the General. "He's the second son I've lost, and you couldn't possibly know that feeling."

She hugged him tightly, and he stared out the window of his study at the garden below, a narrow, long corridor of flowers interwoven with vegetables. If you stood in the middle of the garden, all you could see were flowers. But from a second-story window, the genius of the garden was visible. The garden was such a small urban space that there wasn't room for a flower garden and a vegetable garden, so the General had combined the two, planting rows of vegetables between rows of flowers that concealed them. A herringbone brick walk fanned through the garden, giving easy access to every plant therein. The garden, in fact, was a lot like the General himself. If you stood down there on one of the brick paths, smelling the flowers all around, the garden seemed precise, uniform, gentlemanly. But between the rows, in where you couldn't see, was the real business of the garden—a dirt farm among the peonies and foxgloves and lupines. He had figured out how to have it both ways. The garden told his lie so beautifully you never noticed the food amid the flowers.

The phone rang, and rang again. Belinda broke her hold on the General's neck and kissed the top of his head.

"I'll get it, Buddy," she whispered. He was a tough old goat, she thought, but like most men, he wasn't as tough as he'd like to think he was.

She disappeared into the kitchen, and the phone stopped ringing. The General stared at his garden, making mental notes on how he was going to change it next year. Every spring he drew up a new blueprint for the garden, moving the brick walks, redesigning the layout of the flowers and the vegetables, refining the illusion he took so much pride in having created.

"It's for you, dear," came his wife's voice from the kitchen.

"Who is it?" he rasped.

"It's Mr. Weatherby, from the *New York Times*. He says it's important."

"It's always goddamned important to those assholes from the *New York Times*," said the General.

"Blue here," he said, characteristically blunt.

"Homer Weatherby, General," said the voice on the phone.

"I know who the hell you are," said the General. "Now what the hell do you want?"

"There seems to be more than meets the eye to this White House announcement of your resignation yesterday, sir. My information is that you haven't been in the office for almost a month. What's going on, sir? Did you in fact resign?"

"What goddamned office?" bellowed the General. "What goddamned office am I supposed to have been absent from?"

There was a pause as the reporter from the *Times* gathered himself after the General's outburst.

"Your office over at State, sir. On the third floor."

"You call that goddamned cubbyhole an office, Weatherby? How in hell can I have been absent from there for two weeks if I've never *been* there? Why don't you ask a few of those bastards you've been talking to over at State if they've ever seen me there? Throw that at the bastards, Weatherby. That might be the most constructive thing you could do today. You might wake a few of them up."

"Did you resign, sir?" the reporter persisted doggedly.

"Hell, no. I was fired. Haven't you figured that out by now?"

"That's what I heard, but I had to get it from you, sir."

"One of the things that's always amazed me about you bastards in the press is what you just said, Weatherby. You knew what was going on, but you said you had to get it from me. Why, for crying out loud? If you know the goddamned truth, why don't you just goddamned print it? Why do you have to rouse a tired old coot like me to put the stamp of approval on what you already know? Christ, if I was a goddamned newspaper reporter, I'd do one hell of a lot less bothering of the citizenry, and one hell of a lot more exercising of that goddamned muscle you've got up there between your ears. That would save everyone a good deal of time, wouldn't you say, Weatherby?"

"Yes, but you know, sir . . . my editor. He's going to ask. I've got to have the answer."

"Next time you've got the answer and your editor doesn't, you tell him to call me, Weatherby, if he wants it from the goddamned horse's mouth. I don't want your goddamned questions about my breakfast, if you already know what goddamned cereal I ate this morning. Do you understand me, Weatherby?"

"Yes, sir, I do. I have a few more questions, sir."

"No doubt," growled the General.

"What caused the White House's action, sir? Has anyone told you?"

"Ask them."

"Was it that speech you gave in Lyons last month, sir? The one where you compared Tet to Dien Bien Phu? You said Vietnam was our Algeria. Did you mean that, sir?"

"It's obvious you read the speech. What do you think?"

"It reads like you were taking a walk from the last twenty years of your life, sir, if you want my frank opinion. You've been heading in that direction for some time, but at Lyons you weren't walking away. You were in a dead run."

"You see what I mean, Weatherby? You didn't need to call me this morning. You figured it out for yourself." The General coughed and spat into his handkerchief.

"One more question, if I may, sir."

"What's that, Weatherby?"

"Why?"

"Goddammit, Weatherby! Do your homework! The answer is right there in front of you, in everything I've ever done, in every word I've ever spoken, every stand I've ever taken, right there in the history of every unit I ever commanded. Read my goddamned book. Read what I had to say about the crap Clark pulled at Anzio. Read my damn book, Weatherby. You'll get your answer about Vietnam."

"Thank you, sir," said the reporter from the *Times*.

"Quote me correctly, Weatherby," the General rasped, coughing again.

"I will, sir," said the reporter.

"You'd better, mister," said the General, hanging up the phone.

His wife rubbed the top of his head with the palm of her hand, messing his hair.

"You old coot," she said. "You scared that poor thing to death, didn't you?"

"I doubt it," said the General, staring at his garden again. "He's been around the track a few circuits, and he'll be around again. He'll be on the phone to me tomorrow if he needs something else from me. It's his job."

He coughed and spat into his handkerchief again, and caught his breath after a moment.

"Christ," he rasped through gritted teeth. "It's my job. At this point, it's all I've got left to do, picking up the phone and answering questions, stating the obvious for the ignorant. The little bastard's got his job, I've got my job: spelling it out for them, chalkboarding my life and my opinions over and over again. MacArthur was wrong. Old generals don't fade away. They just answer the goddamned phone and talk to reporters."

"What's on the agenda today, dear?" Belinda asked, rubbing his neck.

"I'm going to work in the garden after lunch. Bruce Pelton is coming over at cocktail hour."

"Will he be staying for dinner?"

"No. He's leaving first thing tomorrow morning for Vietnam on one of those goddamned fact-finding missions for the Secretary of State. I think this is his last one. Old Bruce isn't going to last much longer. He hasn't got it in him, putting up with the crap they're dishing out over there."

"I'm off to the farm to ride, dear," said Belinda. "I'll be home around six."

"Don't you have a show this weekend?" the General asked.

"Yes, the one in Leesburg, remember?"

"The goddamned prissy little assholes from Leesburg," he rasped. "How could I have forgotten?"

She kissed the top of his head and headed out the door. He heard the car back out of the driveway, and he was alone.

The General finished reading the *Post* and walked downstairs to his basement study. A large mahogany desk was along one wall, next to a drafting table where he made plans for his garden and designed furniture. He was entirely self-educated, and it was an education that had begun with his hands. If it was made from wood, he could build it. If it was green, he could grow it. If it was a horse, he could ride it. If it was a polo ball, he could hit it.

The walls of his study were bookshelves, floor to ceiling, except for the brick wall over the fireplace, which was hung with artifacts of the General's thirty-year Army career: a polo ball and mallet, a German Army helmet, a Beretta semiautomatic pistol that had belonged to Field Marshal Kesselring, a riding crop, a Colt revolver of Civil War vintage that the General had found in the attic of a farmhouse he owned just after the war. The General sat down in a deep leather armchair and was drifting off to sleep when the doorbell rang. He struggled to his feet and climbed the stairs. Through the smoky glass of the front door he could make out a slender figure. He opened the door.

"General, I'm awfully sorry to bother you at this time of day, but—"

"Brownie! What the hell are you doing here at this hour? You're not due until the sun's over the yardarm. What's up?" Brownie was the General's nickname for Lieutenant General Bruce Pelton, who had served as a battalion commander under him in North Africa and Italy, and was now Assistant Secretary of State for Military Affairs. He didn't stand much over five feet six inches, and he was as skinny as a college wrestler. He had a prominent, aquiline nose, and his hair, once wiry and black, was now peppered with gray.

"I'm afraid I've got some disturbing news, sir," said Lieutenant General Pelton, still deferring to the General after all those years.

"Well, come on in, Brownie, goddammit. Tell me what's on your mind. Time's a-wasting." He led Pelton downstairs to the study and pointed to a chair. The General took the leather armchair. The two men sat facing each other across an ancient, moth-eaten Persian rug.

"I just received information that your grandson, Matt the fourth, has been charged with desertion in the face of the enemy by his brigade commander in Vietnam. He's under arrest, sir."

"What in hell did you say, Brownie?" The General sat upright in the armchair and leaned toward the other man. The dark study suddenly seemed stiflingly hot, and he fumbled with the top button of his shirt.

"We got a cable on it today, sir. It came in from the ambassador. Every time an American, military or civilian, is charged with a capital offense, the Secretary is cabled immediately. Came in this morning." He handed a file folder to the General.

"Lieutenant Blue was charged late last night and placed under arrest. The technical charge comes under Article 121 of the Uniform Code having to do with discharge of duties under combat conditions. They've charged him with cowardice and desertion in the face of the enemy, sir. They're very serious charges."

The General reached for his half-glasses and flipped on the fluorescent lamp mounted on his desk. He studied the file for a moment and looked up.

"What else have you got?" he asked slowly. He looked and sounded tired.

"That's all, sir. Just the initial cable notifying the Secretary that capital charges have been filed. The rest of the stuff in there is the acknowledgment to MACV and the notations by the duty officer who received the telex."

"Who preferred the charges?"

Lieutenant General Pelton studied the toes of his shoes for a moment, then looked the General in the eye. When he spoke, his words were measured. Just delivering the news to the General was hard enough. Talking about fellow officers made it worse.

"Colonel James Franklin Testor, sir. He's Third Brigade CO in the 25th Infantry Division. You probably know your grandson has been in command of a weapons platoon in the Second of the 22nd, which was attached to the 25th. Technically, he was under command of the Third Brigade, under Testor."

"What could possibly be going on, Brownie?" the General asked, slamming his fist on the arm of the chair. He coughed and spat into his handkerchief and fixed the other man with his huge eyes, a wide-eyed glare that for years had telegraphed his intelligence, intensity, and hatred.

"I know that boy. He spent every summer with me for fifteen goddamned years. That boy would never goddamned *desert,* any more than he'd take a kitchen knife and stab his goddamned mother!" He banged his fist on the armchair, his half-glasses tumbling into his lap from the blow.

"It's unthinkable, Brownie, goddammit. There's something wrong. Something's missing. I can feel it."

"What's missing is young Matt's side of the story, sir. Just because a charge has been brought doesn't mean a crime has been committed. He's innocent until he's proven guilty, sir."

"Of course he is, goddammit, Brownie. I mean something *else* is missing. I told you last week I'd gotten a letter from the boy with news of a unit commendation and the Silver Star he'd been put in for. You goddamned just don't go putting in a soldier for a Silver Star one week and charging him with desertion the next. I know that goddamned war is about as loony a military exercise as I've ever witnessed, but young Matt a deserter? Not on your goddamned life, Brownie. I'll stake my entire goddamned career on the notion that something corrupt is going on, Brownie. And I'm going to be at the bottom of it so goddamned fast, they won't even see me coming."

"I'm inclined to agree with you, sir," said Lieutenant General Pelton, carefully picking his words. "But if you're not careful here, sir, you could end up doing more harm than good. That's why I came over as soon as I got news of the charges, sir. I didn't want you hearing about this from anyone else."

"For which I'm very grateful, Brownie. You can rest assured that I'm aware of the dangers," said the General, biting off his words in crisp chunks. "What do you think we can do? How far can we go and not alert the command over there that one of us, either you or I, is taking an interest?"

"We can cable something about how potentially explosive a charge like this could be, the need to keep the Secretary informed every step of the way."

"That sounds like the ticket, Brownie. Anybody you can call?"

"There's a man out at CINCPAC, in Honolulu, who served under me in Korea. Good man. Albert Kaufman. He was one of my battalion commanders. He's a buck general now, loyal as a hound dog. He's in a liaison slot between CINCPAC and MACV. He's smack in the middle of the paper flow. Everything from Military Assistance Command Vietnam goes straight through him. Everything is in his bailiwick. I'll get him to make the inquiries."

"What about within the 25th Division itself? Who's the CG?" the General asked. He eased his feet into his slippers, which he'd removed when he sat down in the big armchair.

"Major General Lawrence Cardozo, sir. West Point June '43. Don't know him. The word is, he's a comer, a real go-getter. He's one of those men who wants everyone in the division to wear an Infantry blue neck scarf. Spit-shined boots. Anything that doesn't move, paint it white and line it up. Westmoreland and his crew just love him."

"Figures," growled the General, who during the war had worn riding boots, Cavalry britches, and an old leather jacket over an open-necked khaki shirt. The boots were scuffed, the jacket was tattered and frayed, the britches patched in the seat. The war, the *big* war, was a time when commanders wore pretty much whatever they wanted, and the General had taken advantage of the custom. The way he wore the uniform was the way he commanded. He cut a striking figure—a cavalryman who'd taken Infantry divisions and treated them like they were riding, not walking, into battle, marching hard, striking fast, moving on. The man he'd modeled himself on had been Phil Sheridan, whose statue stood in a little park in the middle of New York's Greenwich Village. Sheridan had been suspended from West Point in his second year for having run his platoon sergeant through with an eighteen-inch-long bayonet because the platoon sergeant was making a career out of harassing him. They suspended Sheridan, and he graduated a year late, but he took his rebellious nature into the Army with him. During the Civil War, every time Grant needed someone to raid the enemy—hit them hard and fast at night or at daybreak and get out quick, leaving the enemy wondering what the hell had happened—he called on Phil Sheridan. General Blue was that kind of general. When he was through with you, either in war or in peace, you wondered what the hell had happened.

"So who the hell is this Cardozo? Do we know him?" asked the General.

"He served in the Pacific, sir, from '43 to '45. He was part of the occupation forces in Japan after the war. Then he was a battalion XO, then a CO in Korea, right at the end of the war, in the Second Division. I didn't know him. He went through the schools, got a brigade out at Carson, was Commandant of Cadets at West Point, and picked up the 25th earlier this year."

"Wait a minute. He was Commandant at West Point?" The General stood up and began pacing the study. Lieutenant General Pelton instinctively stood up with him.

"That's right, sir."

"When?"

"Let me see . . . from September '66 to September '68. That's right. Two years."

"Then he would have been there when Matt was a cadet."

"That's right, sir. Matt graduated when? Last year?"

"Yep," said the General. "He sure did. I think we're getting somewhere, Brownie. I want to know more about this Cardozo character. Who can we talk to?"

"Hell, General, the Supe."

"Jesus. You're right. He was in your Battalion, wasn't he, Brownie? In the Ninth Regimental Combat Team? He was with us at Port Lyautey, wasn't he?"

"Yes, sir. He was the best company commander I ever had," said Lieutenant General Pelton.

The General stood at his drafting table, and picked up a pencil. He tapped the eraser on the table as he spoke, emphasizing the points he made.

"I want to know everything he knows about this Cardozo character. What color are his socks? Where did he get his socks? Who darns his socks? Who washes his socks? Who's sending him socks? I want a pair of his goddamned socks! I want him forelock to toes, elbow to elbow. If he burps, I want to know what key he burped in and what he's taking for indigestion. I want the brand of tonic he's rubbing in his hair every morning. Are you getting the message, Brownie?"

He was tapping the pencil on the drafting table and looking at the marks he'd left on the sketch he had been working on. Behind him he heard a gurgling chuckle, a laugh he'd heard for over thirty years, but not very often. Lieutenant General Pelton was a dour man, for the most part a true believer that things could and would get much worse before they got even a smidgen better. It was one of the reasons he had a real affection for his old friend. When he laughed, you knew he had found what you'd said truly funny.

"We're going to get to the bottom of this, aren't we, Brownie?" asked the General, as much to reassure himself as to encourage his friend.

"Yes, sir. We'll knock down some walls."

"Christ. They're like ghosts, aren't they, Brownie, these men are like ghosts. Goddamned ghosts. Sometimes I think I'm living in a dream, Brownie. Everything changes, but everything stays the same. You keep seeing yourself coming, then going, coming and going, like you're looking at yourself in those mirrors in the men's department at Woodward & Lothrop. The same names, the same faces . . . you catch a glimpse and it's goddamned gone, then it's back again, and you're not sure you saw it the first time . . ." The General drifted off, staring at a wall of books, and his friend, the Assistant Secretary of State for Military Affairs, waiting for him to focus his thoughts.

"You know what Carey used to say about the Army, Brownie?" the General asked, referring to his first wife by name for the first time since her death, though his friend had no way of knowing of the years that had passed since the General had admitted to himself, or anyone else for that matter, that she had existed.

"No, sir, I don't," said Lieutenant General Pelton, watching his friend and former commander with no small amount of awe.

"She used to say the Army is just a big small town, Carey did. And I think she was right. Everybody knows everybody. They see you coming, and they watch you going. The Pentagon is like our goddamned county courthouse. And the Army is the county. They're all just sitting over there sipping coffee, watching the traffic, getting their hair cut, exchanging gossip, waiting for something to happen. That's the nature of small towns. Nothing ever happens, so everyone just sits around waiting for something to happen. When it does, then you talk about it. Then you go back to waiting. Hurry up and wait, the troops used to say. That's the goddamned Army, Brownie, in a goddamned nutshell. Carey was about as military as a lace tablecloth, but she knew the goddamned Army. She *knew* the goddamned Army."

"Yes, sir, I believe she did," said Lieutenant General Pelton.

"Where do we go from here, Brownie?" asked the General.

"I'll call you in a couple of hours, sir. I'll have something for you."

"Yep."

"I don't want to touch the situation over in Vietnam, except through official channels. Not for the time being."

"You're right about that, Brownie. I'll wait for your call. When do you leave on your goddamned State Department fact-finding tour over there, Brownie?"

"Not for two days, sir."

"I see. Are you still coming over at cocktail hour?"

"I think I'd better get on this pretty hard, sir," said Lieutenant General Pelton. He paused for a moment, staring across the street.

"Sir?" he asked tentatively.

"Yeah."

"Do you want me to call your son . . . ah . . . Colonel Blue, about this situation?"

The General looked at him hard, then looked away.

"You did the right thing coming to me with this, Brownie. I don't think it will be necessary to notify Matt's father."

"Yes, sir," said Lieutenant General Pelton, uncomprehendingly.

"We'll miss you, Brownie. But I'll be here. You know where to find me."

"Yes, sir," said Lieutenant General Pelton.

The General walked General Pelton upstairs and paused at the door.

"You're a good man, Brownie, coming to me with this," he said, touching the sleeve of Lieutenant General Pelton's jacket. Pelton turned and snapped a salute.

"Thank you, sir," was all he could think of to say. It was the first gesture of affection he'd gotten from the General in the thirty years they'd known each other. He turned and headed down the brick sidewalks of Georgetown toward his car, which was parked around the corner.

No sooner had the General returned to his study, than the phone rang.

"Blue here," said the General. He was alert, but his attention was elsewhere.

"Ma-a-a-atthew," drawled a velvetlike, luxurious voice. "This is your sister-in-law, Aggie."

The voice belonged to the General's first wife's sister, Agnes Randolph. They had never been fans of one another. In fact, they hadn't talked in over twenty years.

"Agnes. Good to hear from you," growled the General.

"I've just spoken to Matt." She paused. "Your son," she said.

"You have," the General said.

"Yes, I have," drawled the velvet-smooth voice. "He has told me about young Matt and his troubles. I think it best that you come down here and talk with your son about his son and your grandson. There is a lot at stake, Ma-a-a-atthew. You know it as well as I do."

"Where are you calling from, Agnes?" the General asked.

"I'm at Wild Acres, where I've always been. Right here in Charlottesville. There is no one else here. It will be just the three of us. Matt is due here at nine. If you drive here directly, you'll be here by then easily."

"We haven't spoken in ten years, you know," said the General, referring to his son.

"All of that must be put aside now, Ma-a-a-atthew," drawled the voice on the phone.

"A boy's life is at stake. Your flesh and blood. Your pride, your son's pride . . . neither of you has that luxury anymore, Ma-a-a-atthew. I'll expect you at nine."

The phone went dead.

The General stared at the receiver, then he leaned his head back against the thick leather of the armchair and stared at the brick wall festooned with the trophies of his trade. He hardly recognized anything hanging there. What good was a gun when there was nothing to shoot? What good a polo ball and mallet when there was no horse to ride, no game to play? What good a helmet when there was no war?

He wondered if it wasn't all just for nothing, the mementos on the walls, the books, the politics . . . the memories. Then he remembered a boy somewhere ten thousand miles away, who was scared and alone, who had no cluttered wall and no politics and, relatively speaking, no memories. He was just starting out, and already someone was saying he was finished.

That had happened to the General nearly fifty years before, when they had told him he'd never make it at West Point. The appointment he'd sought was going to someone else. His hopes for a military career were finished.

Well, goddammit, they had told him it was over before he began, but that wasn't going to happen to his grandson. He stood up and tucked in his shirt and headed upstairs to get his shoes.

Not only was the boy far from finished, but neither was his grandfather, General Matthew Nelson Blue, Jr., U.S. Army, Retired.

3

When Carey Randolph Blue died in September of 1947, she was buried in the graveyard at Monticello next to her mother, Mary Walker Randolph, because she and her mother and her eight sisters were great-granddaughters of Thomas Jefferson. If you are a blood relative of the nation's third President, burial at Monticello is an entitlement, for the graveyard's one and three-tenths acres are still owned by the descendants of President Jefferson, the rest of his property long since having been lost by the family, seized in lieu of unpaid taxes, when President Jefferson died.

It had saddened the General, of course, to bury his wife in a place that had nothing to do with him and everything to do with her. He was destined for Arlington Cemetery, and he would have liked to have had her there with him. But her will dictated the family graveyard at Monticello, and he was loath to go up against the eight sisters who survived her, Aggie at their head. He knew they would stop at nothing to see their sister's will done. Pretty much everything having to do with his wife's family disturbed him. But being commanded from the grave, as it were, where he had to bury his wife of thirty years was on a vastly different plane from the usual disruption of having two sisters stay at the house for a week-long visit, listening to the three of them haggle and argue over people and incidents a half-century in the past with the attention to detail that only two centuries of family history could bring to their disputes.

They were Southern aristocrats from Virginia; they had been raised at Edgehill Plantation, near Charlottesville; when they were girls, their bedrooms had been full of furniture that had come from President Jefferson's house; and when Carey Randolph was sixteen, she had been called with her sisters onto the lawn of Edgehill by her father one morning and told that there was no money left, that Edgehill had to be given up to the state for nonpayment of taxes. The last significant estate in Virginia remotely connected to the Randolph legacy had suffered the same fate as the house and property called Monticello. The life that they had known was over. The nine girls who had been tutored every morning, gone riding every afternoon, taken tea each day at five in long dresses and white gloves—all of them were, as of that morning, on their own. The year was 1910. They were certainly well educated, but having been raised within the cloistered confines of Edgehill, they were hardly schooled in the ways of the world. Carey Randolph accepted what few dollars her father proffered and took a train West.

In Oklahoma she got a job as a nurse in what amounted to a frontier hospital on an Army post on the outer reaches of an uncultivated prairie. A year later she married a young Cavalry lieutenant by the name of Matthew Nelson Blue, Jr. She had her work cut out for her. He was, at the time, a graduate of the eighth grade. The one-room schoolhouse where he had gone to school had lost its teacher to pneumonia when Matthew Blue was fourteen, and *he* had taught the next four years of school. This showed initiative and fortitude, but it hadn't produced a school record or a certificate of graduation. He lost an appointment to West Point to the grandson of Sam Houston, and enlisted in the Army as a private. Two years later he received a direct commission as a second lieutenant, chiefly because of his abilities with horses. His squadron needed him on its polo team, and only officers played polo.

Her sisters had always known she had educated him, that Carey had taken a sharecropper's son from the plains of Oklahoma and turned him into the dashing officer whose picture had eventually appeared on the cover of *Life* magazine. For this reason, chief among many others, they had always resented the General. They felt he had simply used their sister Carey, a woman so tiny and delicate she looked like a doll, with skin as white as porcelain and features, even on the day she died, as free of wrinkles as a magazine cover girl's.

Of course, the sisters had never really known what went on between the coarse, burly General and his petite, demure wife. No one could possibly know the debt the General owed her, or the extent to which it had—or had not—been paid. This didn't prevent the sisters, however, from taking the dimmest of views of the General, and one of those who looked upon him most bleakly was Aggie Randolph Krill, the sister closest to Carey in age and friendship.

Aggie Randolph Krill was widowed, like the General. Upon the death of her husband, a well-regarded professor of criminal law at Yale, she returned to Virginia and settled at Wild Acres, the last piece of Virginia land still belonging to that branch of the Randolphs descended from the family at Edgehill. By the standards of Thomas Jefferson's Monticello or Edgehill, it wasn't much—thirty acres of scrub pine, oak, and maple, on the outskirts of Charlottesville, across from an "outdoor theater," as they called what was popularly known as a drive-in, which specialized in hot-rod epics and five-feature, dawn-to-dusk, moonshine-movie marathons. "Aunt Aggie," as she was called by virtually everyone including the General, was the queen bee of Wild Acres, even though all eight sisters owned the property jointly.

Agnes Randolph Krill knew that her phone call wouldn't sit well with the General. He would be meeting his son for the first time in ten years on ground that was not his, under the supervision of a woman who thought of him, when she thought of him at all, as a philistine who owed his elevated station in life to a dead woman he had wronged on a regular basis when she was alive and his wife.

This wasn't the way the General was used to being treated, but she didn't give a damn. There was something more at stake here than the feelings of an old man who had shown little evidence over the years of having any feelings at all.

Family was at stake. Not the family name, but *family*, the holy notion among those of the South, raised the way she was raised at Edgehill, which dictated that when anyone in the family was down, all family members dropped everything in their lives and came to his or her aid. This is what had made dynasties like the Randolphs powerful over the years—not the fact that a member of the family was a governor or a president or an artist or an industrialist. What made them powerful was the glue that held them together, the shared sense that when they faced it together, the world outside was a far less threatening place than when it was faced alone. In the Randolph family, this held true for sisters and brothers, relatives close and distant, and of course for farm hands' and servants' families who had worked for the Randolphs before, during, and after the War Between the States. Many was the story Agnes Randolph Krill could tell of her father wresting himself from bed at night to bring a sudden halt to the troubles of one of his farm workers who had been stopped on the road by the sheriff because he was walking along carrying six live chickens by their feet, chickens that were braying their discomfiture at a volume usually reserved for roosters at sunrise. Randolphs stood by Randolphs, and if you worked for a Randolph, you might not have the princely status of a descendant of Thomas Jefferson, but your boss did, and you could be damned sure he would exercise it on your behalf, public opinion be damned.

Of course, many called it "taking care of your niggers," but not to the face of Carey or Aggie or Mary Walker or Hollins Randolph himself, because no one wanted to face the wrath of the Randolph family, which, given cause to do so, behaved more like an army than a family.

Indeed, Aunt Aggie had often thought that part of the General's problem with his wife's family was its closeness in spirit to the

Army, which functioned more as a family to him than did his own flesh and blood.

The Army.

She had heard him joke at parties that he was wedded to the Army, but she had always seen the truth behind the joke in the eyes of her sister. Her eyes were alive with intelligence and wit, but wounded from neglect and the hollow feeling within all Army wives that forever they crouched beneath the monolithic Other Woman that was the Army. When the phone rang at 3:00 A.M., she knew he'd be in his boots and out the door to kill rats with a slingshot if that's what the man on the phone told him to do. The terrible thing about being an Army wife, Aunt Aggie thought, having watched her sister for thirty years trying to be as good an Army wife as one could possibly be, was that you didn't just play second fiddle to the Army.

With a man like Matthew Nelson Blue, Jr., you were in the paying audience.

Aunt Aggie and the Colonel were sitting in the living room at Wild Acres, waiting for the arrival of the General. The room wasn't large, but it seemed cavernous from the sofa facing the fireplace. There was a cathedral ceiling, its exposed beams reaching twenty-four feet above the floor at their apex. There was no wall separating the living room at one end from the dining room at the other end of what amounted to a great hall that you entered when you opened the front door of Wild Acres. The dining table, to the right, was a mahogany piece with six leaves that expanded it from a cozy table for six to a behemoth that sat twenty-six. Chairs to seat every one of them tucked themselves into crannies around that end of the room—next to the sideboard, up against a bookshelf, around a card table—so large was the room, they were hardly noticed.

A broad expanse of polished floor separated the dining area from the living area. Off to the left was a hallway leading back to several small bedrooms and one bath. To the right was the door to the kitchen, a great, linoleum-armored, narrow space with windows that looked out on the barnyard next to the house. Down near the fireplace, furniture that had seen better days was gathered in one of those haphazard arrangements that looked so well lived-in you wouldn't dare move a chair. It seemed like a big country house, especially from inside, especially at first glance, but it wasn't.

It was a Prohibition-era roadhouse that had featured a bar, a band, a dance floor, and a basement gambling casino that was reached through a trapdoor. America's flirtation with constitutionally enforced morality had left the Randolphs with a place that exuded character, if not history. Once Aunt Aggie had heard the General actually brag to an old Army friend about the pedigree of Wild Acres. She had thought for a moment there was hope for him yet, then she had watched him pinch the ass of a woman who was not his wife, and who in fact was the wife of the University of Virginia's dean of students. The University of Virginia had of course been founded by Thomas Jefferson, his wife's great-grandfather. It didn't escape her attention that the General had designs—and no doubt would execute those designs—on the wife of another man, in this case the wife of a man who was at least spiritually a retainer of his own wife's great-grandfather. Wives, after all, were just property, territory to him, and he had spent a life taking territory away from other men in war.

He wasn't just coarse, she thought. He was *low*.

The Colonel mixed an old-fashioned for Aunt Aggie and delivered it to her. She was sitting where she usually did, at the end of a chintz-covered couch, and she was perched there like an eagle, because that was the way she looked—like a great bird, about to swoop down on its prey, and its prey was *you*. They sat in the living room of the old place and waited for the arrival of the General, who was on his way down from Washington.

She had her sister's nose, which was assertive, prominent, and, as years went by, even pronounced. Her eyes were slightly hooded, deepset, searching. They made people nervous, her eyes did. Randolph eyes had always made people nervous. Her mother had once told her that all her father had to do was look hard at someone, and he'd buckle. Even the sheriff had no stomach for Hollins Randolph's scowl, a grim, gray ghost of a countenance that could excavate a hundred years of history with the raising of an eyebrow.

Aunt Aggie couldn't drop 'em with an eyebrow, but she could stop 'em with her drawl. When she spoke, the swamps of eastern

Virginia oozed through her teeth. When she was angry, stones from granite outcroppings along the Blue Ridge cascaded down about your feet. Her voice was slow and elegant and cultured and broad in its *a*'s and its *o*'s, but it wasn't her voice that counted. What she *said* was what stopped you in your tracks.

There was the sound of automobile tires on the gravel drive outside, and they heard the iron gate in the stone fence open and shut. The door opened, and a rush of cool autumn air swept through the room.

When the General walked in, she said, "Ma-a-a-atthew." She paused and took a puff of her Fatima cigarette, which she smoked through a long, black holder.

"Say hello to your son, Ma-a-a-atthew. He is a colonel now. I believe he was a captain the last time you two spoke."

The General stood in the open door for a moment, then closed it behind him. He took off his gray fedora and his coat, carefully folding the coat and laying it on a chair next to the door.

"Yes, Aunt Aggie, I believe he was," the General growled. He turned to look at the Colonel.

"How are you?" he asked. He had his hat in his hand, and noticing it, he tossed it atop his coat on the chair.

"I'm concerned about Matt. That's how I am. And I've been hoping that you and I can overcome our differences long enough to do what we can for him. He needs me, and God knows he might even need you before this is over." The Colonel was standing next to Aunt Aggie. He was wearing a pair of khaki trousers and a blue blazer and a tie. Aunt Aggie always liked things on the formal side, and the Colonel was happy to oblige her.

"Bruce Pelton filled me in this morning," said the General. "It looks to me like the boy's got himself into a mess not of his making. It's going to be rough on him, but he's got a few characters on his side. Me, for one. Bruce Pelton's another. He's a lucky young man. He'll come out of this okay."

"I hope you're right," the Colonel said flatly.

"Come over and sit by me, Ma-a-a-atthew," said Aunt Aggie, patting the cushion next to her on the sofa. "Fix your father an old-fashioned, Matt. You do want an old-fashioned, don't you, Ma-a-a-atthew?"

"I'll fix my own goddamned old-fashioned," rasped the General.

The General walked through the door to a bar in the hall just outside the living room and mixed his drink. When he returned, he sat down next to Aunt Aggie on the sofa. She puffed on her Fatima and considered him with her knowing gray eyes.

"You look well, Ma-a-a-atthew," she said. "Your life in Washington must be agreeing with you."

"I got fired two weeks ago. Didn't you hear?" said the General. "Other than that, everything's rosy."

She laughed and puffed on her Fatima, gripping its holder between her thumb and forefinger as she tapped the ash into a large crystal ashtray on the coffee table. The Colonel arrived with another old-fashioned and handed it to her.

"Thank you ever so much," said Aunt Aggie. She coughed, turning her head to the door.

"I'd like to propose a toast," said Aunt Aggie. "To troubles and problems and pain, for these human curses are what truly hold families together." She raised her glass and glanced at the General. He was smiling.

"You're a sly old bitch, aren't you, Agnes," said the General, raising his glass.

"The slyest of the sly old bitches," said Aunt Aggie, raising hers.

The Colonel didn't raise his glass with the others, and said nothing as the others sipped their drinks.

"Is there something wrong, Matt?" Aunt Aggie asked.

"I'll be glad to join any toast after we discuss what we're going to do about my son," he said, looking directly at his father. The General placed his glass on a coaster and slapped his knee.

"Let's get down to it," he said. "What have you been told?"

The Colonel told him about the call from his son, how they were cut off before Matt could tell him anything about the charges and how they'd been brought, what had happened.

The General recounted everything Bruce Pelton had reported that morning. When he got to the name of the division commander, Lieutenant General Lawrence Cardozo, the Colonel stood up and walked over to the window next to the fireplace.

"What's the matter? Hit a nerve?" his father asked, coughing into his handkerchief.

"I had a run-in with Cardozo years ago," said the Colonel.

"What about?"

"About church," said the Colonel, still staring out the window. "He was my battalion commander over in Stuttgart. I had C Company. I was new to the Battalion, there just a week, and he issued an order that all troops would attend church every Sunday. It was part of some big program of his to improve the Battalion's morale . . ."

"Or morals," Aunt Aggie laughed.

"Or morals," said the Colonel, turning to face his father and his aunt. He wasn't smiling.

"I pointed out to him that his order was illegal, that it was unconstitutional to require attendance at church. That didn't earn me many points my first week in the Battalion, let me tell you."

"What did Cardozo say to your amateur reading of the Constitution?" asked the General.

"He said he didn't give a damn, it was his Battalion and he'd do with it what he liked."

"And what did you do? Call a goddamned lawyer?" the General asked.

"I told him I refused to transmit the order, because it was patently illegal."

"Why didn't you just button your lip and go along?" asked the General. "You'd be a general by now. That was the situation that got you sent to that damn munitions depot, wasn't it? Sent to goddamned Siberia?"

The Colonel looked at his father long and hard before he spoke.

"I didn't go along, as you say, because I learned something at West Point that I never learned in your house," said the Colonel, slowly and very deliberately. "I learned honesty. At the Academy they made us attend church every Sunday, and they knew it was illegal and we knew it was illegal. On the one hand, we were being taught that it was our duty to uphold the Constitution, to defend it with our lives if need be. The West Point honor code said that duty and honor and country came before all else, and that honesty was a nonnegotiable demand, an absolute necessity if you were ever to lead men in combat. What was honest about knowingly breaking the law every Sunday by forcing cadets against their will to attend church? The situation was hypocritical on its face and criminal in its effect on the cadets. What I learned, Dad, if you really want to know, is that hypocrisy is a poor substitute for leadership. And I learned that I couldn't stand there and be part of an illegal conspiracy to deprive those troops of the most fundamental of the constitutional rights that they were being paid to defend."

"That's a very noble notion," the General growled. "I'll have to write that down so I can remember it."

"Now, you two," said Aunt Aggie, holding a cigarette aloft on her black holder, waiting for a light. The Colonel stepped forward and lit her cigarette.

"We're not here to fight old battles. We've got a new one to fight, and I don't see that we've done much to that end at this point." She leaned back against the chintz-covered sofa and puffed on her Fatima.

"You seem to know so much," said the Colonel to his father. "Why don't you tell us what we should do?"

The General looked at his son through narrowed eyes. He stood up and walked into the hall and mixed himself another old-fashioned. The Colonel and Aunt Aggie could hear him back there, methodically mashing the lemon rind and maraschino cherry at the bottom of the glass with a wooden pestle. He added the simple syrup and the ice and poured in the bourbon. They heard him swirl the liquid around in the glass for a moment, then he reappeared in the doorway.

"You're such a goddamned self-righteous and pious son of a bitch, and you've done things so goddamned legally and correctly all your goddamned life, boy, tell me this. Are you ready to get on a plane with me and go over to goddamned Vietnam and say to hell with the consequences? Are you ready to go back to Benning and tell your CO that you're sorry but you have to leave for a while so you can take care of your son? Are you willing to cash in your career for the sake of that boy and his troubles?"

"I'm ready to get myself over there and back up my son, but I'll be damned if I'm going to follow along with you and doing things your way. I followed you into the Army and encouraged Matt to do the same, and I'm through following you and your ways."

"You're still the same self-righteous son of a bitch you were when you were twelve years old," said the General. "And here you are back at the Randolph family womb, Wild Acres, hiding behind a woman's skirts, like you used to hide behind your mother's skirts. You'll never change. You were a goddamned mama's boy then, and you're a goddamned mama's boy now." He walked across the living room to the window and took a long, slow sip of his old-fashioned.

"You can do whatever the hell you want to, boy. I've got a plane to catch. Bruce Pelton is heading for Tan Son Nhut tomorrow morning on one of those goddamned State Department fact-finding tours. I'm going with him. I'm going to that godforsaken goddamned country of Vietnam with you or without you, and I'm going to get that boy out of the crap he's found himself in."

"Why cahn't you go together?" drawled Aunt Aggie, her cigarette holder gripped tightly in her yellowed teeth.

The General sipped his old-fashioned, waiting for his son to reply. The Colonel stood and faced his father.

"Do it your way, General. Go ahead over there with Bruce Pelton and grandstand around the countryside and bellow and fluff your damn feathers. I don't care what you do. All you'll be doing, as far as I'm concerned, is getting in my way. And there's a pretty good chance you'll jeopardize any chance that boy has to beat this thing."

"What the hell do you mean by that crack?" asked the General, glowering at the Colonel.

"It's not your war," said the Colonel. "And he's not your son. He's *my* son. You can't treat this situation the way you've treated everything else in your life—with the back of your hand. Things are different from the way they were when you commanded troops in World War II. For better or worse, it's Matt's war. My war was Korea. Your war ended twenty-five years ago. Now it's Matt's turn. It's his war. He called *me* this morning. He didn't call you. And I don't want you over there trying to apply the lessons of World War II to Vietnam. They won't work. This is a new age. It's a new Army. It's a new war. I don't need you over there, and neither does Matt. Do us both a favor. Keep out of this."

"Go to hell," said the General, never removing his eyes from his son.

"Maybe I could be of some help," said Aunt Aggie, trying to put a damper on things.

"This isn't one of those problems great-aunts can solve," said the General. "That goddamned war was started by men, it'll be ended by men, and I'm making it my responsibility to see to it that boy comes out of it not only alive, but with his honor intact."

"I want to propose a toast," said Aunt Aggie, now into her third old-fashioned.

She raised her glass with her left hand, held her cigarette holder with her right, and said, "You're a bastard, Ma-a-a-atthew, and you're not even *our* bastard, but right now I've got a feeling we're going to need more than one." She looked from the General to the Colonel and raised her glass.

"To the two of you," she said.

The General ignored her and turned to the Colonel.

"I'm going over with Bruce Pelton. I don't give a good goddamn what you say, boy."

The General glared at the Colonel, spun on his heel, and left the room. In a moment he could be heard repeating the elaborate process of mixing a fresh old-fashioned, grinding, grinding the lemon rind and cherry at the bottom of his glass with the wooden pestle.

The Colonel stared out the window, drink in hand, his toe beating a slow tattoo to the insistent rhythm of the pestle grinding away in the next room. It seemed as though he'd spent his whole life dancing to his father's tune.

He had been expected to follow in his father's footsteps, and he had. In turn, he had made it clear that he expected his son to follow his father and grandfather into the Army, and he had. War had been their destiny, and war had been Matt's destiny, too.

Not so subtly, the General's distinguished service in World War II and the Colonel's service in Korea had encouraged the boy to volunteer for Vietnam, to take his turn with his war. He was expected to serve as others before him had served. They were a family of warriors, and Vietnam was a war. He wasn't expected to fight in Vietnam to prove his manhood. He wasn't expected to fight in Vietnam for his country. But he had been expected to fight in Vietnam for the Blue name. So he volunteered for a war that by now no one really believed in, and now he was in more trouble than the Colonel could imagine, and the guilt of having encouraged him to volunteer for Vietnam bubbled up inside the Colonel like a bad meal.

The Colonel hated his father most of all because he wished he had been more independent of him. If he hadn't danced to his father's tune, maybe Matt wouldn't have ended up dancing to his. The Blue name was a vicious circle, always threatening to come around and swallow you whole. The Colonel winced at the thought.

Now the almighty family name had swallowed another victim, and this time the victim might not come out alive.

All his life the Colonel had followed in his father's footsteps.

Well, not this time, he thought.

Not while his son's life hung in the balance.

T W O

☆

Eyewash for the Telex-Devil

Firebase Zulu-Foxtrot
Day Two

Eltee! Eltee! It's gettin' on to 0530, so I'm shakin' you, jus' like you said." Dirtball Magee leaned over the Lieutenant and tried to see if he was awake. Dirtball was from Mountain View, Arkansas. He looked like it and he sounded like it. But the amazing thing about Dirtball was the fact that he was a graduate of the University of Arkansas. He'd given some thought to Officer Candidate School but decided against it when he heard a rumor about casualty figures for a typical class of ninety-day wonders: seventy-two percent. Dirtball decided to take his chances as a grunt.

Outside the 113, somewhere beyond the surrounding jungle, the sun was coming up. Lieutenant Matthew Nelson Blue IV turned over on his air mattress and squinted at the face hovering over his own. It was Dirtball, all right. He looked around, trying to focus his eyes. Yeah, there's the cupola, there's the track commander's fold-down seat, there's the lowered back ramp and the berm the track was parked up against. He rubbed his eyes and sat up.

"What's going on, Dirtball?"

"Nothin', sir. Not a fuckin' sound last night. No mortars, no RPGs, no nothin'. Them Charlies musta forgot where we're at, sir. Quiet as a church. Yessir."

"You hear anything about the resupply ship yet, Dirtball? They're supposed to be bringing a hot meal this morning."

"Yessir. They're due at 0600. Two of 'em comin' this mornin'. One carryin' breakfast. The other carryin' the new CO, Lieutenant Colonel Halleck."

"Halleck. Jesus. I almost forgot about him. All right. I better get my ass up and have a look at the perimeter. He's probably going to inspect us with white gloves. Tell Sergeant Davis to start rounding up the troops. I'll be out in a minute."

Halleck. Christ. What a fucking pain in the ass.

Blue pulled on his jungle boots and laced them up. He left his fatigue pants hanging outside the boots, in the manner of all grunts living in the boonies. No bloused boots out here. He put on his fatigue shirt and rolled up the sleeves. Shirts were going to be a problem. There were a few guys who still had them, but he knew there weren't enough to go around. Some would have to stand inspection in their T-shirts. No fatigue shirts wasn't going to go over big with the Halleck-monster.

Halleck was a purebred nut case about dirt and haircuts, but that wasn't all he was. A week before Halleck arrived at the Battalion, one of the officers from the personnel section at brigade headquarters had flown out to the weapons platoon base camp and warned the Lieutenant about him. Halleck was a man on the fast track, said the personnel officer. He'd gotten his promotion to lieutenant colonel on the five-percent list, ahead of his contemporaries. He saw his battalion command as another opportunity for accelerated advancement. And his assignment to Colonel Testor's brigade was no accident, either. Those two went back all the way to West Point. They had been in the same company in the Corps of Cadets, Testor three years ahead of Halleck. They saw themselves as some kind of team, said the personnel officer. And there was a rumor going around that there was more to Halleck's assignment to Testor's brigade than just their friendship. They were up to something, the personnel officer warned. But nobody knew what it was.

The Lieutenant winced when he heard the rumors about Halleck. There was nothing worse than a commander with a private agenda, especially a commander going to war for his own purposes. The Lieutenant was prepared to expect the worst of Halleck. Now he didn't know what to expect.

The Lieutenant crouched and shuffled out the back of the 113. Dirt. That was all he could see. Red dirt, as fine as bath powder. Every step you took sent spoonfuls of the stuff poofing up your pantlegs, down your collar, up your nose, in your hair, in your eyes. Give the place an hour of rain, and all that super-fine red dirt would turn into mud the consistency of soft ice cream—goopy, sloppy, drippy stuff that adhered to everything and dried instantaneously to a metallic hardness that was almost impossible to chip off.

Dirt.

Mud.

VC mortars.

Halleck.

If it wasn't one fucking thing, it was another.

Blue wandered by the other tracks. A half-dozen of the guys could be seen desultorily rubbing down the 4.2-inch mortars with rags that were dirtier than the 4.2s themselves. Rub the dust off this one, it moves over there and gets on that one. Rub the dust off that one, it poofs up and blows over to the 113's firewall. Brush the dust off the firewall, it flies over to the machine gun and happily moves in. Wipe the dust off the machine gun . . .

Christ. The ridiculousness of this asshole Halleck coming out to the platoon firebase and running around checking to see if everything was neat and clean and tidy.

Clean? What clean? Oh, you mean *clean,* like in shiny and bright and polished. Yeah, we got clean for you, shiny boots and gleaming teeth and we got the 113s all waxed and polished, sir. Sure we do.

Neat? Sure, we got lined-up toothbrushes, sir, so if the VC stop by for a night visit, they'll see we're not guilty of inattention to detail.

Tidy? As tidy as your desk drawer, sir, that's how tidy we keep our little asses. In fact, that's all we've got to do out here in the weapons platoon—tidy up, straighten up, make sure the rocks are painted white and the starch in our fatigues is fresh. Sure. Come on out. Just give us a minute to visit the neighborhood barber and make sure our haircuts are regulation length, and while we're at it, we'll have him give each of us an ultra-close shave and a dose of Old Spice after-shave. After all, sir, isn't that what wars are all about?

Neatness, and

cleanness, and

tidiness, and

haircuts.

Lieutenant Blue checked the berm, the dirt levee around the perimeter of the platoon firebase. He checked to see if it was piled high, neat and clean and tidy. It was.

He checked to see if all the tracks were dug in deep and neat and clean and tidy. They were.

He checked the troops, to see if they were all shaved neat and clean and tidy. With the exception of Dirtball, they were.

He checked the concertina wire outside the perimeter to see if it had been laid out in expanding circles, concentric and neat and clean and tidy. It had.

He checked the platoon field of fire, to see if all trees and bushes had been removed for a hundred yards around the firebase perimeter, flat and neat and clean and tidy. They had.

Finally, he made sure that a helipad had been cleared of obstructions so that the CO's chopper could land without blowing up too much debris, all neat and clean and tidy. It was.

"Eltee," called a voice from the other side of one of the 113s. "Can I see you for a short-short?"

The Lieutenant found his platoon sergeant, Elroy Davis, hunkered down over a small fire, cooking his breakfast. A carcass of indeterminate origin was leaning over the fire, skewered on a bayonet. Lieutenant Blue didn't ask what it was. Sergeant Elroy Davis was a couple of years older than the Lieutenant, a career soldier from a place called Hot Coffee, Mississippi, and in Hot Coffee, not much was wasted in the way of edibles.

"What's up, Sarge?"

"We've got three dudes ain't got boonie hats or steel pots neither."

"Who are they?"

"Simpleton, Repatch, and Strosher."

"When did you find this out?"

"This mornin'. I knowed that new major's gonna be dippin' in our shit, so's I had 'em all do a uniform count. Simpleton, he ain't got no fatigue shirt neither."

"Well, you were on the ball checking that out for me, Sarge. Thanks. We'll cover the hat thing, and as far as other missing uniform parts, I'll tell him we've got a lot of shit out to the laundry. What's he going to know?"

"Way I hear it, that new CO couldn't find his ass with a flashlight."

"Watch what you say, Sarge. Stuff has a way of coming back around and biting you right on your tail end."

"Yeah, I hear that, sir." Davis turned his bayonet over to cook the other side of his breakfast.

"You know when this colonel dude be comin', sir?"

"Nobody's even told me he's coming yet, Sarge. I just figure he'll show up, based on what happened last night."

"Yeah, Dirtball done tole me whatchew done on the radio. The men, they be owin' you a trick or two for that one, sir."

"Forget you heard what you heard from Dirtball, Davis. Tell the rest of the men the same thing."

"Me? I heard somethin'? Not this little red rooster, sir." Davis poked at the creature being grilled on the point of his bayonet and licked his finger.

"Mmmm. Y'know what really gets it, sir? I sprinkle me some instant coffee, like a barbecue sauce. Gets that flavorfulness out there where's you can taste it."

"I'll remember that next time I'm cooking in the backyard, Sarge."

Davis smiled, wrinkling his eyes like a Buddha's.

"You gots to get yo'self down to the Delta when this shit war's behind us, sir. I can show you some eatin' you jus' won't believe."

I'll bet, thought Lieutenant Blue. He swallowed hard and nodded.

"Will do, Sarge."

Thwap-thwap-thwap-thwap . . . chopper blades cut the air into great chunks of sound . . . *thwap-thwap-thwap-thwap* . . . down below in the red dirt, it was an unnerving, dangerous noise . . .

thwap-thwap-thwap-thwap . . . but up there in the air over the treetops, out of small-arms range . . . *thwap-thwap-thwap-thwap* . . . pure thriller-diller godlike motion with a rock-and-roll sound-track . . . *thwap-thwap-thwap-thwap* . . . you knew you were on your way when you jumped a chopper and headed out there high above the jungle *swoop-swoop-swooping* deep into the war and safe above it at the same time.

It was magic, it was Coney Island, it was TV, it was noisy, it was supercharged thrillhead willy-dilly, it was the Rolling Stones turned up to 10, it was dreamy and so wonderful and so . . . so . . . so . . . *evil* . . .

The Lieutenant tilted his head back and shielded his eyes, looking over the treetops for the source of the noise. He wondered if it was breakfast or Lieutenant Colonel Halleck. On the one hand, he was hungry; on the other, he didn't give a shit. He was still half asleep, swathed in a cotton-candy fog, nothing could get through to him, everything sounded good, breakfast colonels, colonel break-fast, gimme a hot meal on the objective and I'll float myself over the edge into that daydream zone, a-whapdap slapback lovefalling whoopdeedoo bang-bang-thang like . . .

> Bring it on, man,
> dreamsicle lift-off
> thwapple-popple-dopple
> you know how it is,
> slip it on me
> hang it on me
> yak it down
> baby baby baby
> bring it on . . .

After a while out there you started daydreaming in the Tempta-tions mode, the Platters mode, the Contours mode, the Don Covay mode, the Sam and Dave mode . . . everything had a *beat,* you were always moving and grooving and swaying and baying and wherever you were you were dancing, dancing on "American Bandstand," dancing in the street, dancing up the wall, dancing tight and close and slow with your nose in her neck and your hand on her butt, dancing dancing dancing to the music in your head, and all the girls in your dreams had bouffant hair and tight skirts and high heels all the boys wore white socks and blue jeans and knew the words to "Do You Love Me?" . . .

> *"Do you love me?*
> *Do you love me?*
> *Do you love me?*
> *Now that I can dance . . .*
> *Watch me now*
> *Hey, shoop, shoop,*
> *Hey, whoop it up baby,*
> *Shoop, shoop,*
> *Hey, you driving me crazy,*
> *Shoop, shoop,*
> *Now that I can dance."*

Thwap-thwap-thwap-thwap, in came the chopper, making music over the treetops, dropping dropping dropping straight into the LZ, *whooooooosh* the dusty wind *whooooooosh, shoop-shoop-shoop-shoop* it was shutting down, rotors slower slower slowly slowly dying dying . . .

Hot meal! Yeah! Bring it on!

The weapons platoon emerged from tracks and holes and bunkers and racks and latrines and surrounded the fat bird, lining up eager-faced for scrambled eggs and shit-on-a-shingle and coffee and canned juice and soggy toast and bacon that looked like worn-out shoe leather but smelled just like Mom's kitchen.

Lieutenant Blue watched Sergeant Davis organize a make-believe line, something that would satisfy the mess-hall rats unlucky enough to have been picked for this boonie visit, slopping steaming piles on mess kits, pouring the bitter coffee, always looking over their shoulders like some gook was going to blast out of the treeline with a bullet with their names on it. Over on the side, two company clerks barked out the weapons platoon Mail Call, delivering love letters and bills and third-class promises of cruise

81

vacations and nineteen-inch TVs, if only you'll send for this one-time-special-offer insurance policy, sir.

Sir? they'd joke later. Ain't no sir out here but us assholes, and the only insurance policy we got is paranoia, puking in your poncho you're so scared, eat some speed, eat some more, man, stay awake all night and all day and eat some more speed and wait wait wait wait for incoming wait for 'em to come through the wire on their bellies sappers and dappers and mean-ass little fuckers with knives in their teeth and death in their eyes . . .

Insurance policies, yeah, that was a good one.

The weapons platoon didn't mind the visitation from the real world, hooch-rat motherfuckers or no hooch-rat motherfuckers, they dug into the grits with a blistering determination that could have come from only one thing—three days of C-rations and empty promises and warm canteen swill water and heating up GI instant coffee over little piles of C-4 plastique explosive dug out of the backs of Claymore mines, boonie cuisine, gut-ream ookie-dookie that kept you up holding onto your balls puking and hoping your lunch was all you'd lose.

"How 'bout this shit, Eltee," said Whoopie Cushion Ridgely, who got his name because he was always carrying around some kind of inflatable device the purpose of which was the supposed lessening of the pain of his hemorrhoids. Nobody believed Whoopie Cushion's hemmies. They just thought he was weird. He was hell on wheels with a grenade launcher, though, shot a fat round up a water buffalo's ass one time, clean as a whistle, left water buffalo all over the side of a freshly stuccoed gook hooch, grab-ass good-time graffiti, Whoopie Cushion called it. Weird guy.

"Good grits, Ridgely," said the Lieutenant, digging into his plate.

"They bringin' us more a' this shit tonight, Eltee?" asked Whoopie Cushion with a mouthful of eggs.

"I doubt it, Ridgely. The way things are going, I'm not sure we'll be here tonight."

"Shit, Eltee."

"Yeah, Ridgely, shit."

Before the platoon finished eating, the breakfast chopper lifted up and away and was gone, *thwap-thwap-thwap-thwapping* its way back to the land of hooch honeys and hot showers and deodorant sticks and an immediately noticeable absence of incoming. Hooch-rat cooks and clerks and jerks hung out the chopper door, waving like they were lifting off from a fifty-yard-line appearance at a homecoming game. All that was missing was a marching band in white shoes and hats with big purple pompoms bouncing on top.

It was the middle of the afternoon when the chopper carrying Lieutenant Colonel Halleck *thwap-thwap-thwap-thwapped* its way over the jungle and dropped into Firebase Zulu-Foxtrot. By that time, even Dirtball had dragged a razor over his cheeks, the weapons platoon looked as good as it was ever going to look, and all the red dirt they could find had been redistributed from one weapon to another in a kind of red-dirt musical chairs run to ground on a Wilson Pickett soul man soundtrack supplied by AFN, the Armed Forces Network, the military radio station that supplied the rock-and-roll soundtrack of the war.

He was beautiful.

Lieutenant Colonel Halleck stepped out of the chopper and straightened the crease of his fatigue pants and rubbed each boot toe behind his knees, shining, polishing, getting that mean gleam burnish on his boots.

Halleck looked just beautiful, everybody could see it, like a rock star stepping on stage, he was so fine. His fatigues weren't a uniform, they were pure costume, starched fresh, boots shined, you'd have gone blind if you caught the reflection off his white-sidewall head shave. The sun hit him like a super-trooper spotlight, center stage. He squinted and smiled and shielded his eyes with his hand and he was perfect, just delicious, his own mother wouldn't have recognized him, he was so beautiful.

Lieutenant Blue waited until the chopper's rotors had shut down, then he advanced toward the new CO and reported.

"Lieutenant Blue reporting, sir. Welcome to Firebase Zulu-Foxtrot."

"I thought you called this place Firebase Bravo," said Halleck, returning his salute.

"We changed it, sir. Bravo was bad luck. Zulu-Foxtrot is working for us. We haven't been mortared in twenty-four hours."

"Well, we're going to have to fix that, aren't we, Lieutenant? If you're not drawing fire, you're not doing your job, is what I always say."

"Yes, sir. That's what I say, too." The Lieutenant spun on his heel and headed away from the chopper, concealing the grimace on his face. Over by his track, the weapons platoon was lined up for inspection.

Sergeant Davis saluted.

"Weapons platoon ready for inspection, sir." Lieutenant Blue could smell whatever Davis had grilled for breakfast from ten feet away. Halleck returned Davis's salute and headed down the line, apparently oblivious of the stench. So far so good. Twenty-four of them lined up standing at attention, twenty-one men short of Table of Operations & Equipment regulation forty-five-man platoon strength. Typical. Never enough bodies to go around. Everybody was short. Everybody but the VC. They had a seemingly endless supply of bodies. Their TO&E read "unlimited."

Lieutenant Blue followed Halleck as he walked the line. Halleck paused and executed a left-face in front of each man, bantering with the troops, where-you-froming them, when-did-you-last-write-homing them, how's-the-chowing them. The Lieutenant looked over Halleck's shoulder, down the line. Four men away was Repatch. He didn't have a boonie hat. Halleck was chatting with Whoopie Cushion, and Cushion was laying his hemorrhoid rap on him. Blue saw Thompson's hat pass behind the men's backs down the line until it got to Repatch. Repatch put it on and grinned. Halleck moved down a man. Whoopie Cushion doffed his hat as Halleck left-faced, and Cushion's hat made its way down the line hand to hand. Mallick grabbed it and put it on. Down the line went Halleck, and down the line behind the platoon's backs went the boonie hats. He commented to the six who weren't wearing proper fatigue shirts, and they in turn gave the standard uniforms-out-to-the-laundry-sir excuse, which seemed to satisfy him. He was big on the laundry, bigger still on starch, a panacea for many soldierly ills.

"Starch 'em up and shine 'em up and they'll follow you to the end of the earth," Halleck told Lieutenant Blue as Sergeant Davis dismissed the platoon.

"Yes, sir, I agree wholeheartedly," said the Lieutenant, leading the way to his 113, where Dirtball waited with coffee and doughnuts copped from the breakfast chopper. Dirtball was heating the coffee in a canteen cup over a little pile of C-4 behind the 113. The Lieutenant could smell it. He wrinkled his nose. Nothing like C-4 coffee. No, sir.

Halleck stopped at the 113 and rested a beautifully shined jungle boot on the ramp.

"I want to talk to you about that radio transmission last night, Lieutenant," he said, looking sternly at Blue.

"Yes, sir."

"What happened?"

"I don't know, sir. Radio just went out, I guess."

"I tried to raise you for two hours, Lieutenant Blue. Did you know that?"

"No, sir."

"Where's your RTO?"

"He's making coffee, sir."

"What has he got to say? Does your radio have a dead battery?"

"No, sir. Magee caught a hop back to Battalion yesterday and brought six batteries back with him. The battery is okay."

"Then how do you explain all the static? How do you explain your radio going dead on you?"

"Jamming, sir?" said the Lieutenant, trying hard to sound confused and uncertain.

"Jamming. Mmmmm. Never thought about that," said Halleck. "I've got a memo about jamming on my desk right now. Mmmmm. Jamming. Could be it."

"Yes, sir," said the Lieutenant, trying hard to sound hopeful.

"Now I want to talk to you about the men's haircuts. And *your* haircut."

"Yes, sir."

"You know how I want them."

"Yes, sir."

"Have the men sent back to Battalion three at a time until you get this haircut thing under control. You first, Lieutenant. Understood?"

"Yes, sir."

Dirtball interrupted with a cup of lukewarm coffee and a stale doughnut. Halleck munched and sipped happily, seated on the 113's ramp in the shade. Dirtball gave him a napkin. Halleck used it on his boots, polishing their toes. Dirtball looked at the Lieutenant and shrugged. The Lieutenant signaled him to get the hell away from the track. Dirtball disappeared.

After he was finished with his snack, Halleck took a stroll around the perimeter, checking out the platoon fortifications and fields of fire. He just strolled and nodded, strolled and nodded, hands clasped behind his back in the manner of Winston Churchill. Everything was apparently neat and clean and tidy.

When the perimeter inspection was complete, Halleck reminded the Lieutenant about the haircut schedule and bade him farewell. The Lieutenant saluted. Halleck walked over to his chopper, and the pilot started his engine, the great rotor blades *shoop-shoop-shoop-shooping* through the air. But that's all they did . . . *shoop-shoop-shoop-shoop* . . . *shoop-shoop-shoop-shoop*. The engine wouldn't catch. The rotor blades *shoop-shoop-shoop-shooped* to a stop. Halleck got out of the chopper.

"Do you mind if I use your jeep to get back to Battalion?" asked Halleck. "The chopper won't crank."

"No, sir. Welcome to it," said the Lieutenant. "I'll have Mallick drive you."

The Lieutenant signaled Mallick to get the jeep. In a moment, Mallick pulled up to Halleck and the Lieutenant, who were crouched in the shade of the Lieutenant's 113.

Halleck climbed in the jeep's passenger seat, and Mallick started the engine. Then Halleck said something to Mallick and he cut the engine. Halleck walked over to the Lieutenant. He called him aside.

"Are these roads around here secure?" he asked the Lieutenant, checking his watch. It was seven-thirty.

"Gee, I don't know, sir. You tell me. You've sent me out on three night missions on these roads. You've got better intelligence at Battalion than I have out here. *You* tell *me* if they're secure, sir."

Halleck glared at him. He checked his watch again.

"Lieutenant Blue, I seem to have left my weapon back at headquarters. Do you think I could have the loan of your M-79 until tomorrow?"

The Lieutenant looked at Halleck for an instant and smiled.

"No, sir. That would be against Army regulations, which forbid the loaning of weapons signed to you."

Halleck glared at him. He walked back to the jeep and sat in the passenger's seat for a few moments, obviously calculating his chances of making it back to the battalion base camp, traveling down dirt roads unattended by American troops at this time of night. The sun was low on the horizon, just over the lip of the jungle. There were maybe forty-five minutes until it got dark.

Lieutenant Blue stood there next to his 113, watching Halleck fret. The Lieutenant just stood there, arms folded across his chest. Around the perimeter he could see most of the men watching the scene unfold.

Finally, Halleck climbed out of the jeep and walked over to the Lieutenant.

"I need to use your radio, Lieutenant," he said softly.

"Dirtball? Get the radio," the Lieutenant commanded. Dirtball arrived with the radio, cleared the whip antenna of obstructions, and switched it on.

Halleck called back to Battalion and ordered another helicopter. He did so in a very low voice. Then he glared at the Lieutenant again and walked over to the helicopter and waited.

Twenty minutes later, the replacement chopper *thwap-thwap-thwap-thwapped* into view. The chopper landed and Halleck and the other chopper pilot got on board and the chopper *thwap-thwap-thwap-thwapped* over the treetops into the gathering darkness and out of sight.

The Lieutenant watched the fat bird until it disappeared, then he turned around. The whole weapons platoon was standing behind him, waving their T-shirts and boonie hats good-bye.

"Dude didn't want to spend no night in no boonies with our sorry asses, huh, Lieutenant?" said Repatch, cleaning his nails with the tip of his bayonet, grinning that sick grin of his. Repatch looked like a reject from a bad litter of pit bulls. Nothing pleased him more than walking point on patrol. He'd glide alone out there so quiet the patrol would lose him and he'd reappear in their midst without their ever knowing he was gone. Snake, they called him. The Lieutenant had watched him a few times on patrol and understood why.

"Guess he didn't," said Lieutenant Blue. He was still looking over the treetops, listening to the faint *thwap-thwap-thwap-thwap* of the chopper until it was gone.

"He'll be back," said Repatch, grinning and picking at his nails. "We one up on his ass. He won't forget that."

Yes, Halleck would be back. Not much doubt about that. But if he never showed his face again, it would be too soon for the Lieutenant.

Somewhere on the perimeter in a red hole in the red dirt, one of the troops switched on a radio. Out there on the edge of the boonies, with only three sandbags and a few feet of wire between you and hell, a big bass guitar was thunking and the cymbals were filling and the drums were pounding and you could hear Archie Bell and the Drells chanting softly in the dark:

> *"C'mon now, do the tighten-up,*
> *Do the tighten-up,*
> *Do the tighten-up,*
> *We're tightening-up,*
> *Do the tighten-up,*
> *You can do it to it,*
> *Everything will be outasight,*
> *You can do it now,*
> *Tighten-up, tighten-up, baby,*
> *Tighten-up."*

Dirtball clapped the Lieutenant on the shoulder and handed him a can of C-ration beans and franks.

"C'mon, sir. Let's eat."

"Wasn't Halleck something today, Dirtball? I mean, wasn't he just *beautiful* in the boots and fatigues and all? Did you see his belt buckle? You could use it to read by in the dark, it was so bright. I mean, that Lieutenant Colonel Halleck just makes you want to be as beautiful as he is, doesn't he? I mean, he was inspirational."

"Sure, Lieutenant," said Dirtball, leading the way. "Gonna be a long night, Lieutenant Blue. Sure is."

The Lieutenant folded himself into the 113 and collapsed on his air mattress. He reached for his poncho liner and tucked it around his shoulders. Outside, the jungle treeline disappeared into the darkness and the crickets jumped in and were making music with Archie Bell and the Drells.

That was the thing about Vietnam.

> The smell
> The insects
> The darkness
> The red dirt
> The sudden bright hell of a fire fight
> The songs of the dead on the perimeter.

"Another fucking night in fucking paradise, huh, Dirtball?"

"When you right, you right, Lieutenant. And you right."

Dirtball stood up and stuck his head out the cupola and spat tobacco juice at the jungle and the enemy.

"Take that, motherfuckers," he said.

Yes, indeed.

Take *that*.

4

Where was that noise coming from?

He sat up in bed and cocked his ear. Outside the window, the saberlike fronds of a royal palm swayed in a gentle breeze that had somehow failed to penetrate the confines of his suite even though all three windows and the balcony doors were open, screenless and shutterless to the weather.

He got up and padded over to the balcony and leaned over the rusting rail and peered into the courtyard below. Nothing down there but the usual midmorning clutter. Over in the corner the hookers' resident mama-san squatted next to her clay hibachi, cooking noodles and fish heads and cabbage and lemon grass and God only knew what else. A thin plume of charcoal smoke rose from the fire, carrying with it the pungent aroma of the morning meal. One of the hookers stepped into the courtyard wearing a turquoise *ao dai* slit up to her waist and said something to the mama-san. The mama-san giggled, dropping her head and hiding her mouth with her hand, but he was too far away on his third-floor balcony to hear what all the merriment was about, not that he would have understood either the words or the point of the joke anyway. The hooker teetered back inside on heels that must have made her at least five-one, maybe five-one-and-a-half. Jesus.

There it was again.

He could hear better now. It was music, American music, but where was it coming from? Nobody he knew at the Pension Gravois had a radio, and even if they did, it was doubtful it would be tuned to Armed Forces Network. He padded barefoot back inside and took to his lumpy mattress. He glanced at his watch, a Rolex he'd picked up on the street from a kid with watery eyes and a runny nose and shaky hands, sure signs of a bad opium habit. The kid couldn't have been a day over twelve. He gave him two American dollars and an unopened pack of Marlboros. The kid scampered away down an alley, disappearing in an instant through a doorway no wider than a board. He was amazed to find that the Rolex was a real one that actually worked, and when he saw the same kid a couple of days later, he tried to give him a few more dollars, but the kid ran away before he got his wallet out of his pocket. Weird, what the volatile mix of opium and poverty did to you. Turned you into a rat, you got skinnier and skinnier and skinnier until your fingers looked like claws and your cheeks disappeared and your hair fell out and your ears got pointy and you started scampering into holes and through cracks away from a world that in the absence of your sweet smoke looked more and more threatening and less and less real swimming in the misty edges of a craving that gnawed at you inside . . .

There it was again!

The music was loud now, wafting through the open windows like little bursts of steam from the humid, sunbaked streets below.

> *"Gimme a ticket for an aeroplane,*
> *Ain't got time to take a fast train,*
> *Lonely days are gone,*
> *I'm a-goin' home,*
> *My baby, she wrote me a letter."*

It was a Boxtops hit from a few years back, a song about longing and mistrust and a rabid, nasty kind of need, a song with a melody rooted somewhere down in Mississippi dirt where pride mixed with shame and came up smelling like sweat and meat. Somebody was playing it on a piano, singing the song more slowly than the record to a dirgelike march beat in an accent that sounded like rock and roll played through a car speaker wired to a ceiling fan turned on high—a quavering, wispy, shuddering wail that sent shivers down your spine. The music was funereal, eerie, ghostlike in the emerging heat of the morning.

What did it sound like?

It sounded the way the morning smelled, the way the palm tree waved, the way the mama-san giggled, the way the lizard crawled straight up the wall and across the ceiling flicking its tongue at nightflies and wet mosquitoes, the way the sheets stuck to you like bandages, the way the wind didn't blow in, it sucked out, removing rather than replenishing. The Boxtops at 9:00 A.M. on Phuc Do Street was perfect wake-up music, clearing the debris, emptying you, getting you ready to suck it in all over again.

What did it sound like?

It sounded dead.

It sounded like Saigon.

Danny Jannick lived down at the end of Phuc Do Street in the Pension Gravois because the Pacific News Service didn't pay him enough to live anywhere else. The Pension Gravois was a three-story stuccoed flat-roofed fall-down hovel held together with chicken wire and scavenged paving stones and three-dollar-a-week rents that seemed to have been freeze-dried during French colonial days and preserved like some kind of punishment museum, a reminder that similar fates lurked at the end of similar streets for anyone remaining too long in the zone of bad luck, crushed hopes, and broken dreams that had been Southeast Asia since the beginning of time.

Danny Jannick liked it just fine at the Pension Gravois. He paid ten dollars a week for two rooms and connecting bath that produced hot water for one hour every day. The widowed Madame Gravois, who still lived downstairs in three rooms on the first floor, had a weak spot for reporters. Her son had been an editor at the French-language afternoon daily, *Saigon Après Midi,* before the fall of Dien Bien Phu, the 1954 defeat of the French by the Viet Minh after an eight-year war. Dien Bien Phu was a battle that happened a long time ago, but it was suddenly looking like yesterday as the American "commitment" in Vietnam slogged into its fifth year. Madame Gravois was a handy "source" who provided plenty of historical perspective in the dispatches Jannick wired back to his employers in San Francisco, the Pacific News Service, a kind of left-wing AP that supplied the underground press with an alternative point of view on the war. Jannick, for example, was the only reporter in Vietnam who provided his readers with a monthly *American* body count alongside that of the enemy—a service that hardly endeared him to the handlers of the press over at MACV headquarters.

He was a short, wiry guy who wore granny glasses and looked as though he should have had long hair and probably would have if premature balding hadn't started early and been accelerated by the two and a half years he'd spent in Vietnam scrambling around for the crumbs that fell from the overloaded plates of the wire services, the *New York Times,* the *Washington Post,* and the networks. The Jannick theory of war reporting was simple. Anything considered unimportant enough to be ignored by the big boys was just the right size for the Pacific News Service. The practice of picking up where others left off had provided its share of news plums over the years, including revelations about the massive black market being run by the high-ranking NCOs who ran the chain of officers', NCOs', and enlisted men's clubs in Vietnam.

The Jannick method also made for a more leisurely pace of life than that which was enjoyed by the Dan Rathers and David Halberstams of the establishment press corps.

Nine A.M. was indeed an early morning. Usually the sounds and scents of the Pension Gravois went unappreciated by the man in the third-floor suite until his gradual arousal around noon. Only the mournful wail of the old Boxtops hit had sufficiently disturbed the much-needed sleep of Danny Jannick on this sunny fall morning in Saigon and caused his awakening.

He lay on his cot under an open window, waiting for the breeze that never came. What time was it? Nine-fifteen? Wonderful. Forty-five more minutes of hot water, a luxury he usually missed on mornings that disappeared amid blubbering snores and wheezes that persisted as late as noon.

What day was it?

Was it November?

Did it matter?

He decided not.

Jannick eased his legs over the side of the cot and sat up. He was twenty-five years old. He looked thirty-five. His frame was small, his limbs scrawny, his neck ostrichlike, his nose "pronounced," an adjective on the generous side of the descriptive equation, and his hair—well, his hair was AWOL. He reached under the cot, pulled out his Dopp kit, and rummaged through its collection of ointment tubes and pill containers, finally extracting from its depths a brown glass bottle about the size of a half-pint. He unscrewed the cap and dumped a small pile of white pills into his palm.

"Ah, Ritalin, breakfast of champions," he said to no one in particular, his voice ricocheting from one whitewashed stucco wall to the other. He popped the pills into his mouth and headed for the bathroom, where he found a bottle of Evian water and took a long swallow. His arms vibrated and his legs shivered and his forehead quivered as the pills went down. In a moment the shakes would pass and the pills would take hold and all would be well.

He shuffled back into the other room and sat down on the edge of the cot. Every morning when he woke up, every time he dropped a half-dozen Ritalin and waited for the desired effect, he collapsed under the guilty notion that the ready availability of Ritalin, Dexedrine, Dexamil, Desoxyn, and a score of foreign strains of amphetamines of varying strengths were a good part of the reason he was still in Vietnam after two years. What if he had to go home to Frisco, and he couldn't get the speed to pick him up in the morning? What if those little orange triangles, those little blue squares, those incredible bulletlike black beauties weren't around when the typewriter beckoned, its black keys gleaming like the rotting teeth of the journalism demon, smiling in that come-hither way of all typewriters, whispering across the room the terrifying truth: Within this grinning maw lies victory and defeat, fame and ignominy, fortune and destitution? Would inspiration flee, would words wither, would sentences succumb, would paragraphs *poof?* What then, indeed?

Easier to remain within the comforting confines of the pad on Phuc Do Street, a friendly *pharmacie* dispensing goodies at the end of the block, far from the pokings and proddings of editors, the worried clock-watching of fact-checkers, the prissy thumb-twiddling of publishers, that's what. Where were all those fuckers when the hammer came down, anyway? Where were they when the typewriter sat over there across the room belly-laughing at you, the carriage *tttttttttttthhhhhhhting* back and forth, those black-ass fucking keys dancing their *twick-twick-twick* dance of death in the fading light when all you had between yourself and the beast was a fifth of Scotch and whatever pills you'd been able to gather around yourself, litter-carrier pills toting your sorry carcass past the cathedral of total journalistic failure while attendants of doom danced down a poppy-strewn aisle hungering for a pound of flesh . . .

Where, indeed, were the lousy bastards who sat behind desks screaming for copy from the front? What *front,* you blithering blank-firing zipgun asswipes? What do you know from fucking fronts, or rears or midsections, come to think of it? Zero. Zippo. Nada. El-hole-o. That's what you know. Fucking nothing.

Danny Jannick lifted his right arm over his head and sniffed his underarm.

Yes.

Yes!

The speed was taking hold, dribbling down his ribcage in great rivulets of swamp-stink, delicious tinklings of death-knocker-doom-sweat, clear flowing streams of joy-tears, rot-scent rivers of hope, eyewash for the telex-devil, its bloodsuck black irises staring down the twisted tunnel of the copy-maw . . .

Yes!

Cleareyed at last, Jannick leapt to his feet and stepped into the closet-sized shower and let the rusted shower head dribble some canal water over his head. He soaped up fast, afraid the thing would sputter and quit on him as it usually did. When he was finished washing, he stood under the dribbling shower for a while, letting it rinse away the fear. As he stepped from the shower and wrapped himself in the tissue-thin, pension-supplied towel, he heard a knock at the door.

"Yeah?" he called from the bathroom.

"Danny-san! Danny-san! Message Danny-san!"

He heard the scurrying of small feet as his morning bearer of bad tidings descended the stairs. It was the dead Mr. Gravois's illegitimate daughter's aunt, he knew, a wizened old mama-san who ran errands and cleaned up around the *pension*. Mr. Gravois was ten years in the grave and still the *pension* supported an extended family of a dozen or so, Mrs. Gravois accepting with a shrug her mixed French-Vietnamese offspring and their half-brothers and half-sisters and *their* offspring. There was little sense in fighting the tide while you were swimming in it, she figured. Once Jannick had asked her about the scurrying mama-san, and Mrs. Gravois had smiled a Galoises-stained smile and said, "Henri truly loved this country. Vietnam was Algeria in his dreams."

Yeah you betcha Madame G., Jannick thought. And Saigon is the Paris of the Far East and Beirut is the Paris of the Near East. You keep talking like that, and you're going to be comparing grilled leg of dog favorably with braised breast of chicken, the way the French Foreign Legion vets do after two warm beers and a cigarette. Going native was for dream-besotted romantics with a strong streak of the eager fool in them, the kind of goofs who threw the *I Ching* before sugaring their morning coffee. *Staying* native, on the other hand, could be deadly.

He opened his door and picked up the envelope lying on the sisal mat. Instantaneously, the other three doors down the hall opened a crack exposing low-slung pairs of slanted black eyes squinting into the gloom. The doors closed just as quickly, before the twenty-five-watt hall light could illuminate the dark faces of the watchers. He closed his door and took a bamboo chair out on the balcony and sat down. The sun flickered through the palm fronds and flies buzzed around his ankles. He zipped open the envelope with a switchblade he had found in his desk drawer the first day he checked into the Pension Gravois.

Bush-beater: Check out the TDY assignment roster
for captains over at MACV HQ. Your pal Alvin Dupuy
Esq. from your hometown finally hit it big. He's headed

up to II Corps on some deal they got the lid screwed
down so tight on not even Alvin's talking.

The note was unsigned, but Jannick knew it came from Specialist
Fourth Class Thomas J. Calhoun, one of the clerks in G-1 Personnel
at MACV. Jannick had cultivated Calhoun's predecessor as a
source, and Calhoun had inherited his sourceship when the guy he
replaced rotated home. Jannick kept the personnel poop flowing
with an occasional bribe of a Motown tape that a secretary back at
Pacific News sent over every month. Listening to Motown, sharing
a joint . . . enlisted sources in Vietnam hardly needed encouragement when it came to blowing the whistle on the bullshit. He
wondered if the powers-that-were ever knew how cheaply bad news
could be had. He doubted it. They were safely cocooned inside the
Time-Life and television orbit. Not even the straight newspaper
reporters penetrated the secure perimeter of the top Saigon command, a zone where all enemy body counts were "up!" where
search-and-destroy sweeps always wiped out an enemy command
and control headquarters, where casualties were always "light,"
where the only news that reached the sun-pink little ears of the
staff officers was good news and time on the embassy tennis courts
was easily scheduled.

Alvin Z. Dupuy, Esq., belonged in that zone, yes indeed. Born
with a silver spoon the size of a goddamned front-loader in his
mouth on St. Charles Avenue in uptown New Orleans, Alvin Z.
Dupuy was one of those priss-pot stiff-necked sons of bitches who
had never drawn an anxious breath in his life. He had graduated
from Tulane in the same class as Danny Jannick, followed quickly
by three years at Tulane law school and an ROTC commission. Now
he was a JAG captain assigned to MACV HQ, a duty station he
didn't hesitate to tell you had been engineered by his father's close
friend, Louisiana Congressman F. Edward Hebert, chairman of the
House Armed Services Committee. You could say Danny Jannick
was a draft dodger, though his 4-F draft status had been legiti-
mately come by, owing to chronic asthma. But Dupuy was something worse. He was a rear-area hawk, one of those lily-livered
saber-rattling fucks who spouted opinions from the vantage point of

his air-conditioned quarters in Saigon about the strategic need for more division-sized month-long sweeps of enemy territory by troops who were already worn to a frazzle by an enemy that was as invisible as it was vicious. Yeah, Alvie Dupuy wanted to bomb the north, mine Haiphong harbor, and drive the NVA from their "sanctuaries" across the border in Cambodia and Laos. He was a regular Richard Nixon, that Alvie, always ready to take the old war wagon right down Charlie's alley, as long as he didn't have to ride shotgun.

Jannick wondered what Dupuy was up to, knowing that it couldn't be any good for anyone other than himself. Dupuy had been in-country for six months and this was the first Jannick had heard of him going any farther from the safety of Saigon than an occasional helicopter jaunt to the ersatz beach resort at Vung Tau. He resolved to meander by MACV headquarters later in the day, perhaps in time for the famous Five-O'clock Follies, the chest-thumping press briefing that so amused the collected media cynics every afternoon. Dupuy bore close attention, if only because the bastard functioned as a foolproof weathervane indicating only ill winds, the kind of shit-storms that could land you—but not Alvie Dupuy—in mud up to your neck with sand blowing in your face. Jannick wondered how a place as down and dirty as New Orleans could produce the grand Fats Domino and then turn around and squat out Alvie Dupuy. Next time he got home, he resolved to ask his mother. She'd know. She might have been raised in the far rain forests of the working-poor Ninth Ward, but she sure knew her shit from Shinola when it came to uptown jerks and phonies. She had changed diapers and wiped asses for two generations of them as a uniformed maid. She knew from experience where the Alvie Dupuys of this world got on and got off. Yes indeed.

Jannick pulled on white painter's pants and stuck his feet in a pair of ten-cent flip-flops. He tucked the envelope in his pocket, grabbed a T-shirt with FILLMORE EAST on it, and headed out the door. He didn't leave much behind. Mama-san would comb through his goodies and make sure he wasn't saving anything for tomorrow that could be put to better use today. That was the thing about the Vietnamese. They had a *mañana* attitude that made Mexican siesta-junkies look industrious by comparison. The national mania for procrastination extended to every phase of life except theft, which was regarded more as an obligation than as a crime. If it was there, you took it. Nothing was wasted. A tin can could turn into a stove . . . or a grenade. A belt buckle into a can opener . . . or a shell casing. A length of iron pipe into a drum . . . or a mortar tube. It was all in how you looked at things.

In Vietnam, nothing was as it seemed.

He hit Phuc Do Street and raised a finger. A bicycle taxi appeared out of a fog of exhaust smoke. The driver was wearing aviator shades and a fifty-mission crash pilot's hat. He had betel-nut-stained teeth and fingernails like bear claws.

"You go MACV, Continental, embassy, I take. Cheap-cheap. Twenty piaster. Cheap-cheap. Quick-quick."

"MACV."

Jannick climbed onto the taxi seat and gripped the handrails. Into the fog of exhaust they sped.

Ah! Saigon! Jannick thought as the three-wheeled taxi rounded a corner on two wheels.

Was this the future?

Would he live long enough to find out?

Did it matter?

He gritted his teeth and held on as the bicycle taxi passed an oil-spewing bus with six chickens and three pigs sticking out the window. The bus driver screeched something at the taxi driver, and he screeched back. There was a mutual shaking of fists and baring of stained teeth, and the taxi took another corner on two wheels missing a fruit stand by inches.

That was the thing about Saigon.

With ten bucks in your pocket and a snootful of adrenaline and a decent tip to follow up, you could hire a bike-taxi and be king for a day.

Who could tell you no?

Not your editor back in Frisco. He wasn't around to look over your shoulder.

Not General Creighton Abrams, commander of MACV. He didn't care about pipsqueaks like you.

In Vietnam, no one cared.

The bike-taxi stopped outside the gate of the well-fortified MACV compound. This was where everything was happening. Tan Son Nhut Air Base was just down the road, and huge olive-drab C-141 Starlifters could be seen taking off and landing, two a minute, on the six constantly busy runways that operated twenty-four hours a day. They said Tan Son Nhut had more takeoffs and landings than Chicago's O'Hare Airport, the busiest airport in the continental United States, and Jannick believed it.

Jannick paid the bike-taxi driver and walked over to the gatehouse. An MP checked his press credentials and had him sign the visitors' book. He was in. The main MACV headquarters building was an old French colonial stucco affair that had once housed the myriad bureaucracies that administered French rule in Southeast Asia. Since then, the compound had undergone a U.S. military bastardization. Temporary buildings in a half-dozen shapes and sizes surrounded the headquarters, housing the nerve center of the American military presence. You could stand at the gate of MACV and in a single glance take in the real lesson of Southeast Asia. The Americans had simply taken up where the French left off. They hadn't even built another headquarters.

No one, after all, had learned anything.

For the occupiers, there was no history.

Today was all that mattered.

This was an attitude that fit Jannick's mind-set precisely, because his approach to life was that of the journalist. He lived in the present tense. Nothing counted but *right now.*

Jannick shook his head and headed across the compound to a Quonset hut behind the headquarters. He was looking for Calhoun. If his guess was right, Calhoun was holding out a vital piece of information, as he usually did. Jannick wanted Calhoun's poop. All of it. He was like a junkie who needed to score. He could *smell* Calhoun's little game. His ears pricked up and his eyes gleamed and his fingers tingled. This was what it was all about. Poop. Data. More goodies for the chow-chow monster.

Yes!

Jannick opened the front door and felt a rush of icy air. Ah, the rear-area desk jockeys. They knew how to fight a war.

Calhoun's cubicle was the third one down on the right. Jannick slipped into a chair next to Calhoun's desk before the spec-4 could look up. He tossed an envelope on the desk.

"What have you got, dude?" he asked. "This rascal's half-empty."

Calhoun looked over his shoulder and around the edge of his cubicle. He stood up.

"C'mon. Let's go over to the commissary. They don't like you coming around."

"Well, fuck them. Fuck the Army."

"Yeah, and fuck you," said Calhoun, smiling widely.

They walked out the back door of the Quonset hut and headed for a clump of bougainvillaea bushes near the fence. Calhoun sat down under one of the bushes and wiped his brow.

"Man, when does this heat let up?" he asked.

"It doesn't," said Jannick.

"Listen," said Calhoun, glancing around the compound to see if anyone was coming. "This thing I've got for you—you've got to be careful with it. Don't write anything for a while. Can you do that? Sit on it for a couple of weeks?"

"Sure. I've got no deadlines. You know that."

"Okay, man. But you've got to swear to it."

Jannick looked at him as if he were crazy, but raised his hand anyway.

"Okay, man, I swear on a stack of *Rolling Stone*s. I won't do shit with your poop until you say so."

"Your boy Dupuy is into something big. Real big."

"That right?"

"He's running an Article 32 investigation on some dude they're charging with desertion in the face of the enemy."

"What's the big deal? They've sent guys away on that one before."

"It's an officer."

"No shit."

"Yeah. Lieutenant Matthew Blue. I saw Dupuy's orders. They gave them to me to deliver to Dupuy. I peeked."

"No. You don't say," Jannick teased.

"They're being real hush-hush about this thing. I don't know why. Article 32 shit is routine. But not this one."

"Well, keep your ears open and your eyes peeled. I think I know why they've got the lid on."

"Yeah?"

"If he's the right Blue, he's got a four-star for a grandfather."

"Jesus."

"Yeah. I'm sure they're not real eager for the political fallout from this one."

Calhoun whistled through his teeth.

"You going to talk to Dupuy?" Calhoun asked.

"No. I think I'll hang back and watch for a while. Where'd they send Dupuy, anyway?"

"Dak To."

"A real garden spot."

"Yeah. You going up there?"

"I'm thinking about it."

Calhoun stood up.

"I've got to be getting back. We've got a new deputy G-1 watching us. You've got to damn near ask permission to take a shit."

Jannick walked with him to the Quonset hut, then headed for the gate. He signed out and waited on the street for another bike-taxi.

So Dupuy was investigating a Lieutenant who had a famous grandfather and who'd been charged with desertion in the face of the enemy, huh? Tasty little assignment. He was sure Dupuy saw opportunities for several levels of suck-ass in this one. If he could carry this one off discreetly, turn over as few rocks as possible, focus the investigation right on Lieutenant Blue and not let the thing wander around and get out of hand, Dupuy knew he'd be sitting pretty.

Yeah, Dupuy? That's what your sorry ass thinks.

A bike-taxi pulled up and Jannick climbed on.

"Hotel Continental," he commanded.

The bike-taxi eased into traffic, the driver screamed something, shook his fist, and they were off. Traffic and exhaust fog enveloped them like a flu. The bike-taxi drifted toward the river, ignoring traffic lights, stop signs, and the demented hand signals of every traffic cop at every intersection they passed through. That was the thing about Saigon.

No one was in charge.

Careening through the traffic, Jannick got a whiff of the madness, a tiny glimpse of the future.

Saigon was the future. The future was *now*.

Yes!

Jannick held on as the bike-taxi made a two-wheeled corner, the driver screeching his head off, shaking both fists in the air.

Yes, indeed! Bring it on, Lac To, you wild-ass taxi-man!

Bring it on!

5

Hey, Cathy? Want to get some lunch?"

Catherine Joice was a correspondent for a CBS television affiliate in Kansas City that had sent her to Vietnam to begin building star quality for an anchor slot on the local evening news. She was sitting on her balcony at the Continental Hotel having a cup of coffee and reading *Time* magazine. She looked down. Danny Jannick was standing in the middle of Le Loi Street, holding a copy of *Rolling Stone* over his head, shading his eyes from the midday sun.

"Go away, Jannick. I've got no use for you today or any other day for that matter." Jannick had been asking her out at least three times a week every week since she had arrived in Vietnam, six months before. He wasn't the only one who wanted a date with the dark-haired TV news reporter. Half the staff of the American Embassy, at least a third of all the lieutenants in MACV headquarters, and most of the foreign correspondents in Saigon had asked her out at least once, many twice. But Danny Jannick was by far the most persistent of her suitors. He was the kind of guy for whom "no" was not an answer but a challenge. She peered over the wall of her balcony. He was still standing down there in the middle of Le Loi Street. Trucks, buses, mopeds, scooters, jeeps, and bike-taxis streamed by him in a cacophony of honking horns and shaking fists. He took no notice of the madness around him. He just stood there in the middle of the broad boulevard that ran from the railroad station to the National Assembly, staring up at her.

She was twenty-seven years old, she came from Ipswich, Massachusetts, on Boston's North Shore, she had shag-cut brown hair, and she was so thin and bony she looked like a teenager. She had a narrow, aquiline nose and hooded, mischief-filled eyes and a crooked, wry smile. When she looked at you, she looked at you only one way: skeptically. She had a degree in drama from Smith College, but she was born a reporter. There were a few other female reporters covering the war, but two of them worked for newspapers, and the third had a foundation grant that supported her while she contributed to left-wing magazines like *The Nation* and *Dissent*. All three of them had that driven, studious look that marked them forever as straight-A students who never got invited to the prom, an oversight on the part of their male classmates they would never forget.

To say that Cathy Joice had high visibility in the rumor-strewn bloodthirsty battleground of the news media in Vietnam didn't do justice to the attention she attracted. Catherine Joice could stop traffic on Tu Do Street with a toss of her head. When she attended the Five-O'clock Follies, the daily briefing at MACV headquarters, which wasn't often, briefing officers were known to have dropped their pointers and stop in midsentence when she entered the room. Very few Army officers were ready for female reporters in a combat zone. *None* were ready for the tall woman with a cameraman and soundman who could stand there with a mike in her hand and ask questions and put your awkward answers on TV back home. Despite the flustered reaction she got from most of the brass at MACV, nobody thought to ask the most obvious question about Catherine Joice: What was she doing in Vietnam? What made her so special that she became the first female television news journalist to cover the war?

She was being groomed for an anchor slot back home in Kansas City, of course. That was the answer her bosses at the station would give you. The professional answer. One of her bosses, an enlightened sort, would even question in return: Why *not* a woman as a TV news reporter? Why *not* Vietnam?

They were begging the question. The real answer was far stranger. And more devious.

Cathy Joice was born into the trade of gathering information from reluctant sources. She was a State Department brat, the daughter of Nicholas K. "Nick" Joice, an Irish-American kid from Boston's South Side who had gotten a scholarship-fueled Harvard education, and Michele Phelan Joice, daughter of a North Shore family of Brahmin bankers that owned its own island off Martha's Vineyard. It was a family with a past that gave its daughter something of a leg up in the present. For as long as his daughter could remember, her father had been a "cultural attaché" at embassy after embassy as the family was posted from one country to another around the world. Though it was always said that Daddy worked for the State Department, it was understood differently around the house. Daddy worked for the State Department in name only. His real boss went to work every day out in McLean, Virginia, at CIA Headquarters. Nick Joice had been Chief of Station in every hot spot around the globe since 1947, the year the Agency was formed.

Daughters of men who lead secret lives grow up with a different way of looking at the world. Nothing is taken for granted. Nothing is as it seems. The world, for Cathy Joice, far from being a great big child's playground, had been throughout her childhood a menacing battleground in the war between good and evil. Wars were not things you read about while you did your history homework after supper. Wars were discussed at the dinner table. Wars had reasons for being fought. Wars had uniformed troops, and wars had troops who had no uniforms. Wars had the victors that history taught you about, and then wars had the *real* victors. Cathy Joice's father worked in the world that lay between the two realities, between what was acknowledged and what really was, deep in the shadows between light and dark.

She knew the shady places too. She brought to her job a natural skepticism, and more. She stood before the camera less than five percent of the time. It was what she did with the other ninety-five percent that counted. She moved easily in the swamp of shifting allegiances that was Saigon in 1969. The war was going to be wound down. Everyone could feel it, from the desk men at the embassy to the bar owners on Tu Do Street, from the "laundresses" camped out on the fringes of the base camps to the messengers who rode scooters between the Saigon government and the government hidden in bunkers and tunnel systems in the countryside. The American "presence" in Vietnam would end sooner or later. The American "commitment" wasn't forever. Nobody knew when it would end, so everyone covered his or her ass accordingly. There were many Vietnams, which, of course, caused the need for many allegiances. But the two allegiances that counted most were those demanded by light and dark, by Vietnam during the day and Vietnam at night.

For Cathy Joice, to live in Saigon was to live at dusk. This made her very happy, for she had grown up in a house where it was always twilight, where it was always cocktail hour, and where, Lord knew, there was always a reason to drink.

"Cathy! Come on! Have lunch with me. I've got something for you!" Danny Jannick's voice broke through the din of Le Loi Street again. He was still down there, staring up at her. She folded her paper, took a sip of coffee, and stood up, leaning on the balustrade of her balcony. She was wearing khaki walking shorts, a pair of Keds, and an old blue chambray shirt with the sleeves rolled up. She gazed down at Jannick through a pair of aviator Ray-Bans.

"What do you want, Jannick? What are you concealing from me now?"

"I'm on to something you could use, Cathy. After I use it, of course." He smiled up at her, squinting into the sun.

She considered his offer for an instant. He had been useful in the past. He had a knack for coming up with angles on stories that frequently got answers to questions that hadn't even been asked yet. He was as odd-looking as he was unconventional, and he could be a real bother, but she kind of liked him.

"Get out of the traffic. Meet me downstairs in the bar. Five minutes," she said. She turned around and opened the louvered doors to her room. She looked in the mirror over her dresser, tucked in her shirt, and applied a light coat of lipstick. She gathered up her reporter's notebook and pen on the way out the door.

He was sitting at a table overlooking the hotel's courtyard when she walked in. He waved his *Rolling Stone* maniacally over his head, as if he expected she'd miss him. Typical. There were a grand total of four patrons in the Continental's restaurant other than himself.

She walked over and sat down. A grinning waiter with a name tag that said KIM hovered at her shoulder.

"Coffee, missy?" he said, flashing a set of stained chompers.

"Coffee, Kimmy," she replied.

"You shouldn't tease the help," Jannick said in a scolding tone. "You never know. He could be somebody's uncle. He might know something."

"He *is* somebody's uncle," said Joice, removing her glasses. "His nephew is a province chief down in the Delta, a real slimeball. You've heard of him. Kim Lam Bo. A real beauty, Kim the province chief. He likes to collect taxes in his underwear, preferably in a horizontal position. From the village wives in the province, that is."

"Don't tell me you're shocked," said Jannick. "He isn't the only province chief who has a hard time keeping his pants on."

"He's the only one with an uncle who works in the Continental," Joice said. "How convenient."

"You're not saying old Kim has big ears, are you?"

"And a loose tongue," she said.

"I didn't know he spoke that much English."

"I caught him reading *Newsweek* one day in a linen closet upstairs."

"Maybe he was just looking at the pictures," Jannick said with a shrug.

"Yeah, Danny. That's close."

Kim the waiter arrived with two coffees and placed them on the table with the empty excess of subservience common to all Oriental workers accustomed to currying unneeded favor from unwanted Occidental guests.

"Thank you, Kim," said Cathy Joice. "How is your son, Cam Cao?"

"Cam? Cam fine, missy. Number one."

"And your wife?"

"Wife home, missy. Cook paht noodle. Yum-yum." Kim rubbed his stomach and showed a stained-tooth grin.

"Yeah, Kim. Yum-yum. Run along. We've got business to conduct here."

"Yes, missy. Run-run." Kim the waiter scooted across the restaurant in the general direction of the kitchen, stopping to wipe imaginary dust from nearby tables as he went.

"You think he's VC?" asked Jannick.

"You actually entertain a doubt that he isn't?"

"Just checking. Just checking."

"Are we eating?" she asked.

"Actually, no," said Jannick. "PNS hasn't paid me the expenses they owe me for three months going. However, I do have enough for coffee."

"I figured," said Joice. "What's so important it rated that death-defying act you put on in the middle of the avenue, anyway?"

"I found out about a big court-martial I'm sure you'll be interested in."

"Oh yeah? How big?"

"They've got a Lieutenant up in II Corps for desertion in the face of the enemy."

Cathy Joice's head swiveled as if it were mounted on ball bearings. It was just the kind of story she had been waiting for. Two weeks previously she had filed a story about the alleged fragging of an officer by some enlisted men, but the station had killed the story back in Kansas City. She didn't have enough "color" footage, they said. The fact that no American soldier had been court-martialed for the alleged offense "detracted from the story's legitimacy," according to her immediate stateside superior, the news director. He had cabled his thoughts on the matter in response to a cable she had sent complaining at some length about her stories being held to unequal standards, compared to what she knew they were airing every night in Kansas City.

No matter. The story remained dead, filed away in a library of news film in the station basement.

This one was different, however. This one had a court-martial.

"What's the story, Danny? When did you find this out?"

"Tsk, tsk, tsk," Jannick clucked mockingly. "Don't be getting too eager, now. I haven't actually decided how I'm going to handle this story, Cathy. Then, of course, there is the matter of Friday night."

"You're not going to use your goddamned story to tease a date out of me, Jannick. No way. No sir."

"Who said anything about a date, Cathy? Not I." Jannick batted his eyelashes in an exaggerated display of innocence.

"Then what are you getting at, you worthless creep?"

"I thought maybe if you were sitting in the Hap To Grill on Friday night, and I happened by, I might notice you sitting there all by yourself, and we might have a drink together. Maybe even dinner."

"What about your three months of unpaid expenses, Jannick? I thought you couldn't afford lunch, much less the Hap To Grill."

"Well, I can't, actually. However, Mr. Hap happens to owe me a small favor, on which I have yet to collect."

"I thought you told me you were laying off the black market lately."

"Lately, yes. This favor happens to be several months old. Counting interest, I'd say it would count for a week's worth of dinners."

Jannick was grinning at her, and she couldn't help but smile back. He wasn't a creep, actually. In fact, he was one hell of a lot smarter than most of the newshounds prowling the backstreets and rice paddies of Vietnam, and he was personally about twice as interesting. Somehow, though, she had never featured herself on the arm of a guy wearing a rock-and-roll T-shirt—in fact, the *same* rock-and-roll T-shirt she had seen him wearing only two days before.

"Okay. So maybe I like having a drink by myself at the Hap To

Grill. And maybe by Friday night I'll be lonesome enough that I wouldn't mind some company for dinner. What does two maybe's buy me, Danny? Cough it up."

"You have heard of General Matthew Nelson Blue, Jr., I presume?"

"The roving ambassador? He used to be Deputy Director of the CIA. Big World War II hero. Of course I've heard of him."

"His grandson is up on charges in II Corps. Desertion in the face of the enemy. God only knows what else."

"How did you find this out?"

"I cannot reveal my sources," said Jannick, drawing himself up in mock seriousness.

"Come on, Jannick. You're talking to Cathy."

"Seriously. I can't tell you how. All I can tell you is the info is legit."

"When did you hear about it?"

"This morning."

"So you haven't done anything on the story? You haven't called anybody?"

"No. I was just heading back to my room when I saw you on the balcony. . . ."

"Then don't. They're only going to give you the runaround for the first week you ask questions about it, anyway. You know that."

"What, you think you can do better?"

"I *know* I can do better, and you know it, too."

Jannick took a sip of coffee. She was right, and he knew it. The Pacific News Service was not exactly at the top of the Army press spokesman's "preferred" list. In fact, it wasn't even on a list. The credentials Jannick carried had been left to him by an AP guy who had left Vietnam over six months ago. Officially, as a reporter Danny Jannick didn't even exist.

"Okay. I admit my chances of breaking anything for a while aren't the best. But we've got to come to some kind of agreement on this thing. It's *my* story. I ought to be able to file at least a day ahead of you. It's only fair."

Cathy Joice thought for a moment. The chances that something appearing on the PNS wire would find its way into the establishment press within twenty-four hours were slim to nil. She'd be on CBS national news days before anyone picked up Danny's stuff.

"Sure," she said, smiling widely. "That's fine with me, Danny. Now let's get down to it. I want everything you've got."

"Well, that's pretty much it. The big General's grandson is getting court-martialed. That's about all I know. That, and it's supposed to be big-time hush-hush, natch."

"What's his name?"

"It's Matthew Nelson Blue the fourth. He's an Infantry platoon leader up there. Or he was."

"Isn't that something? Those generals pass their names along until they pick up so many Roman numerals they just about tip over."

"Yeah, weird. A real WASP thing, I guess."

"How old is the news?"

"It was fresh this morning. They just started the Article 32 on him yesterday."

"Do you know who's handling the prosecution?"

"Yeah. They've got a real dickhead from MACV, a JAG captain called Alvin Z. Dupuy."

"He doesn't sound like your favorite person."

"He's not. My mother used to work for his family back in New Orleans. The world could do with a few less Alvie Dupuys, I assure you."

"Who's the defense attorney?"

"Terry Morriss. He's a Harvard dude. He's okay."

"Listen, Danny, why don't you let me work this for twenty-four hours, and I'll give you a call and let you know what I've got."

"Sure. Fine with me."

"Okay. It's a deal."

"And Friday night. That's a deal too?"

Cathy Joice stood up and took a final swallow of coffee. She looked at Danny Jannick. If his face had been any more hopeful, you could have used it for the March of Dimes.

That was the problem with the men who had chased her and asked her out and called her and left messages for her at the hotel's front desk, and yes, stood down in the middle of Le Loi Street, staring up at her. They hungered for her, and it was their eagerness that left her feeling empty. They hadn't fallen in love with her, they had fallen *for* her, and there was a difference. She didn't want anybody who fell. She wanted love to be difficult and foreign and terrifying and . . . *lonely* . . . as though you were the only two people in the world who were in love. Nobody else understood.

She wanted love to be dark, and so far, love was still 6:00 A.M.

"I was planning on going to the Hap To Grill anyway," she said. "Talk to you tomorrow."

She strode toward the door of the restaurant. In the corner, Kim the waiter watched her with black, knowing eyes. The woman the help at the Continental called "Teeveemissy" was up to something. It would take Kim the waiter a few hours, but by suppertime he would know what it was that had "Teeveemissy" so excited.

For this was the way of Saigon.

Danny Jannick's credentials said he wasn't really Danny Jannick, he was the AP guy who had left the country six months ago. Kim the waiter wasn't really Kim the waiter, he was a province chief's uncle and probably more than that. Catherine Joice had legitimate credentials that identified her properly. Kim the waiter had seen them himself, one morning while his niece was cleaning her room.

But in Vietnam, nothing was as it seemed.

No one was who he claimed to be.

6

T here was a story the Colonel used to tell about his father. He had told the story up until ten years ago, when he and the General stopped talking to each other. He hadn't told it very often, and he hadn't made a big deal about it, though maybe he should have, for it was a story that had come back to haunt him.

One day in the 1930s, at Fort Leavenworth, when the General was still a Captain and the Colonel was a young boy, his father was playing polo on the big flat polo field out behind the movie theater. He played every afternoon at four o'clock in preparation for the summer tour of the Army polo team. The boy accompanied him, holding his father's spare polo ponies between chukkers. Near the end of the game that afternoon, the score was tied and there was a loose ball. Captain Blue and a man on the other team rode at top speed toward the ball, which was bouncing slowly toward the goal. The other man was closer to the ball and he started to swing his mallet to hit the ball and send it away from the goal. Captain Blue spurred his polo pony and ran into the opposing player, nearly dismounting him. Captain Blue wheeled his pony and whacked the ball across the goal, scoring a goal. When the game ended a moment later, Captain Blue's team had won.

Young Matt Blue dipped under the white rail fence around the polo field and walked over to take the reins of his father's polo pony. The other men on the field dismounted and wandered down the field to a grove of oaks where every afternoon after the game, they gathered at the rail and were served tea by strikers, black soldiers who tended the polo ponies up at the stables. The polo players would take their tea and cool down in the shade of the oaks and talk about the game. On this afternoon, all the rest of the players, even the other officers on his father's team, gathered down the rail at the end of the field in the sun, a good distance from Captain Blue and his son, who had taken their places under the oaks.

"Why are the other men standing down there today?" young Matt asked his father. "Why aren't you having tea with the rest of the men, Dad?" For indeed he and his father were standing alone at the rail, sipping tea by themselves.

"Because of that last score, son," said his father. "You know in the game of polo, when there's a free ball like that one, members of both teams can ride for it. But there's a tradition in polo called the 'give.' The second man to the ball is expected to veer away from the other man's shot. The rules don't require that he veer away, but it's considered the gentlemanly thing, the proper thing to do."

"And you ran Captain Walters down and stole the ball and made the shot," said the boy.

"That's right. I failed to give, and I scored the winning goal. That's why we're not having tea with the others today. Because I didn't behave like a gentleman. They're letting me know it."

"Why didn't you give, Dad?"

"The point of the game is to score goals and win, boy. You're not out there to act like a gentleman. You're out there to win. I rode him down and I took the shot and my side won."

"And they're mad at you, huh, Dad?"

"They're mad at me, boy." His father took a sip of tea and took the boy by the shoulders and looked him in the eye.

"Sometimes in life, my boy, if you're going to get what you set out for, you've got to be a son of a bitch. That's what those men are telling me. That I'm a son of a bitch."

"And you don't care what they think, Dad?"

"I won the game, boy. That's all I care about."

The son looked at his father. He was dirty and tired and he smelled of leather and horses and sweat and pride. His father had found it necessary occasionally to be a son of a bitch in life, and he wanted his son to know that when the time came, that's what you had to be. A son of a bitch.

As it turned out, the Colonel didn't follow his father's advice, and it became a sore point between them as the years wore on. He never forgot what his father told him, however. Never again in his life would he see such a pure look of down-and-dirty, mean-ass, go-to-hell determination as he saw on his father's sweat-and-dirt-stained and horse-smelling face that afternoon. He was different from the other men, his father was, and he looked like it and he talked like it and he acted like it.

As he grew up, the boy who had held the reins of his father's polo ponies that afternoon discovered how different he was from his father, a difference of which he was very proud.

But he learned that he was a bit like him, too.

Now it seemed the Colonel was going to find out just how much like his father he was, for he had caught a whiff of panic and madness in his son's voice on the telephone from Vietnam. The fear in his son's voice wasn't at all like him. He was a levelheaded, logical sort, not given to doom-struck imaginings and dread. The moment he heard his son's voice, he knew the time had come when he had to be a son of a bitch. He wondered how much of a son of a bitch he really was.

The Colonel recalled the story about the polo game as he drove from the Atlanta airport back to Fort Benning on the morning after the meeting with his father and Aunt Aggie at Wild Acres. Things were going to happen fast now. He had to talk to his wife first, tell her everything he'd found out from his father the night before. He knew she would agree with him that he had to get himself over to Vietnam as soon as possible. Then he had to get in uniform and tell the commanding general, Lieutenant General Ralph Hunter, that he was taking all the leave he had accumulated in order that he would be able to travel to Vietnam and aid in his son's defense.

Lieutenant General Hunter wasn't going to like it. The brigade had a major field exercise coming up, joint maneuvers with the 82nd Airborne Division out of Fayetteville, North Carolina. The brigade would be in the field for three weeks, not including the four weeks it would take to prepare for and stand down from the exercise. It wasn't the most convenient seven weeks for a brigade commander to be gone. He would have to make Lieutenant General Hunter understand. Nothing was going to keep him from flying to Vietnam and helping his son.

There was another problem. Money. He and his wife had never been able to save much of it, Army pay being what it was, which wasn't much. He would have to empty their savings account and hope for the best. He wished they'd been able to accumulate some assets along the way—a house, a few pieces of art, maybe some stocks. Here he was, more than twenty years in the Army, and he didn't own appreciably more today than he had as a lieutenant. It was a sad state of affairs, and many were the times he had felt sorry for his wife, who had suffered alongside him as the rest of the world took the middle of the twentieth century by the lapels and shook it for everything it was worth. He had the feeling that all they'd been able to do while the civilians got fat and happy was pick up a few crumbs dropped under the table.

The worst thing was, he had always suspected that something would occur that would make him regret the financial inadequacies of a military career, regret the fact that when all was said and done, he had passed up several opportunities to get out of the Army and really make some bucks. Now here he was, a middle-aged man with the son he loved in big trouble, and he was lacking just about every resource that was necessary to help him out. He racked his brain, trying to remember something that would give him an edge on this thing. He knew it was there, a memory of something in his past that would give him a leg up. He knew it.

The Colonel's old Ford crested a hill and started a long bend to the left. Up ahead, past the curve, he could see a small rural airstrip. A light plane was taking off; the path of its climb took it over the Colonel's Ford into the cloudy distance.

That was it. The weekly courier plane out of Saigon. It was a C-141 Starlifter that left Saigon every Monday and made twenty stops in seven days as the plane completely circled the globe and returned to Tan Son Nhut Air Base with classified documents and passengers it had picked up along the way. He could catch a ride on the courier flight. It stopped every Friday at Warner Robins Air Force Base near Macon, only forty minutes from Fort Benning. If he took the courier flight, he'd be in Saigon on Monday. Sergeant Gilbert, his battalion motor pool sergeant, could get him on. He had spent ten years as an aircraft maintenance specialist in the Air Force before he got tired of it and switched enlistments to the Army. He still had pull with the flyboys over at Robins, and he was well known around the brigade for playing fast and loose around the edges of the motor-pool supply rules. If anyone could arrange a free flight halfway around the world to Saigon, South Vietnam, it was Sergeant Wilbert W. Gilbert.

There it was. The first little curve in the road through his past, a quick jog around the conventions governing who was and who wasn't allowed to fly the courier flight. Sergeant Gilbert could get him on the flight. There was no doubt about that. He could pull the strings necessary to get you on Air Force One. The fact that such string-pulling would bend and stretch the protocols of flying military standby a little would simply have to be overlooked—just as his father had overlooked the convention of the "give" in polo that afternoon so many years ago.

The Colonel clucked his tongue against the roof of his mouth and shook his head slowly from side to side.

I'm going to scrape a few shins before this thing is over, he thought to himself. The time had come to be a son of a bitch. It was going to be a long trip—into the future and through the past—and it was going to hurt. The Colonel rolled down his window and spat into the wind.

"The hell with it," he said out loud. He could barely hear himself in the sixty-mile-an-hour noise inside the Ford.

"The hell with it!" he yelled. That was better, much better.

"THE HELL WITH IT!" he screamed.

He felt about twenty years younger, and he had a hunch he was going to need to feel that young during the next couple of months. He was going to have to think like a younger man to understand how his son had gotten himself into so much trouble. And he sensed that he was going to have to act like a younger man to get him out of it.

All wars are young men's wars, and Vietnam was just like the rest of them. He thought back to Korea, when he was a young man fighting his own war. He remembered the feel, the smell, the sounds of the war in Korea—the boom of the big guns, the scream of F-80 close air support overhead, the rattle of machine guns in the night distance. And he remembered the hollow, empty feeling after the armistice, when the war was over, neither won or lost. It wasn't as if it had all been for nothing, but it was pretty close. All those mothers and fathers he had written to when their sons had died . . . how would they feel now that the American Army had simply given up, drawing a line in the dirt at the Thirty-eighth Parallel, calling a truce a victory? What happened to the invincibility of the Army of his father, who had marched through ten countries on two continents, finally driving Hitler to suicide in his bunker? It wasn't fair, the Colonel remembered thinking. They sent us to war, now they're sending us home, and they never told us why either time.

His son's war, the war in Vietnam, was showing disturbing signs of turning into another Korea. The Colonel had never really been free to engage the enemy down in the Delta when he'd commanded a Battalion there. Too much time had been devoted to "pacification" and the establishment of "strategic hamlets" and other nonmilitary, essentially political activities. The war in Vietnam was another "limited" war. Korea had been a "police action." This one was a "brushfire war." The Colonel wondered when they would stop labeling and start fighting.

The war in Vietnam had all the sounds of Korea, but there was a soundtrack to the war in Vietnam, too, a rock-and-roll soundtrack. He'd heard it every day in his Battalion over there, radios playing, tape recorders blaring, guys hooking up tape decks so they'd play through the headsets on helicopters, guys whipping rock tunes on the psy-war chopper speakers that were supposed to broadcast anti-Vietcong propaganda down on rice-paddy-treading villagers, blasting the villagers with Ike and Tina Turner instead.

Somehow his son had run afoul of his war, and the Colonel only hoped he could understand why and how and when. It was going to take a lot out of him, but then he had a lot to give.

The Colonel took the exit off I-185 and drove down Victory Boulevard. He pulled up to a stoplight opposite Honest Frank's Used Cars. Something clicked in his memory, taking him back twenty years or more. He had bought his first car from Honest Frank. Things were coming back to him now, memories, images, sounds, feelings. He made the turn onto Marshall Avenue and headed west. A warm feeling reached his neck and his face. He was almost home.

THREE

☆

———

Thunder in the Sun

Firebase Zulu-Foxtrot
Day Three

The operations order came at 0130. Lieutenant Blue's weapons platoon had already broken out of its night defensive perimeter. It took them from 0200 to 0500 to pull in the Claymores, roll up the concertina wire, and rebox the trip-flares. When they were finished, the whole platoon went on alert. Until they left, they were essentially defenseless. At 0515, the tracks were fueled up and idling at the treeline. Then the radio crackled to move out.

Lieutenant Blue gave the word.

"All right," he said into his CVC mouthpiece. "Let's go."

The lead track, the two-four, jerked forward, commanded by Lucky Lemon, rattling and clanking into the bush. Blue's track followed, trailed by the two-three, Platoon Sergeant Davis's track, and the two-two, Repatch's, and the two-one, Mallick's. They made a hell of a racket, tracks churning dirt and crushing small trees and rumbling over rocks and *sluuuuurping* through mud bogs, throaty exhausts echoing across the clearings like kids goosing their Chevies at a stoplight.

Whoopie Cushion Ridgely was standing in the two-six, the Lieutenant's track, manning one of the M-60 machine guns mounted behind the commander's cupola, covering either side of the vehicle. The M-60 jerked and bucked against his grip as the track rolled over fallen tree trunks and dipped into streambeds.

"Fuck this Army and fuck this war and fuck this gun and fuck this track and fuck it all is what I say, you ask me," said Whoopie Cushion with his usual eloquence.

"Nobody axed you, Cushion, you white-ass motherfucker." Moonface Samuels grinned from his position at the other M-60, swaying with the awkward rhythm of the track.

"I got a higher callin' than your sorry ass, Moonface," said Whoopie Cushion over his shoulder.

"Yeah? Who dat? Yo' mama?"

"My Lord God and Savior," said Whoopie Cushion, intoning the words like an evangelist. "I got the ear of the big dude, the master of 'em all, my main man."

"You got yo' ear stuck upside yo' ass thinkin' it be yo' haid," said Moonface. "Sound you be hearin' be last night's beans and franks, dude. You listenin' to refried C-ration, Cushion. Yo' shit be in de street, man. As per us-u-al."

"Knock it off back there," said the Lieutenant, without turning around. "We're supposed to be maintaining combat road-march discipline. We could use less wisecracking, and more examination of the state of our flanks."

"Yes, sir," said Whoopie Cushion Ridgely.

"You got it, sir," said Moonface Samuels.

The radio crackled a couple of times and cleared.

"Rattail Two, this is Rattail Six, over."

It was the company commander, Goose Gardner, a loose-limbed captain out of Elizabethtown, Kentucky, who had played first-string basketball for Vanderbilt University before he passed his physical and got drafted and opted for OCS. He had been told he'd flunk the physical because of his knees, both of which had been operated on twice, one of which still locked up when it got cold. The only problem was the X-ray machine was broken the day of his physical, and as the doctor said during his interview, "It doesn't get very cold in Vietnam."

"Rattail Two, over," said the Lieutenant.

"We're passing the line of departure, over," said Captain Gardner.

"This is Two. We're on it right now," said the Lieutenant.

"Six out."

"Roger that."

The brigade was making a "sweep," also known as a search-and-destroy mission, of the region west of Dak To. This meant that three battalions crashed around out there in whatever boonies showed on the map, spoiling for a fight—and, in the case of the troops, hoping like hell that nobody took the bait and actually took a shot at them. The weapons platoon was running parallel to the rest of the Battalion, about four kilometers to its south. This was necessary, since in order to support the Battalion with close-in mortar fire around the perimeter, the platoon had to be far enough away for effective mortar firing. It was a little lonely, way out on the flank of a larger unit like a Battalion. But there were side benefits out there on the side.

For instance, the battalion commander couldn't see what you were doing, so he had to take your word for it on the radio. A unit the size of a Battalion, some sixty tracks strong, made a huge ruckus and got most of the attention from those in the vicinity who had an interest in loud, lumbering things like American Mechanized Infantry Battalions . . . such as Battalions of North Vietnamese Infantry regulars. The NVA would definitely be interested in an American Mechanized Infantry Battalion. Thus it was in *your* interest to remain clear of anything that drew their attention . . . like an American Mechanized Infantry Battalion.

Then, of course, there was the satisfaction of taking your own path through the wilderness, going it on your own, and still having the rest of the Battalion count on your knowing *precisely* where you were and where they were at all times.

Artillery or mortar support fire demanded exact locations of firebase and target. Not approximate. Not close. Not almost.

Exact.

In order to place accurate fire on a target, you had to be able to plot your position and the position of the target on the map precisely as you set up to fire. Once the mortars were zeroed in, you could fire on the target and begin receiving adjustments of fire from the unit commander whom you were supporting.

This was known as adjusting fire, and it necessitated definitive manipulation of the weapons and absolute accuracy in map-reading, a skill the Lieutenant had picked up from his father when he was a boy.

His father, who was then a captain of Infantry, would mount on the refrigerator door a scale-drawn map of the area the Blue family lived in, cover it with a piece of acetate, and hang a grease pencil from the map on a string. Every day, the boy and his brother would have to plot with a grease pencil where they intended to play, and the route to and from their destination. This entailed placing a circle around the woods or creek or tree house or recreation center they intended to play in for the afternoon, and tracing a route from the house to the place of intended play. One or two mistakes at playground or woods or creek or baseball diamond route-plotting, such mistakes having their attendant punishments and restrictions-to-room of varying severity, had a tendency to create a precociously adept map reader. This the budding Lieutenant had indeed become.

As a kid, he had considered all the map nonsense an enormous pain in the ass, but now he had to admit that his early trials as a refrigerator-door map plotter were paying off. If there was one man in the entire battalion who knew where he and his unit were virtually all of the time, it was Lieutenant Blue, the former boy map-reader. The other lieutenants derisively called him "Path-finder" behind his back, and he knew it, but he didn't care.

Many was the time that one of them would quietly radio his approximate position in grid coordinates to the Lieutenant, and then describe the surrounding terrain features for him. The Lieutenant would plot the alleged grid coordinates on his map and match them against the observed terrain features . . .

Let's see, he's got a mountain on his left and a river on his right and he just crossed an ungraded dirt road . . .

In a minute he'd have new grid coordinates and relay them to the lost platoon leader on the other end of the radio. They kidded him a lot, but that's all it was. Kidding. Not only did Pathfinder Blue know where he was, he fucking knew where *you* were, and that was spooky.

The battalion and its attendant weapons platoon ambled west at a pretty good clip. The Lieutenant checked his platoon's progress against his map periodically, noting his position with red grease-pencil marks on the acetate.

Sometimes his mind wandered, and the very process made him feel like a kid again . . .

He was in the boonies . . . the *deep* boonies . . . woods all around . . . *big* woods . . . trees and trees and trees without end . . . *scary* woods, so damn scary the first hundred yards made your hair stand on end, and the second hundred yards just plain froze you with fear . . . and he could hear the voice of his old man echoing in the trees . . .

You could get lost out there in those woods, son . . . that's why I want you to plot your route and your destination on the map . . . I'm not trying to harass you, I just want to do what's right, I just want to handle this thing efficiently, I just want to know where you are in case something happens . . .

The old man's voice would ring in his ears, deep and caring and truthful and honest and sincere to the point of fucking tedium . . .

He'd always wondered if his old man knew how goddamned *boring* it was, being efficient and logical and useful and helpful and caring and . . .

The tracks rumbled and clanked and grunted forward, but in his mind he was back at Wild Acres with his brother in the forest. He remembered just what it felt like.

It felt like these woods do right now . . . foreign and dark and wet and mossy and smelling of sweat and dirt and musk and fear . . .

They were Southern woods, and you could walk endlessly through the stands of stately white pines and scrub oaks and mountain laurels and maples and you'd never get anywhere but deeper and deeper into more and more woods. They were thick and impenetrable except insofar as they could be explored on foot by little boys, and somehow they felt more uncharted and wild than even the massive expanses of forest he would come upon later in life in the West, most of which had been declared national forest and seemed for that reason to feel like a gigantic governmental tourist attraction.

People *owned* the forest around Wild Acres. The Randolphs owned Wild Acres of course, but farther back in there were other woods, owned by other people. There were good old boys he remembered who could lead you to the biggest whiskey still in the county, or show you the pond where you could catch the biggest bass, or take you to a tree where the buzzards gathered at dusk to roost, looming overhead, black and sinister and forbidding against the graying sky.

There weren't any fences or dirt roads that wandered into the woods in search of how far they went back, or where they ended up. So when you went into those woods, you went in tentatively. Maps didn't help much. Those woods were *way* beyond the meager control of maps . . .

They were sinister . . .

Provocative . . .

Sensual . . .

That was why you always wanted to wander off the refrigerator map, heading back in there, way beyond what was called "whistling distance," the extent of the old man's quite substantial whistle, which he created, two fingers tucked tightly beneath his tongue, with an entire lungful of air. His high-pitched shriek would simply deaden and drop off when it hit the deep woods. So anyplace you went in there was technically beyond "whistling distance," and thus deliciously illegal.

Ravines were back in those woods. Bridges that were crumbling and had only enough timbers left for a boy to scamper across. Swamps sprang up out of nowhere, damp and mossy and foggy and mysterious. Turtles. Snakes. Wild things.

Occasionally a buzzard would circle overhead . . . you could see him through breaks in the canopy of leaves above you . . . and when he thought of the woods around Wild Acres, that's what the Lieutenant remembered best:

A buzzard circling, waiting for some little kid to get lost and fade into the big pines to a deep beyond "whistling distance," a place only the buzzards knew about, from which you'd never return . . .

The Lieutenant shook himself and rubbed his eyes and splashed water from his canteen on top of his head.

Fuck it, he told himself reassuringly. All in a day's work, huh? Yessir, that's what we're out here for . . . getting deeply into woods, weirdness, whatever . . .

The Lieutenant skipped an entry on his route plot during the hour after the Battalion halted for a brief lunch, and when he checked the platoon's position an hour later, he was brought up short by what he found.

He checked it again, scoping out the terrain, comparing it to the lines on the map.

Yeah, there's that little saddle between two low hills. Yep, there's the creek we just forded. And over there's a clearing we could see through a break in the trees. And right up ahead is the dry reservoir edged by a swamp that Sergeant Davis just reported on the radio.

Jesus.

They were in Laos.

Nobody knew it but the Lieutenant, of that he was sure. Laos hadn't been part of the ops order. They were supposed to skirt the border, watching for crossings by elements of an estimated NVA reinforced battalion known to be operating in the region.

The Lieutenant tried to imagine what had happened. Somebody had forgotten to hang a right back there somewhere, and they had poked into a piece of Laos like a finger pressing into the side of a balloon. There weren't any signs out there in the boonies reading Attention: You Are Now Entering Laos. No fences. No roads. Just woods. They were pushing the balloon, all right. Only this time the finger was an American Infantry Battalion, and the balloon was the nation of Laos, and the balloon had just burst.

They were in.

Fuck.

What was he going to do? Get that dufus Battalion CO Halleck on the horn and tell him he was violating the sovereignty of an allegedly noncombatant nation?

Ri-i-i-i-ght. And the Pope's gonna get married and the rabbi's gonna eat pork and the redneck's gonna trade in his pickup for a Volkswagen Beetle.

S-u-u-u-u-re.

Christ. They didn't offer a course in how to correct your battalion commander as an elective at the Infantry School. If they had, the Lieutenant would have been number one on the sign-up list. He had found himself caught between entirely too many rocks and too many hard places with his old man when he was a kid to relish the notion of making a career out of it in the Army.

Besides, what if they were supposed to be in Laos? What if the ops order this morning had been subterfuge? He'd heard of Battalions in the 101st Airborne Division making sweeps into Laos through the Ashau Valley, and another platoon leader had told him that their ops orders never had them crossing the border.

"What's up, sir?" asked Whoopie Cushion Ridgely, who had noticed that the Lieutenant was being fairly quiet for the last klik or so.

"Somepin' I can do?" asked Dirtball, who was sitting on a pile of sandbags on the floor of the track, picking his nails with the whip end of the PRC-25 antenna.

"We just crossed into Laos, men," said the Lieutenant.

"Shit, man, I always wanted to add me another one of these tropical garden spots to my list of vacation destinations," said Whoopie Cushion. "Lay-ose. I wonder if they got them some bumper stickers say 'Land of the Pissant Motherfucker, Home of His Mama'? I got to get me one, fer sure."

"Ain't pronounced Lay-ose, Cushion," said Moonface. "Say . . . La-a-a-ose, man. Say it."

"La-a-a-ose," said Whoopie Cushion.

"Dere. You got it. What we doin' in La-a-a-ose, anyway, Eltee? I don't remember hearin' no La-a-a-ose in them plans you was layin' out for us this mornin'."

"You didn't, Moonface," said the Lieutenant.

"Den what we doin' here?"

"I don't know."

"Maybe we better find out, 'fore Charlie learns we in de vicin-ity."

"Yeah."

"You think they know where we at? At Battalion, I mean?"

"I'm sure they do," the Lieutenant said slowly, not knowing exactly what he was going to say. He didn't want to panic them, and there was nothing more certain to panic a bunch of men who were already so scared and jumpy they felt cold to the touch.

"Eltee, this shit's gettin' serious, huh?" Dirtball asked from his perch atop the sandbags on the floor of the track.

"Vietnam . . . Laos . . . what fucking difference does it make?" the Lieutenant joked, trying for levity.

He didn't make it.

"Hey, Eltee, how much longer we got till we go into a night logger?"

The Lieutenant checked his watch.

"Not much longer, Dirtball. We ought to be hearing something within the hour."

"What time you got, sir?" asked Moonface.

"Sixteen-fifty," said the Lieutenant, giving the military version of 4:50 P.M.

The radio crackled.

"Rattail Two, this is Rattail Six, over."

It was Goose Gardner, the company commander, coming through the Lieutenant's CVC.

"Six, this is Two, over."

"We've reached our night logger. Suggest you do same. Contact me with grid coordinates when you're dug in, over."

"Roger that, Six. Out."

The Lieutenant took off his CVC helmet and looked around. The tracks were moving through a rolling field on the edge of some woods. The Battalion was several thousand meters to the northwest. He checked his map.

They were about ten kilometers inside Laos.

He punched the button on his CVC.

"Whooooa!" he called, western-style.

He watched the tracks ahead of him and behind him jerk to a halt.

"See that little hill on the left, on the other side of that clearing?"

"Roger."

"Roger."

"Yo."

"Gotchew, Eltee."

"Let's get on it and make it ours, men," said the Lieutenant.

He could hear the whooping from the other tracks. Everybody was in the same mood he was in. Everybody wanted to dig in.

"Dig 'em deep, guys," the Lieutenant called over the radio. "I've got an idea this is going to be a long night."

"Roger that," said Repatch.

"That's a rodge," said Lemon.

"Yo," said Sergeant Davis.

"Gotchew," said Mallick.

All five tracks started for the little hill on the other side of the clearing, clanking and bucking and rattling their way toward the dark.

7

From the air, looking out the oval window of a Pentagon jet at 35,000 feet, the coast of Vietnam resembled the Eastern Seaboard of the United States—hundreds of square miles of verdant green space and tilled farmland, interrupted only by the occasional street grid of a seaside town, all of it edged by perfect white beaches. It was hard to see the country of Vietnam as the seething sweathole of hate and terror that it was. Altitude afforded you a sleepy luxury that horizontal distance did not. Being up there amid the clouds allowed you to dream. You weren't looking at Vietnam, that was New Jersey down there! The resort town on the coast, that's not Vung Tau, that's Asbury Park! The airport on the horizon, that's not Tan Son Nhut, that's Newark!

Too soon the ground rushed up to envelop dreams in dank reality. Lieutenant General Pelton's jet taxied to a stop on the tarmac at Tan Son Nhut and lowered the stairs. Ten hours on a 707 had left its mark. General Matthew Nelson Blue, Jr., unfolded himself from his seat, crackling and squeaking like a new book binding. He was wearing a set of World War II khakis, long-sleeved, open at the neck, and a pair of brown Army oxfords. On his head was a panama hat with a wide brim and a black satin hatband. It was the uniform he wore while gardening at home, and he wore the same khakis when he received visitors late in the afternoon on the screened porch overlooking the garden. It was his way of reminding his visitors—and, not incidentally, himself—not of who he was, but of who he had been. The khakis were devoid of military decorations, of course. He had retired in 1947, but seemed as unable to give up his one last vestige of his beloved Army as he was unwilling to stop drinking martinis.

He and Lieutenant General Pelton walked down the aisle to the jet's door. As it opened, the fetid heat from the tarmac swept over them like bad gossip, wet and nasty and mean.

An olive-drab staff car pulled up and the two generals started down the stairs. Halfway down, the General halted and shaded his eyes against the sun. He was looking across the tarmac at a nearby C-141 Starlifter, a fat green tube of a cargo jet that had its rear ramp lowered to take on a payload destined for the United States. When he reached the bottom of the ramp, he instinctively returned an aide's salute and barked:

"Captain, is that what I think it is over there?" He pointed to the cargo jet that was inhaling shiny aluminum coffins from an automatic belt loader at the rate of one every thirty seconds.

"Yes, sir, it is," said the Captain. "Those are some of our KIAs on their way home."

He looked over at Lieutenant General Pelton. A grimace of bewilderment and disgust showed on his face.

"Brownie," the General said, "can you imagine us boxing up our dead on the beach at Anzio and shipping them home? Can you imagine such a goddamned travesty?"

"No, sir, I can't," said the man who had been a battalion commander under the General from Anzio through Italy and France and Germany until the General had relieved Patton at Garmisch-Partenkirchen after the war, and Pelton became his chief of staff.

"What's the reasoning behind that business?" the General asked the aide. He had been dispatched from the military affairs section at the U.S. Embassy to chaperon the visiting dignitaries and prevent just such a display of discomforting imagery from disturbing their visit.

"I'm not sure, sir," the aide said nervously. "I guess if you have the technical ability to ship your KIAs home, you do it, sir. Then there's the families to consider. I'm sure they want them home. I think that's the main thing, sir. What the families want."

The two generals got in the backseat of the staff car. It was air-conditioned. The driver, a young GI with long sideburns and a pair of Air Force flying glasses, looked as if he knew he had the cushiest job in the war. He glanced in the rearview mirror and announced in the dulcet tones of a tour guide, "Welcome to Saigon, sirs. I hope your stay will be a pleasant one."

The Captain got in the front seat next to the driver and whispered, "Shut up and drive, Bisket."

The driver put the staff car in gear and turned left in an arc that took them within a few feet of a forklift loaded with shiny aluminum coffins heading for the belt loader.

"Stop the goddamned car," the General ordered.

The driver slammed on the brakes and skidded to a halt next to the stack of coffins.

"What happens when they reach home?" the General asked.

"I'm not sure, sir, but I think they're put on a train with an escort and shipped to the dead man's hometown."

"That's correct," said Lieutenant General Pelton.

"Whatever happened to the cemeteries like the ones at Anzio and Normandy and Belgium?" the General asked, sounding truly bewildered. He turned in his seat to watch a forklift full of coffins drop its load at the end of the conveyor belt and turn around for another.

"If they buried them over here, parents would want to come to the funerals, sir, and technically, we wouldn't be able to stop them. You can get a commercial flight to Saigon from Los Angeles, San Francisco, Honolulu, Tokyo, just about anywhere on our West Coast or in the Pacific. We'd have a logistical nightmare and a considerable public-relations problem."

"What do you mean, 'a public-relations problem'?" The General coughed out the words like a mouthful of bad meat.

"Well, sir, I heard they don't want the TV showing a bunch of funerals at a big cemetery over here every night. It wouldn't look good. A cemetery would create more problems than it would solve. But the parents are the big thing, sir."

"Hell, I'm sure the fathers and mothers of my boys killed in North Africa or Sicily or Cassino or Anzio, or any other goddamned hellhole for that matter, would have wanted the bodies of their sons home. But what families wanted us to do with our dead just wasn't among our major concerns. In Italy, my business was to run Kesselring to the ground and keep his army from becoming reinforcements at Normandy. We didn't have the goddamn time, much less the goddamned inclination, to go through the machinations of sending our dead back to the United States. They fought in Italy. They died in Italy, and they're buried in Italy, like soldiers ought to be, where they fell."

"I guess I never thought of it that way, sir."

"Do you know what those coffins are saying to the Vietnamese, young man? They're saying that it doesn't mean as much to us as soldiers, and to the public back home, to have given your life in Southeast Asia as it did to have been killed at Anzio or Salerno or Cassino or on Omaha Beach. They're saying we don't goddamned mean it over here. We're not willing to fight and bury our dead and drive on and fight again. When those coffins disappear into the belly of that airplane, they're telling the Vietnamese that we don't want our presence here felt when we are gone."

"I'm not sure I understand what you're getting at, sir," said the Captain.

"I'm not sure you do either, Captain," said the General.

The driver drove toward a gate in the fence around the tarmac. An MP dressed in perfectly starched fatigues and spit-shined boots motioned them through with a flip of his white-gloved hand. The General shook his head in wonder. MPs directing traffic on the beachhead at Anzio were immediately recognizable by the layer of mud that had been thrown on them by passing trucks and tanks. The only spit-shine the General had seen during the entire war was on the boots of a German general the day he surrendered twenty-five divisions of troops in northern Italy. And in war he'd never seen a pair of white gloves on anybody wearing a uniform.

An air-conditioned staff car in a combat zone was another first for the General. He rolled down his window and sniffed the air. He wanted to get closer to the ground beneath him. Vietnam had the same hot, humid, wilted indifference of every country at war. The road to Saigon was like every road the General had driven from North Africa to Germany. Its surface changed within a mile from asphalt to gravel to dirt to dust to mud and back again. Where rice paddies had overflowed their banks, the staff car splashed through slimy puddles.

All wars were fought in the hole between rage and indifference, in the heart between love of God and sympathy for the devil, down rubble-strewn roads between mud and dust. The only thing different about Vietnam was a spit-shine of cheap technology that tried vainly to hide the truth.

Sweat still glistened.

Mud still stuck.

Cannon fire still rang alarms in the ear.

Gunpowder still burned sweetly in nostrils immune to anything but the smell of fear and pain.

Blood still flowed the color of heat and hate.

The truth about this war, like all wars, still hurt.

A newly polished escort jeep with an M-60 machine gun mounted behind the driver kicked up a cloud of red dust ahead of them. Along the sides of the road, peasants slapped the broad flanks of water buffaloes, driving them from one flooded rice paddy to another. The roads were hot and straight and dusty and the fields were muddy and the peasants were poor and the war was someplace else, a low thunder in the distance, audible and unforgivable but ultimately forgettable. The war after all was only visiting; the dust and the mud and the water buffaloes and the peasants and their bottomless hunger for a calm day and a good night's sleep and a bellyful of rice that had escaped them for twenty years would still be here long after everyone else had gone home.

Six F-4 Phantom fighter jets roared by overhead at low altitude, standing on their tails, heading for the sun. The staff car shuddered under the backblast of twelve fully lit afterburners spraying burnt kerosene at the ground like a hot yellow curse.

One of the water buffaloes spooked, running in front of the car. The driver hit the brakes, missing the man driving the buffalo by inches. The General turned and looked out the back window. He was about the same age as the General, a deeply wrinkled man, bent over like a question mark from working in the fields. He was wearing peasant's pajamas and a straw hat and he was standing in the middle of the muddy road, scowling and shaking his fist at the retreating staff car.

The General leaned back and closed his eyes. He could still see the scowl on the man's face, his fist in the air. He was in North Africa, Sicily, Italy, France, Germany. It didn't matter where. Wars never changed. The men who made wars didn't change, and neither did those against whom they made war. The victims of war varied in diet, costume, skin color, and location, but they all spoke the same language.

The General opened his eyes and turned around to look out the back window of the staff car again.

The grizzled little man's fist stood still in the air, brave and eloquent and alien, like thunder in the sun.

A pair of remote-controlled cast-iron gates opened silently and the staff car pulled into a walled compound somewhere on the outskirts of Saigon. Inside the compound was a flat-roofed, stuccoed villa in the Mediterranean style that had been the great house of a French rubber plantation. The United States Embassy used it to house visiting dignitaries. It had the advantage of being a secure location far enough from the seamier side of Saigon that it was reminiscent of simpler times, when the colonial impulse came not from ambition but obligation. The villa had hosted several visits by a prominent senator on the Armed Services Committee who had been so taken by its well-stocked bar and gourmet kitchens that he never left the compound, leaving to his staff the messy rounds through base camps and captured tunnel complexes.

"I'll see you downstairs once we're settled," said the General to his former aide.

"Righto, sir," said Lieutenant General Pelton. Both men were tired, and they both had a lot to think over before they got started.

The two generals were shown to their quarters by one of the white-jacketed Filipino house staff. General Blue's room was at the back corner of the house on the second floor, overlooking a tropical garden that had goldfish ponds and a stream cascading down an artificial waterfall that appeared to be constructed of fiberglass and painted rocks. The General picked up the phone extension next to his four-poster mahogany bed, and when an operator came on the line, he barked, "Give me the goddamned embassy."

"One moment, sir. To whom would you wish to speak?"

"That's my goddamned business. Ring the goddamned embassy."

The operator rang the embassy.

"Put me through to Rousseau," the General growled.

"Who may I say is calling, sir?" asked an officious female voice.

"Put me through, goddammit."

The phone clicked a couple of times and rang through.

"AID," said another female voice.

"Give me Rousseau," said the General.

"Who may I say is calling, sir?"

"General Blue," said the General.

"One moment please, sir."

"Jake Rousseau, sir," said a voice.

"Jake, goddammit, I want to know what in hell is going on over here."

"General Blue, sir, it's good to hear from you, sir. Where are you?"

"I'm inside some kind of goddamned compound looking at a goddamned waterfall and a bunch of flowers. Come and get me, Jake. I want a goddamned briefing on this situation over here, and I want it now."

"When did you get in, sir?"

"Five minutes ago."

"Get yourself a shower, sir, and I'll be there in twenty."

The General hung up the phone and sat on the edge of the bed, exhausted. Silently he blessed the day he had stolen one of De Gaulle's young staffers from him in Tripoli before the attack was launched against Sicily. Lieutenant Jacob "Jake" Rousseau was then in the Free French Army and served as a logistics specialist on

De Gaulle's personal staff. He was one of the few people working for De Gaulle who spoke passable English. The General demanded the services of Rousseau ostensibly as a liaison officer. The real reason he stole him had nothing to do with "liaison." The General simply liked the cut of his jib. Rousseau was loud, profane, and so completely shot full of his own adolescent genius that he reminded the General of himself at age twenty. Rousseau stayed with the General through the end of the war and, after receiving U.S. citizenship, was the General's personal aide when he took over deputy directorship of the CIA to run European operations in Berlin from 1947 to 1955.

He was a giant of a man, standing a good half-foot taller than the General. He had coal-black hair and black eyes and a crooked smile from nerve damage suffered in a fistfight as a child in Marseilles. His father and his father's father had been fishermen, and his mother's father was a shadowy figure who never seemed to have a job but managed to command the respect if not the fear of every man on the Marseilles waterfront. When she met him after the war, the General's wife, Carey Randolph, said Jake Rousseau had been born an aide. He was another on the list of what she called "Grandpa's boys."

Of all of "Grandpa's boys," she liked Rousseau the least. Perhaps like the General, Rousseau reminded her of a time when her husband was as coarse and unmannered as he was loud and profane. His wife never let on why she didn't like Rousseau, but she made a point of warning her husband never to trust him.

"He'll be loyal to you so long as it's in his interest," she cautioned. "He'll be smiling like a cat the day he walks away from you, and you'll never see it coming."

The General dismissed the warning from his wife as one of her delusions. He figured, she misunderstood the truths of what went on between men. This came from her upbringing in a culture that had long been dependent on the work of slaves, and without them crumbled into a well-mannered heap of disappeared dreams and lost illusions.

Now "Grandpa's boy" was no longer an aide. For twelve years Jake Rousseau had been CIA station chief in Saigon, using the

Agency for International Development as a front. It was a job he had trained for all his life, the equivalent of the General's position at the top of the Agency heap in Europe after the war. All CIA operations in Asia were coordinated by the station chief in Vietnam because, presumably, what was done behind closed doors in Bangkok or Singapore or Tokyo was bound to have its effect on the ground in Vietnam. But the practical dictates of CIA Asian policy were only a minor source of Jake Rousseau's wide sweep of influence. What lay behind the enormous scope of his power were the years he had spent under the General in Europe. The entire top floor of the CIA's present command structure at Langley had cut its teeth in Germany after the war. They had all worked for the General, and because Jake Rousseau was the man closest to him, he was the man in the position to do the most good for the most people. Jake Rousseau had a pile of IOUs from those early days in Berlin that he had only begun to dig through. The net effect was, what Jake Rousseau wanted, Jake Rousseau got.

Now his mentor the General had come calling. Rousseau knew it wouldn't take the General long to let him know why.

Rousseau drove himself from AID headquarters to the Chateau, as the VIP quarters were called. He knew the General would appreciate the fact that their meeting was being kept private. When he arrived at the compound, he found the General standing in front of the main house wearing the same khakis he had been wearing the last time he had visited the General's for cocktails in Georgetown almost a year ago. He could see the General's gray eyes squinting under the brim of his panama. He remembered when a flicker of those eyes in his direction had sent shivers of fear down his spine. Rousseau parked the jeep and stepped out. The General didn't move, but he followed Rousseau with his eyes. They still sent shivers, Rousseau was less than amazed to learn. Even twenty years later, he still wilted under their gaze.

"Sir, it's good to see you," said Rousseau with a nervous half-salute.

The General still didn't move. He waited until Rousseau was standing exactly in front of him, only a foot or two away.

"I want to know what in hell is going on over here, Jake. Either this is the most fucked-up theater of operations I have ever had the misfortune of seeing, or I've lost my grip. And just between you and me, I don't think I've lost my grip, despite the noises you may have heard emanating from the most recent occupant of the Oval Office."

"Well, sir, we've got our hands full over here, that's for sure," Rousseau said nervously, his voice losing its American tone, slipping back into its French accent.

"Looks to me what you people have got your hands full of is your own dicks," said the General. He wasn't grinning.

"Yes, sir. I get your point, sir," said Rousseau. "There is certainly some of that, sir."

"More than some, Jake. I just saw the damnedest thing I've ever seen in my life. They were loading goddamned coffins on a cargo plane headed back to the States. Coffins, goddammit! They're shipping the bodies of our boys back to their hometowns, wasting time, wasting money, wasting men, wasting materiel . . . God only knows what else they're wasting. But more than anything else, goddammit, they're wasting lives! Over here, those lives *count* for something. They *died* here, goddammit. You send those bodies home and you may as well tell Ho Chi Minh his boys count for more than our boys. You may as well tell him we're *all* going home. He won."

Jake Rousseau looked at the old man. The General was seething with rage. His teeth and his fists were clenched, and his khakis were stained at the armpits, dark brown around the neck, wet down the chest, dripping at the cuffs. Everything he had spent his life believing had been violated before he'd even put a foot on Vietnamese soil, and it showed.

Rousseau didn't know what to say. Things were different now? That wouldn't hold any water with the General. Political considerations made the shipment of KIAs home necessary? The General hadn't given a good goddamn for politics all the way through World War II, through hundreds of battles in a dozen countries, through twenty years in the CIA. He had told the politicians not what they wanted to hear but what the General wanted them to know. And judging by the events of the last week, he hadn't stopped. He'd just been fired by the White House. He wasn't any more inclined to cosset politicians right now than he'd ever been.

"I don't know what to say, General," Rousseau said haltingly, his tongue thickening in a familiar way. He felt like a lieutenant again, tall and skinny and shuddering under the General's withering gaze.

"I don't know what to say either, Jake. But some goddamn body better start knowing what to say to me, and they better do it quick."

"What do you mean, sir?"

"I want to know what in hell's going on with my grandson up in II Corps. I want to know what this court-martial shit's about, goddammit. That boy didn't desert in the face of the enemy any more than you did, goddammit. I want some answers, and I want them quickly, Jake. Uncork your minions. Call in your goddamned markers. Get on it. You hear me?"

"Yes, sir," said Jake Rousseau. "Give me the afternoon, sir, and I'll be back to you by dinnertime."

The General stepped forward and put his arm around his former aide and squeezed the big man tightly.

"It's good to see you, Jake. Makes a man proud."

"Yes, sir. Good to see you, sir," Jake Rousseau said stiffly.

His body was rigid. He glanced over the top of the General's hat and saw that he'd left his jeep idling on the gravel drive. He hoped the General hadn't noticed.

There was nothing the General hated more than a subordinate in a hurry.

8

The C-141 Starlifter courier touched down at Tan Son Nhut. The Colonel was braced against a wall of olive-drab webbing, seated on a stack of military film cans on their way back to MACV from the Department of Defense. He was staring at another wall of webbing with more film cans strapped down on its far side. Somewhere down there in the bowels of the Pentagon, in a dark screening room, generals had reclined in armchairs and watched last week's home movies from the front. It was almost too ridiculous to imagine. The Colonel wondered if they served popcorn, if they cheered when the choppers came in low with their miniguns blazing, the stereo sound of a 105mm artillery battery's support fire *cruuuump-cruuuump-cruuuump-cruuuumping* all around them.

The Colonel had picked up the courier flight forty-eight hours ago. It made three stops on its way East—Frankfurt, Teheran, Bangkok, then Tan Son Nhut Air Base, Saigon, Vietnam. The

C-141 taxied to a stop and lowered its rear cargo door. The wet heat of the tarmac curled into the open cargo door like a wave. The Colonel unstrapped himself from his web seat and stretched.

"Told ya you'd git here sooner 'er' later, suh," drawled an Air Force technical sergeant wearing a blue-gray crew jumpsuit. The Colonel looked around for his duffel.

"Gotcher duffel rightcheer, suh," said Tech Sergeant Brewster. "Looks like a downright purty day out there, suh."

"Every day's a good day if you wake up on the right side of the bed, Sarge," said the Colonel. "But I'm not sure I had a web seat in the belly of a 141 in mind when I thought up that particular little kernel of wisdom."

"I hear that, yes, suh, I do," said the tech sergeant, guffawing deeply from the vicinity of his considerable belly.

"The last time I arrived here, it was on a damn troop ship," said the Colonel. "They supply only one side of the bed on board one of those merchant marine luxury liners."

"They evah try ta git me on one a' them tubs, I'll cash in mah stripes, that's fuh *damn* sure, suh."

"It's been good talking to you, Sarge."

The tech sergeant blushed and turned his head.

"We ain't nevah had no *colonel* fly this here courier flight with us, suh. Been a real, *real* pleasure havin' you aboard, suh."

"You do that coffeepot justice, Sarge. Best damn coffee I ever had at five hundred miles an hour."

"Glad ta serve ya, suh . . . yes, suh," said Brewster. "Have yersef a real fine stay in Saigon, suh, and don't fergit to tell ol' Minh Cao that Sergent Brewster said hey."

"I won't, Sarge."

The Colonel took his duffel from Tech Sergeant Brewster and started down the ramp into the heat. He wasn't wearing a uniform, because this wasn't that kind of trip. He was wearing a pair of Levi's, a tan polo shirt, and an old pair of rough-out cowboy boots. A floppy-brimmed golf hat covered his salt-and-pepper crewcut and a pair of cheap dark glasses concealed his steel gray eyes.

As he started across the tarmac, an old 707 taxied to a halt and began disgorging a load of replacements. The Colonel stopped to watch. They came down the mobile stairs from the plane in a sea of khaki, each man shouldering his duffel as he reached the ground. A young sergeant wearing starched jungle fatigues and a racy-looking black baseball cap organized the men into two ranks and started calling names.

"Stevens!"

"Here!"

"Dobrowski!"

"Yo!"

"Brown!"

"Here, Sarge!"

"Bernstein!"

"Yeah!"

"Tomilson!"

"Here!"

The sergeant called off ninety names and marched them across the tarmac to the in-country processing station. The Colonel headed for the passenger terminal. As he passed through the gate in the chain-link fence around the terminal, he could still hear them, unloading from another tired old 707 with the Flying Tigers logo on its tail.

"Anson!"

"Here!"

"Bronstone!"

"Yo!"

"Jaworski!"

"Yay!"

Farther away down the flight line he could see the ranks of khaki figures forming below a third plane. Faintly, he heard but couldn't see another group double-timing in the distance:

> *"I don't know*
> *But I been told,*
> *Streets of Saigon*
> *Paved with gold,*
> *Sound off,*
> *One, two,*

Hit it again,
Three, four,
Take it on down,
One, two,
Three, four,
ONE . . . TWO!"

The Colonel shuffled through Immigration and followed a crowd past a makeshift counter made out of old packing crates with a hand-lettered sign above it reading Customs.

Outside the terminal, the Colonel put his duffel on the curb and waited. Taxis in various forms rattled past carrying everything from human cargo to crates of chickens. Finally an old diesel Mercedes screeched to a halt next to him, and a brown face with a cigar stuck in it like a fencepost showed in the window.

"You go Caravelle . . . Continental?"

"Sure," said the Colonel, not knowing where he was headed exactly. He climbed in the backseat shoving his duffel ahead of him.

The brown face turned around and grinned. The fencepost cigar was stuck in a row of corn kernels.

"You pay dallah? Big-time cheapy-cheapy, dollah!"

"How much?"

"Two dallah . . . two dallah, cheapy-cheapy."

The Colonel looked at a sign posted on the dash. In piasters, the fare amounted to five dollars. He pulled a folded wad of dollars from his pocket and showed them to the driver.

"Cheapy-cheapy," said the brown face, nearly ejecting the fencepost from his smile.

He dropped the Mercedes into gear and with a great grinding of gears and slipping of clutch and spewing of rancid exhaust and screaming of epithets, the taxi entered the traffic flow. The driver kept his left hand on the horn, and it yelped like a drowning dog all the way into the city.

The Colonel hadn't spent much time in Saigon when he'd commanded a Mechanized Infantry Battalion down in the Delta in 1966. Saigon had been the headquarters that disgorged a never-ending flow of action memos and field directives, each more incredible than the last. There was a shifting cadre of generals and colonels serving on various division, corps, and command staffs, all of whom saw their jobs as improving the manner in which "their war" was being fought. In each of their minds, Vietnam was definitely "my war," for every last one of them had a proprietary sensibility when it came to "the only war we've got," as had been said more than once about Vietnam, most prominently by the recently departed occupant of the White House.

According to the Saigon generals, there were simply an infinite number of ways that the fighting men of the U.S. Army could improve their battlefield performance. The Colonel remembered one command improvement directive as if he'd read it yesterday.

The Colonel had a little tent fly his driver had set up behind his M-113 armored personnel carrier. He used it like an office, and he sat on a folding camp chair under the tent fly at the end of the day, reading the stack of poop sheets that had arrived from Saigon while he was out crushing boonies somewhere with the Battalion. Every day the poop-sheet pile deepened, and every day the flurry of directives from on high grew more and more amazing.

"I didn't know you couldn't fight a war without paper, Top," the Colonel said to his battalion sergeant major one evening. "Look at this."

He held up a fistful of mimeographed lunacy and shook it.

"Damn stuff weighs a couple of pounds, did you know that?"

The Sergeant Major stubbed out his cigarette with his boot toe and chuckled.

"Wisht we still had us some mules, sir. We could feed 'em that shit," he drawled.

The Colonel laughed so hard he almost choked. Sergeant Major Theodore Bennett was an old Cavalry troop, the kind of man he had grown up around as a kid. In fact, he felt like a kid sometimes around the old soldier. More wisdom had passed through the Sergeant Major's ears than would ever be produced by the cabal of Saigon bureaucrats who thought they were running the war.

The Colonel turned arbitrarily to one of the pages in his hand and began reading aloud:

" 'Subject: Nightly anti-mortar ambush patrols. Distribution: one each battalion command. One: Each battalion-sized base camp will send out six, parentheses figure 6 close parentheses, squad-size ambush patrols each night in order to depress enemy mortar pressure on night defensive perimeters. Ambush patrols will patrol and establish ambushes at a radius of three hundred meters from battalion perimeter, considered effective range of enemy sixty-millimeter mortars. Patrols will begin thirty minutes before dusk and will end at first light. Reports on effectiveness of night defensive perimeter anti-mortar patrols will be made on a daily basis with body-count supplied by each command. Failure to institute adequate anti-ambush patrols will result in disciplinary action by next highest command. Signed: William P. Richter, Brigadier General, Corps G-3.' "

Sergeant Major Bennett spat in the dirt outside the tent fly.

"Shit," he intoned under his breath.

"Do you believe that, Top? Every Battalion in this division has been wasting time and energy and *lives* on those goddamned ambush patrols every goddamned night, and we're getting mor-tared more today than we were when we got here two months ago."

"Yes, sir. Sarenmajor Cunningham done tol' me the same thing when I seen him at division yesterday for that damn command sarenmajor briefing. Waste a' fuckin' time, damn patrols and briefings, both."

"I'm inclined to agree with you there, Top," said the Colonel, lighting a cigarette and passing it to his stocky Sergeant Major. "I'll see if we can't do something about this policy."

Chuckling over the corps directive on ambush patrols that afternoon had proved a turning point in the Colonel's career that he couldn't have foreseen at the time. He had kept meticulously accurate figures on mortar attacks suffered by his Battalion ever since it had arrived in Vietnam. He plotted the mortar attacks on a graph against strength of ambush patrols and proved that there was no link whatsoever between ambush patrols and the incidence or aggressiveness of nighttime mortar attacks.

He filed a memo on the subject appending his graphed statistics with the brigade commander, addressing it to the corps G-3,

General Richter. A week later he made his first official trip to Saigon, to the mahogany-paneled office of Brigadier General Richter.

Richter ignored the Colonel's statistics and memo. Without letting the Colonel get in a word edgewise, he ordered the Colonel to destroy both his data and all copies of his memo and commanded him not to discuss the subject with any contemporaries, inferiors or superiors. The G-3 raged and screamed at the Colonel at the top of his lungs. He sent the Colonel back down to the Delta with orders to shut up and forget that he had ever filed a memo on ambush patrols.

The Colonel stayed quiet for a few weeks, sending out patrols and counting bodies. American bodies. The patrols, as he had predicted, did nothing but suffer casualties. Mortar attacks went unabated.

At the end of the fourth week, the Colonel generated another memo on his ambush patrols, this one plotting American casualties against mortar attacks on two graphs. One showed casualties suffered when no ambush patrols were dispatched. The number of casualties was zero, and its graph was flat. The other showed casualties suffered when ambush patrols went out every night. The number of casualties went up in direct proportion to the number of patrols dispatched.

The message of the memo and graphic analysis was simple: Enemy mortar attacks produced zero casualties. American anti-mortar ambush patrols produced casualties in direct proportion to the number of patrols that were demanded.

The Colonel never heard anything about his second memo, and assumed that it had traced a trajectory through the bureaucracy similar to that of all bad news: a steep slide straight into the circular file.

The Colonel made a final trip to Saigon at the end of his tour with the Battalion. He was ordered up to corps headquarters the day before his flight departed from Tan Son Nhut. The purpose of his visit became clear when he saw who was waiting for him at Headquarters.

Brigadier General Richter.

The G-3 called the Colonel into the mahogany-paneled, air-conditioned office and read him his officer efficiency report out loud. Somehow Brigadier General Richter had gotten his hands on the Colonel's OER, and he had changed the score in every category to a substandard rating. He finished reading the OER to the Colonel, then he just stood there behind his desk, grinning from ear to ear, as if to say, *You thought you'd have the last word on those ambush patrols, but now you know. I had the last word, and there's nothing you can do about it.*

The Colonel stared at the grinning apparition for a moment, then saluted and turned an about-face and walked out of the G-3's office.

It wasn't the last he heard about his OER, a black mark on his record that followed him to this day. Once or twice the Colonel wished that he had simply ignored the memo and faked his ambush patrol reports, the way he knew all the rest of the battalion commanders were doing. If he'd just knuckled under and played the damn game, if he'd just kept his own memos and statistics and graphs to himself . . .

Nah. I did the right thing by the troops, and I did the right thing by the system. What does it matter in the end, anyway? What's more important? A high OER or one eighteen-year-old GI taking a bullet that he shouldn't have taken?

The OER followed him around, but Brigadier General Richter didn't.

He read in the pages of *The Army Times* one day that Brigadier General Richter had been killed in Vietnam while on an inspection tour of base camps in the Delta.

He was mortally wounded in a night mortar attack on a battalion defensive perimeter. Six ambush patrols had protected the perimeter from mortars that night.

The taxi rattled to a stop under the canopy of the Hotel Caravelle, and the Colonel handed the driver a couple of dollars.

"Dallah number one. Piaster number ten," the driver said, grinning, shifting the fencepost cigar from one corner of his mouth to the other.

The Colonel pulled his duffel behind him and walked through the hotel doors into the lobby. Ceiling fans turned lazily overhead, stirring the moist air. A young woman signed him in, taking no notice of the fact that he omitted any mention of his rank or indeed of the fact that he was an Army officer. A stooped little porter showed him to a balconied room on the back side of the hotel. The porter threw open the louvered doors to the balcony. The Colonel stepped outside. He was high enough to see over the rooftops along Tu Do Street to the Saigon River, brown and littered with junks and sampans and house barges, flowing toward the sea.

He turned to tip the porter, but the porter had slipped silently away, closing the door behind him. The Colonel opened the door and looked up and down the hall. He'd spent only an instant on the balcony, and the stooped little man was gone.

He was back in Vietnam, all right. There was no doubt in his mind about *that*.

The Colonel sat down on the edge of the swaybacked double bed in the middle of the room and picked up the phone.

"Give me the NCO Club at Cam Rahn Bay," said the Colonel.

"That is a military call, sir," said the voice of the telephone operator.

"Then get me a military line," said the Colonel.

He waited for several moments while the phone clicked and screeched and clacked and crackled.

Finally he could hear a dim, hollow ringing, like an alarm clock going off at the end of a long, empty hall.

Somebody picked up.

"Cam Rahn NCO Club," said a man's voice.

"I'd like to speak to Sergeant Major Theodore Bennett," the Colonel said authoritatively, hoping the voice on the phone wouldn't ask him to identify himself. The Colonel was going out of his way not to advertise his presence in Vietnam. So far he'd been successful. He held his breath.

"Wait one," said the voice.

The phone crackled and popped a few times. The Vietnamese phone system, through which he knew the call had been routed, was the technological equivalent of two juice cans and a piece of Mom's kitchen string. He hoped the line would remain open long enough . . .

"Sarenmajor Bennett, sir," said a voice. It was Top's.

"Sarenmajor," the Colonel said slowly, making sure he could be understood, "this is an old friend from down south."

"Come again, sir?" said Sergeant Major Bennett.

"Top, it's me," said the Colonel.

"Sir? Colonel, sir, that you?"

"Yep, it's me, Top."

"Sir, whatchew doin' back over here? I thought maybe you'd . . . you know, sir . . ."

"Retired."

"Yes, sir. Where ya at, sir?"

"Saigon. Don't use my name, Top. You hear me? Don't say my name."

"Yes, sir. Trouble, sir?"

"You've got it, Top. I need to see you. Soon."

"Name place and time, sir. I'll git myself there soon's I can."

"Where was that spot you were always talking about, Top? The restaurant you went to all the time when you were on your damn resupply missions."

"Madam Ky's."

"That's it."

"Down along the river, sir. In Saigon. It ain't hard to find. Any bike-taxi take ya there, sir. Madam Ky's place is a wee hole-in-the-wall down where the Ben Nghe Canal meets the Saigon River. Right there by the bridge, sir. It ain't much, but she got herself a new sign a coupla months ago."

"I can find it, I'm sure."

"What's up, sir?"

"Can't talk right now, Top. When can we meet?"

"I'll catch a hop first thing in the mornin', sir. Be there by noon fer sure."

"Bring your kit with you, Top."

"Y'mean my *stuff,* sir?"

"That's what I mean, Top."

"*Pas de problème,* sir," said the Sergeant Major, giving the French phrase a Kentucky kick in the ass.

"Sir?"

"Yeah?"

"This don't have nothin' to do with—"

"It's private, Sarenmajor. Don't talk to anyone about me. You hear?"

"Yes, sir. Gotchew."

"I'll see you at Madam Ky's, twelve hundred tomorrow, Top."

"That ya will, sir," said the Sergeant Major.

"Take care not to . . ."

"Righto, sir. Don'tchew go worryin' yourself none. Ol' Top's on top a' things. You kin count on it."

Outside the louvered doors, across the rooftop, the sun had gone down and the lights of Saigon had begun to twinkle in the wet heat.

The Colonel cradled the phone and fell back on the bed. He was so close he could taste it . . . the Delta only a few miles away down the road . . . the smell of the dust . . . the sound of the big guns on the edge of town . . . the heat of the sun . . . the icy stillness of the night . . .

9

————

Cathy Joice heard scratching coming from her balcony. It was eight o'clock, and the sun had just gone down. She walked over to the middle doors leading out on the balcony and peeked between the louvers. Below her room at the Continental Hotel, the yellow lights of Saigon sparkled in a soft rain.

There it was again, louder, only a foot or so away!

It wouldn't surprise her if it was a thief. A week after she had arrived in Saigon, she walked into her room one night and interrupted a burglary in progress. She slammed the door and ran downstairs, yelling for the police. Five minutes later, accompanied by hotel security officers—two off-duty "white mice," South Vietnamese Military Police—she unlocked the room to find the burglar gone and her balcony doors ajar.

If they came in this way once, they could try it again. Saigon burglars weren't notable for their criminal genius, but they did show a certain daring as they went about their business.

She turned and looked around the room for something big and heavy. Not a few of the correspondents staying at the Continental had firearms stashed in their rooms, though most avoided carrying them while on assignment. She had done her best to ignore the handgun issue. Now she wished she had sprung for the twenty-five dollars or so it would have taken to pick up a black-market pistol.

She tiptoed over to the standing lamp in the corner. It was a thick-stemmed behemoth with a circular cast-iron base. She unplugged the lamp and quickly unscrewed its shade. Grabbing the lamp in both hands like a baseball bat, she tiptoed back to the balcony doors. With her left foot she kicked open the louvered doors. She stepped onto the balcony swinging. Something fluttered overhead brushing her hair. She dropped the lamp at her feet and looked up.

A dozen bats were hanging upside down from the door frame above her, apparently escaping the rain.

She collapsed in a chair, gasping for breath.

In Saigon, nothing was as it seemed. Every day when she woke up she repeated the maxim to herself, and every day she proceeded to forget it.

In Vietnam, your eyes played tricks on you . . .

Your ears heard things that were not there . . .

Your memory slipped out of gear like a car's transmission gone lame with age . . .

Your skin crawled with insects and fungus and scales and maladies for which there were no cures . . .

Your feet stank . . .

Your hair stuck . . .

Your makeup melted . . .

Your eyes stung . . .

Your lips cracked . . .

Your nails split . . .

Your button threads rotted . . .

Your zippers rusted . . .

Your sweat poured . . .

Your lonely dreams swam thickly with creatures carved cruelly from the deepest darkest reaches within you . . .

There were times when Cathy Joice wondered what the hell she was doing in a hotel room in Saigon getting ready to go out there and strip the mysteries from a world that didn't particularly relish the idea of being shown naked by a girl. This was one of those times.

She hit the arms of the captain's chair on the balcony and hit them again.

Bats!

If you tried to write home about what had just happened, nobody would believe you. They'd dismiss such a letter as the ravings of a malaria-induced fever and send you a get-well card, that's what they would do.

No one would believe Saigon the way it truly was. That was one reason news pieces sent back to the States featured correspondents standing in the sun clad in their best foreign-correspondent gear— khaki bush jackets with epaulets and bellows pockets and floppy hats and dark glasses dangling from a breast pocket—staring emotionless into the unblinking eye of the camera reading scripts that carried piles of facts to the viewer like buckets of water to a house fire. Few of the television correspondents working in Vietnam could be said to have an ounce of faith left in anything at all, but what little faith still burned beneath their hairy chests was invested in the notion that exposed film coupled loosely to found facts represented a form of truth that was at least palatable and maybe even powerful.

Which was the problem, of course. There wasn't a man in that gang of self-important talking heads in khaki bush jackets who could get beyond the daily grind of stating the obvious with brow furrowed as seriously as possible in vocal tones as close to those of Edward R. Murrow as they dared. They could gather facts and stack them like slices of cheese and salami on a poor-boy sandwich, but they couldn't tell a story to save themselves.

Cathy Joice wanted to tell stories about America's war in Vietnam. This was her source of trouble, as well as her greatest strength. She knew that at least some of the stuff she filed would never be aired and was destined for film cans in the basement library. But she filed her stories anyway and hoped for the best and kept looking for more stories to tell.

Now she had one by the throat and she wasn't about to let go. The grandson of a four-star general, indicted for desertion in the face of the enemy? Are you kidding? It was bound to be a story that spoke reams about the Army, the war, the military leadership in Saigon and Washington . . .

There wasn't a single element of the American dilemma in Vietnam that the story of Lieutenant Matthew Nelson Blue IV wouldn't touch. Of that much she was certain.

Now all she had to do was get the story and tell it.

Danny said they had the lid down on this one tight, and she didn't doubt him. It was going to take more than a little digging to get at the heart of the story. Hell, just getting in to see this Lieutenant Blue would tax her abilities to the limit. Cathy Joice was going to have to turn the crank on her little box of tricks, and she knew it.

She got up from the chair on the balcony and went back inside, closing the louvered doors behind her. The wind was coming up, and rain had begun pitter-pattering on the balcony. It was time to get ready to go out there and fool them yet one more time.

She sat down at her dressing table and contemplated the girl in the mirror. Maybe if I lift my hair like this and roll it and tuck it with some bobby pins . . .

She began the process of becoming—ta-ta!—*Cathy Joice!* And as her fingers flew across the dressing table's potions and lotions and tubes and jars, her mind drifted off to a time long ago when she had first discovered that when she wanted to, she could fool them and fool them good . . .

She was sixteen, all legs and arms and neck and teeth, and her family was spending Christmas day with her grandparents on her mother's side. They were Phelans and they owned banks and horses in the United States and England and France and they had a sixty-room house in New Hampshire that sat on a piece of property groomed so meticulously for the gentlemanly sports of hunting and jumping and polo that the U.S. Equestrian Olympic Team considered itself privileged to train there once every four years.

The Phelans were beyond opulence. They existed out there somewhere in that realm of wealth where having *things* has lost meaning, where all that matters is civilized conversation . . . the acrid twang of martinis sipped from slender stemware amid the leathery elegance of a dark study . . . fresh-mown lawn stretching away out the windows to the sides and front and back . . . ladies powdered and perfumed and coiffed, the kids sparkling from the tub scrambling underfoot in pressed linens and seersuckers . . . dinners tinkling with laughter and candlelight and china and crystal . . . the gifts of breeding and bearing and attitude and charm . . .

Every time her family was in the United States for the holidays, which was every other year between postings to one embassy or another, they spent Thanksgiving with the Joices and Christmas with the Phelans. Every year old Mr. Phelan, her maternal grand-father, fixed an obligatory martini for her father, chatted with him until each man had taken his first sip and commented upon its wonderfulness, then the old man dropped him dead and never passed another word with him. The rest of the family followed his example. No one talked to her father after old Mr. Phelan had fixed him a martini. The Phelans's disrespect for her father went on year after year, and there seemed nothing anyone could do about it.

At the grand old age of twelve, she had first noticed the way the Phelans treated her father. They acted as if he weren't even there. When she was fourteen she watched them cut her father dead again. And she swore to herself she would find a way to get back at them, to make them stop treating her father like part of the furniture. She waited for the Christmas of her sixteenth year with a mixture of dread and anticipation. She didn't know what she was going to do, but she was going to do *something*.

As she watched her grandfather prepare the obligatory martini for her father that Christmas, she saw her chance. Old Mr. Phelan went through a procedure peculiar to the Phelan family in order to mix a martini. It was called the Phelan Martini, naturally, and its preparation was a sight to behold.

"Who'll have a Phelan Martini?" the old man began, taking a sterling silver shaker in his left hand. That was the signal for her father and anyone else in the vicinity to gather round. Usually it was understood that the first Phelan Martini was intended for Mr. Phelan and Mr. Joice, so the others kept their distance.

"First we take the ice—two kinds of ice, mind you, shaved and cubed—and we liberally pack the shaker." Old Mr. Phelan liberally packed the shaker with his two kinds of ice from two separate ice machines under the bar in the corner of the study, an imposing room with twenty-foot ceilings and leather furniture and ancient Persian carpets on the floor and the heads of many endangered African animals killed on many safaris mounted on the wall.

"Then we add the gin—Bombay Gin, no other will suffice." Old Mr. Phelan added the Bombay Gin.

"Then we wave the neck of the vermouth bottle over the shaker . . ." Old Mr. Phelan waved the neck of the vermouth bottle in the direction of the shaker and a few drops found their way into the icy mix.

"Then we add the special secret of the Phelan Martini." Old Mr. Phelan reached into a locked cabinet and pulled forth the special secret of the Phelan Martini.

"A hint of aged Spanish sherry does the trick. Just a hint . . ." And old Mr. Phelan dribbled a few drops of aged Spanish sherry into the shaker, by now frosted and dribbling icy drops of condensed water on the ancient Persian carpet under his feet.

"Then we *shake,* we do *not* stir the Phelan Martini." Old Mr. Phelan grabbed the sterling silver cap and tapped it into place atop the frosty shaker. He gripped the shaker in his hands, and holding it at an angle at chest height, he began shaking. He took a deep breath and he shook and he shook and he shook. The more he shook, the redder he got, and still he shook some more. Just when it looked as though he would burst a blood vessel, he stopped and exhaled, and so did everyone witnessing the event.

He poured the contents of the shaker, by now extremely well shaken, into iced martini glasses on the bar, and handed one to Cathy's father and took the other himself. He took a sip of the martini, smacked his lips, canted his head to one side, and said:

"Ahhhh, now that's a good martini."

"Yes, sir, it sure is," said her father with a thin smile. He knew he was something approximating the brunt of a joke to these people, but he gritted his teeth and hung in there, deferring to his wife's wish that the holidays not be ruined by her father's ungracious behavior or her husband's anger.

This was just one of many reasons Cathy Joice admired her father, and it was the source of her determination to stand up to her grandfather and let him know that if you pushed one Joice around, you'd better count on pushing all of them.

So, at age sixteen, having waited two years for her chance, she stood next to her father in mock admiration of her grandfather's performance. She waited until the two men had tasted their martinis and pronounced them ideal. Then she stepped forward, smiling with youthful enthusiasm, and announced excitedly, to her father's amazement:

"Daddy, Daddy, let's fix a Joice Martini for Grandpa!" She smiled at her father and nudged him and pinched his hand and smiled so wide she thought she'd burst, and nodded her encouragement.

"Daddy, Daddy. *Please.* I've watched you so many times, and you showed me how and I make them at home. *Please,* Daddy. Let me make a Joice Martini for Grandpa. *Please . . .*"

Her father looked at her and she winked. Her grandfather was bending over the sink, washing the martini shaker, and missed the exchange between father and daughter.

"Okay, Cathy, make us a Joice Martini," said her father.

She took the shaker from her grandfather.

"Grandpa, have you ever had a Joice Martini?"

He looked bewildered and shook his head.

"I . . . I . . . don't believe I've had the pleasure," he stammered.

"Well, it's a little different from a Phelan Martini, but it's just as good. I know, because Daddy always gives me sips. Don't you, Daddy?"

"Just little ones," said her father. "A martini isn't really the proper drink for a sixteen-year-old girl."

"I know, Daddy. I know."

She stepped up to the bar and made sure she had her grandfather's full attention. On the edges of their little group at the bar in the study, various Phelan cousins gathered. Something was going on. They could feel it. The old man hadn't taken his seat at the end of the leather sofa and begun holding court. Cousin Cathy had him trapped behind the bar, up against the sideboard.

"Grandpa, you make a Joice Martini in a shaker, just like you make a Phelan Martini," she began, tossing her pigtails in an exaggeratedly cute way. Her grandfather smiled.

She had him now. She *knew* it.

"The Joice Martini got invented, I think, five years ago when we were in Sri Lanka. Isn't that right, Daddy? You have to correct me if I'm wrong, Daddy. Help me."

He played along.

"That's right, Cathy. In Sri Lanka."

"Sri Lanka is kind of backward, Grandpa, and the electricity went out all the time, so quite often we didn't have ice. Did we, Daddy?"

"Not much of it, no we didn't," he said, picking up her flow.

"And we didn't have much gin, either, did we, Daddy?"

"Ahhh . . ."

"You remember, Daddy. They were always running out at the store. You remember."

"Oh yes, of course," said her father.

"But we always had plenty of vermouth, didn't we, Daddy? The Italian ambassador always gave everyone a case of vermouth for Christmas. Remember?"

"Oh yes, Antonio Lombardi. I remember him well. I think his family owned the company that made it. The vermouth, I mean."

"That's right, Daddy. He did."

"Good man, Antonio. Didn't have much of a taste for a martini, but he did like his vermouth. Drank it as an aperitif, as I recall."

"That's right, Daddy. So . . ." She put the shaker on the bar and straightened her skirt. She had their attention now. No doubt about it.

"Daddy still wanted a martini before dinner, so he invented the Joice Martini, didn't you, Daddy?"

"Yes. Out of necessity, of course." He was into it now.

"So Daddy would make a Joice Martini. First he poured in six jiggers of gin, didn't you, Daddy?" She picked up the bottle of gin and a jigger and measured six jiggers into the shaker.

"Then, because we didn't have much gin but we had lots of vermouth, Daddy poured in three jiggers of vermouth." She picked up the vermouth bottle and measured three jiggers into the mix.

"Then he would take a long spoon"—she picked up a bar spoon—"and he would stir the Joice Martini until it was nicely mixed."

She stirred the mixture with a look of sublime happiness on her face, as if she had been making Joice Martinis all her life.

"And Daddy would pour one for himself and one for Mommy, and there they had it! The Joice Martini!"

A look of abject terror crossed her grandfather's face as she picked up two fresh martini glasses and poured half of the warm mixture into one and half into the other. She was actually going through with it! He was going to have to drink that vile stew! He steeled himself. Protocol was protocol. It would . . . *upset the balance of things* . . . if he failed to go through the Joice Martini process to the end, to the tasting and smacking of lips and pronouncements of delight, as his son-in-law had gone through the Phelan Martini process to the end, to the smacking of lips and pronouncements of delight.

She handed one brimming martini glass to her father and one to her grandfather. Her father took a big sip from his glass and smacked his lips.

"Ahhh, now that's a good martini!" he exclaimed.

Old Mr. Phelan took a sip from his glass and smacked his lips with something less than a look of relish on his face as the two-to-one mixture went down.

"Yes indeed, that *is* a fine martini," he said. "I'll remember this . . . uh . . . for those times when we don't have ice."

"Isn't it good, Grandpa! I'm so glad you like it!" Cathy Joice hopped up and down with excitement.

Her grandfather excused himself and headed for his perch at the far end of the leather sofa.

Her father wrapped his big arm around her shoulders and whispered:

"I won't forget this martini, either, daughter."

Then they parted, so that nobody would suspect the conspiracy.

It was her first con job. The fact that she'd straddled the delicate line between the opposing sides of a single family made it all the more difficult.

She wouldn't forget it, either. She remembered that day every time she readied herself to go forth and wring them dry, every time she convinced the reluctant to talk, the imperious to listen, the just plain dumb to shut up . . . every time she went out there and fooled them one more time.

Thirty minutes later she was walking through the front door of the Tan Son Nhut Air Base Officers' Club. She was wearing a simple black short-sleeved dress that was hemmed just above her knees, and a pair of plain black pumps. Her hair was twisted into a French roll. The heat hadn't melted her makeup yet, and her purse contained a reporter's notebook.

Get ready, here I come, she said under her breath.

She walked over to a telephone and dialed the number for the Officers' Club bar, a large room at the end of the corridor.

"Captain Terrence W. Morriss, please," she said to the bartender when he answered the phone.

Then she let the receiver dangle and hurried into the bar. She was standing at the curve of the horseshoe-shaped bar when a man in blue slacks and a white shirt reached the phone.

"Captain Morriss, sir," the man said into the receiver. He waited a moment and said it again, looking perplexed. "Can I get another beer here?" he asked, raising his hand.

Cathy Joice slid down the bar a step at a time, slowly, shouldering her way past two lieutenants, a captain, and a colonel. He still had his hand in the air, and now he was waving at the bartender.

"Bartender . . . bartender!" he called, to no avail. The bartender, an off-duty GI twenty ranks below Captain Morriss, was rolling dice double-or-nothing for the price of a beer with a crewcut flyboy lieutenant about nineteen years old at the far end of the bar.

So *that* was Captain Morriss, the man who would be defending Lieutenant Matthew Nelson Blue IV.

Hmmmmmmm.

Maybe getting in to see the prisoner accused of desertion in the face of the enemy wasn't going to be as difficult as she'd thought.

"Bartender," she called across the horseshoe softly. His head wheeled around as though gimballed on a ring of greased ball bearings.

He scurried around the horseshoe past Captain Morriss and presented himself in front of Cathy Joice.

"Yes, ma'am? What's your pleasure?"

"That man down the bar has been trying to get your attention longer than I have," she said, indicating Captain Morriss with a nod of her head.

"Give him whatever he wants and bring me a martini. Very dry. Very cold. Bombay Gin."

"Yes, ma'am."

Cathy Joice put her purse on the bar and slipped onto a barstool.

"Thanks," said Captain Morriss, heading her way.

She opened her purse and pulled out her lipstick and compact.

"Don't mention it," she said.

She gazed into her compact mirror and applied the lipstick slowly, first her top lip, then the bottom. She pursed her lips together, distributing the color evenly. She put the cap back on the lipstick tube and closed her compact and shoved them into her purse.

"I'm Terry Morriss," said the man being served a draft beer by the bartender.

She closed her purse with a snap and turned her head.

"I know," she said.

"Really?" he asked.

"Sure. I heard you answer the phone as I walked in."

The bartender delivered her Bombay Gin martini and she took a sip, leaving a large red lipstick mark on the edge of the glass.

"Sorry," she said, looking up at the bartender. "I guess you'll have to wash this glass separately, won't you?"

"No problem," said the bartender. "Anything for a pretty lady."

"I'll get the next round," said Captain Morriss.

"Why . . . thank you, Captain," she said. "That's very nice of you."

"You're that television news reporter, aren't you? Cathy . . . ah . . ."

"Joice. From KCKA. It's very nice to meet you."

She turned to him and they shook hands.

"I've always wanted to do a story on what you lawyers are doing over here in a combat zone."

"There are many kinds of war, Cathy. My specialty happens to be the kind that takes place in the courtroom."

"Fascinating. See? I was right. I always knew there'd be a story among the forgotten men of this war. I'll take that martini now, bartender." She smiled broadly at Captain Morriss.

"I hear you've got yourself a big case."

The drive from Saigon to Long Binh the next morning took thirty minutes over a road that would have qualified for emergency repair in the United States. Route 316 was regularly swept for command-detonated mines, and potholes where they had been dug up blemished its surface like pockmarks.

Captain Morriss's jeep bumped and careened across the road's two lanes like a bumper-car at an amusement park.

Cathy Joice held on to the jeep's windshield and braced herself for each pothole. Even when she raised her butt from the seat, the jeep hit the holes with such force that she would discover, when she got back to the hotel, that the blue flesh of bruises completely covered her lower back and bottom.

"Only a mile to go, Cathy," said Captain Morriss. "I told you it wouldn't take long."

"It might be a short distance in kilometers," said Cathy Joice, "but it's considerably longer in potholes."

Captain Morriss threw his head back and laughed out loud. The jeep careened from the roadway into a shallow ditch and out again. They crossed the Dong Nai River on a temporary floating bridge that had been thrown across the river by the Army Corps of Engineers when the main bridge was damaged for the twenty-third time by satchel charges detonated by VC sappers. Up ahead, the chain-link fence of the Long Binh post complex could be seen. It was surrounded by the traditional shack city that sprang up around every American base camp in Vietnam in response to the American soldiers' insatiable appetites for beer, booze, hookers, and, for the first time in an American war, drugs.

Captain Morriss was waved through the camp's front gate with a snappy salute from an MP clad in starched fatigues, spit-shined boots, and white gloves. Captain Morriss drove the jeep straight to the Long Binh stockade, a complex-within-a-complex in the far northeast corner of the camp. The stockade was a group of six temporary buildings built out of corrugated aluminum, surrounded by an elaborate perimeter of tall fences and barbed wire. Guard towers stood at the four corners of the stockade, and uniformed soldiers armed with M-16s could be seen on the tower balconies, standing guard over the yard full of prisoners below.

Captain Morriss stopped his jeep at the stockade gate. An MP checked his papers. He went back into the guard shack, talked on a field phone for a moment, then nodded. Both the outer and inner gates to the stockade opened, and Captain Morriss drove the jeep to a parking area on the far side of one of the stockade buildings.

He turned to Cathy Joice and said:

"Here we are! The lovely Long Binh Jail."

Captain Morriss led the way into the first building, which housed the stockade administration. He cleared them past a receptionist and they entered the stockade itself. All the aluminum buildings were connected by covered walkways. Morriss picked up some papers from a desk at the rear of the administration building and they headed down the first walkway.

"That's as far as you go, miss," said Captain Alvin Z. Dupuy, the prosecuting attorney.

"What do you mean?" asked Captain Morriss.

"No press. No farther," said Captain Dupuy.

"This is bull . . ."

"This is orders from MACV," said Captain Dupuy. "This is as far as she goes. This is as far as *anybody* goes. You ought to consider yourself lucky to be getting an audience with your so-called client, Morriss."

"Will you wait for me here?" asked Captain Morriss. "This shouldn't take long."

"Sure," said Cathy Joice.

A half-hour later, he returned, looking grim.

"What's going on?" she asked.

"They're railroading this kid," said Captain Morriss.

"Why?"

"I don't know why, but what I do know is this: a court-martial procedure that normally takes six to eight weeks has been screwed down to seven days. They want to get this kid in front of a court-martial and out of here. That's why you're not welcome. They don't want press. They don't want anybody to know what's going on. It's scary."

Captain Morriss looked across the barren grounds of the Long Binh Jail and shook his head.

"I think they're trying to kill this kid, and I don't know why," he said. "I just hope I can figure this whole thing out before it's too late."

"Hasn't Lieutenant Blue told you what you need to know?" asked Cathy Joice.

"No. He just sits there staring. That's what's really scary. He doesn't seem to care what happens to him. He just sits there, looking at the wall. I hope I can get through to him before it's too late."

F O U R

☆

A Slit in His Face Called a Smile

Firebase Zulu-Foxtrot
Day Four

Night came fast. The Lieutenant was glad the brigade had stopped its sweep and had dug in early. He had been in more hospitable spots than the little knoll identified on the map as Hill 448 which by his reckoning was ten kliks inside the nation of Laos. The ops order he'd received that morning had said nothing about Laos. The alleged purpose of the sweep was to stir up some action with an estimated NVA Battalion, reinforced, which division intelligence said was active in the AO, or area of operations.

What area, you dufus base-camp hooch-rat G-2 motherfuckers? The area known to the rest of the world as goddamned Laos? Who in hell dreamed up this chickenshit operation, anyway? Halleck? Testor, the goddamned brigade CO? Maybe it was General Cardozo, who to his great surprise wakes up every morning and looks in the mirror of his air-conditioned trailer back there in the big base camp and sees a division commander. S-u-u-u-re, Gen-

Gen. Two stars and a clap on the back and a brand new guidon and you think your shit doesn't stink anymore, old God himself reached down and bopped you on the head and made you the military equivalent of bishop. Yeah? Tactical genius by divine ordination? That what you think your gig is, General, sir, er . . . ah . . . Bishop, sir? Well, General, sir, Bishop, sir, haul your starched ass out here and see if you can't figure out what the hell we're doing in Laos, dug in on a little hump in the ground no bigger than a baseball field, sitting here in the dark waiting for something to happen. C'mon, chopper on out here to us, General, sir, Bishop, sir. Award yourself another Air Medal while you're at it. We've got a spot for heavily decorated heroes like you. In a hole next to Whoopie Cushion Ridgely who figures he's got a pipeline to the same dude upstairs who stuck stars on your cap. Cushion sees stars, too, sir. Only problem being, Cushion sees them when they aren't really there. You'll love him, General, sir, Bishop, sir. Cushion's one of those American Fighting Men who makes guys like congressmen and generals and bishops get all teary-eyed every time they give a speech about the selfless sacrifices he makes, his dedication to his duty and to the ideals of Democracy . . . Why, they're so proud of the idea of Whoopie Cushion they just plain forgot ol' Cushion himself. Hell's bells, General, sir, Bishop, sir. Drop what you're doing, sir, hop a Huey and visit us here on Hill 448. We'll put you in a hole with Cushion and I personally guarantee you'll spend a night you won't soon forget. Any justice left in the world, you'll qualify for another Air Medal . . . an Air Head Medal for Bravery in the Face of Lunacy . . .

The Lieutenant stood in the commander's cupola of his track, his back pressed up against the foam-edged rim of the cupola, gazing out at the perimeter. Concertina wire, vicious stuff with razor-sharp barbs laid around the hill like a gigantic Slinky, had been uncoiled and bounced around until the little hill had a three-deep barbed wire necklace. Concertina was SOP stuff—standard operating procedure—intended to discourage VC sappers from coming inside the perimeter to wreak havoc with grenades, explosive charges, whatever was this week's flavor at the VC Sapper Shop. Thing was, it hardly even slowed them down. The concertina probably just pissed them off a little, made 'em want to kill even more round-eyes.

Outside the wire were Claymore mines, neat little jobs that looked like an olive-drab paperback book open to the middle. Detonated by remote control or trip-wire, Claymores spewed a fan of thousands of tiny flechettes, steel arrowheads with sharp points, in front of them. Claymores were nice to have out there protecting you, if you could find enough of them that were operable. The problem with Claymores was coffee. Guys were always unscrewing the backing plates from the mines and digging out and lighting up the C-4 explosive, with which they would heat canteen cups of coffee.

The Lieutenant had often marveled at the essential ingenuity of the average troop.

He had also often marveled at the essential stupidity of the average troop, whose priorities ran to hot coffee in the morning rather than live Claymores at night around the perimeter.

Aaah, well . . .

What are you going to do, Lieutenant?

Or, as Dirtball put it:

"Whatchew gonna dew, Eltee?"

It was an organic thing, a living creature, a platoon. You woke it up in the morning and you fed it and you told it to come on and do this thing, whatever thing, anything, then you fed it again, and you took it somewhere and did another thing, then you dug it in and you fed it again and you slept with it and you did the same thing all over again. In return, the platoon would keep you safe and dry (sometimes) and warm with its embrace.

A platoon was not a pet and it was not a possession and it was not a career position and it was not positive and it was not negative. A platoon was what you made it and what it made you. It was men banded together to do the work of war and the glue that bonded them was not political or legal or practical or mental; it was love that held a platoon together in sun and storm and pits and glory.

And to command a platoon in combat was like playing the game of Three Wishes for keeps. Every kid, at least once, tried the most obvious first wish of all, that all your other wishes would come true. And that was the thing about commanding a platoon in combat. You had to take the chance that your first wish would not come true, that you might lose the game, or it was all for nothing.

Combat was different from the real world. It was somewhere out there in the zone where the normal rules didn't apply anymore. It was like a game, and you began with these men and these weapons and these tracks; you started with no rules, with all of the pieces on the board. The game was combat, and *you really got to use them.* Stateside, all you could do was take them out in a big field somewhere on the military reservation and drive around and shoot blanks.

In combat, everything counted. The guns fired real bullets. The 4.2s lofted real rounds. The M-79s fired real grenades. And when you hit somebody out there in the bush, he bled real blood. Few would talk about it, and if they talked, nobody would admit it, but the thing about commanding a platoon in combat was that it was fun. It *was* like a game.

But out there in the woods in the dark, you left the gameboard.

Out there, everything depended on how good you really were, how much you really meant it, how much courage you really had.

Out there beyond the wire in the woods in the dark, running that platoon was frightening beyond all your poor powers of imagining how it would be.

Out there, *you* had to make your first wish come true, or *they* died.

Sometimes you'd lose track of what a platoon was and what it was not and what it was doing to you and what you were doing to it, and the guilt would settle in back there behind your eyes where memory lived, reminding you of who you were and what you meant to the platoon and what it meant to you. You'd stand there alone at night and watch it out there on the perimeter playing the game for you for real, and you'd love it all over again and swear you wouldn't forget this time . . . this time you'd always remember that a platoon was a gift from God, a blessing bought wholesale that really was just like Grandpa's Battalion . . . a platoon was the most perfect thing in the world, and don't you *ever* forget it, boy, don't you *ever* forget what those men do for you . . .

Okay . . . okay. I won't, Grandpa. And yeah, I'll remember, Dad. Just stop hammering me with your rules and reminding me of the wonderfulness of it all. It's only a platoon. We're only men trying to fight a war. Weirder more wonderful stuff has happened to lesser collections of people. Like families.

The Lieutenant's track was dug in defilade, down between two bumps in the ground that protected it from direct fire from its flanks. But standing in the cupola, he could see all the way around the perimeter and beyond it to the treeline looming like a wall in the distance. He could see them out there in their holes doing their thing for him in the dark.

What in the hell was going on? They were in Laos, to be sure, yeah, but what were they doing there? And why wasn't Laos on the ops order menu this morning? And why wasn't there any acknowledgment by Battalion of their position inside the Laotian border? And where in hell was this so-called NVA Battalion, reinforced? And what in hell were they supposed to do with a NVA Battalion, reinforced, if it happened along the goddamned pike? Shake fucking hands with it?

Questions flew through the Lieutenant's mind like fireflies, each one briefly illuminated without shedding any real light on the situation.

He felt something tugging on his pants leg and looked down. It was Dirtball.

"Hey, Eltee. It's the CO on the horn for ya, sir."

The Lieutenant stooped down through the cupola and sat down on his air mattress up against the firewall. He took the mike from Dirtball.

"Rattail Six, this is Rattail Two, over."

"This is Six," crackled Goose Gardner, the company commander, over the radio.

"I just got a mission for you from Saltlick Six," said Gardner, referring to the battalion commander, Lieutenant Colonel Halleck. "You are to send out an ambush patrol at a distance of two thousand meters from your perimeter on azimuth two-niner-zero. Radio your coordinates when you're set up, over."

"Roger," said the Lieutenant, "that is ambush patrol at two thousand meters, azimuth two-niner-zero, come again."

"Roger that," said Gardner.

"Rattail Six, this is Two. Back to you with those coordinates when we get out there in a short-short. Out."

The Lieutenant handed the mike to Dirtball.

"Rattail Six says we've got to put an ambush patrol outside the wire, two thousand meters northwest of here."

"Whatchew gonna dew, Eltee?"

"Put the damn patrol out there, that's what," said the Lieutenant. "Where's Davis?"

"He's out behind his track, over there," said Dirtball, pointing out the back of the track to a bump in the ground.

"I'll be back in a minute," said the Lieutenant.

He found Platoon Sergeant Elroy Davis behind his track, as advertised. He was picking at something gray and soupy at the bottom of his canteen cup.

"Want some, Eltee?" he asked thickly, holding up the cup, his mouth full of gray soupy stuff.

"No thanks," said the Lieutenant.

"What's up, Eltee?" asked Davis.

"I just heard from Captain Gardner that we've got to put an ambush patrol out there, two thousand meters from the perimeter. I think I'm going to take it out myself, Davis. I don't like the looks of this shit around here. There's no telling what we're going to run into, or what's going to run into us. I want to make sure we're set up and we know right where we are, so fucking Battalion doesn't put a patrol out there that runs into us."

"I can dig it," said Sergeant Davis.

"You run things back here while we're out there," said the Lieutenant. "I want that perimeter so fucking tight I'll be able to hear their assholes puckering at two thousand meters, you got me?"

"Gotchew, Eltee. I'll keep 'em awake. Don'tchew go worryin' yo'self 'bout that."

"They better be, Sarge. There's no telling what manner of hell might be raised by that fucking NVA Battalion that's supposed to be out there."

"Who you gonna take, Eltee?"

"Dirtball, Repatch, Woodley, Cushion, Moonface, and Strosher."

"I'd keep an eye on Cushion, sir," said Sergeant Davis. "He been seein' things again, sir, talkin' t' God and weird shit."

"I know," said the Lieutenant. "I'm going to have to live with it, Sarge. Cushion's the only one who knows where Repatch is when he's on point. It's like they've got some kind of radar between them."

"I hear that," said Sergeant Davis. "Spooky mo'fo's, you ask me, sir."

"Maybe having those two spooky mo'fo's with us will scare the shit out of the NVA, they'll check out Cushion and Repatch and just cash their check and keep their distance."

"I hear that."

"Stay by your radio. I'll buzz you, let you know where we are when we get settled out there."

"Rodge, Eltee. Me an' the platoon gonna keep our shit together. Nobody gonna fuck with our shit. No, sir."

The Lieutenant walked the perimeter, rounding up the troops. Each of them grabbed his M-16, a pouch of ammunition clips, a half-dozen grenades, and as many Claymores as he could stuff in the pockets of his rucksack. They tucked ponchos and poncho liners into web gear and waited at the wire in a file, pissing and moaning and swearing off dope and cigarettes and booze and chicks, if only they can make it through this fucking patrol in one piece, promise you, God, every one of our sorry asses promises we'll be good forever, yes indeed, God, sir, just get us through this one fucking patrol alive.

Repatch, picking his teeth with a skinny nail he carried around, humming a James Brown tune, rolling his shoulders, swiveling sideways, doing an eerie soft-shoe in the dark . . .

Dirtball, shouldering the prick-25 and an M-79 and a bandolier of '79 grenade shells and a homemade sack carrying his stash of C's, scratching his ass, spitting tobacco juice toward the wire . . .

*   *   *

Woodley, the medic, skinny as a twig, silent and brooding and hawk-faced under the camouflage-stick he'd rubbed all over his face like an Indian . . .

Whoopie Cushion, hugging himself, rocking back and forth, back and forth, talking to God, listening to the devil, goosing Moonface, scratching his nose and farting and rubbing his weapon like it was a girl . . .

Moonface, M-60 slung over his shoulder like a smoked ham, chest crisscrossed with belts of linked ammo, twitching every time Cushion ribbed him, grinning that toothy grin, laughing, jiving nervously . . .

Strosher, blond and jolly, claimed to be eighteen, looked fourteen, eager, loaded down with his M-16 and six M-72 LAWs—light antitank weapons, folding bazookas you fired once and threw away—Strosher's favorite, called them his roman candles . . .

The Lieutenant, traveling light, M-79 and a load of shotgun shells, binoculars for better night vision, face rubbed with camouflage, spitting anxiety through the gap in his teeth, trying to go steely and cold and knowing it wouldn't work, he was sweating and shuffling at the edge of the night with the rest of them . . .

Mallick lifted the wire and pointed out the Claymores and their trip-wires, and they moved out silently from the perimeter, heading across the high grass for the trees. It was black-dark, no moon, light cloud cover, no stars, nothing, a good night for a patrol, if there could be said to be any time of the day or night, bright or dark or rainy or shiny, that was truly *good* for shit like crawling around out there in a place not of your choosing, spoiling for a fight with persons painted green and black and scared and alone . . .

*   *   *

. . . and, like you, strangers once they were beyond the wire.

They moved softly through the tall grass and disappeared into the black hole of Laotian woods.

Repatch on point, gliding silently up ahead somewhere, Cushion following, finding the way behind him through signals only the two of them understood . . . crushed grass . . . bent twigs . . . little clicks and clacks they did back and forth with their tongues . . .

The Lieutenant behind Cushion with his compass and his map, counting paces, counting, counting, estimating distance from the wire, gauging his position by terrain and just plain old instinct . . .

Dirtball on the Lieutenant's tail, ticking his back with the prick-25's antenna, mike/receiver glued to his head like a new ear . . .

The rest of them trailing behind, picking their way carefully through a forest of sweating trees and midnight brambles, cursing to themselves in a velvety chorus of dull fear and black hatred . . .

They had moved fifteen hundred meters by the Lieutenant's estimation, and they were cresting a low hill, when the signal came back that Repatch was frozen, pointing into the dark.

"Eltee . . . Eltee . . ." whispered Whoopie Cushion.

The Lieutenant crept up a few yards and ran into Whoopie Cushion's rucksack. Cushion was crouching next to a tree, vibrating.

"Yeah. I'm here."

"Repatch's got somethin' up there, sir."

"Where is he?"

"Don'tcha see 'im? He's right *there*," said Whoopie Cushion, pointing into the dark with the barrel of his M-16.

The Lieutenant squinted but couldn't make out a thing. He grabbed his binoculars and screwed his eyes to the glass.

Repatch was standing at the crest of the hill like a statue, his back to the Lieutenant. He looked like a tree stump or a fallen branch or *something*. He didn't look like Repatch.

The Lieutenant scooted forward until he could reach out and touch Repatch.

"What's going on, Repatch?" he whispered. He was kneeling and couldn't see past Repatch's broad back.

"Eltee? Gotcher binocs?" Repatch whispered.

"Sure." He handed the binoculars over and waited.

Repatch looked through them for a very long moment, then crouched down next to the Lieutenant.

"You ain't gonna believe this shit, sir," he whispered, turning his head.

The Lieutenant could hear him, but he couldn't see his face.

"What's going on? Spit it out."

"There's a fuckin' airstrip up there, Eltee, and they're loading some fuckin' plane. There's a whole bunch of 'em movin' around. Take a look."

He handed the binoculars to the Lieutenant and moved to the side.

The Lieutenant slithered forward on his belly and, leaning on his elbows, had a look through the glasses.

"Jesus, you're right, Repatch. It's a fucking DC-3, and they've got a grass strip lit up out there somehow."

"Little cans fulla kerosene or diesel. You can smell 'em," whispered Repatch. "Jus' enough light to land the fucker."

The Lieutenant handed the binocs back to Repatch.

"Can you make out who it is?"

Repatch studied the scene for a moment.

"Nope. I mean, no, sir. Jus' a buncha fuckers movin' around the plane. Not enough light, an' we're too fuckin' far away."

"Let's move up," said the Lieutenant. He turned and crawled back to the rest of the patrol. He gathered them into a bunch and whispered, "There's something going on about two hundred meters ahead. Somebody loading a plane. We're going to have a look."

"My Lord and Savior," said Whoopie Cushion. "He's come at last. Flyin' first class."

"Shut up, Cushion, you dull-ass mo'fo'. Yo' Lord and Savior hadda knowed your ass was comin' along, he'd a' done took hisself a wife and settled down and done him some bass fishin' and your ass woulda been grass long time ago," said Moonface.

Whoopie Cushion started praying softly in the dark.

The Lieutenant signaled the patrol forward and they began to move.

Repatch led the way down the hill, breaking trail, not making a sound. The rest of the patrol followed just as silently. They approached the makeshift airstrip from its far end, sticking to the treeline. The grass strip had been well taken care of. It was freshly mowed and lined, just as Repatch had said, with tin cans full of diesel flickering yellow in the black night. The wind was blowing their way, masking any noise they made in the woods.

Halfway down the strip, the Lieutenant called a halt. He pulled out the binocs and had a look.

"Jesus, Repatch, they're ours! Those are Americans! Round-eyes! They're wearing civvies but they're ours! What in hell are they doing out here?"

He handed the glasses to Repatch.

"Damn. Weirdest shit I ever seen, long as I been in 'Nam," he said, handing the glasses back to the Lieutenant.

"We're not in 'Nam," said the Lieutenant. "We're in Laos."

"No shit."

"No shit."

"Whatchew gonna dew, Eltee?" asked Dirtball, radio receiver screwed to his ear.

"Let's move on down farther and see what the fuck is going on," said the Lieutenant. "Then we'll make our move. We don't want to come strolling out of the woods and spook them. No telling who they might take us for ... VC, NVA ... Anything might happen."

They glided through the treeline in Repatch's wake. That was the thing about Repatch. With him on point, you couldn't help but pick up his rhythm. Inside of a couple hundred yards, you were moving just like he did, soft and quick and happy. It was spooky. Behind the Snake, you stopped sweating and swearing and sucking wind. With Repatch on point, you were inviolate, walking hallowed ground. Even Whoopie Cushion stopped his mumbling and praying. The only god out there on point was Repatch, and he worked just fine, thank you.

The Lieutenant called a halt when they were opposite the plane, about fifty yards away across the airstrip. They could see the action around the plane clearly now. A half-dozen Americans in blue jeans and olive-drab camouflage T-shirts were loading something on the plane, boxes it looked like, tightly wrapped with tape and rope. Another dozen men, also American, also in jeans and fatigue T-shirts, were standing guard in a circle around the plane. They were heavily armed. Every man carried at least one weapon in his hands and one slung over his shoulder. Two of them carried M-79s.

"Eltee. Check it out," said Repatch. "Dudes are carryin' Kalashnikovs. One of 'em's got a RPG. That's some weird shit, Eltee. 'Merican dudes carryin' that shit."

The Lieutenant raised the glasses. It was exactly as Repatch had said.

"Give me the radio, Dirtball," said the Lieutenant.

Dirtball unlatched the receiver from his head and handed it to the Lieutenant.

"Rattail Six, this is Rattail Two, over," he whispered into the receiver.

Static.

"Rattail Six, Rattail Six, Rattail Six, this is Rattail Two, this is Rattail Two, over."

Static.

Break.

Dead air.

Static.

"Dirtball, check and see if you got the right freek," said the Lieutenant.

Dirtball unshouldered the prick-25 and peered into the dim glow of the radio frequency dials.

"S'right freek, Eltee. We're on the company net solid."

"See what you can do, Dirtball," said the Lieutenant, handing the mike/receiver to his RTO.

Dirtball knelt next to the radio, whispering into the receiver. The Lieutenant turned around and looked through the glasses at the scene on the grass airstrip.

"I got nothin' on this mo'fo' radio, Eltee," said Dirtball. "Either this fucker's shot, or they ain't monitorin' the freek. And I *know* this fucker's in good shape. We was talkin' to the captain only an hour ago, sir. I *know* my radio's strac, sir. I *swear* it."

"Okay, okay, Dirtball," said the Lieutenant.

"Whatchew gonna dew, Eltee?" asked Repatch.

The Lieutenant looked around. The patrol was gathered in a semicircle, kneeling on the forest floor. Twelve eyes were gazing up at him shining so brightly they looked like oncoming headlights in the distance down a long flat road . . . wet, glowing, expectant, hopeful, scared, trusting . . .

. . . loving . . .

"Well, they're Americans, just like us. They're ours. They're in our AO. We may as well see what's going on, men," said the Lieutenant. "Come on. Let's see what the fuck is up."

The Lieutenant led the way through the treeline onto the grass. He had taken three steps when Repatch tackled him. He looked up as he went down.

One of the men in jeans and T-shirt wheeled around and shouldered his Kalashnikov.

The Lieutenant heard a brief burst of fire, then he heard a dozen bursts of fire and another dozen bursts and the night was ablaze.

He looked up and waved his arms over his head and yelled as loud as he could, "Hey, assholes, we're American! Weapons platoon, Triple-Deuce! Hey!"

He knew they heard him, but it didn't matter. Gunfire kept coming.

Rounds splattered the ground around him and he found himself crawling at top speed back to the treeline. Moonface, who hadn't left the trees when the shooting started, had dropped and was firing his M-60 at an ungodly clip, spraying the airstrip as if he was watering it with a garden hose.

The Lieutenant reached the treeline and dropped and turned around. Strosher was hit, lying on his back in the tall grass at the edge of the strip. Woodley was lying next to him, holding a compress over his stomach.

"Get the fuck in here!" yelled the Lieutenant.

Strosher looked back at him, a look of shock blanketing his features as though he'd woken up in the middle of a bad dream. Woodley scooted backward toward the trees, dragging Strosher by the arms behind him.

Gunfire was still coming, tree branches cracking and falling as rounds *thwack-thwack-thwack-thwack-thwack-thwack-thwacked* into the woods around them.

Moonface laid down heavy machine-gun fire, and the others cut loose with their M-16s. Whoopie Cushion had Dirtball's M-79, and he pumped grenade rounds at them as fast as he could load. The first few grenades hit, and most of the men around the plane dropped, easing up on their fire.

The Lieutenant looked back at the plane. One engine was going, and the other was turning over. Some of the men were up and running for the opposite treeline. Three of them were crouched next to the plane, under the near wing, firing at the patrol. Three more were still tossing burlap bales through the side door of the DC-3.

The Lieutenant wondered what three men would be doing in the middle of a savage firefight, throwing bales into an airplane. He pulled out the glasses and squinted through them.

Another volley of rounds from the Kalashnikovs *thwack-thwacked* into the trees, and everybody ducked.

The DC-3 was roaring down the airstrip, taking off.

Moonface followed the plane with the barrel of the M-60, firing until the plane rose and disappeared over the trees and into the night.

The barrel of his M-60 was glowing white-hot in the dark, like a magic wand. Any minute Moonface was going to wave it and all their wishes would come true.

Yeah, the Lieutenant thought. Real fucking likely.

All of the American men in jeans and camouflage T-shirts were gone. Nothing was moving. Everybody crouched in the treeline and listened.

No engine noise. No firing. No movement.

Nothing.

"Anybody other than Strosher hit?" the Lieutenant asked, looking around at the patrol.

Everybody shook his head no.

"You okay, Strosher?"

There was no answer.

"He's dead, Eltee. In the stomach. Nothing I could do." Woodley looked up at the Lieutenant blankly. All business, Woodley. Coldly efficient. Dropped out of Kansas University. The men said he could stem the tide of a good-sized creek with a Q-tip, he was that good at stopping a wound from bleeding. The Lieutenant wouldn't trade him for three real docs. There was no one like him in the whole Battalion. Good man. This time, however, as at several other times in the past, there was nothing he could do. Strosher lay there on the ground under the trees, under the black night sky, staring up with wide-open eyes that saw nothing.

The Lieutenant looked down the airstrip to where the plane had disappeared. The cans of diesel were smoking densely. Several had burned themselves out. Others were flickering and dying.

"Dudes knew how to time them runway lights," said Repatch. He was picking his teeth, watching the diesel cans go out one by one. The plane hadn't been gone sixty seconds.

"Where'd they go?" asked the Lieutenant, stunned by the sudden silence.

"They gone, Eltee," said Moonface, sweat pouring from his brow, eyes sparkling, teeth glistening in the dark.

The Lieutenant stood up and walked to the edge of the woods. He started onto the grass, heading toward the spot where the plane had been loaded.

A single round *thwacked* into the branches next to him. He ducked, watching and waiting.

Nothing.

He felt a tugging on his pants leg and looked around.

It was Dirtball.

"C'mon, Eltee. More a' them than us anyways. Nothin' we can do for Strosher now. Let's set up our fuckin' little ambush like Rattail Six done said, an' settle on down for the night."

"Nobody gonna believe this shit." The words came from the dark.

"*I* don't believe this shit," said the Lieutenant.

A man was dead, killed by friendly fire.

Somebody shouldered Strosher. Repatch slithered into the dark and they were gone behind him, sucked up into the black woods like smoke.

10

They say betrayal can happen only in the presence of love, but they are wrong.

When the General got to Vietnam, he turned to Jake Rousseau before anyone else because the scrappy Frenchman-turned-American had been his most trusted aide for eight years in Berlin after the war, when the General headed up the CIA in Europe and he needed someone he could trust in his first civilian job in thirty years.

From the start, Jake Rousseau owed the General his career, indeed his citizenship and his identity as an American, as a CIA man.

But the General remembered someone who wasn't there anymore. He was an old man who had fought an old war and was still playing by old rules. This was a new war. And there were new rules.

The General had made an error typical of military men. He confused one currency for another. Jake owed him something old:

loyalty. But he paid him off the Vietnam way, with something new: crushed hopes and broken promises and disappeared dreams.

In Vietnam, truly, nothing was as it seemed.

The General, waiting for Rousseau in his room overlooking the ersatz waterfall in the courtyard of the VIP Villa, wasn't really part of the American royalty he had aspired to through his marriage to Carey Randolph, not to mention his marriage to Belinda Thomason. He was a sharecropper's son who had made good the hard way, by taking everything he could get and giving nothing back once he had it.

The Colonel, sweating under a ceiling fan stirring the wet air in a hotel room in Saigon, wasn't just boring and pedantic and honest and thorough—he was *brave* and boring and pedantic and honest and thorough.

And the Lieutenant, who by now was languishing some thirty kilometers away in the stockade in Long Binh—a place the troops jokingly referred to as LBJ, Long Binh Jail—who looked just like his grandfather had looked in a photograph taken when he was twenty-four, also a Lieutenant and a platoon leader—who had patterned his life on the General's every utterance and motion, wasn't really like him at all. For the first time he had just seen life through his father's eyes—boringly and pedantically and thoroughly and honestly. It happened because, like his father, he was a fool for love and a sucker for a sad thrill.

And Jake Rousseau? He wasn't AID, he was CIA, and he was above all in vogue. He betrayed the General with a shrug of his shoulders the modern way, on the phone, through a slit in his face called a smile.

It was 9:00 A.M., and the General was shaving when the call came. He wiped the soap from his face and picked up the phone.

"General Blue," he growled, sounding like an unmuffled car engine turning over for the first time, grinding, snarling to life.

"General, please hold for Mr. Rousseau," said a woman's voice, obviously his secretary's.

A moment passed, and Jake Rousseau came on the line.

"General, sir?" said Rousseau.

"Goddammit, Jake, what in hell's going on over there? I want to find out what's happened to my boy. I want to *see* him, for crying out loud. Let's get on with it."

There was a long pause before Jake Rousseau answered him.

"I'm afraid that's not going to be possible, General," said his former aide.

"Not possible! Goddammit, Jake, what in tarnation are you talking about!"

"Your grandson has gotten himself into some very serious trouble, sir, and I'm afraid it's completely beyond me to affect the situation at all from my end."

"Your goddamned *end?* What the hell does that mean?"

"It means I can't do anything for you, sir. And I certainly can't do anything for young Matt."

"Goddammit, Rousseau, you were that boy's age when I took you onto my staff in Tripoli. We've been through two lifetimes together, Jake. I counted on you. I still count on you." The General's raspy voice was tarnished and tired, thickened with half-tones of desperation and despair.

"I'm afraid this time your trust was misplaced, sir," said Rousseau.

To the General, Rousseau's words came from the bottom of a well.

"There is only so much I can do, only so far that I can go. A man in my position must tread carefully when it comes to matters of the law. You yourself taught me that, General, in Sicily, when you ordered a court-martial for that soldier who shot himself in the foot. We were standing down on the beachhead, the Third had been in combat for fifty-six consecutive days, and there was a rash of self-inflicted wounds, thirteen in all, as I recall. You ordered every officer in the division to watch for self-inflicted wounds and catch a soldier in the act. You wanted to make an example of him. I will never forget it, sir. And I'll never forget what you told me just after the man was found guilty and sentenced to hang, a consequence you had not foreseen."

"Get on with it, goddammit," the General growled. He remembered the incident too.

"You said, 'The goddamned law is an impenetrable thicket, Jake. You turn to it at your own risk.'"

"I don't give a good goddamn what I said in Sicily, Jake. That's all behind us now. History. This is different. My grandson's life is at stake. I want to know what happened to him. When is the court-martial? Who's the prosecutor? Were there any witnesses? What's going on up there in II Corps? Goddammit, Jake, don't you understand me? I want some help on this."

"I understand only too well, General. That man's life was at stake then, too. He made an understandable mistake, under the circumstances, which happened also to be a crime. Your grandson seems to have gotten himself in similar trouble. You sent the soldier in Sicily to the gallows. Now you want me to intervene in some way on your grandson's behalf. I will not do it. The law is the law, General. There is no difference."

"There's a big goddamned difference, a blood difference, Jake. You know that. Damn it."

"All lives are equal in combat, sir. All men are equal under the law. Apparently your grandson did not understand this, and you have certainly forgot it."

"You don't sound like the Jake Rousseau I knew," said the General.

"I am not the same person you knew. You are no longer my boss. I am the CIA station chief in Saigon. I will not involve myself or the Agency in matters which are currently being prosecuted by MACV. Neither would you, when I was your aide. You would not risk either the Agency or yourself for personal gain. That was your rule. It is still my rule."

The General stared out the back window of his room at the VIP Villa. The waterfall cascaded down its fiberglass path over painted rocks, but it made no sound. Neither did the two men on the telephone for what must have been a full minute.

"You are a great, great disappointment to me, Jake," said the

General, choosing his words carefully, coughing each syllable as if it were his last.

"And so are you to me, General. I am sorry our friendship had to end this way."

"We never had a goddamned friendship, Rousseau. We depended on each other, that's all."

He hung up the phone and walked back into the bathroom. He filled the sink with cold water and dipped his face into the water for a long time. When he came up for air, he looked in the mirror. The man he saw staring back at him wasn't his friend, either. He was just someone he had depended on.

The General slowly put on his khakis, every motion an effort. His brown shoes felt as if they weighed ten pounds each. He had just finished dressing and was heading for the door when he heard a knock.

"Come in," he growled, not really meaning it.

"General, it's me," said Lieutenant General Pelton.

"Ahhh, Brownie. Just the man I want to see," said the General, genuinely relieved that it was his old compatriot, a man he knew he could trust.

"I've got some word on young Matt, sir. Do you want to eat breakfast? We can discuss what I've found out downstairs in the garden."

"I don't know if I'll be able to keep anything down," said the General.

"What's the matter, sir?"

"Jake Rousseau is the goddamn matter. I just talked to him. He refused to get involved. He refused any help at all for Matt. I've never heard any man talk as coldly as he talked to me. And I've known some goddamned cold ones."

"I'm not sure we need Rousseau, sir."

"I don't care if we need him or not. He *owes* me. There is something he knows about II Corps operations that he isn't telling us. He's covering something up. I can smell it."

"What do you mean, sir?"

"The Agency is always privy to intelligence that no one else has. He could pick up the phone and make one call and determine what in hell is going on up there in II Corps, and he probably did. He's hiding something. He was insubordinate and disrespectful. I could hear it in his voice. That man is so frightened of this thing with Matt, he wouldn't drive over here and look me in the eye when he told me to go to hell."

"Didn't they call him Happy Jack Rousseau during the war, sir? The other young men on the staff, I mean. Wasn't that his nickname?"

"Yes, and I never understood how he got it. He never acted happy around me. He was the most driven individual I ever had the misfortune to come across, I'll tell you that."

"And now he's got his station."

"Now he's got his station. By the looks of things around here, he hasn't done much with it. We're going to lose this war, Brownie. Mark my words. We're going out of here with our tail between our legs. I may not live to see the day when that happens, but it's in the cards. These Vietnamese peasants are going to nibble at us like mosquitoes until we scratch ourselves to death."

"Unfortunately, I think you're right, General," said Lieutenant General Bruce Pelton, the Assistant Secretary of State for Military Affairs. "I don't know how we got into this war, and I don't know how we're going to get out of it. But what we're doing over here makes Korea look like Normandy, and the truce at the 38th Parallel like a gift from God. I don't think it's possible to prevail militarily in Asia in the classic sense, to achieve the victory we won in Europe. We won the war with Japan only when we dropped the bomb. Short of that unacceptable move, we'll never contain them here in Vietnam. Never. They will fight us until we leave. It's as simple as that."

The two men left the General's room and went to the garden to have coffee. The General looked at the fiberglass waterfall. You could hear the electric motor driving the circulatory system for the water. It sounded like a gas pump.

"You know what is wrong with the way we're fighting this war?"

"I'd like to hear what you have to say on the subject, sir. Maybe I'll include it in my report to the Secretary when I get back."

"We're letting technology drive tactics, instead of the other way around. The almighty helicopter is a good example. First, we bought thousands of them. Then the challenge seems to have become, now that we've got them, what can we do with them? So the airmobile concept was born. Ride the helicopter to battle in the morning, ride it home in the evening, and eat a hot meal and sleep between sheets that night. Is that any way to fight a war?"

"No, sir."

"One of these days, I'm afraid this fascination with technology will bring us to the point where men are obsolete on the battlefield. War will be fought by robots, by remote control. But men will die. When that happens, we'll be in big trouble."

"What do you mean, sir?"

"When you remove men from the battlefield, you inevitably make war more and more of a logical option in the furtherance of policy, because you reduce the cost of lost lives. It's happening over here. You take the influence of the helicopter on this war. We let the helicopter dictate tactics, when we should have formulated tactics and made use of the helicopter in their furtherance. We've got it ass-backwards. The same goes for the base-camp concept and the strategic hamlet concept and every other goddamned concept they've come up with. And most especially, the same goes for the body count as a measure of whether or not we're winning the war. You do not count bodies and add them up and allow arithmetic to determine strategy and tactics. To do so is to deny the truth about war. Wars are fought by men, but they are fought over land. Warfare since the beginning of time has measured men against territory. You need the one to get the other. One's ability to take and to defend land is the gauge of military strength and, ultimately, the measure of victory. You cannot count bodies and expect a raw number on a piece of paper in some rear-area headquarters to suffice as a rhetorical declaration of victory. There is no substitute for victory over the ground. None. Without domination of the land, we have done nothing here but waste lives in the pursuit of a corrupt policy in a futile quest for a hollow victory. It is criminal, what's going on here. The way this war is being fought, the reasons we're fighting it—it's a criminal enterprise, and it makes me so sad to see what they've done to our Army . . ."

The General's gravelly voice trailed off in a harsh, hacking cough. He pulled out a handkerchief and spat into it. When he recovered, his eyes were red and he had trouble getting his breath. Lieutenant General Pelton averted his eyes and waited.

The General took a sip of water and sat back against his cast-iron chair.

"What have you got on Matt?"

"Not much, sir. They preferred charges six days ago, instituted the Article 32 two days ago. The Article 32 investigation is proceeding now."

"Where is he?"

"The stockade at Long Binh, sir. In isolation."

"When can I see him? Can we get up there this morning?"

"No, sir. No visitors are allowed, other than those permitted under the UCMJ—his attorney and any medical personnel that might be requested."

The General reddened.

"You mean to tell me they're going to refuse admittance to the man's grandfather, a retired General?"

"Yes, sir, they are."

"And you? You're the Assistant Secretary of State. You too?"

"Even if I could get in to see him, sir, it wouldn't be proper. It would be tantamount to command influence."

"I know. I know," said the General, dejected.

"It's a capital charge, sir. Desertion in the face of the enemy is punishable by death."

"Who's the attorney? Maybe we can talk to him."

Lieutenant General Pelton shuffled through a sheaf of papers and extracted one.

"Captain Terrence W. Morriss, sir. He's a JAG stationed at Long Binh."

"Do you know anything about him?"

"They say he's the best they've got up there. All the men charged with serious offenses put in to get him. He's got a reputation as a lawyer who will do almost anything to defend his man. He's an ROTC man doing a four-year hitch in the JAG Corps. He's won some pretty big cases, sir. Last month he won a rape case. Seven men in a squad were charged with raping a civilian woman while they were on a combat operation. He took on all seven of them and got acquittals for all seven. Matt must have heard about him in the stockade."

"Or the lawyer heard about Matt."

"I doubt it, sir. They've got the lid down tight. No one even knows he's in the stockade at Long Binh but us and the lawyer."

"No doubt. What about him? The lawyer, I mean. Anything else?"

"He graduated from Southern Illinois University and went to Harvard Law School. He was drafted right out of law school and took the JAG option right away. He went through Advanced Individual Training at Knox, then he went to the JAG school in Charlottesville and was commissioned a reserve captain, like all JAGs who start out as draftees. He served a year at Fort Carson, and he's been over here for six months, with six months to go. He's unmarried and he likes expensive cigars and Jack Daniel's whiskey. He has no known associations with dissident groups in his intelligence file, and his OERs from Carson are in line for a non-regular-Army JAG officer of his background. In short, he's a typical twenty-seven-year-old American male who would probably rather be back in New York getting his paychecks from a three-name law firm than from Uncle Sam. He is good at what he does, and he doesn't care who knows it. If I were charged with a capital offense, sir, I'd want him at my side."

"Well, at least the boy's in good hands," said the General, staring across the garden at the fiberglass waterfall.

"Can you think of anything else? Anything we could do for Matt without violating any protocols or laws?"

"No, sir. I can get a message to him. That's about it, sir. There's not one hell of a lot we can do."

"Then do it, goddammit. Let's get with the program!"

"Sir, I have to make a command appearance at a reception at the embassy."

"A reception for who?"

"The board of directors of the Association of the United States Army, sir. The AUSA. I'm sure you've heard of it."

"Of course I have. It's a loose consortium of Army officers and defense industry executives that spends all of its time and money trying to get the United States of America to buy more gadgets and doohickeys and popguns and helicopters and God only knows what-all. A consortium we could well do without. I have never approved of the illicit bump-and-grind that is done daily between the military and its civilian military hardware contractors. The dance that goes on between us and them is entirely too cozy for the good of the Army or industry. I'll wager the reception tonight at the embassy will provide more evidence of the kind of systemic whoring I'm talking about."

Lieutenant General Pelton watched the General in rapt fascination. He was a man who never failed to fascinate. In war, he was intense, demanding, unrelenting in pursuit of the enemy. He had proved himself one of America's true battlefield tactical geniuses. He was unafraid to take risks that other commanders would dismiss as too costly.

Not the General. He was supremely confident of himself and of his men and their ability to carry out what he demanded of them. If it meant double-timing, *running* the entire length of Italy, then that is precisely what they did. They *ran* where others walked. He moved the Infantry at a speed that Armored divisions couldn't match. By the end of the war, they said there was nothing he could not do with an Army, and Lieutenant General Pelton, then a colonel who had served under the General for three years, believed it.

"I've got to get over to the embassy, sir. They've prepared a dozen briefings for me, and I can't disappoint them."

The General turned to his friend with a cheerless look on his face.

"This is what it's come down to. Right here." He pointed at the fiberglass waterfall and shook his head. "Here we sit, two old soldiers who came over to Vietnam expecting to enter a combat zone, and they've got us in goddamned Disneyland."

Lieutenant General Pelton nodded, and a white-jacketed waiter arrived to clear the table. He placed a sterling silver coffeepot in the middle of the table and stood at attention.

"Can I get you a Bloody Mary, sir, or perhaps a vodka and orange?"

"What time are we going to the embassy?"

"Twenty-one hundred," said Lieutenant General Pelton. Nine P.M.

"I'll tell you what you can get me, young man," said the General. "Come twenty-one hundred hours, you can get me the hell out of here."

At 2100 hours, the American embassy was floodlit by two M-60 tanks with xenon spotlights. They were parked across Thong Nhut Street, swiveling their turrets, raising and lowering their gun tubes, splashing icy light across the U.S. Embassy as if it were a movie theater, giving downtown Saigon the feel of Hollywood the night a major motion picture opened on Sunset Boulevard.

At the embassy gate, lieutenants scurried from one arriving car to another, checking identification, rechecking, monitoring the flow. Captains monitored lieutenants. Majors stood around in groups of three, critiquing the captains. Somewhere a colonel hovered on the edge of the lights, worried about his majors. It was a very big night on Thong Nhut Street.

The reception was one of those open-necked-shirt affairs that embassies throw once or twice a month in Third World countries where it would be considered bad form to black-tie it in the presence of the hunger and poverty nibbling at the edges of the capital city. Saigon in the fall of 1969 differed from the Third World norm only in that Vietnam was a combat zone and the starving proles out there were carrying guns along with their empty rice sacks. The Tet offensive of the previous year may have left its mark. The embassy was still pockmarked with bulletholes in the stucco walls, and the compound fairly bristled with troops and weaponry, but nothing was going to disturb the feeding and watering of the AUSA directors and their minions.

When Lieutenant General Pelton and General Blue arrived at the gate, their staff car was met by a phalanx of MPs, rifles at the ready. As he stepped from the car, the General could see the dim outlines of snipers atop the embassy roof.

"They're not taking any chances, are they?" he said as they brushed past the wall of MPs.

"It wouldn't look good if an embassy reception turned into a bloodbath," said Lieutenant General Pelton.

"That's probably the extent of the Ambassador's concern, too. How it would *look*."

"Probably."

The generals were guided into the main reception room of the embassy by the captain who had met them at the airport. Along the walls of the room, curtained booths displayed weapons systems from various defense contractors. This one displayed the Infantry soldier's best friend, the M-16, and you could pick one up and fire light beams at little VC targets, just like in a booth on a carnival midway. Over there was a mockup of a Phantom F-4 cockpit you could climb into and make mock bombing runs on North Vietnam on a television screen inside the cockpit. Another booth displayed the interior of an M-60 tank, and next to it you could actually climb into an M-113 armored personnel carrier that had been driven into the room through the folding French doors leading to the rear of the embassy compound.

A white-jacketed waiter brought the generals a drink, and Lieutenant General Pelton was directly pulled away by an aide to the Ambassador.

"I'll be back in a moment, sir. Official duties," he said apologetically.

General Blue smiled and lifted his glass of bourbon in a toast.

Just then he spied Jake Rousseau stepping out of the mock Phantom F-4 cockpit. Climbing out of the cockpit's rear seat was a Vietnamese woman a good thirty years younger than Rousseau. Her hair was coiffed into a beehive and she was wearing an embroidered silk *ao dai* slit to her navel. The General averted his eyes, but Rousseau had noticed him watching them.

He walked over to the General's side.

"General Blue, I'd like you to meet Miss Dzu. Miss Dzu, this is General Blue, from the United States. He is a very important man over there."

The girl bowed her head, closing her eyes, in an Oriental gesture of respect.

"Get me a drink, dear, and get one for the General, too."

She scurried in the direction of a bar.

"I didn't know embassy protocol allowed the display of in-country mistresses," said the General.

"Many things have changed since your day, General." Rousseau towered over the General and was smiling crookedly as he spoke.

"You always had a bit of the pimp in you, Rousseau. You've always liked to display your wares. Protocol may have changed, but you haven't."

Rousseau started for the General, but pulled up short at the sight of Lieutenant General Pelton and the Ambassador, who were heading their way.

"I guess we are more different than I'd ever supposed, General," said Rousseau. "Your tastes ran to Clare Boothe Luce, and mine to barmaids and belly dancers. And I see where our tastes have taken us. You're over here with your hand out, wanting something, and I've got what you want. In this way you remind me of Miss Dzu. She has her hand out, and I've got what she wants. What does that say about you?"

"Volumes, Rousseau. But I see you now in a way I was never able to see you before. Carey was right about you. You always were a field hand, and you'll always be a field hand. You had shit on your shoes when I pulled you in out of the rain in Berlin, and you've still got shit on your shoes. I'm glad Pelton talked me into coming tonight. I wouldn't have missed this for the world."

Just then Lieutenant General Pelton and the Ambassador arrived at the General's side. The Ambassador whispered in Rousseau's ear, and the two men were gone, heading in the direction of the M-16 booth, where little electronic *pop-pop-pop*s could be heard as grown men fired the toy rifle at miniature VC targets.

The General turned to his friend. For the first time since he had arrived in Saigon, he felt truly relaxed, at peace. Jake Rousseau was firmly behind him now, a dim corner of his past where a night light still glowed, showing the way in the dark.

"Who are these people? The civilians, I mean?"

"That man over there is the president of General Dynamics, and the man next to him is his rival at McDonnell-Douglas. The man in the F-4 cockpit is the executive in charge of Dow

Chemical's napalm division. The man in the backseat is from the Ford Motor Company. He makes M-60 tanks like those out front tonight."

The General put his empty glass on a tray carried by a waiter and picked up a full one. He took a long slug of bourbon and swallowed hard. His eyes teared as the bourbon went down.

"A lot of people are making a lot of money from this war, aren't they? Look at them. They're over here feeding like pigs at a trough."

"Yes, sir. They are."

"You know something funny? Funny in a sad kind of way, I mean? I learned this many years ago playing polo at the Gates Mills Country Club. I captained their team every summer while I was at Leavenworth. George Patton had the Old Westbury team out on Long Island, and Marshall had the North Shore team up in Boston. All of us were released from our military duties in the Army every summer for three months so we could play polo with important men, industrialists in the main, whose political and economic influence made their friendship important to an Army that had weakened considerably between the wars. You remember, Brownie. When you graduated from West Point, you played for a summer with the team from Webster Groves, Missouri, as I recall."

"Yes, sir, I remember."

"What I learned those many summers ago was this: anybody can make money. But there are only a few of us left who can still make war, either on the polo field or the battlefield. I'm afraid we're a dying breed. I despair for this nation of ours when we're gone."

The old generals stood for a moment watching the swirl of defense contractors and Army officers and embassy officials. Then they turned and walked out the door, heading for the staff car. They were blinded momentarily as the big xenon spots mounted on the tanks across the street painted the front door of the American embassy with broad strokes of blazing white light.

Then the General stepped into the shadows and stood alone with his thoughts.

This is what it's come to. Grown men playing with their toys in the safety of Saigon while out there in the dark men are fighting and dying in a war that is more about toys than it is about those men and what they stand for.

It's criminal, he thought. *And I'm a criminal unless I get myself back to Washington and do something for Matt and for those men out there in the dark.*

11

===========

Years ago, when the Colonel was a young man and the Lieutenant was a boy, the Colonel used to stand in the doorway of his sons' bedroom and serenade them to sleep with his harmonica. Matt and Terry, who was two years younger than Matt and as different from him as night from day, used to lie in bed listening to the old man wail away in the dark. He played a long Hohner with a flat bar and twenty holes, and his hands were so big he could cup the Hohner and the instrument would disappear within them. His hands would swallow the Hohner, and he'd blow a few notes to warm up, then he'd start to play, making the notes *wha-wha* by cupping and uncupping his massive hands, feathering the music as it flowed from the reeds of the Hohner. He'd play standards from the 1940s and 1950s like "In the Mood" and "Begin the Beguine," music he had grown up with, the latter tune flavored with the exotic syncopated dance beat of Martinique and St. Lucia, the dusky islands soaked in rum and sun down in the south Caribbean. He'd play hot stuff from the radio, like "Mack the Knife," and ballads by Nat "King" Cole and horn solos by his favorite musician of all time, Louis Armstrong. The Lieutenant often mused, lying there in the dark, that if his father could have been anyone else in the whole world, he'd have wanted to be Satchmo.

Then there were the nights when the old man would stand in the door and play something the boys liked—some of "your music," he called it—like "Devil or Angel" by the Clovers, or "Georgia" by Ray Charles, or "Up on the Roof" by the Drifters. This would usually occur, of course, a night or two after he had punished one or both of the boys for some domestic offense, real or imagined, such as failure to clean out the day's ashtrays, which were full of his and their mother's cigarette butts and ashes.

He would come home in the middle of the night from a party and wake his oldest son, Matt, and march him around the house silently, pointing to ashtrays that had not been emptied or wiped clean, then he'd stand him in the living room in the dim light of a lone table lamp and talk to him very slowly and very deliberately about how disappointed in him he was, about how this was "the third goddamn time this month" that those ashtrays had failed to have been cleaned by the time Matt went to bed; about how, as the oldest child, Matt had to accept responsibilities the others didn't; and about how maybe a couple of weeks restricted to his room would help him remember to clean the ashtrays next time.

The Lieutenant never understood his father's mood swings, from warm and loving to cold and exacting, until he got his platoon. Then he understood his father in a way he could never have predicted. With his platoon he learned the power of guilt to cleanse you in its backwash. The Lieutenant's platoon reminded him of those nights he and his brother would lie in their beds in the dark. They had been young and vulnerable and imperfect. So was the platoon.

As much as he tried not to, he treated the platoon the way his father had treated him.

First you whack them over the head for some shortcoming that has more to do with you than with them, then tomorrow night you learn "Yesterday" by that damn bunch of British longhairs the Beatles, or "Lonely Avenue" by Ray Charles, or "Cry to Me" by Solomon Burke. You stand in the bedroom door and play the old mouth harp well enough to earn forgiveness—your own as well as theirs. On those nights his harmonica would soar with passion and swoop with pain and on those nights usually he played the blues.

The Lieutenant had no way of knowing what his father felt in those moments or why, because like most fathers in those days, he didn't talk much about his feelings to his sons. He couldn't find a way to tell them that the most painful thing about being a father of a son or two or three was the split personality you sank into as naturally as falling asleep.

On the one hand, you didn't want to repeat the mistakes of your father. On the other, you wanted your sons to turn out at least as well as your father's son—*you*. For this reason you wanted your sons to emulate and love the man who had sculpted you and made you who you were. That man was, of course, your father, their grandfather. But by the same token you were afraid that if they listened to him and loved him too much, they'd forget you and lose track of their love for you.

It was hard enough being the father. If you were the son, caught in the vise between father and grandfather . . . the Colonel could only imagine what it must have been like for the Lieutenant and his brother, growing up in the narrowing space between a Colonel no longer on his way up and a General on his way down.

And what of his wife, Martine, Matt's mother? She was caught where mothers usually are, in the middle of the middle between her husband and her son, who was caught between her husband and his father. It was painful and it was confusing and the whole thing was going somewhere she didn't want to go, but what choice did she have? When you're caught, you're caught, so you buckle down and wait it out and hope for the best, the way girls have been taught by their mothers as long as there have been mothers to teach them.

The Colonel and the General hadn't talked in ten years—with the exception of the other night—and they were bound to collide, the way things were going. The Colonel could only hope that Matt wouldn't be caught between them when the collision came . . . or that there wouldn't be a clashing of egos, out there on the edges of the psychic battlefield where sons and fathers cling desperately to their maleness hoping against hope it will save them.

That was the other thing about being a father: more often than not, fatherhood stripped you bare of earned and learned abilities and left you with only one thing:

Hope.

It wasn't much to go on, but it was all he had. Like his wife, the Colonel had to buckle down and wait it out and hope for the best, and one blessing he'd picked up somewhere along the way was patience.

For one reason or another, he had never been in much of a hurry in raising his sons. There was always time to try something over and over again, and if that failed, there was always punishment. A week or two restricted to one's room, he knew from experience, tended to stop time.

But now his son Matt was, for better or worse, *raised*. There was no time left for doing it over again, or for punishment if it wasn't done right the first time, or for Matt or he himself to "grow into" a new situation.

Now someone else held the reins of the punishment demon, and was whipping them on Matt with a vengeance. The Colonel's son was facing a capital charge, an accusation that could take him to the gallows, to the grave. Someone else had stepped in and stopped time.

There wasn't a moment left for mistakes or apologies or corrections. His son's life was at stake and every second counted. He was learning just how much he truly loved his son—both of his sons. He could only hope—there it was, *hope* again—his son loved him just as much.

Maybe the Colonel and his son stood a chance of meeting halfway between love and hate instead of wasting time as he and his father had done. They were still burning away their lives, like waiting for the passing years to cook off the ills between them. The only place left for them was halfway between tomorrow and the end of their lives. If they wasted any more time, the Colonel knew, death would solve the problem for them, and guilt would come visiting again to cleanse him in its backwash.

Heaven had always been advertised to the Colonel in Sunday School and church as a good place to mend the wounds in your past, but he knew now for the first time in his life that heaven could wait.

He wanted the love of his son and his father *now*.

Maybe if he and his son succeeded in overcoming the trouble his son found himself in, he and his father could heal their wounds.

Maybe.

He hoped. Good *God* did he hope.

The Colonel picked up his stride then broke into a run as he passed through an alley on the way to Madam Ky's. Dark faces peered at him through cracked doors, and he could hear the soft shuffle of feet on the cracked pavement behind him. Overhead, laundry dangled on lines run between windows across the alley. Down the dim sidestreets he could smell the aroma of charcoal-burning hibachis boiling fishhead stew, sauteeing hindquarter of yellow mutt with cabbage, warming last night's fricassee of scrawny street pigeon.

It wasn't yet noon.

It felt like midnight.

He was *in-country*. He was back.

He rounded a corner on Ham Nghi Street and headed for the river. When he reached the docks he turned right and followed the river until he reached the Ben Nghe Canal, then he followed the canal until he saw the bridge. On the corner was Madam Ky's. The Sergeant Major had been right. It was a wee hole in the wall. It was also a *dark* hole in the wall. He entered.

In a far corner he could make out the glowing tip of a long cigar. Sergeant Major Bennett had beaten him to Madam Ky's. As he approached the table, the Sergeant Major stood and pulled out a chair for him.

"This here's how the other half lunches, sir," said the Sergeant Major. "What's your pleasure? I'm partial to the local beer." He held up a brown bottle. It didn't have a label.

"Sure. I'll have some. How've you been, Sarenmajor?" The

Sergeant Major heard his rank and title said the way it was supposed to be said and he smiled.

"I'm pretty happy with the way life's treatin' me, sir. Health's good. Recently I socked in a goodly supply of these here Cu-ban-o seegars ..." The Sergeant Major took a long puff and grinned. "That's one of the things about hardship duty, sir. There's ways you can sorta reduce the hardships, if you get what I mean."

"I see you're not having any trouble keeping down the local cuisine," said the Colonel, pointing to the Sergeant Major's ample gut. "If you were still in my Battalion, I'd have that spare tire off you in a month."

"I hear that, sir," laughed the Sergeant Major. "That's one of the side benefits of my new situation, sir, up at the NCO Club. No colonel standin' around lookin' over my shoulder, worryin' about my waistline."

A waitress in a miniskirt and white go-go boots shuffled over to the table, blew a bubble-gum bubble and said:

"Madam say beer on house, Sar-jant, special deal special guest."

"That's right nice of the Madam, ain't it, sir? We'll have two more of these." The Sergeant Major held up the brown bottle and tapped it with a gold ring the size of a roll of Scotch tape.

"You've known the Madam for a while, Sarenmajor?"

"Since '62, sir. She's okay. Her old man's definitely VC, but she don't give a shit either way. Us or them, she don't care, long as she can move enough beers and rice to keep herself and the kids fed good. Her old man don't come around much. He's down in IV Corps messing up our riverine patrols, probably. When he does come around, he don't do nothin' for her. Takes a month's profits and buys himself some black-market M-16s and a few boxes of ammo and heads south to fuck up a few more patrols. You know how it is with these people, sir. They got to get by any way they can."

"Yeah, I know how it is, Sarenmajor. What's your connection with her? Supply her with a few surplus sodas, maybe a case of Scotch or two?"

The Sergeant Major puffed nervously on his cigar and shifted this way and that in his chair.

"Oh, you know how it is, sir. We got to win their hearts and minds. Only way I found to do that is through their wallets. We don't keep the local saloonkeepers supplied with a little good cheer to spread aroun' to their friends, ain't much sense in us bein' over here, is there now, sir?"

"That's the line they're putting out in Washington these days, Sarenmajor. It seems we aren't fighting to win a war anymore. We are fighting to win hearts and minds. I'm glad to see you're up to snuff on your political poop. Don't get too close to that political heat, Sarenmajor, or you'll burn your nose." The Colonel lifted his beer in a toast and took a sip.

The Sergeant Major laughed so hard he almost choked.

"You sure do get to me, sir," he coughed. "I mean, I never had it so good as when we had you in the Battalion. I don't guess I knew it at the time, but that was the best damn unit I ever had the pleasure of bein' in, sir. Yes, it was. *Fine* outfit. Damn fine." He sat back and pulled on his cigar.

"Yes, it was, Sarenmajor," said the Colonel. "I miss the old Battalion." He gazed out the door at the canal. Sampans brushed against one another going in opposite directions as they plied their trade up and down the busy waterway.

That was the thing about Vietnam. They took up every inch of the place busying themselves at whatever it was they were busying. Not even a sewer like the Ben Nghe Canal was passed up. They used it for a highway, a shopping center, a supermarket, a restaurant, an apartment complex. They traveled the canal, bought food there, ate there, lived there, and slept aboard sampans and barges and floating docks tied there.

Vietnam. Whew. It didn't take up much room on the map, but as a culture of many and varied ethnicities, customs, and habits, it was as big as all outdoors.

"Damn fine outfit, sir. The best. Yes, sir. Here's to the ol' Battalion." The Sergeant Major raised his bottle of beer and tipped it toward the Colonel and stared out the open door too.

They were doing the Dance of the Old Troopers, the Colonel and the Sergeant Major. Sergeant Major Theodore Bennett was literally an old Cavalry trooper, having served in the horse Cavalry when the horse Cavalry still had horses. The Colonel was the son of a horse Cavalryman, having grown up on one Cavalry post after another, getting up before dawn to feed and water his old man's polo ponies, holding their reins during the polo matches, seeing to their grooming afterwards. Once or twice the old man had even let him accompany the troop when they were on maneuvers, living out in the field for a week with the men and the horses. That's what the Dance of the Old Troopers was all about—the shared memories of a time when boots were still brown and sabers still rattled along the flanks of a pony at full gallop and taps was still played on a real bugle and soldiers still shot straight and drank straight and stayed out late and never missed reveille (played on a real bugle, not a tape recording) in the morning.

"I've got a real problem, Top," said the Colonel.

"That's what you was sayin' last night, sir. You were soundin' pretty low."

"It's Matt, Top. Somehow he's been charged with desertion in the face of the enemy. He called me at Benning a couple of days ago, and I got over here as fast as I could. Now I can't even find out where they're keeping him. When he called he said he was under arrest, whatever the hell that means in a combat zone."

"They probably got him in LBJ, sir. Up to Long Binh."

"I called up there first thing when I got in, and nobody has heard of him. Either they're lying or they've got some pretty sloppy record-keeping, or they've got him stashed someplace else. I don't know. I just don't know. After that, I called his unit up in II Corps and I couldn't get anybody in authority to come to the phone. Not the battalion CO, the brigade CO; I couldn't even get his company commander. I asked one of the clerks I talked to what was going on, and he said, 'We've been told not to discuss Lieutenant Blue or anything about his unit, sir.' Can you imagine? They've got lips buttoned up right on down to company clerks."

"Damn. I never heard of anything that could shut up a damn *clerk*. They're as full of nasty bile and bad-ass poop as a damn washerwoman."

"I know, Top. That's why I'm worried."

"Desertion . . . that's pretty serious stuff, sir. Do you know what happened?"

"No. All I know is, Matt said he didn't do it. And he said things were crazy. He said I wouldn't believe what was going on."

"I don't doubt that one bit, sir. I don't believe the shit that's goin' on with this war, sir. It's the damnedest thing I ever seen, and I've seen the better part of two wars 'fore this one. I been three years in 'Nam now, and I can tell you this: there's some weird shit happenin' over here, sir. I didn't know nothin' 'bout it when we was here with the Battalion because we spent all our time in the boonies down in the Delta, but I sure as hell have been seein' it and hearin' 'bout it this time."

"I don't know what I'm going to do, Top. I can't find him. And if I can't find him, I can't talk to him. And if I can't talk to him and determine what happened, I can't help him."

"Don't you worry 'bout that no more, sir. Top's got a handle or two he can still crank when he's got a mind to. We'll find out where they got him by retreat today, sir. That I promise you. Time they lower the flags around here, we'll know where that boy is and we'll know what he done and we'll know what happened to 'im."

"How are we going to do that, Top?" The Colonel sounded tired and exasperated, which he was.

"I brought my stuff, sir. Like you said. Let's get us a bite to eat and slap back another of these here cheap beers and we'll get my stuff out and see what we can do."

"I sure as hell hope we can find him soon, Top. Every day that passes, Matt is one day closer to being court-martialed and facing the death penalty. We've got to get to him quickly. If we don't move fast, it may be too late. I can't let that happen to my son, Sarenmajor. Over the years I know there were times when I wasn't there for him. I can't let him down now."

"I know, sir." The Sergeant Major put his hand on the Colonel's shoulder and squeezed. The old man was trembling. Sergeant Major Theodore Bennett had never seen an officer so upset he was trembling. Not in thirty-three years in the Army. But then, this wasn't the Army. This was something different. This was family.

"I just hope we can find him before it's too late," said the Colonel. The Colonel tried to smile at the Sergeant Major, an old Cavalry trooper, a man with whom he had literally shared a foxhole and dodged a bullet. He winked.

There it was again, in Top's eyes ... vibrating through the Colonel's shoulders. Hope. All he had was the Sergeant Major and his hope. Such a fragile thread from which to hang your dreams, on which to gamble your life and that of your son. He had to hurry before the thread frayed and broke his heart.

12

Danny Jannick was the kind of wiry little guy who gnawed at life like a terrier; once he got hold of something, nothing could make him let go. It had to do with his physical stature, of course. All his life he'd been the little guy: he was the last one picked in gym class for choose-up-sides touch football; they never passed to him in basketball and he never got a shot. As for varsity athletics, forget it. They even laughed at him the day he went out for track, bony arms and skinny legs jutting from his track outfit like cheap golf clubs. In track, your size wasn't supposed to matter. All you had to be was fast, and Danny Jannick was fast, but not in track.

A little guy had to go at things harder than big guys if he was going to tear off his piece of life, and Danny Jannick started ripping away at life early and never stopped. In his little piece of the world there was a new definition for the term *single-minded*. Editors at PNS back in Frisco hated to work on his copy. If he took issue with something you'd changed, there was no stopping him. He'd flood you with cables, bury you in phone calls, weigh you down with poison-pen postcards. One editor even got a phone call late one night from a local ham radio operator. On the other end of the line, sailing through the air on short waves, was Danny Jannick. He had talked the local ham into patching the cross-Pacific transmission from the radio to the phone. The ham-radio call was emblematic of the Jannick Method. Once he got on your case, he'd come at you from every angle.

From the *heavens,* even.

When Jannick smelled a good story he was like a rabid dog with a mouthful of fresh blood, and right now he smelled one. Cathy Joice's reaction to the tip about Lieutenant Blue was classically intense, practically wild. He knew she would pursue all of the legitimate, aboveground angles in her distinctive, high-profile way. Thus it was now time for Danny Jannick to disappear.

Jannick had disappeared into every big story he'd ever gotten. He had learned the trick from a photographer in Washington, D.C., with whom he had worked on a few stories for *Rolling Stone.* The photog was short, like Jannick, and beyond that, he was baby-faced. He got carded every time the two of them hit the D.C. bar scene. At thirty, he looked seventeen. When he hadn't shaved that day.

Over the years the photog had learned a trick. He looked so young that he seemed completely unthreatening. He'd walk into a reception in Washington full of important dignitaries, he'd stand around listening to them, and soon he found they were talking to each other as if he weren't there. The thing was, he *wasn't* there. He had disappeared, turned into a piece of furniture, a lawn decoration, somebody's son, a tousle-headed teenage tourist with a camera around his neck. The dignitaries hardly noticed him. Anybody that young and innocent couldn't understand the importance of what was being said in his presence.

Jannick watched him pull his disappearing act one afternoon when he accompanied the photog on an assignment from *Time* magazine to shoot an important political adviser to President Johnson who happened also to be gay. Jannick carried three bags of photographic equipment so he could go along on the assignment. He was little and he was young and he was just a photog's assistant, so he dropped out of sight, too, as soon as they entered the big man's office.

The photog put the man at ease with a few initial words of banter, then he suggested the adviser go about his business while they set up the photographic equipment. The adviser buzzed his secretary and told her to start putting calls through again. He took one call from a Cabinet secretary—he made sure to mention his complete name before he started first-naming him in every sentence—then he took another from a senator. No name this time. Just "Yes, Senator," and "No, Senator," and "I'll get back to you on that, Senator."

Two more calls went through while they were adjusting lights. Then the important presidential adviser took a call that didn't appear to have a business purpose. He lapsed into a lisping Southern twang, a cross between Truman Capote and a bird dog. He talked to his friend for a good five minutes before hanging up, and when he did, the photog had to remind him they were still there, waiting to get the shot.

Jannick had learned to disappear that afternoon, and it was something he never forgot. All you had to do was go ahead and be the guy everyone had always ignored and shut out, and you were home free.

It made sense that disappearing within the bowels of Saigon was easier than making yourself scarce in Washington, D.C. Vietnam was a country that in many ways didn't really exist. Every time you turned around and tried to establish that you had indeed seen what you thought you'd just seen, it wasn't there anymore. Something else was in its place. And the place itself had changed. And so had you. When you really sat down and tugged at the doors of the mental filing cabinet, trying to figure out what was going on, Vietnam popped out as the terminal example of Heisenberg's Uncertainty Principle. Everything is changed by the exercise of observing it, Heisenberg said.

Over on the curving coast of Southeast Asia, they didn't need Heisenberg to tell them which way the wind was blowing. In Vietnam, nothing had ever been as it seemed. Neither was Danny

Jannick. He seemed to be there, but he wasn't. He was somewhere else, somewhere you can't see him or hear him, but he's okay. So don't worry about him. Just go ahead and do your thing. Let the good times roll. He'll be along when the time is right.

Now? Nah.

Then? Maybe.

When? You got me.

Danny Jannick didn't play by conventional journalistic rules because he was not a conventional journalist. Thus, when he decided it was time for him to journey north into II Corps and find out what the hell had happened to Lieutenant Matthew Nelson Blue IV, the last thing he thought about doing was going over to the MACV public-relations office and checking in, securing from the clerks and jerks who had the job of packaging the 'Nam news a pass to whatever theater of combat operations he wanted a ticket to.

No, life for the slight and self-effacing Danny Jannick was much, much easier than it must have been for Dan Rather or Walter Cronkite or David Halberstam or Homer Bigart or Fox Butterfield. When Danny Jannick wanted to head north or south or east or west, he simply hied himself out to Tan Son Nhut and hung around the maintenance shack until he heard about a recently repaired chopper that was on its way back to whatever "front" it had limped in from. Jannick took his skinny carcass and his skimpy shoulder bag of personal belongings and sat in the chopper until it took off. When it landed, he got out. That was it.

So when dawn broke, Jannick was already up and padding around his rooms at the Pension Gravois, admiring himself in the mirror. The way not to be noticed when you traveled out of the comparatively safe and unrestricted orbit of the Saigon/Bien Hoa/ Tan Son Nhut vicinity was to costume yourself in a manner that distanced you as far as possible from the Epaulet-Shouldered-Khaki-Bush-Jacketed-Foreign-Correspondent-in-an-Exotic-Locale Look. This much Jannick accomplished without even trying. All he did was get up and slip into his jeans, Fillmore East T-shirt, and sneakers. With the addition of his United Airlines shoulder bag, he looked like a student from the Sorbonne who had seriously lost his way and was more to be pitied and helped out than warned away.

The instinct that Jannick counted on arousing was the same one aroused by whipped puppies.

There's a good boy. Come on over here and we'll give you something to eat and a warm place to sleep. Ye-e-e-e-s. Good boy. Come to Mama.

Years of experience had yielded unto Jannick the secret within the secret of the journalism game. Everybody wants to be found out. The only thing is, they don't want to meet the guy who's doing it to them.

Jannick made a quick call to his pal Specialist Fourth Class Thomas J. Calhoun over at MACV Personnel and got the name of Lieutenant Blue's unit. They were still up in II Corps, over near the Laotian border, searching and destroying, sweeping and mopping up. The Battalion was loggered in at a semipermanent base camp a few kliks north of Dak Sut, along the Ya Krong Bolah River. Jannick knew the Ya Krong. He had been in a chopper that lost power one afternoon and autorotated onto a sandbar on the river. They spent a nervous night on the sandbar waiting for a rescue chopper that came at midmorning the next day. Jannick swore he'd never go back. The Ya Krong was like all the rest of the rivers in Vietnam. It flowed brown and slow and nasty like an open wound to the sea. In its waters lurked a variety of tropical evils. Leeches. Snakes.

Who could know the mysteries held in the depths of such a river? The way things were looking, Jannick was going to get another shot at the Ya Krong and its myriad evils after all.

He caught a northbound chopper out of Tan Son Nhut with no problem. It turned out this one had been sent in to be fitted with new passenger seatcovers. The brigade commander wanted his name and unit crest embroidered on the canvas seats. This had been accomplished by employing six elderly Vietnamese women who reported for duty at the air base every day and spent ten hours working their embroidery needles through the thick canvas at a cost to the taxpayer of $100 per seatcover. There were four seats, four hundred dollars' worth. Jannick reclined against the unit crest and yawned. It was a three-hour flight with two stops for refueling. He might even get in a nap before the chopper put down at Dak To, which was as close to the "front lines" of Dak Sut as he could get by air.

They stopped at Phuoc Binh and Pleiku and reached Dak To about suppertime. The chopper put down at a forward-area brigade base camp commanded by the colonel who was desirous of helicopter-seat embroidery. By the time the Huey's skids scraped the dirt, Jannick was out the side door and gone into the maze of bunkers and hooches that characterized a base camp of that size. It took him twenty minutes to reach the base-camp perimeter, and with a few words to a bored GI standing guard at the camp gate, he beat it down the dirt road to Dak To.

He spent the night swilling beer and swapping stories with some American engineers who had been more or less permanently employed for the past year rebuilding the bridges over the Ya Krong that the VC blew up about once a week. Jannick waited until it got light outside and caught a ride in the back of the engineers' deuce-and-a-half on its way north to Dak Sut. By 9:00 A.M. he was snooping around the Triple Deuce base camp. They were in a stand-down after the sweep that had carried them into Laos.

He talked to a few guys standing around their tracks drinking coffee. All the while he was looking around, scoping out the base camp. It didn't take Jannick long to locate the weapons platoon. They had been pulled into the battalion perimeter for the stand-down, a time when as many men as possible were removed from the tension of standing twelve-on-twelve-off watches, of living every day and night, if not in the enemy's lap, at least at his dinner table.

Jannick sauntered over to the little semicircle of tracks that constituted the weapons platoon and struck up a conversation with a sergeant who looked old enough and tired enough to be the platoon sergeant. He was twenty-five, he looked thirty-five, and this was his second tour in Vietnam with a Mech-Infantry Battalion. Last time, he'd been stationed down in the Delta. He was glad as hell to be out of that morass of mud and bugs.

Jannick oozed the conversation around to questions about the rest of the guys in the platoon, the platoon leader. What were they like? What was he like? Average dudes, the sergeant opined. About like any other collection of male American bodies in Southeast Asia. Some good. Some bad. Some indifferent. Platoon leader was an okay dude. A bit fresh. Other than the new-guy jitters, he was okay.

This was a new platoon leader he was talking about?

Yeah, new guy. Outta Salt Lake City. Mormon-type dude.

What had happened to the old platoon leader?

Transferred out of the Battalion, out of the brigade, out of the division, way he heard it. Him and the rest of the platoon. All twenty-five of them. Nobody really knew what it was about, and nobody in authority was talking. Something about a mutiny, some kind of revolt they were investigating. Very big deal. Not a man left of 'em. No, sir.

Jannick recoiled. Bumping along all this way by chopper and truck, cozying up against the dread Ya Krong once again . . . all of it for *nothing?* Not only had they removed Lieutenant Blue from the scene, they had managed to do the same with the twenty-four men left under his command? It was almost too fantastic to contemplate.

Jannick slipped away from the platoon sergeant's track and was heading for the mess tent when he felt a hand on his shoulder. He turned and stared into a pair of red-rimmed eyes deeply set into a face only a mother could love.

"I know what happened to the weapons platoon, man," said the man with red eyes.

"You do? How?"

"I was in the weapons platoon, man. Bigger'n shit I was there for more'n a year."

"Really? How come you didn't get transferred with the rest of them?" Jannick watched the red-eyed man warily. Something about him looked seriously off-kilter. He looked like he'd been awake for about a week and had spent most of his time eating nails and drinking diesel and snorting gunpowder. He smelled like the inside of an automobile muffler and looked just about as dirty.

"They missed me," the man with red eyes said.

"How did that happen?" asked Jannick. "That they missed you, I mean?"

"I'm not here."

"What?"

"I don't exist, man. Ain't on no mornin' report, nothin'. They sent 'em all away last week, but they missed Repatch, man. Bigger'n shit they missed my ass."

"You weren't on the platoon roster?"

"Not on no platoon roster, not on no company mornin' report neither."

"How did you accomplish that?"

"Got two names."

"And one of them is Repatch."

"That's right, man. Other one is Fish."

"And Fish is on the morning report."

"That's right, man. But he ain't in the weapons platoon, neither. Repatch was in the weapons platoon. Fish works in supply, but they already got them one Fish in supply, and they think he's me."

"I think I'm beginning to get it," said Jannick. "You got yourself substituted for another guy, then you created a new identity, and you've been living that identity all this time."

"Goin' on two years now, man."

"You've been over here two years?"

"You got it, man."

"Didn't you want to go home when your tour was up?"

"Home? Where's that?"

"How come?"

"Nothin' for me back in the world, man. At least over here I had the weapons platoon, man."

"You'd rather stay with the weapons platoon than go home?"

"Hey, dude. It's what I *do*. Like, I *walk point*, see? 'S what I *do*, man. They ain't got no jobs walkin' point back in the world, man. Even you got to know that."

"And you did this . . . you walked point . . . for the weapons platoon?"

"Yeah, man. We had it fuckin' *good*, man. Had ourselves our own little logger out in the fuckin' bush, man. Nobody out there jumpin' in our shit alla time. Jus' the Lieutenant and Sergeant Davis and the rest of the dudes and me. Like a *family*, y'know, man? They was like the only family I ever had."

"And now they're gone. The old weapons platoon, I mean."

"Yeah. Now I got nothin'. Now I ain't even got my platoon no more. They done disappeared, just like me."

"What happened? Where did they go?"

"Gone like immediate, man, *w-w-w-w-w-w-h-h-h-h-h-h-t-t-p-t,* just like that, man." The man with red eyes lifted his hand and waved it away, like he was shooing a fly.

"Gonzo, man. So fuckin' quick you'd a' thought a fuckin' typhoon done got 'em. Gone, man. *W-w-w-w-w-w-h-h-h-h-h-h-t-t-t-p-p-p.* In the fuckin' air, gonzo, man, *whew,* like that. Speed-a-light style, man. Scary."

"What happened to the weapons platoon? How come they, uh, disappeared them?"

"We was out on this patrol one night, 'bout a week ago, man. I was, like, walkin' point. Jus' like always."

"Who? Who was on the patrol?"

"Me. The Lieutenant. Whoopie Cushion. Strosher. Woodley. Moonface. Dirtball. That's all of 'em."

"You were on patrol . . ." Jannick reminded the red-eyed man. His eyes kept drifting off, and his head would loll to the side and he'd look as if he was going to fall asleep, then his head would snap upright, his eyes would focus, his jaw muscles would tense, and he'd start talking again.

"We was on this little ol' patrol one night, supposed to go outside the wire a coupla kliks and set up a little ol' ambush. We was jus' about two kliks out when we come up on this clearin' and there was this plane and they was loadin' it fulla these big bundles and the Lieutenant, he sees it's a bunch of 'Merican dudes around the plane, so he stands up and says, 'Hey, fellas,' and they started firin' at us with about twenty Kalashnikovs, and Strosher got hit, an'—"

"Wait. Wait! *Who* was loading *what* plane? Who fired at you? Who shot your guy Strosher?"

"Buncha 'Merican dudes wearin' blue jeans and T-shirts. They was throwin' them bales on that plane to beat the fuckin' band, man. They start firin' at us, and all hell broke loose. Moonface, he laid down some M-60 fire on 'em, and we pulled Strosher in, and the plane took off and the dudes, the 'Merican dudes I mean, they went into the woodline across the clearin' and the whole fuckin' thing was over, man, in like a minute."

"What kind of plane did you say it was?"

"I didn't say. The Eltee, he said it was a fuckin' DC-3, but I wouldn't fuckin' know one fuckin' plane from another fuckin' plane. I guess it was a fuckin' DC-3. Eltee said it was."

The red-eyed man was losing it. He kept drifting off, head lolling from side to side. Jannick took his arm and sat him down behind a sandbagged ammunition bunker.

"Then what happened?"

"We set up our little fuckin' ambush, and in the mornin' we got ourselves back inside the wire, and the Eltee, he goes to see the CO about Strosher gettin' killed by friendly fire . . . you know, you got to file one a' them reports every time a dude gets hit by friendly fire. Anyway. The Eltee goes to see the CO and he comes back out to the perimeter later that afternoon and the next mornin' he was gone and by afternoon the whole platoon comes back in here from the bush for the stand-down, and the rest of 'em was gone."

"Except for you."

" 'Cept for Repatch."

"They just disappeared."

"One minute they was here, next minute a coupla choppers come in and they was gone, man."

"Did you get a chance to talk to the Lieutenant before he left?"

"Nope."

"What was he like? Lieutenant Blue, I mean?"

"Lieutenant Blue? Pretty good dude for a Pointer, you know what I'm sayin'?"

"Not really."

"He was straight, didn't take no shit from us, none from upstairs neither. Good platoon leader, Lieutenant Blue. Best one I ever had. Don't 'spect I'll see 'nother like 'im."

"How about the others? Did they feel the way you did about Lieutenant Blue?"

"You fuckin'-A right they did. Dude stood up for our asses more'n once, tell you that. Got our asses paid by Finance out in the bush when that Battalion wasn't payin' nobody in no bush. Used to chopper us back to Division so's we could go to the PX an' shit. Not many men in this man's Army care no more. But Lieutenant Blue, he cared about shit. He cared about *us*."

"Did you see or talk to any of the others before they left?"

"Nope. Soon as I seen what was happenin', man, I hightailed my ass back to my hole and I laid low for a while. Them choppers lifted off an' that was the last I seen of 'em."

"When did they get these replacements in?"

"Next day."

"How about you? Nobody noticed you were still here?"

"Hey, man. Nobody notices Repatch, 'less I care for it to happen, you dig?"

"Yeah. Sort of."

"I ain't here, man."

"Right."

"You didn't see me, man. You ain't seein' me right now. It ain't me you're listening to."

"Got you."

"You turn around, man, and I'm gone from here, 'fore you know it, gone like a cool breeze on a hot day, man."

Jannick looked into the man's red eyes. The man put his hand on Jannick's shoulder, right where he had first felt it. The man gave a little push, turning him around. Jannick staggered a few steps and looked around.

Repatch had disappeared.

F I V E

☆

A Refuge in the Facts

Firebase Zulu-Foxtrot
Day Five

He sat on the aluminum side bench inside his track, typing on the Olivetti his mother had given him, which rested on a stack of sandbags across from him. He typed automatically, half-dead with fatigue from being awake all night on patrol, half-alive from the adrenaline that poured through him like hot sauce, spiking his emotions, zeroing him out, focusing every cell in his body on the task at hand. He licked his lips. They were dry and cracked, and his mouth felt as though hot wind was blowing across sand on his tongue. Sweat poured off his brow into his eyes. He blinked in the dim light inside the track. He couldn't see the paper in the typewriter, so he followed a form in his head like a path through the madness.

Subject. To. Thru. Paragraph one. Paragraph two. Paragraph three . . .

And in there, too, he could hear the echo of his father's voice, softly chanting . . .

Just tell the truth, son. Just tell the truth, son. Just tell the truth, son.

Okay, Dad . . .

The Lieutenant was angry and afraid. He'd lost a man to friendly fire, and it was his fault. If he hadn't stepped from the treeline and hailed the men loading the plane . . .

If . . . if . . . if . . .

If he could just get through this report, somehow things would be different. Somehow he'd understand. Somehow he'd make *them* understand . . .

The men could hear the *click-click-click* of the Olivetti through the open ramp of the track as they sat around on ammunition crates and C-ration boxes, shoveling in cold breakfast C's. They were still dug in where they'd been the night before, in a perimeter some six kliks south of the battalion night logger.

They were still in Laos.

Subject: Casualty Due to Friendly Fire

To: Lt. Col. Henson W. Halleck, Bn CO

Thru: Capt. Henry G. Gardner, Co CO

1.   The Weapons Platoon suffered a KIA due to friendly fire last night, 12 Oct 1969, at approx. 0200 hrs.

2.   The dead man is Cpl. Lester G. Strosher, Serial #865–09–3466, U.S. Army Reserves.

3.   The circumstances surrounding the casualty due to friendly fire are as follows:

At approx. 0100 hrs., I was contacted on the company net by Rattail Six, Capt. Gardner, and ordered to send out an ambush patrol approx. 2,000 meters NW of my plt. position at grid coordinates 77560834 on Bn sector map 24-Lima. I immediately organized a six-man ambush patrol with myself commanding. We left the wire at 0125 hrs. and headed NW for approx. ½ hr. Approx. 1500 meters out, near a trail intersection in the approx. area of the intended ambush, I halted the patrol. At that time, my patrol point man reported the sighting of something suspicious about 150 meters ahead. I joined the point man and using my binoculars determined that a crude grass airstrip had been fashioned in a clearing in the trees, and what looked to be an unmarked DC-3 was being loaded at the far end of the field. Approx. 15 men were loading and guarding the DC-3. Because I did not at that time know the status, friendly or unfriendly, of those loading and guarding the DC-3, I ordered the patrol forward along the woodline next to the grass airstrip.

When the patrol was opposite the DC-3, I determined, again using binoculars, that those doing both the loading and guarding of the DC-3 were American male civilians dressed in what looked to be blue jeans and camouflage T-shirts. The guards were armed with weapons appearing to be Kalashnikov assault rifles. We could hear the guards closest to us conversing in English. At this time I attempted to contact Rattail Six on the company net, but due to a malfunction of the PRC-25 or the distance of our position from Rattail Six's location, I was unable to raise him on the radio. Because the civilians were clearly American, I stepped out of the woodline and attempted to contact the civilians verbally. The moment I called out to them, the guards turned their weapons and laid down intense fire on our position. Cpl. Strosher was hit in the stomach by this fire and died shortly thereafter.

I dropped back into the woodline and ordered the patrol to return fire. There then ensued a firefight lasting approx. three minutes. During this time, the civilians completed loading the DC-3 and the airplane took off. Once the DC-3 was gone, the remaining guards retreated into the woodline on the far side of the grass strip, and I gave the order to cease fire.

4. Because the wound suffered by Cpl. Strosher had killed him, and no one else was in need of medical attention, and because I had no way of knowing the intentions or the whereabouts of the American civilians who fired on the patrol, I decided against attempting to return to the platoon night defensive perimeter and risking running into the American civilians with whom we had the firefight. I continued the patrol and established a patrol ambush at

grid coordinates 76420941, Bn sector map 24-Lima. There was no further contact with either NVA regulars or American civilians for the duration of the hours of darkness.

5. Ambush patrol was terminated at 0515 hrs., 13 Oct, and the patrol returned to platoon night defensive perimeter at 0535 hrs.

6. The DC-3 observed during last night's patrol was unpainted and unmarked. The civilians loading the plane and guarding it wore no distinguishing insignia of unit, rank, or branch of service, though all were dressed similarly in a mock uniform of blue jeans and camouflage T-shirts.

7. The packages being loaded into the DC-3 were approx. 1 ft. by 2 ft. by 2 ft., brown in color, appearing to be burlap-wrapped.

8. Cpl. Strosher was medevaced at 0545 hrs. and removed to the battalion night defensive perimeter to graves registration.

9. There was no other loss of platoon manpower or duty hours due to the friendly fire taken by the patrol.

Matthew Nelson Blue IV
2nd Lt., Inf, USA
Plt Ldr, Wpns Plt

The Lieutenant signed the casualty report with a pen his grandfather had given him on the day he graduated from West Point. He attached a memo cover slip to the casualty report, shoved both into an inter-unit routing envelope, and waited for the resupply chopper.

Thwap-thwap-thwap-thwap-thwap ... the resupply chopper's rotors cut the early morning mist ... *thwap-thwap-thwap-thwap-thwap* ... chopping the mist like meat ... *thwap-thwap-thwap-thwap-thwap* ... chunk-chunking in over the trees ... *shoop-shoop-shoop-shoop-shoop* ... settling into the red dust ... *shoop-shoop-shoop-shoop-shoop* ... shutting down the green bird ... *shoop-shoop-shoop-shoop-shoop* ... the sad sweet song of the air war coming to rest.

Mallick and Sergeant Davis and a few others unloaded boxes of ammunition, Woodley picked up some medical supplies, Dirtball sniffed around, looking for warm food, Whoopie Cushion was directly in front of the chopper with his arms out, twirling twirling in the dust, imitating the chopper coming in for a landing.

The Lieutenant wandered over and handed the routing envelope to the pilot, instructing him to hand-deliver it to Captain Gardner when he got back to Battalion. The pilot, a warrant officer who couldn't have been a day over eighteen, screwed his face into a look of Official Recognition and bassoed as low as he could:

"Rodge, suh." He drew out the word "rodge," short for "roger," like an F-4 pilot who had fifty missions too many under his belt and a twenty-year fondness for cheap cigars and John Wayne. The Lieutenant looked at the kid and shrugged.

Whatever.

He wandered back to his track and lay down on his air mattress. Dirtball brought him a cup of coffee hot off Sergeant Davis's breakfast fire.

"You oughta check on Repatch 'fore he gits himself into somethin' he ought'n to, sir. He's looking a bit blinky, you ask me, Eltee. But then agin, you didn't ask me . . ."

The Lieutenant didn't have to penetrate the grime on Dirtball's face to see concern in his expression. They needed Repatch. The platoon needed him. The next night patrol needed him. The Lieutenant needed him. Repatch seemed to be able to make a kind of awkward sense of the war. At times the Lieutenant thought Repatch was all that stood between himself and madness.

"Where is he?" he asked.

"Over there behind his track, sir," said Dirtball. "He ain't lookin' too good, Eltee. I wouldn't be botherin' you, sir, if'n it wasn't that Repatch . . . you know, sir . . ."

"Yeah, I know," said the Lieutenant.

He shuffled through the dust to Repatch's track and found him standing on his head beside the track, his back and legs against the outer aluminum wall of the track, forearms forming a V with his forehead resting between his index fingers and thumbs, which were joined together in a triangle.

The Lieutenant was so tired he could barely move or think. But this was Repatch. He needed Repatch tonight. He would need him tomorrow night. He had to do something. He tried to think fast, but all he could come up with was:

"Hey, Repatch, what's going on, man?"

It wasn't often that he was "familiar" with his troops, but this was one of the times. They said at West Point that an officer should never get "familiar" with his troops, but they were full of shit, and the sad thing was, they knew it. How do you fight a war next to a man and not care about him and show that you care?

You can't.

"Gettin' me some rest, sir," said Repatch. He opened his eyes and looked at the Lieutenant and grinned.

"You okay, Repatch? I mean . . ."

"Looks a little funny, I know, sir, but it's good for the circulation," said Repatch. "Clears things up, ya know?"

"I guess."

"Some bad shit last night, sir. Out on patrol, I mean. Them dudes was serious 'bout gettin' in our shit. You know who they was, sir?"

"I don't have a clue, Repatch. I imagine I'll be hearing something about them tomorrow. I just filed my casualty report. Battalion ought to get back to me pretty soon. My guess is, either they'll know what that was all about, or they'll be as curious as I am about what was going on out there last night."

Just then the morning resupply chopper *thwap-thwap-thwap-thwapped* its way overhead on its way back to Battalion.

"Get some sleep, Repatch. We're probably going to be putting out another patrol tonight. It's looking like we're going to be here for a while."

Repatch slumped into the dust and rolled to his feet like a cat. It was surprising how agile he was, especially after having been out on patrol all night. His eyes were coal black, red-rimmed with fatigue. His fingers were long and bony and clawlike, and when he rubbed his eyes he looked like a great bird grooming himself.

"Right on, sir," said Repatch. "I'll be ready for ya."

He glided away, soundless and scrawny and hawklike in the morning sun.

The Lieutenant took his own advice and shuffled back to his track and curled up on his air mattress atop the sandbags. He was asleep the moment his head touched the rolled-up olive-drab towel he used for a pillow. He did not dream. He just lay there like he was dead, but he wasn't. He was alive.

It was noon. Sunlight flooded the inside of the track when the Lieutenant opened his eyes. Someone was tugging at his shoulder.

"Eltee! Eltee!" It was Dirtball. "Eltee! Cap'n wants you on the radio."

"Yeah? What's up?"

"Rattail Six callin' you, sir. Here ya go." Dirtball handed him the receiver.

"Rattail Six, this is Two, over," the Lieutenant said sleepily.

The receiver crackled with static, then cleared.

"Two, this is Six. Saltlick Six wants you in here this afternoon by 1600. Roger?"

"Saltlick Six? Come again?" the Lieutenant said groggily, raising himself to a sitting position. Dirtball was standing in the track with his head out the top hatch, spitting tobacco and scratching his balls. It was taking the Lieutenant a moment to orient himself. He rubbed his eyes and yawned and tried to pretend he wasn't where he knew he was, somewhere deep in Laos in the middle of a war.

"Saltlick Six is sending a chopper for you at 1530, roger?"

"Roger the chopper at 1530, Rattail Six. What's this all about, Six?"

"Couldn't tell you, Two. Just be ready at 1530. Rattail Six out."

"Two out."

The Lieutenant handed the receiver back to Dirtball.

"What's up, Eltee?"

"Halleck wants me back at Battalion at 1600. They're sending a bird out to pick me up at 1530."

"Whatchew gonna dew, Eltee?"

"I'm going to be ready for them," said the Lieutenant. He checked his watch. It was just past noon. He had three hours.

*   *   *

231

The Huey wound its rotor like a giant fan, picked itself up a couple of feet, tilted forward, and with a great shuddering and *thwap-thwap-thwap-thwapping* of its spinning wings, it rose into the air and over the wire and over the trees and it was gone.

The Lieutenant sat behind the pilot and copilot in the open door of the cargo bay. He hung his feet over the edge of the Huey's floor and braced them against the skid. He held his M-79 grenade launcher between his knees. Next to him, a spec-4 in a fatigue jumpsuit and flight helmet manned an M-60 door gun that dangled from the chopper's ceiling on a steel wire. He aimed the M-60 at the green blur below them, which the Lieutenant knew to be Laos. The ground rushed past so fast you couldn't focus on any distinguishing features of terrain; all you could do was sit there and brace yourself against the skid and buzz through the air like a fly.

For a person accustomed to knowing precisely where he was at any moment, the sensation of traveling by helicopter over ground that you had walked through was an eerie one. The Lieutenant knew that most officers serving in Vietnam would consider that to be above the ground at, say, two thousand feet was to be in control of all that was below you. Several times, the Lieutenant's platoon had been engaged with the enemy in a firefight when through the earpieces of his CVC helmet would come the voice of the brigade or even the division commander, directing his platoon's fire, ordering squad maneuvers, instructing him, the platoon leader on the ground under fire, where to call in and direct supporting fire from the Artillery, or air strikes from Air Force F-4s. This was the function of the helicopter in Vietnam: to control the action on the ground from the air. It was why they were called command-and-control ships. The Lieutenant understood where the terminology came from, but as far as he was concerned, they could take their C&C ships and ship 'em up where the sun didn't shine.

To be in command, to be in proper control of your platoon, you had to *be on the ground* so you could identify fields of fire and places of concealment and cover, so you could gauge the strength of the enemy and the accuracy of his fire, so you could direct fire and maneuver on terrain that you yourself had walked over and under and around and through.

You could not know from the air how high was a hill, how tall a tree, how thick the underbrush, how deep a stream, how fast-flowing a river, how impossible the mud, how thick the dust, how acrid the smoke, how hot the sun, how fatigued the men, and how determined their enemies.

You had to be down there *in it,* you had to be down there so you could *feel it,* you had to be down there *among them,* you had to be down there and *walk through it,* you had to be down there in the heat and the dust and the smoke *under enemy fire* in order to command the men who were down there going through it anyway, who didn't have C&C ships they could hop into and fly over battles like the sky ride at Disneyland. If you wanted those men to do for you what they were capable of, you had to stand next to them and take the risks they took. Only on the ground could you make what little sense of combat that could be made.

Only on the ground could you pierce the madness and see the truth. To lead was to share highs and lows, risks and rewards, anger and love. To lead was to get dirty and dusty and muddy and wet, and you couldn't get dirty, dusty, muddy, or wet in a C&C chopper two thousand feet overhead.

The Huey's *thwap-thwap-thwap-thwap* fell off to a muted *thwop-thwop-thwop-thwop,* and they began their descent into the battalion logger. The Lieutenant was relieved to see it was as hot and dusty and nasty at Battalion as it was out with the weapons platoon. Maybe the heat and the dust and the relentless sun would bake some sense into them. Maybe if everyone was waist-deep in the same load of shit, a way could be seen.

Maybe.

In Vietnam, it was always fucking *maybe.*

Shoop-shoop-shoop-shoop the chopper shut down and the Lieutenant hit the ground and scuffled through the dust toward the battalion commander's bunker. It was an elaborate affair the size of a small house, dug into the ground maybe six feet, topped with logs and four layers of sandbags, with sloping sandbagged sides and a twisting entrance designed to absorb nearby artillery explosions and keep the interior of the bunker from being sprayed with shrapnel. It had been done by the book, and the Lieutenant estimated that it had taken twenty, maybe thirty men the better part of five hours to complete. One hundred to one hundred fifty man-hours' worth of the kind of security money couldn't buy, security that came from trees felled, sandbags humped, holes dug.

The Lieutenant zigzagged through the bunker entrance and paused inside so his eyes could become accustomed to the darkness.

"Come on in, Lieutenant Blue," said a voice the Lieutenant knew belonged to Lieutenant Colonel Halleck, the battalion CO.

"Yes, sir," the Lieutenant said reflexively. He stepped forward gingerly. He still couldn't see anything. Then, in the far reaches of the dimness, he made out two human forms standing in the glow of a kerosene lamp.

"Lieutenant, you know Colonel Jim Testor, your brigade commander, don't you?" Halleck's voice had a tinge of sweetness the Lieutenant had never heard before.

He wanted something.

Of that much the Lieutenant was certain.

The Lieutenant groped his way forward. He ran into a folding metal chair, toppling it with a soft thud against the sandbagged walls of the bunker. Then his thighs hit the edge of a table and the Lieutenant stopped.

He unslung his M-79 and snapped a salute.

"Sir, Lieutenant Blue reports as ordered."

In the dimness he made out the blur of an answering salute, and he dropped his hand to his side.

"Sit down, Lieutenant," said Lieutenant Colonel Halleck.

The Lieutenant looked around. His eyes were finally growing accustomed to the darkness, and he saw the folding chair he had knocked over. He righted the chair and sat down, holding the M-79 across his lap. He faced Lieutenant Colonel Halleck and Colonel Testor across a folding camp table that was covered with maps and coffee mugs with the unit crest emblazoned on them.

The two commanders sat down on folding chairs that were padded with canvas cushions emblazoned with the battalion insignia. Halleck waved his hand at someone the Lieutenant couldn't see.

"More coffee!" he commanded.

The Lieutenant heard the shuffle of feet through dirt as someone went for coffee.

"You must wonder what you're doing here," Halleck began, allowing a smile to cross his lips. It was supposed to be a joke.

The Lieutenant didn't say anything. He stiffened his back. He didn't know what was coming, but whatever it was, he didn't like it. You didn't get called into sandbagged battalion bunkers in the deep boonies by not one but *two* colonels to listen to their jokes.

"We want to go over the after-action report you filed this morning, Lieutenant Blue. It's got some problems."

The Lieutenant sat still. He said nothing.

"First, this patrol last night—it was a little out of the ordinary, wasn't it, Lieutenant?"

"No, sir. I do not believe it was." The Lieutenant gave his answer in a measured tone, choosing his words carefully. He didn't feel nervous. He didn't feel frightened. He didn't feel. He just *was*.

"Are you in the habit of taking ambush patrols outside the wire yourself, Lieutenant?" It was Colonel James Franklin Testor, the brigade CO. He was built like a bulldog. He had no neck, and a crewcut that made Yul Brynner look hirsute. He stood five feet ten, maybe five-eleven in jungle boots. Each time the Lieutenant had seen him, he had an unlit cigar jutting out of his mouth. He chewed the cigar and shifted it from one side of his jaw to the other in a manner that made him look like he'd made a study of tough generals on "The Late Movie." He wasn't a cliché, exactly, but he was right on the edge.

"Sir, I lead ambush patrols when I feel that it is necessary. Last night I made a determination that it was necessary. I led the patrol. I have led perhaps twenty-five such patrols since I've had the weapons platoon. There was nothing out of the ordinary about taking command of the patrol myself."

"That's not the way I see it, Lieutenant," said Colonel Testor.

No one said anything for a moment.

The Lieutenant sat there stonily. He had picked out a stain on one of the sandbags against the back wall of the bunker, and he stared at the stain whenever he wasn't addressing one of the colonels. It was a trick he had learned at West Point, a variation on something his father had taught him.

Don't speak unless spoken to, his father had always said.

Okay, Dad. And I don't look at them unless spoken to, then I look them right in the eye.

"Whatever possessed you to take that ambush patrol out yourself, Lieutenant?" Colonel Testor asked.

"Sir, I made a determination early yesterday afternoon that the movement of the battalion sweep had taken us off the map. Off the map sector mentioned in the ops order, 22-Lima, I mean, sir. My platoon's position is on another map. For that reason, when the ambush patrol was ordered, I was concerned that the patrol be able to report its exact location once in position. I didn't want my patrol running into any other battalion patrols, sir, walking into any other friendly ambushes. I knew I could pinpoint exactly the patrol's ambush location, so I took the patrol out myself, sir. That was my reason, sir. I knew we were off the ops order sector map. I didn't want my men getting lost."

"You don't have anyone else in that platoon who can read a map?"

Testor had removed the cigar from his mouth and was studying its well-chewed tip with some satisfaction. He spit an imaginary bit of tobacco on the dirt next to his chair and reinserted the cigar. The Lieutenant noted that he looked better with it, somehow. More like a brigade commander, less like an instructor in the Physical Education Department at West Point, which, as the Lieutenant recalled reading in a brigade newsletter, Testor had been when he was a captain.

"Yes, sir. There are several men in the platoon who are good map readers," said the Lieutenant.

"Then why didn't you send out the patrol with one of those men in command, Lieutenant?"

Testor had taken over the questioning completely now, and he drilled the Lieutenant with a stare the Lieutenant knew he should feel was intimidating. He wondered if he would ever respond in an appropriate manner to such a stare from a man as high-ranking as a colonel. Remembering the number of times his grandfather, the

General, and his father, the Colonel, had fixed him with their huge eyes and pasted him up against a wall in silence, he decided not. The simple truth was, he was not properly prepared for the glares and stares of men like Colonel Testor, and this was a problem for him as a Lieutenant. You were certainly supposed to be frightened by colonels, and he was not.

"Because I was concerned about the fact that we were out of the AO designated in yesterday's ops order. I wasn't sure it should get around that we were operating about twenty kliks inside Laos, sir. I didn't feel it was in the interest of the battalion operation for that knowledge to get spread around indiscriminately, as I knew it would if I sent out one of my sergeants with a map indicating our true position inside Laos. Sir."

The Lieutenant tacked on the "sir" not as an afterthought but as a punctuation mark. He wanted it clear to the Battalion and brigade commanders that he knew precisely where the Battalion was located, even if they didn't.

"What made you think you were in Laos, Lieutenant?" Testor pulled the cigar butt from one corner of his mouth to the other, making a sucking noise as he chewed it across.

"I put the grid coordinates of the incident in my casualty report, sir. They are accurate."

"Oh, they are, Lieutenant? Are you telling this colonel that he can't read a map?"

"No, sir."

"Then what are you telling him, Lieutenant?"

"I'm telling you, sir, that the casualty report I filed is accurate. My platoon position is accurate. The position of my ambush patrol is accurate. We are in Laos, sir. All of us. We were in Laos last night, and we are in Laos today, sir. Nothing has changed since I filed the report with Captain Gardner this morning."

"I'm of the opinion you're trying to put one over on us with that casualty report, Lieutenant."

The Lieutenant said nothing. He stared at his sandbag stain, sitting straight in his chair, as close to attention as the chair allowed.

"Lieutenant?"

"Yes, sir."

"Did you hear what I said?"

"Yes, sir."

"Do you have a response?"

"My response is this, sir: My report is accurate."

"Well, Lieutenant, let me try this on you: I think you took that patrol out last night, and I think you diddled around out there, and I think you made contact with an enemy unit probably no larger than your own, and I think you took that KIA, and I think you got no enemy body count, and I think to cover up your little patrol, you created this incident, this so-called casualty due to friendly fire. That's what I think, Lieutenant. I think you screwed up, and now you're covering up."

The Lieutenant said nothing. There was a long pause, then Colonel Testor took the cigar out of his mouth and leaned to his right so his face came into the Lieutenant's view, which was fixed dead ahead on the sandbag stain behind Halleck.

"What have you got to say for yourself, Lieutenant?"

"My casualty report is accurate, sir. What I reported this morning happened last night, exactly as I reported it. Sir."

"You expect us to believe you took fire from fifteen American civilians who were loading a DC-3 in the middle of the jungle in the middle of the night? You expect us to believe they were carrying Kalashnikovs, and that's how your man got killed? A bunch of blue-jeans-wearing civilians shot him? You expect us to accept this utterly fantastic nonsense as fact?"

"Sir, my report stands. It is accurate. I have nothing to add to it. Whether you accept the report or not is your business, sir, not mine."

"I think you're lying, Lieutenant." Testor glowered at the Lieutenant and pulled at the cigar in his teeth with a smacking noise, like a kid working on a candy sucker.

The Lieutenant said nothing.

"I want you to change your casualty report, Lieutenant."

The Lieutenant stared straight ahead, saying nothing.

"Did you hear me, Lieutenant?"

"Yes, sir."

"I want you to change this report so it says you got hit by a VC ambush and took one KIA, this, uh, Corporal Strosher. You got me?" Colonel Testor shoved the Lieutenant's casualty report across the table. It was lying on top of the inter-unit routing envelope, just as he had typed it that morning.

"That's not the way it happened, sir."

"I don't give a good goddamn if it happened that way or not, Lieutenant. I want that report changed to read the way I said it should read. Am I making myself understood, or is there something wrong with your hearing?"

The Lieutenant looked Testor in the eye and held his gaze for an instant before he spoke.

"There is nothing wrong with my hearing. Sir. But what you say didn't happen. Sir."

"Listen to me, Lieutenant. If I tell you down is up and up is down, that's the way it's going to be, sport, you got me?"

"No, sir."

"What did you say to me, sport?"

"I said, 'No, sir.' "

Testor glared at him, rolling the cigar back and forth across his mouth, rolling, rolling, chewing, glaring. Then he took the cigar out of his mouth and looked down at the table for an instant. When he looked up, the glare was gone, and so was the cigar. He was going to take another tack. The Lieutenant could smell it.

"You've got a lot to lose here, son. You know that?"

"I already lost one man, Corporal Strosher, to friendly fire, sir. I don't want to lose another, sir."

"I'm not talking about your corporal, son."

The Lieutenant waited, saying nothing.

"I'm talking about your career. You understand what I'm saying?"

"Yes, sir. I think I do."

"This is a very serious situation you've created here. You've got to pick the fights you fight carefully, son. That's the way life is. You've got to examine the situation and estimate whether you're going to win or lose, and you've got to pick your fights on that basis. You're going to lose this one, son. Am I making myself clear?"

"Yes, sir."

"All you've got to do right now is do what I say, and this will all go away and be forgotten. Lieutenant Colonel Halleck and I here will just forget we ever saw this report, and we'll forward your new one up the chain of command and everybody will be happy, and you'll go on to have a great career in the Army just like your grandfather, and you'll probably be a general by the time you're my age. It's all right there for the taking, son. All you've got to do is change this report. You get me?"

The Lieutenant looked Testor in the eye.

"No, sir."

"I'm ordering you to change this report, Lieutenant. Now do you get me?"

"I understand your order, sir. But what happened happened. Nothing will change that fact, sir, and because nothing will change the way Corporal Strosher was killed, I see no reason to withdraw or change my casualty report, sir. It is required by regulations, every time a man is killed or wounded by friendly fire. I was taught at West Point that a casualty report due to friendly fire is one of the most important reports one can make, sir. The intent of my report, and the intent of any casualty report due to friendly fire is the same: to avoid such an occurrence again. I cannot withdraw my report, sir. Most especially I cannot withdraw it if doubt is cast on its accuracy."

"Who the fuck do you think you are, Lieutenant?"

"Sir?"

"I said, who the fuck do you think you are?"

"Lieutenant Blue, sir."

"Don't crack wise with me, Lieutenant."

The Lieutenant said nothing. He looked at Colonel Testor unflinchingly.

"You're not getting it, are you, son?"

"Getting what, sir?"

"That I want that fucking report changed, and I want it done right here and now, that's what."

"Yes, sir, I understand that."

"Would it help if I told you that changing your report will help the war effort?"

"I understand, sir."

"I'm ordering you to change the report, Lieutenant. It's for the good of the brigade, son."

"Sir, my job is to file the report, and I've done my job, sir. What you do with the report after I have filed it is your business. You can accept my report, sir. You can reject it, sir. But my business is finished. My report has been truthfully written and filed according to regulations. My man was killed in a firefight with approximately fifteen American civilians. I've had some pretty crazy things happen to me and happen to my men since I've been over here, sir, but last night takes the cake. I couldn't have made up what's in my casualty report if I tried. It is as accurate and detailed as I could make it. My report stands as I wrote it, sir."

"Listen, you little shit—" It was Lieutenant Colonel Halleck.

Testor held up his hand and silenced him.

"All you've got to do is change the report, son, and this will all be behind you. You must understand that. It will all be forgotten and this whole business will be over."

The Lieutenant looked at Testor and started to say something. He checked himself and looked down at the table, at his report. Then he began to speak hurriedly, as if he weren't really in control of the words flowing from him in a torrent of pent-up anger and exasperation.

"What about Strosher, sir?" said the Lieutenant, expressing his bewilderment and anger for the first time since he'd been in the bunker. He checked himself and looked at Testor imploringly. Maybe he could make him understand. Maybe he could make them understand how guilty he felt for what he had done. He stepped out of the woodline and called out to those men and they turned and fired and Strosher went down and a moment later he was dead. It was all his fault.

"What about Strosher, sir? Do you want me to forget him, too?"

"You don't understand, do you, Lieutenant?"

"I don't guess I do, sir."

"I don't give a damn about your man and if he died or how he died. What I give a damn about is that report and getting it changed. You change it like I've ordered you to, and we'll forget this whole thing."

The Lieutenant didn't stop this time.

"Sir, I can't change the report. If I change that report about how Corporal Strosher got killed, it will be like forgetting he ever existed. It will deny that he died, and deny how he died, and deny what he died for. And that's not going to happen. Strosher is not going to be forgotten. Not while I'm still here to do the remembering, he won't, sir."

Colonel Testor stuck the cigar back in his mouth. He had a half-smile on his face, and he shook his head slowly from side to side.

"That is all, Lieutenant Blue," he said levelly.

The Lieutenant picked up his M-79 and saluted. Colonel Testor returned the salute and the Lieutenant executed a crude about-face on the dirt floor of the bunker. He zigzagged out the entrance and walked up the dirt ramp from the underground bunker.

The sun had begun to set, and the sky in the west was ablaze with riotous color. He shouldered the grenade launcher's strap and started looking for a ride back to the weapons platoon's night logger. He was going by air again, he knew. Nobody would send a vehicle outside the wire this close to dark.

He took a deep breath of hot air and squinted into the red sunset, a sky the color of a rose blossom in the morning, an embarrassingly deep, rich, blushing crimson soaked with heat and passion.

A gust of wind passed through his sweat-soaked fatigues and he shuddered. Suddenly he was cold, and he stood there at the entrance of the bunker and he shivered with hate and fear and disgust.

I lost him, Dad. I stood up and I yelled at those men and they started firing and Strosher was dead. Do you know how I feel right now? Do you know how empty I feel? I wish I could blow away, just like this dust, Dad. Just blow away and I'd be gone.

He walked toward the chopper pad, heading for his platoon, heading for home. Later he would remember what he was thinking as his boots kicked the dust and he tried to forget what had just happened in the bunker, what had happened last night. He was trying to forget Strosher, that was what he was doing. It wasn't working and he knew it wouldn't work, ever. He'd never forget

Strosher, and he'd never forget what he had done that had caused his death. Never.

Laos is one hell of a beautiful spot for a war, he mused entirely inappropriately as he strode toward the setting sun, looking forward to a new day, trying to forget the last one.

Jesus. One hundred twenty-seven more days to go.

13

They were somewhere over the Pacific, east of Hawaii, when his friend Bruce Pelton turned to say something to the General and found him slumped in his seat, chin on chest, barely breathing. Lieutenant General Pelton grabbed his wrist and felt for a pulse. He wasn't good at it, and he moved his fingers from one side of the General's wrist to the other three times before he detected a heartbeat. The pulse was completely normal, sixty beats per minute. He studied the General's face, moved his ear close to the General's mouth. His breathing was shallow but regular, with a slight wheeze on the intake and a rasping rattle when he exhaled. But you had to get your ear right next to his mouth to hear him breathing at all. It was the first time Lieutenant General Pelton had looked at his friend and been startled by the thought that he wasn't going to *goddamn* his way through another decade, leveling everything in his path with the brute force of his energy and his home-grown but finely honed intelligence. He had seemed invincible for so long, Lieutenant General Pelton couldn't remember when he was ever frightened for him. Even when the General had had a heart attack back in '47, which had occasioned both the end of his thirty-year Army career and the abrupt end of a forty-year love affair with Camel cigarettes, he had come through it growling and spitting and chewing on the necks of doctors and nurses alike, threatening their goddamned careers if he didn't get a goddamned drink pretty soon, and charming them into childlike blushes and giggles as they went looking for the booze. Lieutenant General Pelton relaxed in his seat across from him. The General was heavier than the man he had followed ashore at Anzio, and he was grayer. His skin seemed to sag from his face and jowls like curtains drawn across a life. He wasn't just *getting* old anymore. He *was* old, and he would probably die soon.

The General never felt the ministrations of his old friend Bruce Pelton. He was somewhere else at the time.

He was sitting on the front porch of his quarters at Fort Leavenworth, the house he had occupied for the duration of the Depression, from 1932 to 1939, before he had departed the United States for Great Britain, in command of the First Ranger Battalion, on its way to the British Commando School in Largs, Scotland.

The year was 1935, and he was sitting on the front porch with his wife, Carey, and they were drinking gin and tonics a few minutes after retreat on one of those summer nights that were all too rare along the banks of the Missouri River. Someone had worked a miracle on Kansas. It wasn't hot. It wasn't even humid. It was cool and crystal clear, and a pale sliver of early moon was visible above them in the darkening sky. If there had been a brass plaque on the outside wall of the front of the house, it would have identified the structure as the first building erected by white men west of the Missouri River. The house sat just a hundred yards off the intersection of the Oregon and Santa Fe Trails. You could walk across the street and down the hill toward the river and find the tracks of wagon wheels cut deep in the rock of the old trail coming up from the flats. The house was the cornerstone of the walled fortress that had been Fort Leavenworth in 1820, just after the Louisiana Purchase, when the Army was pushing America west by pushing

American Indians farther west in front of them. Quarters Number Two (the commanding general's house, which had come much later, had the distinction of being Quarters Number One) had stone walls three and a half feet thick, and hardwood floors that had come from trees felled just across the river in what was to become the state of Missouri. By 1935, of course, the house had indoor plumbing and electricity, but neither of those modern creature comforts did much to dispel the feeling that you were living in an old stone fort. The windows were small, and the walls were so thick that each window was set deep enough to be cushioned as a window seat. Interior doorways were narrow and low, in the manner of a building that made few concessions to its occupants but many to its antagonists, the Plains Indians, whom Quarters Number Two had displaced.

From the kitchen porch you could see the river, and across the river the State of Missouri, green and hilly all the way to the horizon. The front porch looked over the parade ground, a meticulously groomed central greensward edged on three sides by newer sets of quarters and on the fourth by a stretch of the fort's original stone wall, complete with battlements and firing slits facing south and west.

The General (who was then a captain) and his wife would sit out on the front porch every night and watch the sun go down across the wooded ridge to the west. He would have been finished with his late-afternoon polo game, and she would have completed most of the preparation of dinner. Captains in those days had a number of servants, including a married couple who functioned as cook/housekeeper and footman, called a "striker" in the Army, and they would have been in the kitchen, getting ready to serve a formal dinner in the candlelit dining room.

As usual, the General was wearing a coat and tie, required attire for all males on the post after 6:00 P.M. unless one was in uniform, which at that hour was Army Blue, a formal uniform worn to formal occasions at the colonel's house, to dinner at the officers' club, to a battalion dining-in, to weddings, and to funerals. Army Blue was a stunning uniform that dated to the 1800s: sky-blue trousers with wide gold-thread stripes down the sides; a dark royal blue jacket with brass buttons and gold-thread stripes at the cuffs and gold epaulets with gold inserts indicating the Cavalry and silver-thread captain's bars embroidered into the epaulets; a stiffly starched white shirt and a black tie. His wife wore the long, pale pastel cotton dress of an officer's lady. His son, Matt the third, had just served the drinks and disappeared inside to listen to the radio, which was allowed only before supper, the hours after supper having been decreed study hours by the Army captain who would become a four-star general who had never completed the eighth grade.

He was on the porch at Leavenworth in 1935, and it was as real as if it had happened yesterday, except for the fact that his wife was talking to him about the present day, 1969, and about the past and about the future.

"You know you'll have to go back there, don't you, Ma-a-a-atthew?" she asked, drawing out his name in thrushlike quavering tones and broad vowels, the way Virginia ladies did back then.

"Where?" he asked, at first annoyed that his cocktail hour reverie was being interrupted at all.

"Vietnam," she said. "You'll have to go back to put things right with your son, Ma-a-a-atthew. It's the only way you can help the boy."

"What do you mean?" he growled, looking at her sideways through squinting eyes. He found it almost impossible to look straight at her, and he had never been able to argue with her the way he could argue with virtually anyone else in the world, including Churchill and De Gaulle and Montgomery and even Ike, both during the war and after, when he served the President as Deputy Director of the CIA. He had fought with other generals and he had fought with heads of state, but he had never won a fight with her, because he couldn't fight with her.

She would look at him with her sad, drooping eyes and she would purse her lips and words would come out of her mouth and bounce around his head like a flurry of soft fists. Then her voice would flow over him like warm, soapy water over a baby, soothing and gentle and easy, and when she was through he would feel cleansed and free of anger but not free of her. He had never been free of her, not while she was alive, not now that she was dead. In his dreams he still sat with her on the porch at Leavenworth, listening to her soothing talk and watching her warily, at once entranced with and afraid of the second woman who had given birth to him, his mother having birthed a baby and his wife having birthed a gentleman.

"I know you were never able to love him as you should have," she said, ever so slowly, sipping her gin and tonic, gazing across the parade at the sunset. "You couldn't love him as he needed to be loved. What you never understood, Ma-a-a-atthew, was that it was all right to feel as you did toward him. You're his fa-a-a-ather. Fathers and their first sons fall out of love so soon for a reason, you know."

"And what might that be?" he growled. He looked over his shoulder for his son and took a final slug of his gin and tonic. He wanted another.

"Because we were so young. It was the only way you could continue to love me as your wife."

The General pretended he didn't hear her, and turned his head and called to his son.

"Boy! Bring me another goddamned drink out here!"

"Leave him alone, Ma-a-a-atthew," she drawled. "He was only here for a moment. I sent him back to Vietnam. I just wanted you to see him as he was. I wanted you to remember him the way I do, as a towheaded boy full of dreams and promise and wild ideas. I wanted you to see how much your son is like your grandson, Ma-a-a-atthew. You love him, don't you?"

"Sure, I love the boy," he said, staring into the bottom of his empty glass.

"Which boy, Ma-a-a-atthew?"

"That one," he said, pointing back into the house.

A face appeared in the door and was gone.

"That boy, Ma-a-a-atthew?"

"Yes, that one."

"That was your son, Ma-a-a-atthew. Your grandson brought your drink."

"You're confusing me, goddammit," he said, slapping the arms of his wicker chair with his thick hands.

"Of course I am, da-a-a-arling," she said. "I always confused you. Why should things be any different today than they were yesterday?"

"Because you're dead now."

"Of course I am, Ma-a-a-atthew. But my death didn't change anything."

"I lost you, didn't I, goddammit?"

"You'll always have me with you, my deah. Always. You know where I am now. I am where you found me tonight, on the porch at Leavenworth. This was our favorite set of quarters, remember?"

"Why don't you go away? You're dead, for crying out loud."

"You still need me, Ma-a-a-atthew."

"I know," said the General, looking down at his hands, which were clasped together as in prayer on his lap.

His wife stood up and walked over to his chair and stood behind him, hugging his huge head to her tiny frame with arms that didn't look as if they could pick up a salad fork, much less do the daily work of taking care of a house and children.

"Watch, darling," she whispered in his ear.

A boy walked out the door of the house dressed in a dark suit, carrying a corsage. The General heard something and turned to see what it was.

There he was, a young captain standing in the door with a cigarette in his mouth, calling to the boy.

"Boy! You be home by midnight, goddammit, and don't you take that girl downtown, you hear me?"

The boy turned. It was his son, Matt. He was leaving to pick up his date, the daughter of another captain who lived just across the parade.

"I'll be home on time, Dad," his son called.

"You come in one minute after midnight, and you'll wish you hadn't come home at all, boy!"

"I know, Dad," said the boy. He sniffed the corsage and headed across the parade field at a gallop.

"What are you doing to me?" the General asked.

"Sssh. Just watch, Ma-a-a-atthew. There is nothing you can do now but watch."

The boy walking across the field disappeared into the misty gray dusk. A moment later he emerged from the dusk, walking back toward the house. He climbed the front steps and knocked on the door. It was answered by someone the General had never seen before, a tall man with gray hair wearing a sweater and tan slacks and loafers.

"Come in, Matt. Wendy will be down in a moment," said the man. He was smoking a pipe, and the General could smell its sweet aroma. The door to the house was ajar, and inside were furnishings the General had never seen before. The glow from a television colored the sitting room, and an overcoat with a full colonel's insignia was hung on the hook by the door.

"We didn't have a goddamn television, Carey! That's not me! That's some goddamned colonel. What in hell is going on in there?"

"Ssshh," said his wife, wrapping her arms more tightly around his thick neck.

The boy appeared in the door. He was beaming as though he'd just been handed his first shotgun, and his hair was slicked back with grease, and as he moved he seemed to float an inch or two above the floor. He pushed the screen door open and held it for a girl about his age, who emerged wearing a long pink chiffon dress. Her hair was piled atop her head and she was wearing pale blue eye shadow and pink lipstick. She was beautiful, and the tinkling of her laughter sounded like pebbles rolling down iron stairs. She was self-assured, womanly, feeling sexy for the first time in her life, and she looked it. Her high heels tap-tap-tap-tapped on the boards of the porch as the two of them descended the stairs. A 1955 Plymouth station wagon was parked on the road in front of the house, and the boy and girl got in the car and switched on the radio to a rock-and-roll station and drove away.

"Who was that?" the General whispered, barely able to talk.

"That was your grandson, going to a dance on his first date in 1959. The girl is the daughter of the colonel who lived here in our house. She had Matt's room, the one at the back, remember? Your son lived across the post, over where the old firing range was, where you took the men for rifle practice. Your grandson lived in the basement with his brother. Remember?"

"A goddamned colonel's daughter! These aren't colonel's quarters! These are captain's quarters!"

"Not in 1959, Ma-a-a-atthew. Colonel Williams lived here then. That was his daughter, Wendy."

"I don't understand," said the General in a low, hoarse voice. "I don't know what you're doing to me."

"I'm not doing anything to you, Ma-a-a-atthew. You're doing it to yourself."

"What? What am I doing?"

"You're re-creating yourself, Ma-a-a-atthew. In those boys. In your son. In your grandson. This is a glimpse of how it works."

The General took a deep breath and looked into the far distance, across the parade, across the rooftops, across the treetops, across the ridge into the evening sky.

"You created me," he said softly. "I'm yours, just like those boys."

"I know," said his wife, stroking his silver hair with her thin fingers, bony with enlarged knuckles from arthritis, from age, from being a Randolph, from the grave.

"You can kill me. You can take me with you," he said. He was still looking away, unblinking, just staring.

"I want out, Carey. Nothing is the same as it was. It's all gone to goddamn hell. All of it. The Army. That goddamned war over there in Vietnam. The country. All gone to hell."

"I can't take you with me," she said. "If I could, I would not. Your place is with your son, and with his son. It is why you were left behind, Ma-a-a-atthew. It is why you were spared. So you could love them, so you could leave something of your love behind for them. Before, you did not have the time. You didn't have the heart."

"I know," he said. He reached up and took her bony hand in his and held it to his cheek and kissed her fingers.

"I know."

His voice sounded very far away, as though it had carried from far across the parade, from the trees atop the ridge in the distance. His words boomed against the roof of the porch and shook his teeth and made his eyes hurt. He clung even more tightly to her thin, bony hand and began to cry.

"What was it you always said, deah? That you must lead by example?"

"That's what I said."

"Now that is what you must do with your love. Lead them by the example of your love. If you do that, everything will turn out all right. You'll see."

"Why did you always know so much, Carey?"

"I don't," she said, stroking his cheek with the backs of her fingers. "I always thought I did. Now I know differently. There is so much that escaped me. You hid from me, for a while."

The General felt his face easing into a smile.

"Powerful Katrinka. That's what I called you after the war. Remember?"

"Not-so-powerful Katrinka. That's what I was. I died, Ma-a-a-atthew. It is you who has the power now."

"What about you? Can't you help me?"

"You can help yourself now, Ma-a-a-atthew. You have it within you."

"How?"

"You know what your problem has always been, deah?" She leaned forward and he tilted his head back so they looked in each other's eyes.

"I guess if you won't take me away, you may as well tell me," he said.

"You never saw the opportunities in your children," she said. "What has happened to your grandson is a great tragedy, but this is your chance! Your chance to set things straight! Do it out of love, Ma-a-a-atthew. Don't do it because you feel you have to. And for God's sake, don't do it to show them that you *can*. You've shown the world what you can do. Now show your son, and your grandson. Do it for them, and for me, and for the memories we will share when we are together again. Do it for love."

"It is so hard," said the General, still staring at the burnished bronze ridge, the golden sunset, the place where he had felt as happy as he had ever felt in his life.

The General heard a sharp noise like a door slamming. He turned his head. His son was standing in the door grinning at him, the same handsome young man of twelve or so who had left on the date. He was leaning against the door frame, and as the General watched, his grandson materialized next to him, and his son dropped his arm around the other boy's shoulder and the two of them melted into one.

Then they were gone.

"What's happening?" he asked his wife, who just as suddenly was again seated across the porch from him.

"You're finding out how much you love those two boys, Ma-a-a-atthew. I know it's not easy. Just let it happen to you. You will see the power of your love."

The General leaned back in his chair and closed his eyes and he heard a wind, a strong wind, a storm wind, sustained and frightening, whipping through his ears like a freight train, then he opened his eyes and they were gone, all three of them, and he was alone on the porch at Leavenworth, and it was fall, and leaves blew from the trees around the parade ground, swirling around his feet, swirling, swirling, and the wind stung his eyes and he closed them again.

He blinked open his eyes, and he still heard her voice, but he was in the seat of a jet at 33,000 feet, and Lieutenant General Bruce Pelton was sitting next to him reading a magazine. He leaned back in his seat and blinked closed his eyes and listened.

"Ma-a-a-atthew. Ma-a-a-atthew. Can you hear me?" she called as if from far away, across the parade. He could hear her, but he couldn't see her.

"Yes. I can hear you, Carey."

"Do it for me, Ma-a-a-atthew. Hold me tightly and love me so much that you can love your son, too, Ma-a-a-atthew. It's all there is for us now. There is nothing else."

"I love you, Carey. And I love that boy, goddammit. I love him and I love his son and I'll die for them if that's what it takes."

The General felt something on his arm and turned his head. It was Bruce Pelton.

"Are you okay, sir?" his friend asked. He had turned in his seat and was holding the General's wrist, feeling for his pulse.

"I'm okay. You goddamn right I'm okay. Where are we?"

"We've begun our descent into Washington, sir," said Lieutenant General Pelton. "We'll be there in a few minutes."

"Good," said the General. "I've got a lot to do."

By the time the plane's wheels touched ground at Washington National Airport, his course of action was clear. If the boy had as good a lawyer as Bruce Pelton said he did, then the boy should be freed from the Long Binh Jail so that he and his attorney could mount a defense. The fact that Jake Rousseau had stabbed him in the back didn't mean the General had exhausted his store of people in power he thought he could count on. Rousseau's defection, however, had given the General pause. There was something behind the indictment of his grandson that he couldn't figure. Rousseau wasn't talking about it, and if he didn't talk, no one would. The General was on his own with this one. It had been years since he had undertaken something completely by himself. It felt good. He felt empowered, and for some reason he didn't really understand, he felt twenty years younger.

"When you get to State, I want you to call the Pentagon and make an appointment for me to see the Secretary of Defense."

"When would you like to see him, sir?"

"This afternoon. Five o'clock," said the General.

"I'm sure he'll see you then, sir, if he doesn't have a full calendar."

"Just tell him I want to see him. He'll clear his goddamned calendar for me."

The office of the Secretary of Defense was an outside suite on the Pentagon's E-Ring, overlooking the Washington Monument and the Lincoln Memorial. The General had spent his share of time in the Secretary's office when he was Deputy Director of Central Intelligence. The look of the office hadn't changed much over the years, and neither had the men who occupied it. They were almost without exception confidants of the sitting President, men with a background in industry or finance who seemed to have spent half their lives making a living and the other half stuffing the coffers of the political party to which they owed the good fortune of their friend's election to the presidency and their subsequent appointment to the Cabinet.

The current Secretary of Defense, Samuel Hamilton, was no different. He was a Midwestern industrialist who had spent the Eisenhower years toiling in the vineyards of the Republican National Committee, during which time he had cozied up to the current President, for whom he had been campaign finance chairman in 1960 and 1968.

Now Mr. Hamilton was reaping the rewards of seeds well sown in a twenty-five-year career as a party functionary. He sat at the top of the greatest dollar-expending machine mankind had ever put on the face of the earth—the Department of Defense of the United States of America. It was a little like winning the lottery. One day someone called you on the phone and said your checking account had swollen to the tune of about a hundred billion dollars, and you had a year to spend it. Secretary Hamilton, like any good party fund-raiser, was going to spend his winnings at the stores owned by the men who had helped put his President and himself in their present jobs.

He was doing just that—calling his friends at various defense industries to report on his recent fact-finding journey to some twenty-five military installations around the globe—when the call came from Assistant Secretary of State Bruce Pelton that his friend Matt Blue wanted to see him at five o'clock. He hadn't seen the old warhorse since they had run into each other at a polo match down in Charlottesville a year or so ago. He had heard that the President had moved one of his California buddies into the Ambassador-at-Large slot that General Blue had occupied for the past few years. The General was probably looking to do some part-time consulting for DOD. The cloak of retirement wasn't going to ride very comfortably on the General's broad shoulders. He'd have to find something for his old friend to do that would get him out of the house a few days a week. Shouldn't be too much trouble. Maybe he could put him in charge of the study group that was looking into closing down some under-used military posts overseas. The General's extensive military and foreign-relations background made him just right to head up such a difficult inquiry, one that would step on all kinds of military toes domestically and an equal number in NATO.

The buzzer on his intercom startled him.

"Mr. Secretary, General Blue is here to see you," said his executive assistant, whom he'd brought with him from Kansas City. She couldn't get over the fact that he was really the Secretary of Defense, and insisted on calling him "Mr. Secretary" even when they were alone and she was taking dictation or bringing him coffee. She'd been with him for twenty years. They knew each other as well as if they were man and wife. It was a cute affectation, and he let her indulge herself, but he teased her about calling him by his title.

"Send him in, Miss Secretary," he barked into the intercom. He hoped the General had heard him tease her. It was the kind of familiarity he enjoyed.

The door opened and General Blue strode purposefully into the office. The Secretary of Defense stood up and walked around his desk to greet him.

"Matt! Good to see you! You know, I was going to get Jill to call you to arrange lunch next week, then Bruce called and said you wanted to come over."

The two men shook hands. General Blue was a full six inches shorter than Secretary Hamilton, a man who was ten years his junior but didn't look it. All those years of arranging rubber-chicken speaking engagements for party hopefuls across the country had taken their toll on him. He was fifty pounds overweight, nearly bald, and dark circles under reddened eyes and a tremor of hand belied a somewhat more than recreational interest in gin.

"What can I get for you, Matt?" he asked, walking over to a wet bar behind his desk. He threw a switch, and overhead spots came on, illuminating crystal decanters with gold labels reading Scotch, Bourbon, and Gin.

"What was it you used to say, Matt? Sun's not over the yardarm until the bugler's blown retreat and left his post? Those were the days, huh, Matt? The smell of wet leather on heaving horseflesh . . . you had me convinced you could ride down a polo ball and swat it downfield without giving either the ball or the goal so much as a glance. I'll tell you. Those were the days . . ."

He looked over his shoulder at the General.

"Sam," said the General, "as much as I'd like to, I didn't come here to reminisce about our days on the polo field back at Gates Mills." The General's face was set sternly, his mouth downturned, his huge eyes hooded by a gravely wrinkled brow.

The Secretary of Defense poured a shot of bourbon into each of two glasses and tossed in a few cubes of ice. He handed one glass to the General.

"You look like you could use a libation," he said. "I know I sure as hell could."

He sat down on a leather sofa facing the windows, and sighed audibly. The General sat across from him in an armchair that matched the sofa.

"All those years I dreamed about this office, and now it's mine, Matt. I've been here almost a year and I still have to pinch myself every once in a while to remind me that it's real."

"I have come to talk to you about my grandson, Sam," the General interrupted. "He is in a great deal of trouble over in Vietnam, and I want your help."

"What? Your grandson? What's happened, Matt?"

The Secretary of Defense looked genuinely surprised, which startled the General. He had figured the Secretary would have been well briefed on the situation.

"He has been charged with desertion in the face of the enemy, Sam. They've got him locked up at the Long Binh stockade, and I want you to issue an authorization to release him pending trial by court-martial."

The Secretary of Defense took a long drink of bourbon and stood up.

"I don't know anything about this, Matt. I'll have to look into it and get back to you. I can't imagine why I haven't been informed, unless it was overlooked by my daily briefing officer while I was on my trip. I just returned from—"

"Jill was telling me outside," the General interrupted. "I'll wait, Sam."

"Wait? For what?"

"For you to look into young Matt's situation. I want this taken care of *now,*" said the General. "I've been getting the goddamned runaround on this thing, Sam, and I want you to authorize that boy's release tonight. *Now.*"

The Secretary of Defense looked stunned as he sat down at his desk and punched his intercom.

"Jill, get me Colonel Tomkins," he said.

"One moment, sir," came the reply.

"Jim Tomkins is my military aide," the Secretary explained. "A fine, fine man."

The intercom buzzed.

"Colonel Tomkins on line one, sir."

The Secretary of Defense picked up the phone.

"Jim, I want to know what you've got on the arrest of . . ." He turned to the General and covered the receiver. "What is he? A lieutenant? Infantry?"

"That's right, Sam," said the General.

"I want everything you've got on Lieutenant Matthew Blue, Infantry, Jim. Apparently he's been arrested and is being held in the stockade at Long Binh. Get back to me ASAP."

He hung up the phone.

"What do you know about this?" asked the Secretary of Defense, turning to his old friend the General.

"Not much more than you do, Sam. They've got him incommunicado over there, and I can't find out a thing about the facts surrounding the charges against him. I was over there yesterday and the day before, and this whole goddamned thing stinks to high heaven if you ask me."

The two men sat drinking and talking for several minutes when the intercom buzzed.

"Colonel Tomkins for you, sir," said the intercom.

The Secretary of Defense picked up the phone.

"What have you got, Jim?" he asked.

He listened and nodded his head slowly.

"What about it?" he asked.

More listening. More nodding.

"What did he say?"

The Secretary of Defense stopped nodding and listened intently. He picked up a pen and made a few notes on a pad of paper on his desk.

"Sit tight, Jim. I'll be back to you in a moment."

He hung up the phone and turned to the General.

"I'm afraid what I've got to say isn't what you came to hear," he said gravely, tapping the desk with the end of his pen. The Secretary stood up and paced back and forth behind his desk.

"The charges against your grandson are very grave, as I'm sure you understand," he said. He stopped pacing and turned to face the General. "Anything I undertake to do on his behalf at this point would be seen as command influence. I know you understand how seriously this is taken by all the services, Matt. Anything smacking of command influence could jeopardize the possibility of a fair trial for young Matt. I know you don't want to do anything to lessen his chances to clear his name of this . . . this very serious charge."

The General sat on the leather armchair for a moment, staring at the Secretary of Defense. Then he rose slowly from the sofa and straightened his suit jacket, smoothing its front with his palms. He walked across the room and stood in front of the Secretary's desk. He leaned forward at the waist, placing his palms on the desk to support his weight. He stared at the Secretary of Defense as only the General could—a wide-eyed, half-smiling stare, like a mean dog's.

"I want you to listen very closely to what I've got to say, *Mr. Secretary,* because I'm only going to say it once." The General intoned his friend's title slowly and deliberately, making the point that while he understood their respective positions, he'd been there before.

"I want you to remember a day about twenty-five years ago, the day I got my orders in North Africa that would take me and my division across the Mediterranean to Sicily, and from there to Anzio and up the boot of Italy to Milan and from there to Marseilles. I was in Tunis, and I received a letter from you that had been sent over in the Chief of Staff's pouch from Washington. In this letter, you asked me to do what I could to secure your steel holdings in Italy

259

and France, and you were good enough to remind me, on two subsequent pages, where each and every one of the Hamilton Steel plants was located. Do you remember that letter, *Mr. Secretary?*"

The Secretary of Defense nodded.

"You knew I'd do what I could to safeguard your steel holdings overseas, didn't you, *Mr. Secretary?*"

The Secretary of Defense nodded.

"We had been friends for—what?—twenty years at that time? About that?"

The Secretary of Defense nodded.

"We played polo together at the Gates Mills Polo Club for every one of those twenty years, every summer.

The Secretary of Defense nodded resignedly. He knew what was coming.

"And I proceeded to establish my command headquarters in a dozen of your plants over there. We swept wide of your largest plant outside Milan, avoiding the artillery barrage that would have been inevitable if we'd gone the other way. We established military government headquarters in your other plants. No, it was eight. Is my recollection correct?"

The Secretary of Defense nodded, looking down at his feet, which were pigeon-toed on the deep blue carpet of his office.

"I've still got the letter you sent me, *Mr. Secretary.* And I've got a very strong memory of the work your company did for the Agency in '48, before the Italian election. I talked to George Marshall and got you into your post on the Committee on European Reconstruction, a position that couldn't have done any harm in your efforts to get your companies going again over there."

"Are you threatening me, Matt?"

"Hell no, I'm not threatening you. You ought to know me better than that. I'm reminding you of a favor, a very significant favor I did for you a number of years ago. Now *I* need a favor. I want the boy out of the stockade, and I want him out now."

The Secretary of Defense looked at his friend and spoke slowly. "This could go very badly for you and me both, Matt," he said. "What I asked you to do wasn't wrong. You know that as well as I do. And neither was what you did for me. That was a different time.

A different war. But it would make a difference for both of us if you were to bring this out now. I'd probably lose my job, as I'm sure you know. And your reputation for integrity would be besmirched forever. What you're asking me to do for Matt just isn't possible. I can't go into it right now, but when I can tell you, I will. And you'll understand. I'm sure you will. National security is involved, Matt."

"I'm not sure you're getting my message," said the General, standing up. "I don't give a good goddamn what the fallout is. I want that boy out of the goddamn stockade, and I'm not leaving this office until you give the order."

The Secretary of Defense studied the General's face for a moment. He was looking for some glimmer of understanding, some recognition of the value of twenty years of friendship. There was none.

"You really are the son of a bitch they've been saying you are all these years, aren't you, Matt?"

The General didn't answer the Secretary of Defense for a moment. He stood in the front of the Secretary's desk, impassive, silent, fists clenched, his whole body a club ready to strike at any moment. Then he took a deep breath of resignation and stepped back and collapsed into the armchair. He nodded at the Secretary of Defense, indicating he should sit down across from him. He did.

"You know, Sam, you spend your whole life trying to find a way to live on this earth that *fits*. Do you know what I mean?"

The Secretary of Defense looked puzzled.

"I'm not sure I do, Matt."

"You spend your life trying to find a way to make yourself and your family . . . comfortable. You try and you try and you try, and I'll be goddamned today if I know any more than I knew forty years ago. Sometimes I sit alone in my study, looking out at the garden, and I wonder where it was exactly that I went wrong. What path I could have taken that would have made things turn out differently. And I'll be goddamned if I know where it is, or where it was. I just don't know. I really don't, Sam."

The General stared off out the window at the Washington Monument for a moment, then took a sip of bourbon and looked at his friend.

"I'm still not sure what you're getting at, Matt," the Secretary said.

"It's *family,* Sam. You're talking about national security, and I'm talking about my *family.* You know, Sam, you wear a family like a suit of clothes. They keep you dry and warm, and your family conceals the essential truth that from the day you're born until the day they lay you in the ground, you stand naked before the world. It's taken me sixty years to admit this to myself, Sam. Sixty years to admit to myself what a goddamn fool I've been all these years. How much I have owed and how little I've repaid them."

The General took a deep breath and looked into his friend's eyes.

"Young Matt is in trouble, big trouble. I know it and you know it. But that's not why I'm here, Sam. I'm here because of my son. My son has been like a pair of shoes that I never broke in, that bound and blistered my feet for years, and I always blamed the shoes, not myself for not breaking them in. All these years, Sam, I've blamed my son for problems between us that I have caused. Well, this time I'm not going to make the mistakes of my past. Nothing anyone can do to me now can ever compare to what I've done to myself and to my family. If I'm going to take some heat about young Matt, then so be it. I don't give a goddamn anymore. I'm an old soldier whose time has come and gone. Nothing convinced me of this more than my brief trip to Vietnam. We're fighting a war over there that is wrong, Sam. We're fighting it the wrong way, we're fighting it against the wrong people, and we're losing that war, Sam. It's almost as if we're punishing ourselves for all the indiscretions we've committed since the last war. Now young Matt has run afoul of that war in some way I don't understand. But I'll tell you one thing I do understand. I'm going to stand by that boy, and I'm going to stand by my son and see this thing through. And damn the goddamned consequences. I'm pleading with you, Sam, but I'm also telling you this: you can stand with me, Sam, or you can stand against me."

His friend studied the General's face. He drank his bourbon to the bottom of the glass, then stood up and grabbed the decanter and poured each of them another stiff shot.

"All right," said the Secretary of Defense. "I'll give the order. I'll get him released from the stockade. But I'm not sure it will do him any good, Matt. He's in the kind of trouble that is bigger than both of us. Nothing I do, nothing you do, can help him get out of this. Of that much I'm sure."

He walked over to his desk and punched a button on the intercom.

"Get me Arthur," he said, referring to General Clifford Arthur, the Army Chief of Staff.

The General stood in front of the desk at attention. He had gotten what he had come for. He had used the force of his personality to get the Secretary of Defense of the United States of America to bend to his will. But he could threaten and cajole no longer.

The easy part was over.

Now he would have to deal with his son.

14

Catherine Joice had always found a refuge in facts, in the process of research itself, in the mounds of data that could be accumulated and pawed through and fussed over and analyzed and organized and reorganized until finally you did not *understand* a subject as much as you *absorbed* it, allowing the data to shower over you like cool rain on a hot day, cleansing, refreshing, restorative . . . pure.

That was the thing about facts. They were more than separate bits of data. Brought together under the rubric of a story, facts were chewy little bursts of energizing soul food that satisfied you like rich, dark chocolate poured over a vanilla ice cream sundae bought with money lifted from your mother's purse the day you cut French and biology with your best friend who had a Ford convertible with a floor shifter and didn't mind driving around on a sunny afternoon until the tank ran dry.

And there was something else about gathering and organizing

and reporting facts. If you surrounded yourself with enough facts, she knew, you could forgo the bother of feelings.

This was, of course, what had driven her into journalism. Pursuit of facts wasn't a means to an end, it was an end in itself. So when the story of Lieutenant Matthew Nelson Blue IV presented itself to her nearly devoid of facts yet so front-loaded with emotion it was flammable, Cathy Joice knew what she had to do, but she didn't know how to do it.

She had to get to Lieutenant Blue because he had all the facts. This made his story different from any she had ever worked on. Usually in journalism what you did was run around and collect facts, and then you confronted the object of your story with the assortment of facts you had collected. Afterwards, you retreated to a room somewhere to lash together the facts and the interview into some kind of cohesive whole.

But this time, where could she run to collect facts? What facts were out there to collect? Besides Lieutenant Blue, from whom? They had the lid down so tight on Lieutenant Blue it made your eyes bulge. So what was left? She had a room, but she had no facts. This made her extremely nervous. It also gave her a headache.

She was lying in a tub full of lukewarm water, resting her neck on a rolled towel at the lip of the tub, when the phone rang.

Wouldn't you know it!

She hauled herself out of the tub and wrapped a dry towel around her torso and dripped into her room and picked up the phone.

"This better be good, because I'm in no mood for small talk," she announced to the caller. The anger in her voice was trip-wire taut, on the edge of control. Suddenly, out of nowhere, the phrase "mad as a wet hen" jumped into her mind and she covered the receiver and giggled.

"Who is this?"

"Terry Morriss."

"How did you get my number?" Cathy Joice was standing in her room with the phone crooked into her shoulder, toweling her hair with one hand and grabbing for a notepad and pen with the other.

"It wasn't hard. I called the desk."

Cathy Joice laughed and dropped her towel on the floor. She sat naked on the edge of the bed and looked out the doors to her balcony and across the rooftops of Saigon into the acid-black Southeast Asian night. Somewhere out there was a story that contained the answer . . .

"As a matter of fact, I'm across the street at the Caravelle."

"Listen. Give me a few minutes, and I'll meet you downstairs in the bar."

"I understand you're good at that."

"At what?"

"Meeting lawyers at bars."

"Oh. *That.*"

"I'll treat you to a martini, but I can't promise it'll match the one you had at the club."

"I know what you mean about the martinis at Tan Son Nhut," said Cathy Joice. "Ten minutes. Downstairs in the bar. We'll see if we can get my friend Nha Sang the bartender to improve his technique."

She hung up the phone and finished drying her hair. The call from Captain Morriss was a sign. It had to be. The facts were starting to flow her way.

Cathy Joice put on a white cotton short-sleeved blouse, a tan skirt, and a pair of white sandals. Blow-drying her hair had left it tousled. She wore a light pink lipstick that matched her nails, and enough eyeliner and mascara to lend some mystery to her pale blue eyes. It was almost nine o'clock. It was still cocktail hour in Saigon, where pretty much any hour you could find a reason for a cocktail, but what hour was it back home at the Joice house? What were they doing over at the Phelans? Was the President still pushing papers across his desk at the White House? Hanoi was in the same time zone, but was it time for a drink in Hanoi, too? She wondered what they were doing up at Long Binh Jail. Eating a cold supper off aluminum plates, she presumed.

She wondered what they had served Lieutenant Blue, how he could even stand to eat in a cell inside the stockade, facing the charges he was facing . . .

Wait a minute.

What was she doing, thinking about the diet of a Lieutenant

charged with desertion in the face of the enemy? He was somebody she didn't even know, and if she did know him she'd probably hate him. Sure, she was obsessed with getting her story, but this was different. This time she couldn't get the image of the Lieutenant out of her mind. At odd moments, like right now, he would reappear in her mind's eye and she would massage the memory to keep him there.

What was this shit?

She leaned over and shook her head and ran her fingers through her hair, teasing it into a neat bundle of contradictions. It was flying every which way, unkempt, alive.

That was the way she wanted to look—a little disorganized, but focused on the matter at hand. It had helped her occasionally, being seen as something of a ditzy girl when beneath the surface was a cunning woman. You use what's available, thought Cathy Joice. You do what you can with what the good Lord gave you.

But now there was a problem. Every time she thought about the Lieutenant up in Long Binh, she lost focus and she floated . . .

She started imagining what his cell looked like, she wondered what he was feeling, alone and adrift from everything he had spent his life believing in . . .

That was the problem. *He* was the problem.

Every time she thought about him, all she got was a jumble of feelings. His feelings. Her feelings.

And no facts.

Captain Morriss was already standing at the hotel bar when she walked in.

She slid onto a barstool and lifted her hand for the bartender.

"I didn't see you come in," said Captain Morriss, also signaling the bartender. "I'm sorry. I should have been looking for you."

"Nha Sang? About that last martini you mixed for me . . ." she began.

"Sorry, missy. Got new martini mix for you," said the bartender, smiling a little too sheepishly to be totally believable.

"Oh yeah? Let's see what you've got, Nha Sang."

The bartender reached for a bottle of Bombay Gin, and Cathy Joice turned to Captain Morriss.

"Anything new you tell me about Lieutenant Blue—about his case, I mean?"

"What makes you so interested in my client? There are other stories around. I heard about a fragging in the 25th Division yesterday. It's a little unusual. You might be interested."

"Oh? What makes it so unusual?"

"They killed a black platoon leader. Somebody told me he's the first black fragging victim."

"That *is* something new," said Cathy Joice. "But I'm still interested in *your* platoon leader. What can you tell me?"

"They're out for his ass, I can tell you that much. This whole thing is coming from very, very high up. He claims he was set up, and I believe him."

"Set up? How?"

"Er . . . uh . . . here's to the war effort," said Captain Morriss, raising his glass. Cathy Joice reached for her martini and matched his toast.

"What is it the flyboys yell all the time out at Tan Son Nhut? Nuke 'em!" She clinked glasses and smiled and sipped her martini.

"You were asking about my client," said Captain Morriss. He was a thickset man who looked as out of place in civilian clothes as he had in uniform. He was wearing a pair of Bermuda shorts and a golf shirt that wasn't tucked in. On his feet were the black Army-issue lace-ups he had worn with his khakis all day. They were unshined, scuffed, and dusty. His socks were also Army issue, and one sock had slid down his heel into the shoe. He wore a pair of gold-filled Ben Franklin glasses on the end of his nose, which was bulbous and red from the sun. He had a contagious smile, and behind the granny glasses his sparkling eyes shone with a mischievous delight that belied his image as a cynic. All in all, he looked about as much like a lawyer as he looked like a captain.

Cathy Joice studied him. He was a familiar type, probably Law Review at Tufts or Harvard, maybe Yale. He had spent so many years in the bowels of a law library that he had completely missed the sixties and was getting ready to miss the seventies. A few young men like him had clerked for her father when she was growing up. They were allergic to the sun, and every time she had met one of them, the young clerk had avoided her eyes, too embarrassed to speak. This one wasn't having any trouble talking, however. He was about as sure of himself as you could be at twenty-seven, twenty-eight years of age, which she figured he was. She took a guess.

"Let me see, you're Harvard Law '67, right?"

"Sixty-six. How'd you guess?"

"Just lucky."

"And you're . . . Smith College '65, am I right?"

"Yes. You are." She blushed and turned her head and took another sip of her martini. She made a face and slid the martini across the bar.

"Nha Sang? Take this away and bring me a gin and tonic."

"Now that we've got the formalities out of the way," said the captain, "what do you want to know?"

"I want anything you've got on Lieutenant Blue. Anything."

"He's charged with desertion in the face of the enemy. That's the most serious charge that can be brought against you in the Army. Maybe treason is as serious, but I doubt it. He could get the death penalty. Death by hanging, that is. The Army has yet to move into the twentieth century when it comes to doing away with its own."

"And you think he's innocent?"

"I'm paid to think he's innocent."

"I realize that," said Cathy Joice, tapping her right index fingernail on the bar, twirling her hair with her left one.

The bartender scurried behind the bar, filling a glass with ice and gin, adding tonic almost as an afterthought.

"Nha Sang is going to get you drunk if you don't watch it," Captain Morriss said with a laugh.

"It's his job," said Cathy Joice. "And what about you? You said it's your job to think Lieutenant Blue is innocent. But that doesn't answer my question. Do you think he's innocent, or are you just going through the motions, saying so because you have to?"

Captain Morriss took a swig of beer and stared into the middle distance for a moment. Then he looked at Cathy Joice. His eyes seemed to have receded gravely into hooded holes in his face, and his lower lip quivered as he spoke.

"I don't know as much about the case as I'd like to, but I think Lieutenant Blue is as innocent as you are. He claims it's a frame, and I believe him."

"But why would anyone want to trump up such a charge against a young officer with his background? Whoever charged him would have to know that he was asking for trouble. His grandfather isn't exactly a house painter from Biloxi. He's a very big man in Washington, and he must still have a lot of pull in the Army. Have you heard anything from him?"

"From the grandfather? General Blue? Not directly. I heard he was here a few days ago. Some inquiries were made. Somebody was making calls for him. I don't know who he was, but he carried a big enough stick to pry answers loose from my office faster than I've ever seen them pried."

"That's all? The General was here and somebody made some calls for him and he left?"

"He wanted to get in to see the Lieutenant, but they drew the line on him. They wouldn't let him near his grandson. They're railroading this guy, Cathy. They moved Lieutenant Blue around like crazy for a couple of days, apparently afraid that the General would pull enough strings to get through to him."

"What do you mean?"

"They moved him out of Long Binh, stashed him in a locked room. He doesn't know where he was. They had him blindfolded all the time. Then they moved him again, this time to a sandbagged bunker somewhere else. They drove him in the back of a three-quarter-ton truck from place to place. He said it took about an hour to get to the first place, the locked room, and two hours to get from there to the bunker. It looks like they kept him around the outskirts of Saigon somewhere, probably Bien Hoa, maybe down at Vung Tau. It's hard to tell. All we know is, he was on the move the entire time his grandfather was over here. When he left, they put him back in Long Binh."

"Did you hear from anyone else in his family?"

"Just today I heard from the Lieutenant's father, Colonel Blue. I'm supposed to meet with him tomorrow. He's here in Saigon, but I don't know where he's staying."

"Do you think I could come along?"

"I don't know. I'd have to ask Colonel Blue, but as I said, I don't know where he's staying, so I don't know where to call him."

"Has he tried to see Lieutenant Blue?"

"He tried, but he didn't get any further than General Blue did. They won't let anyone but me near him, and for a couple of days there, even I couldn't see him. They're not real thrilled every time I show up."

"Is that standard? Not allowing visitors?"

"Not to my knowledge. I've never heard of them shutting the door on everyone but the defense lawyer. Lots of prisoners up there get visits from guys in their units, from their company commanders; one guy gets visits from a Vietnamese girl he married."

"Are they awaiting trial or serving time?"

"Both."

Just then a white-jacketed boy passed through the bar, calling Captain Morriss's name. Morriss stopped the boy.

"I'm Captain Morriss. What do you want?"

"Telephone, Captain, sir," said the boy in halting English. "In lobby. Quick-quick. Very important, man say."

Morriss followed the boy into the lobby and returned five minutes later.

"What do you know about that!" he exclaimed as he sat down next to Cathy Joice and gulped the last of his beer.

"What's up?"

"That was Alvie Dupuy. They're releasing Lieutenant Blue to my custody tonight. The order came down about an hour ago from Washington. He's on his way down here with him right now."

"You weren't expecting this, were you?"

"Hell no, I wasn't. Alvie sounded pissed as hell, but the release order came down and specified they let him go immediately. They pulled Alvie out of his weekly card game to go pick up the Lieutenant."

"Can I talk to him?"

"Dupuy said he has given Lieutenant Blue orders not to talk to the press. Normally I'd counsel him to obey orders, but these aren't normal circumstances. I'll talk to him about it, but I'm sure you understand that I'll have to respect his wishes."

"Where are they taking him?"

"Over to my quarters. I've got to be there . . . let me see . . . in twenty minutes."

"Where are your quarters?"

"Out by the MACV Compound. A BOQ. *Très* luxurious."

"Well, you know where I'll be. Please give me a call if Lieutenant Blue decides he'll talk."

"Don't get your hopes up. It's been all I could do to get what little I've gotten out of him. It's like he's in a trance. One moment he's lucid, the next, he's staring at the wall. It's pretty strange, I've got to tell you. He doesn't behave like a man who's facing the gallows. Most of the time, even when he's in a trance, he's more relaxed than I am behind three martinis."

"That *is* strange," said Cathy Joice, sipping her gin and tonic. "Why do you think he's behaving like that?"

"I don't know. It's not like he doesn't care what happens to him. He does. And I've seen flashes of anger, real molten-lava stuff, from way down deep inside him. Every time he blows up, he starts talking about some kid called Strosher. Then he'll drift off into the trance again and just stare at the wall. God only knows what he's going to be like when they let him out."

"You sound worried about him."

"I've seen guys with more emotional stability, I'll tell you that much." Morriss stood up. "I've never represented anybody in this much trouble before," he said. "Most of the time I have this feeling I'm in a dark room with a gun, shooting at targets I can't see. I don't know what's behind these charges against him, but I'll tell you one thing. They're very serious about putting this kid away for a long time or hanging him, one. I hope I'm hitting a few of the targets I've been shooting at. But that's all I can do. Hope."

"Hanging him?" asked Cathy Joice. "Are you serious? Do you really think they would hang him if they convict him?"

"I don't know," said Captain Morriss. "Seems to me I recall that the last time they hanged anyone for desertion was World War II, although I'm not sure that little detail would get in their way. One thing is for sure. It's a hanging offense. If they convict him and they want to hang him, they can ask for the death penalty. Whether they could get a jury to sentence him to die, I just don't know."

"What do you think his chances are?"

"At this point? Not good. He's going to have to start cooperating in his defense for him to have any chance at all."

Captain Morriss shook hands with the television reporter.

"It's been nice getting to know you," he said. "You're kind of a legend around here, you know. They just love you over at the Five O'clock Follies."

"They're going to adore what I do with Lieutenant Blue, if I ever get to him."

"I'll let you know what he says about talking to you, one way or the other," said Captain Morriss.

"Sure. Thanks," said Cathy Joice, as Captain Morriss turned and walked out the door of the bar.

But with you or without you, I'm going to get to him, she thought. She finished her gin and tonic, tapped the bar with her fist, and called out, "Put it on my tab, Nha Sang."

"Yes, missy," she heard him say as she headed across the street to the Continental.

15

Danny Jannick was about to get up. It was the middle of the night, and the noise downstairs was loud as hell, but loud noise wasn't the problem. It was *Vietnamese* loud noise. All the weird banging and clanging and thumping and screeching and sounds you'd never heard before and sounds you hoped you'd never hear again. He had been in the Pension Gravois for two years and by this time he knew what made one of the sounds. It was a mynah bird, and the damn dirty bird had been taught to say "fuck you" in English, but it was *Vietnamese* English with that awful Vietnamese accent, and the damn dirty bird sat there all day and all night squawking *fawk ooo! fawk ooo! fawk ooo! fawk ooo!*

Nobody could sleep through a mynah bird squawking *fawk ooo!* all night to the delight of the collected hookers and mama-sans who owned the damn dirty bird and had taught the damn dirty bird his delightful little trick.

Delightful! My ass delightful! Oh shit there he goes again . . .

Fawk ooo!

Tee-hee-hee . . .

"FUCK YOU!" Danny Jannick yelled from his bed.

He rolled over and faced the window, the better to scream out the window and downstairs into the ears of the hookers and the mama-sans and whoever the fuck else was down there tee-hee-heeing . . .

"FUCK YOU!"

He was bellowing now, the words coming from deep within his chest from down in the place where he lived down below his heart in his belly . . .

Jannick rolled over and looked for something to pick up and throw down in the courtyard, something he didn't care about, something cheap and heavy that would make a big noise and do some real damage if it hit the bird or one of the hookers or a mama-san or two . . .

His typewriter!

He sat up and squinted through the dimness at his desk. There sat an old steel portable grinning its black toothy grin at him and beckoning to him and reminding him forever reminding him that he hadn't filed in two weeks . . .

C'mon over it was saying *c'mon over* and it was saying *I've got some words for you . . . they're right here hidden down in my little black keys . . . all you've got to do is find the hidden words . . .*

There was something next to his typewriter, something that hadn't been there when he went to bed last night. The something was large and wide and the something was sitting in his chair and the something had two beady eyes and the something had arms and the something had legs and the something had feet and the something had white shiny teeth and the something was grinning at him . . .

Jannick bolted from the bed and opened his mouth to scream and nothing came out but dry air and a rasping noise as he tried to get his breath again. He crawled into the corner and turned around with his back to the wall and pulled his knees to his chest and asked in a voice that sounded very small and very far away . . .

"Who are you? What do you want?"

The something reached out with an impossibly long arm and turned on the light next to the typewriter on the desk and the something opened its mouth to speak . . .

"Hey, dude," the something said softly.

It was Repatch.

"What the hell are you doing here?" asked Jannick, releasing his knees and trying to stand up.

"I needed a place to stay, man."

"How long have you been here?"

"I don't know. I been here last coupla nights. I know that. I just needed a place to sleep, man. Hey! Some weird shit goin' on downstairs tonight, huh? What is that noise, man? A fuckin' parrot?"

"A mynah bird." Jannick could barely get the words out of his mouth. He was in shock and his mouth was dry and his palms were wet and he still couldn't stand up.

Repatch walked across the room and held out his hand and helped Jannick to his feet.

"You've been staying in this room with me for three nights, and I've never seen you," Jannick said in a tone of stunned amazement.

"That's right, man. I didn't want to disturb you. I was just gonna let you sleep like I done last night and catch a little shut-eye for myself."

"You have been sleeping bolt upright in that wooden chair? For three nights? Really?"

"Hey, man. Rack is rack. I've packed some serious Z's on my eyeballs in worse spots."

"Like where? What could be worse than a ladder-back wooden chair?"

"Foxhole fulla rainwater during the rainy season. Thing about a foxhole is when it rains you got to pull yourself up on a little ledge you dig in there just so's you can sit on it when it rains. You see what I mean? I ain't seen a hole and for sure I ain't *dug* a hole big enough for a ledge that would really hold you comfortable-like. Know what I mean? I mean, a hole is a hole and they're all miserable as hell when it rains, right? Fillin' up with water and shit is what holes *do*. You see what I mean?"

"Right," said Jannick, sitting down on the bed. The mynah bird had shut up and it was strangely silent in the room, a condition to which neither Jannick nor the room was accustomed.

"What are you doing in Saigon?" he asked blankly. He wasn't focusing. He knew it, but there was nothing he could do about it except to try to force words from his mouth and hope like hell they added up to something.

"I come down to keep an eye on the Lieutenant. I got to be there if he needs me, you know what I mean? The Lieutenant, he's a real good guy and all that shit, but he needs somebody to look after him. You know?"

"Lieutenant Blue? He's in LBJ."

"Not no more, he's not. They let 'im out tonight. He's in Saigon now."

"Jesus! I've got to get up and find him!"

Repatch grinned. "I know where he is."

"Where?"

"He's at a hotel 'cross town."

"Here? In Saigon?"

"Yeah. I followed him in from Long Binh tonight."

Repatch sat there with his brow furrowed and his eyes glistening and shining wildly in the light from the desk lamp.

"You want to get some sleep?" Jannick asked, surprising himself at the ease with which he had accepted his new roommate. Something about this guy Repatch made you trust him. Jannick didn't know what it was about him, and didn't *want* to know what it was, that simply made you feel better that he was there.

"I think that damn dirty bird has shut up for a while. We'd better get to sleep while we can."

"Sure," said Repatch.

"Do you want me to see if I can find you a cot? They've got a few of them rattling around this place somewhere."

Repatch held up his palm.

"Nah. I been gettin' real good rack right here. Anyway, I'll be goin' out after a while to check up on the Lieutenant."

"Whatever," said Danny Jannick, his head finding the pillow automatically. The damn dirty bird was quiet and Repatch was already asleep in the chair and the thing was it all seemed somehow so *right*.

*   *   *

She had been asleep for two hours when she heard the noise at her door. She sat up in bed and looked at her alarm clock. It read 2:20. Outside the lights of Saigon had dimmed as businesses closed their doors and sleep settled over the city.

She slipped into her robe and walked across the room to her door. She stood there for a moment, listening.

Nothing.

She turned and walked back across the room to her bed and was slipping out of her robe when she heard the noise again. She hurried to the door and pressed her ear against the wood. Then she stepped back.

"All right. That's enough. What the hell is going on out there?" she called in a loud, assertive voice.

"Miss Joice?" The voice was low, almost a whisper.

"Who's out there?" she called again, louder this time.

"Miss Joice? It's Lieutenant Matt Blue."

She stepped forward and opened the door. The Lieutenant nearly fell on her. He had been leaning against the door, and he staggered to regain his footing. By the time he was standing upright, he was in the middle of the room.

"I didn't mean to wake you, but Captain Morriss said—"

"That's all right," Cathy Joice said hurriedly. "Wait right here. Give me a minute to get dressed."

She grabbed some clothes and went into the bathroom and closed the door behind her. It was dark, and she hadn't seen him very clearly, but what she had seen was gaunt and drawn. He was wearing a set of khakis about two sizes too big for him, and his shoes didn't look as though they belonged to him, either.

"Are you still there?" she called from the bathroom.

"Yes, ma'am," said the Lieutenant.

"Don't call me 'ma'am,'" she called through the closed door. "My name is Cathy."

"Yes, ma'am," he said.

"Hey! Cut it out with the 'ma'am' stuff, I said."

"Sorry."

She opened the bathroom door. He was standing right where he'd been when she left the room, lost in a tent fly of khaki.

"You look like you could use something to eat," she said, switching on the light next to the bed.

"I sure could. Food isn't one of their priorities at Long Binh, I found."

"How long were you in there?"

"A week. A week and a day. Eight days," he said haltingly.

"You lost some weight I see."

He looked down at his uniform.

"Oh. This. It's Captain Morriss's. I took it out of his closet."

"Does he know you're here?"

"No. I left after he went to sleep."

"What are you doing here at this hour of night?"

"I don't know. I needed to talk to someone. Captain Morriss put me in a room in the BOQ and went to sleep. I knocked on his door trying to wake him, but I didn't get any response."

"Captain Morriss told you about me."

"Just before he went to bed. Yes."

"He told me you were under orders not to speak to the press."

"He said something about talking to you off the record. I could talk to you and you wouldn't tell anyone. He said he trusted you."

"I'm glad. I trust him, too."

The Lieutenant smiled, then dipped his head and gulped air as if he hadn't taken a deep breath in weeks.

"Are you okay?" Cathy Joice asked.

He looked up blankly.

"I've got to get out of here," he said. "I've got to get to someplace bigger than a little room like this. Being in that cell got to me. I've never been locked up before."

"Okay," she said. "Come on. Let's go get a drink."

"I wanted to go back to my unit, but Captain Morriss told me it doesn't exist anymore."

"Really?"

"He said they shipped everybody out right after I was arrested."

"Won't you be needing those guys as witnesses?"

"I think that was the point of shipping them out," said the Lieutenant.

"Of course."

The Lieutenant was staring out the open door to her balcony, staring, staring, shoulders hunched forward, arms dangling at his sides.

"I'm in big trouble. You know that, don't you? I mean, Captain Morriss, he told you, didn't he?" he asked.

"Yes. Captain Morriss . . . Terry told me."

The Lieutenant continued to stare out the balcony doors, breathing in shallow, forced gasps of air. His chest was heaving convulsively, and beads of sweat had formed on his forehead and were dribbling down his face.

"Are you okay? You sound like you're hyperventilating."

"Just . . . a . . . minute . . ." he gasped. "Give . . . me . . . a . . . bag . . . paper . . . bag."

She rummaged in her closet and found a paper bag and handed it to him. He held the open end of the bag tightly over his nose and mouth and breathed into the bag quickly, shallowly. The bag inflated and deflated with every breath. Slowly his breathing grew deeper and more even. In a moment he removed the bag from his mouth and nose and turned to look at Cathy Joice.

"I'm . . . s-s-s-sorry," he stammered. "I didn't mean to put you through this."

"That's okay. Are you feeling better?"

"Yeah. I guess so."

"Can I get you anything?"

"I think I need a drink."

"I think you do, too," she said, leading him to the door.

"I'm finding it harder and harder to give a shit what happens to me," said the Lieutenant, following her. "So much bad has happened already, I don't care what happens from here on out."

"Let's go find someplace open and get drunk," she said.

"I know a place," he said. "One of the guys in my platoon told me about it. It's down on the waterfront somewhere, near a canal."

"What's it called?" she asked.

"The Kit Kat Klub."

"Let's find it."

They wandered from the Continental down Tu Do Street toward the Saigon River waterfront, and from there south, past the Hotel Majestic and the Club Nautique, across the Ben Nghe Canal into

South Saigon, a thick undergrowth of shacks and alleys and backstreets along the Saigon River.

As they crossed the canal, the Lieutenant asked what Captain Morriss had told her about him.

"Not much," she said. "Only that he thought you were innocent."

He followed her as they headed down one alley after another, each darker than the last, all of them spookily hooded by line after line of laundry blowing softly in the breeze overhead.

They rounded a curve and the street dead-ended. Ahead was a barnlike structure made from sheets of tin and scavenged sides of corrugated aluminum shipping containers from the States. The logos of a dozen American companies stared down at them from the side of the building like testimonials. Over the door, a single lightbulb illuminated a childishly hand-lettered sign reading KIT-KAT-KLUB.

"This is the place," said the Lieutenant. "They said it looked like a warehouse."

He pushed open the door and they entered.

It was a long, narrow, rectangular room with a high cathedral ceiling and a bar at one end. A post-and-beam structure held the roof aloft, and the insides of the scavenged packing crates and tin sheets could be seen along the walls, many of them stenciled CAM RAHN BAY, the place they were shipped. Three rows of bleachers ran along either side of the room, and they were filled with Vietnamese men, every one of whom seemed to be smoking. The air hung thick and low with the acrid cloud of smoke from their cigarettes. The room was utterly silent. The only sound that could be heard was the soft shuffle of slippers along the wooden floor as a half-dozen *ao dai*-clad waitresses scurried back and forth to the bar, carrying trays of large earthenware jugs.

"What kind of place is this?" Cathy Joice asked.

"I'm not sure," said the Lieutenant. "One of the guys in my platoon told me about it a couple of months ago. He said it was open around the clock and that you'd never find a place like it back in the States."

"I guess not," she said, standing perfectly still, taking in the scene.

A short Vietnamese man with a wispy gray beard and a gray ponytail materialized next to them. He was wearing a black silk robe with a purple and yellow orchid embroidered on the back. The cuffs of the robe were turned back, revealing a purple and gold patterned silk lining, the same colors as the flower.

"This way, please," he said in unaccented English. He bowed and moved his arm as if sweeping aside a curtain, and shuffled down the bleachers. From the way he moved, he appeared to be in his seventies or eighties, but his face was completely unlined and his eyes shone with energy and intelligence.

He stopped halfway down the row of bleachers. Three men hurriedly stood and moved away, disappearing in the smoke.

"Please," he said, bowing and gesturing with his robed arm.

They sat down on the bleachers where he pointed. He bowed and snapped his fingers. One of the waitresses appeared out of the smoke and bowed to him and to the Lieutenant.

"You want to drink," said the robed man, more as a statement of fact than a question. He snapped his fingers again, and the waitress disappeared, her black *ao dai* rustling against her thighs as she scurried into the smoke.

"Many pleasures," said the old man as he backed away from them, bowing as he went. He clapped his hands twice and was gone.

The lights went out.

"What's going on?" Cathy whispered.

"I don't know," said the Lieutenant. Instinctively he reached for her hand and found it clammy with nervous sweat. He gripped her hand tightly and hugged it to his stomach.

The waitress emerged from the darkness, handed each of them a tall ceramic jug. Before they could pay her, she disappeared into the dark.

The Lieutenant took a sip from the jug.

"It's rice beer," he whispered. "It's strong. Kind of sweet. Try it. It's good."

Cathy raised the jug to her lips and swallowed.

"Hey, you're right. I wonder why you can't get this at the hotel."

"I think they make it here," said the Lieutenant.

"Where? In a back room?"

"Here. In this part of Saigon. It's home brew, I'm pretty sure."

"I think this is exciting. I've never seen this side of Saigon."

"Neither have I."

A spotlight blinked once, twice, then snapped on, flooding the empty floor between the bleachers with yellow light. A sound could be heard floating softly into the room from somewhere behind the bar.

Tick-tick-tick-tick-tick-tick . . .

"What's that?" the Lieutenant asked, leaning over to whisper in her ear.

"Sssshh."

Suddenly the tin-walled space was awash in light and a hundred men were before them holding drums and cymbals and lance-sticks and garbage-can lids and iron chains and tin cans full of pebbles nailed to the ends of sticks and jeep wheels and long strips of tin that quivered eerily in the smoky light.

The men were half-naked, wearing jockstraplike loin wrappings and sarilike lengths of dyed cloth wrapped around their necks and upper arms. Some of them had hair that had been tied in a topknot and festooned with bright pieces of string that dangled to their waists, and others had heads shaven bald except for a single thick tuft of hair that emerged from the backs of their heads and cascaded down their backs like black waterfalls.

The spot blinked *off-on* and the men began to move, shuffling about the room haphazardly, but on the same beat.

Shuffle-*stomp*-shuffle-*stomp* . . .

They wandered the floor in aimless patterns, turning left then right then left, stopping, spinning on bare heels . . .

Stomp . . . they found the beat.

Clang-clang-clang-clang the pounding began on drums, garbage-can lids, pieces of steel, old jeep wheels . . .

And a high-pitched wavering sound blew like an ill wind through the air, *wheeeeee-eeeeeeeeessssssh* it came, teasing the ear with tickling weeping tender tones of doom . . .

Stomp . . .

The spot blinked *off-on-off-on* again, and the room began to shake with light and heat and noise.

They were both riveted on the mass of flesh and noise in front of them.

From the other end of the room twenty women emerged from the smoky gloom in single file wearing floor-length *ao dai* skirts and tight silk body wrappings and towering headdresses of feathers and painted palm fronds and bead strings and cascading strips of colored foil . . .

Stomp . . .

The men began to circle them . . .

The women danced fluidly, hands over their heads, bodies swaying to the *shuffle-stomp-shuffle-stomp* beat, eyes down, chins left right left right left right, hips swiveling, bare feet gliding across the floor soundlessly . . .

A noise riffled through the dark room like dry leaves blowing across gravel . . .

Thunk . . .

The lances hit the floor and it began again . . .

The men circled the women in tighter and tighter circles and the women swayed faster and faster and faster until the circling of the men and the swaying of the women became one black aqueous wave of wet bodies and black hair and wavering headdresses and shuddering feathers and pounding instruments . . .

The women were in the middle of the floor, lying in a wet circle, undulating to the beat . . .

Stomp . . .

Bright lights flooding everything, a hundred bodies whirling madly, blazing eyes caught trancelike by the spots, unblinking, wet eyes, black-rimmed eyes, flashing whites, black face holes whirling and spinning and twisting and crying . . .

Whoosh . . . the wind the spinning mad wet white eyes whirling tin strips twirling arms sweat spraying *thud-thud-thud* wall of clanging noise . . .

"Matt, those women aren't really women," Cathy whispered, tight against his ear.

"I know."

The Lieutenant turned his head to look at Cathy. Her face was dripping with sweat, hair matted to her head, eyes wide, taking it in . . .

The lights went out and he couldn't see her. He reached for her hand.

It wasn't there.

The noise washed over him, laying him back against someone's knees . . .

"*Cathy!*"

He gripped her more tightly, pressed her against his chest, buried his face . . .

He held her and he could feel her breathing and her wet hair stuck to his face and her neck smelled like sweet wine vinegar and sugar poured over fresh dirt like the edge of a lake where water licked mud and brushed your face with birth air birth wet birth fog birth black birth white . . .

"Cathy . . ." He whispered in her wet ear.

"*Cathy!*"

They screamed her name banging jeep wheels and tin cans and sabers and lances . . .

"Cathy . . ." He whispered and he held her to him and they shuddered in the thunder . . .

"*Cathy!*"

They screamed and her name slapped at him through the smoke crushed him smothered him and he bent over and he whispered in her ear . . .

"Let's go."

He clutched her to him and stood up . . .

Stomp . . .

He looked to see where he was going and a hundred brown sweating faces stared at him, black eyes gleaming in the blinking spots like buttons sewn on the surface of a nightmare . . .

He tried to move, but he couldn't . . .

Stomp . . .

He looked down . . .

Thunk . . .

Both of them were tethered to the bleachers with wire wrapped around their ankles wrapped around the bleacher supports tying their feet to the floor . . .

Stomp . . .

Whoosh . . .

"Let us go! Let us go!"

They mocked him and they moved as one and a hundred wet bodies stared at them and moved sideways left and stared and moved sideways right . . .

Shuffle-stomp-shuffle-stomp . . .

He tried to walk and his feet wouldn't budge and he reached down and tugged at the wire but it was tight too tight . . .

Stomp . . .

He was holding her with one arm and tugging at the wire tugging tugging and his hand was bleeding and sweat ran off his forehead into his eyes and dripped on his hand and a stream of sweaty blood covered his shoes and the wire bit into his ankle and his ankle bled and mixed with the sweat and the blood on his shoes and ran onto the wet floor and . . .

Thunk . . .

The lances came down pounding the floor as one . . .

He tugged and tugged and tugged and she fell from his arm onto the bleachers in a heap and he tried the wire holding her feet to the bleachers and nothing gave way and his hand bled onto her feet and her feet turned wet red wet red wet red . . .

He felt something . . .

Stomp . . .

He looked down . . .

Thunk . . .

A hand reached through the bleacher supports holding a bayonet and the bayonet severed the wire and his feet kicked out from under him and he landed on the bleachers atop Cathy and he looked down and the hand and the bayonet slashed through her wires and her feet flew forward and he lifted her arm and wrapped it around his neck and he stood and he started walking . . .

Stomp . . .

He felt the weight of her body ease up from his shoulder and he looked to his left across her wet bowed head and Repatch grinned at him crazily in the smoky dark . . .

Repatch.

The lances hit the floor . . .

"This is some shit, huh, Eltee?"

Repatch yelled at him over Cathy's head and the stomping bodies parted and black eyes followed Repatch warily and they carried her to the door and Repatch lifted his foot and kicked the tin door and it flew open and the cold night air hit them like a wet sheet and they carried her out the door and down the narrow alley with laundry waving over their heads like flags of doom in the dark . . .

They reached the end of the alley and the Lieutenant felt Repatch turning left, so he followed him, then Repatch turned right, and he followed him, and the alley opened up and they were walking next to the canal and crossing the bridge and they were back in Saigon proper and Repatch stopped at a bus stop bench and they eased Cathy down onto the bench and the Lieutenant collapsed next to her and he looked up.

"Repatch. What in holy hell are you doing here? How did you find us?"

"I been with you for a while," said Repatch. He was looking to his left and his right and his hand was on the handle of the bayonet which was stuck in his belt and in his other hand he held a .45-caliber pistol. A figure materialized out of the misty dark.

"Who's that?" the Lieutenant asked.

"Danny Jannick," said the figure. "I'm a friend."

"He's okay, sir. He's some kinda reporter. He come up to see me in the boonies."

"Are you okay?" Jannick asked.

The Lieutenant nodded.

"What in hell is going on, Repatch?" he asked.

"Some weird shit, huh, Eltee? Ever since the clearing and the plane, huh? Some *weird* shit, that's fo' sure, sir."

"How did you get here?"

"I walked."

"I mean, from the unit. From the platoon."

"Ain't no platoon no more, Eltee. They disappeared 'em, every one. I jus' walked outta the base camp and hitched me a ride from Dak To."

"How long have you been here?"

"Here? Saigon?"

"Anyplace."

"I been here in Saigon tonight, last coupla nights. Been stayin' with Jannick."

"What are you doing down here?"

"Waitin' fo' you, Eltee. That's what I been doin' for the past week. I been up Long Binh every day, waitin'. Nights, I been down here."

"Jesus, Repatch."

"I know, sir. Some weird shit, ain't it?"

Cathy began to stir, and the Lieutenant brushed the hair from her face and crooked her neck against his shoulder.

"She be okay, sir. Jus' give her a minute."

The Lieutenant held her and rocked her and she coughed and looked up.

"Where . . . where are we?" she whispered.

"We're out of there," said the Lieutenant.

"I want to go home," she said.

Repatch reached down and hooked her arm around his neck and the two of them stood up and gathered her legs under their arms, and with Danny Jannick leading the way, they carried her the six blocks back to the Continental. When they reached the hotel, Repatch turned left and led them through a side entrance, down a dark corridor, and up a set of back stairs.

The Lieutenant dug into her purse and pulled out her keys and opened the door and they carried her to the bed and eased her gently against the pillows.

"I'll be aroun' if you need me, Eltee," said Repatch as he backed out the door.

"If I could get a word with you tomorrow . . ." Jannick said. Repatch grabbed his arm and they disappeared down the hall.

The Lieutenant watched them go with a mixture of awe and superstition. He knew Repatch had been there tonight. He was certain of it. Still . . .

He wasn't certain of anything.

Cathy stirred and reached for him and he held her to his chest and spoke softly in her ear . . .

"It's okay now. You're all right now. Just go to sleep."

She opened her eyes and saw her room and she moved her head and she saw him and she closed her eyes and clung to him and shuddered against his chest until she stopped and her breathing told him she was asleep.

He rolled from the bed and found the bathroom and washed his face. He took a towel and cleaned the dry blood from his ankles and wrapped his hand with a washcloth. He wet another towel and removed her shoes and wiped the blood from her feet and her ankles and pulled a bedspread over her and sat on the edge of the bed and stared.

She was just plain beautiful.

He wiped her brow with the wet cloth and stroked her hair and tucked the bedspread around her shoulders. Then he went back in the bathroom and leaned on the sink and looked at himself in the mirror. He had dark circles under his eyes, and his cheekbones were stark and pronounced. A two-day stubble darkened a pasty, sallow complexion.

He'd looked better.

He turned off the bathroom light and felt his way into the bedroom. As he passed the bed, a hand reached out from the spread and grabbed his arm and pulled him down on the bed beside her.

"I thought I heard Jannick," she mumbled.

"You did. He was here, but he's gone now." He stood up to leave.

"Stay. I need you," she said, eyes closed, as her arm wrapped around his neck and eased his head onto the pillow next to hers. She lifted the bedspread for him, and as he slipped in next to her, he felt her bare, cold skin.

She had undressed.

Then he felt her hand unbuttoning his khaki shirt and tugging at his web belt. He worked his pants free and kicked them on the floor and sat up and he felt her removing his uniform shirt and he reached up and pulled his T-shirt over his head. She tugged at the waist of his drawers and he slid them over his knees and kicked them free. She wrapped around him like a child and whispered in his ear something about the morning and he closed his eyes and the sound of her and the smell of her rocked him to sleep.

S I X

When Colonels Go to War

Firebase Zulu-Foxtrot
Day Six

Repatch was cleaning his weapon and Sergeant Davis was cooking a skinny creature over a campfire he'd built down in a hole and Whoopie Cushion Ridgely was standing alongside his foxhole baying at the moon which had just risen above the horizon and Mallick was tugging at Whoopie Cushion's pantlegs trying to get him to stop and the Lieutenant was sitting on a pile of sandbags in his track playing cards with Dirtball when the radio split the silence and crackled and *screeeeeed.*

Dirtball grabbed the receiver.

"Rattail Two," he said, crooking the receiver against his shoulder and dealing another hand of stud.

In a moment he put down his cards and handed the receiver to the Lieutenant.

"You're gonna love this one, sir," he said.

"What's up, Dirtball?"

" 'Nother patrol, sir. They want 'nother fuckin' patrol from us, sir."

The Lieutenant took the receiver from Dirtball.

"Rattail Two, over," he said.

"Two, this is Six," said the company commander. "Saltlick Six wants another patrol tonight."

"Where do they want it this time, Six, over?" the Lieutenant asked.

"Same general area, coupla kliks out and back. That's all. Over."

"Righto, Six," said the Lieutenant.

"Six here. Saltlick Six stated specifically in his order that you're to lead the patrol tonight, Two. Do you copy? Over."

"Roger on leading the patrol, Six," said the Lieutenant. He waited a moment, then he said, "Six, Two. Did he give you any reason why I'm ordered to lead the patrol, over?"

"This is Six. Negative. Over."

"Christ, over."

"This is Six. I don't like this crap any more than you do, Two. But don't pull anything, Two. I don't know what's going on, but they're going to be watching you tonight."

"Roger on the watching, Six."

"Call in the patrol's grid coordinates once you're set up, Two."

"Rodge."

"Six out."

"Two out."

The Lieutenant put the receiver on top of the radio and stared at his hand of cards and tossed the hand on the sandbag and rubbed his face and blinked in the dim red light inside the track.

"Same old shit, sir?" Dirtball asked.

"SOS, Dirtball. You got it."

"You want me to get Sergeant Davis, sir?"

"May as well."

Dirtball headed down the back ramp of the track. In the distance the Lieutenant could hear artillery booming softly in the night. The sound of artillery reminded him of something from his boyhood, but he couldn't quite put his finger on it. Then it came to him. Distant artillery sounded like somebody was beating on big cardboard boxes about a block away. He remembered how much fun a kid could have with something as simple as a box that had contained a washing machine or a refrigerator. You could turn it into a fort or you could beat on it like a drum or you could cut it up with your pocketknife and slide down a grassy hill on a big piece of cardboard, holding the front edge before you like a bobsled.

Sergeant Davis appeared in the door of the track with something black and crusty on the end of his bayonet. He was chewing hard and he stopped at the back ramp and bent over and spat a bone into the dirt then he duck-walked into the track and sat down across from the Lieutenant on a sandbag and looked up with his sad eyes and he said:

"What you got goin', sir?" He finished a bite and spat another bone into the dirt.

"They want another patrol tonight, Sarge. The word came down. I've got to lead this one, too."

"Roger that, sir. Me and the boys will watch the farm while you're out there. They try anything back here, we'll take it to 'em for you."

"They want it same as last night. Two kliks northwest and set up an ambush. And they want the grid coordinates. I'll call 'em to you when I get out there."

"Yes, sir. Sounds good to me."

"Get Repatch for me, will you?"

"You got it, sir."

Sergeant Davis drifted into the dark and returned with Repatch a few minutes later. The two of them came up on the track so silently that they startled the Lieutenant when he looked up and saw their faces peering in the ramp door.

"We lost Strosher last night," said the Lieutenant. "I don't want any casualties tonight. It's fucking criminal to have lost a man on one of these bogus goddamned patrols. So . . . Repatch, I want you to take us there again and set up tonight right where we were last night, and I want to be dug in so deep you could walk on top of us and never know we were there."

Repatch nodded, looking at something over the Lieutenant's shoulder.

"That a picture of your girl, sir?" he asked, pointing to a photo pasted to the firewall of the track.

"That's Dirtball's girl, Repatch."

"Mighta knowed. Fuckin' Dirtball. How does he get 'em, huh, sir?"

"They home in on his smell," said the Lieutenant.

Everybody laughed, including Dirtball, who was dangling his feet over the top edge of the track and listening in.

"Sergeant Davis, Repatch knows right where I'm talking about, and I've got the grid coordinates marked here, but I'll let you know on the radio if there is any variation whatsoever from where we were last night."

"Rodge, sir."

"Okay, Davis. Round them up."

"You want the rest of this bird, sir? He's better tastin' than he looks."

"I'm sure he is, Sarge, but no thanks."

"Okay, sir. I'll leave him right here for Dirtball." Davis pulled the creature off the end of his bayonet and placed it carefully on top of a sandbag under the photograph of Dirtball's girlfriend.

"Tell him it's with my compliments, sir."

"He's right up there on top, Sarge, tell him yourself," said the Lieutenant, pointing to Dirtball's feet and legs.

"Dirtball, the grilled bird is fo' you," said Sergeant Davis. "You goin' tonight?"

"Thanks, Sarge. Eltee told me to stay back here with you. Take care out there tonight now, you hear me, Eltee?"

"Yes I will. You know I will Dirtball."

"Who you want me to give the radio to, sir?"

"Give it to Cushion," said the Lieutenant. "Maybe carrying that extra weight will keep him from dancing around."

"Got you," Dirtball said, dropping into the track and picking up the radio and heading down the ramp.

The Lieutenant followed him to the perimeter, where Sergeant Davis was shaping up the patrol. Watching Davis gave the Lieutenant the opportunity to study the process in a way that he couldn't when he was the one shaping them up. He stood in the dark and marveled.

Who was it that had figured out the concept of a patrol? Caesar? One of those guys? Whoever invented the patrol came up with a beautiful thing, the Lieutenant thought.

There they stood . . .

Repatch, silent, face blackened, almost invisible against the dark treeline, shuffling his shuffle, breathing slowly, in and out, in and out . . .

Whoopie Cushion, wearing the radio like a new suit of clothes, proud and erect, almost stately, staring at the moon . . .

Mallick, crouched on one knee, resting his chin on the barrel of his M-79 grenade launcher, looking out past the wire like a dog ready to hunt . . .

Moonface with his M-60 over his shoulder, twenty-five pounds of steel he carried like a baseball bat . . .

Lucky Lemon, hair so yellow it looked like somebody spilled mustard on him, scratching at the dirt with the toe of his boot, humming "Orange Blossom Special" . . .

Simpleton Sample, two sacks of Claymores over each shoulder, M-16 stuck between his knees like the third leg of a tripod holding him up . . .

Woodley the medic, steady and reliable and well turned out in clean fatigues and neatly bloused trousers, always a man to pay attention to detail, always watching, ready to sprint . . .

And back there at the end of the patrol . . . nobody . . . a blank spot where Strosher would have been, the terminal teenager, jolly and giggly, always cracking jokes and enjoying being the brunt of more than his share, but now he was gone and nobody was there to take his place, so the night filled in Strosher's spot with silence and humid air and heat and doom . . .

Sergeant Davis picked up the wire. The Lieutenant ushered them across the perimeter and through the cleared brush and into the woodline and they were gone, sponged up by the woods and the darkness like a stain on the night.

They had been gone for an hour when the radio crackled and the Lieutenant called in the grid coordinates, the same as the night before: sector map 24-Lima, 72548869. Sergeant Davis cross-checked the coordinates with those the Lieutenant had given him from the night before and satisfied himself they were exactly the same.

The Lieutenant told him to call in the patrol's grid coordinates to Rattail Six. He did.

Sergeant Davis carefully folded the map and laid it out on top of the track's bench and mixed himself a cup of cold instant coffee and got ready to wait them out. That patrol would be inside the wire before he put his head down and racked out.

Dirtball shuffled the deck of cards for a while, then got out his notebook and started writing a letter to his girlfriend. When Sergeant Davis had finished his coffee, he scooted down the ramp and took a walk around the perimeter, checking the men in their holes, prodding one or two awake, ordering others to relieve the ones on guard.

It was a night like many others he had spent with the weapons platoon. Quiet. Strangely still. You could hear every noise made inside the wire and a virtual racket from the night birds and creepy-crawlies out in the woods. The danger on a night like this, he knew, was complacency. You could let the night noises lull you into a sense of security that wasn't yours for the taking, not in a platoon perimeter somewhere inside Laos, it wasn't.

And then there was the patrol, out there somewhere in the dark, dug in, crouched down, breathing in quick shallow little gasps of air, waiting . . .

Waiting . . .

Waiting . . .

Waiting . . .

Waiting . . .

The Lieutenant was out there waiting . . . cranky, jittery, spastic, humorless and ugly and nasty and mean, hunkered down in the dark.

They waited another hour and the silence broke with the *pop-pop-pop-pop* sound of gunfire in the night.

The Lieutenant was lying on his back in a slight depression in the ground, staring up at the stars, and when he heard the gunfire he sat up straight and listened and heard it again and he poked Cushion in the shoulder and grabbed the radio and whispered:

"Dirtball. Dirtball. Give me Davis."

He was breaking radio procedure, but he didn't care. He just sat there drumming his fingers on the side of the radio, waiting for Sergeant Davis.

"Eltee, it's me," came the sound of Davis's voice on the radio.

"What's going on back there?"

"I don't know. There's some shootin' over to the east of us, but it ain't much. Sound like somebody blew a bush. We sittin' tight, Eltee. Everything's cool."

"You let me know if the fighting picks up."

"Rodge, Eltee," said Davis, whispering into the mike. "Will do."

The Lieutenant handed the receiver to Cushion and leaned back against the ground. He was completely soaked with sweat and his back felt clammy and soggy and sweat poured off his brow into his eyes, and his eyes ran and his nose ran and he sniffled and sneezed.

He sat up and switched the radio to the company net.

"Rattail Six, this is Rattail Two, over," he whispered.

He waited.

"Rattail Six, this is Rattail Two, over."

He waited.

"Two, this is Six, over," the radio crackled.

"Six, Two. What's going on, over?"

"Two, this is Six. We're taking some fire from the south of us, over."

"Six, Two. We're standing by."

"Roger, Two. It's not much, so far. We'll let you know. Out."

"Two out."

"What's up, Eltee?" Repatch asked. He had appeared next to the Lieutenant out of the dark.

"The Battalion's taking some fire. Captain says it's not much so far."

"You want me to get them ready to move out, Eltee?"

"Yeah, Repatch. Do it."

Repatch crept along the ground to each man on the patrol, warning them to be ready to move out.

There was no telling what the distant fire meant. The fighting could move toward them. It could move away. By the time Repatch got back to the Lieutenant, the distant gunfire had picked up. A fight was going on somewhere out there between the firebase and the battalion base camp, a distance of about three kilometers. The Lieutenant heard the distinctive pop of a 60mm mortar, the handheld weapon carried by the VC. He heard another pop, and another.

Then he heard the skittish rattle of a VC machine gun and the answer of an M-60.

The radio crackled.

"Eltee."

It was Sergeant Davis on the platoon frequency.

"Yeah, go ahead."

"There's some shit out there. They shootin' 60s and shit. They must be getting pretty close to you."

"We're keeping our heads down, roger?"

"Roger that. Our heads is down, too. *Way* down."

"Is anything coming your way, over?"

"Nothin' so far."

"Stay by the radio, over."

"Rodge. Out."

The Lieutenant left his hole and made a quick inspection of the rest of the patrol. Everybody was tense. He could smell them sweating in the dark.

He returned to his hole and squatted down and looked out through the jungle into the night. He could hear it but he couldn't see it. There was a war going on but he wasn't in it and he didn't want to be in it and he didn't want his men in it but he knew that soon it would come to him and he and the weapons platoon would be at war.

The radio crackled and Cushion grabbed the receiver and whispered to the Lieutenant:

"Battalion's callin' for a fire mission, Eltee!"

"Give it to me," said the Lieutenant. He took the receiver. The radio was tuned in on the company net. He pressed the receiver to his ear and listened.

On the radio, Dirtball took the fire mission coordinates from Captain Gardner and relayed them to Sergeant Davis. He would call them out to his fire direction control sergeant, who would compute the coordinates and call out the azimuth and elevation to the gun crews, who would dial them into the mortar sights. Then the mortars would fire.

The Lieutenant switched the radio to the platoon frequency and whispered into the receiver.

"Davis, hold it." He said the words slowly, deliberately, to make sure Sergeant Davis received his message.

"Rodge, sir," said Sergeant Davis.

The mortar crews were waiting for their settings. The fire direction control sergeant was waiting for his coordinates. Dirtball was sitting by the radio, ready to take adjustments of fire from company commander, who was the one calling in the fire mission.

Everyone was waiting for the Lieutenant. He had taken out a penlight and was studying his map under his poncho. The radio crackled.

"Six wants to know where his rounds are, sir." It was Sergeant Davis, calling on the platoon net from back at the firebase.

"Tell him to wait one," said the Lieutenant.

He plotted the coordinates Gardner had called in to his platoon. They plotted nowhere even near the vicinity the sounds of war were coming from.

"Ask him which map he's using," the Lieutenant whispered into the receiver.

Davis relayed the question over the company net and called back:

"Double deuce-Lima, sir."

"Christ," said the Lieutenant.

He dug into his pocket and pulled out the map on which he had plotted the platoon's position, the battalion base camp's position, and the location of his patrol.

"Six is screaming for his rounds, sir," Dirtball called over the radio.

"Wait one!" whispered the Lieutenant.

He plotted the grid coordinates Dirtball had called to him.

Fuck.

He plotted the coordinates again, and he plotted them again. He was sure of it.

They were calling in fire on his patrol's location. Either they didn't know it or they had screwed up the grid coordinates and they thought they were calling it in somewhere else, or . . .

Then it hit him.

They were calling in the fire mission on purpose.

They had ordered him to lead the patrol after questioning his judgment about leading last night's patrol.

They knew where he was. They knew right where the patrol was. They were trying to kill him.

"Give me the radio, Cushion," the Lieutenant whispered. "Put it on the company net."

Whoopie Cushion handed him the receiver.

"Rattail Six, this is Rattail Two, over."

"This is Six. Where is my fire, over."

"Six, this is Two. You're calling in fire on my patrol, over."

"What?"

"Six, you're calling in fire on my patrol. Right on top of us, over."

"I couldn't be, over."

"Six, you plotted them on the wrong map. Check it yourself, over."

"Wait one," said Rattail Six.

The Lieutenant tapped the map under his poncho in the dark, waiting.

"Two, this is Six. Fire mission stands, over."

"Six, this is Two. We're out here about halfway between Firebase Zulu-Foxtrot and you, Six. The fire mission you've called in will place fire right on top of me. Please confirm, over."

"Roger, Two. I've got you now. Wait one. I'm going to relay the situation to Saltlick Six and get back to you. Six out."

"Two out."

"What's up, Eltee?" Repatch stuck his face under the poncho. His face was stained with sweat. He looked as though somebody had painted white streaks down his brown cheeks.

They are calling in fire on our asses, Repatch."

"Do they know that, sir?"

"They are fucking *supposed* to know, Repatch. But sometimes I wonder if they could stand in the middle of a goddamned PX parking lot and find their correct position. Jesus. What a trip."

"Whatchew gonna do, Eltee?"

"I'll tell you what I'm *not* going to do. I'm not going to let them call in fire on this goddamned patrol, that's what."

The radio crackled and the Lieutenant picked up.

"Rattail Two," said the Lieutenant.

"Rattail Two, this is Saltlick Six. Your Six tells me you have refused an order for a fire mission. Over."

It was Lieutenant Colonel Halleck.

Fucking perfect. This is all I need.

"Saltlick Six, this is Rattail Two. Negative. I have not refused an order for a fire mission."

"Then where is my fire on target, dammit?"

"Saltlick Six, this is Rattail Two. I explained it to Rattail Six. If my guns fire that mission, every round will go right on top of me."

"You don't know what the hell you're talking about, Rattail Two. You've got order for a fire mission. Order your men to shoot the fire mission or I'll have your ass."

"No, sir."

"What!"

"Saltlick Six, I said negative. I will not call in fire on this position, over."

"I gave you an order, Rattail Two. Are you telling me that you are disobeying my order?"

"Saltlick Six, I am telling you I will not fire a mission on this position, and the coordinates you gave me will put fire right on top of me, over."

"Rattail Two, this is Saltlick Six. Who is in command of this battalion? You or me?"

"You are, Six."

"Then give me my goddamn fire mission or I'll come down there and set the sights and fire the guns myself."

The Lieutenant tilted his head back against the wet ground.

This fucking war is so fucked up and these fucking so-called commanders are so fucking fucked up I always fucking knew it would fucking come to this. I fucking knew it.

"Saltlick Six, this is Rattail Two. Negative. Over."

"You give me that goddamn fire, Rattail Two, or I'm coming down there and I'll personally have your ass, and I'll personally fire those guns, you hear me? Over."

"Then come on down, Six. Because that's the only way you're going to get that fire mission out of my guns. Rattail Two out."

"Jesus, Eltee. You're wadin' in some deep shit tonight. That's all I got to say." Repatch smiled a thin, nervous smile.

"Repatch, I've never seen bullshit this deep in my life. Get me Davis, Cushion."

Cushion switched frequencies and raised Sergeant Davis on the radio.

"Here you go, Eltee," said Cushion, handing him the mike.

"What's going on back there?" the Lieutenant asked.

"They got some fire on them, but it ain't much, Eltee. 'Tween us and the Battalion, 'bout a squad raisin' hell. They got 'em a 60 and a rattletrap machine gun, but they be gone in a minute. You watch."

"How close are they to you, over?"

"Maybe a klik or two. They be gone pretty quick, Eltee."

"So they're not right on top of Battalion?"

"Negative. They five, maybe six hundred yards due north of Battalion, and they be settin' up and shootin', then movin' a hundred yards, settin' up and shootin' again. Typical VC shit, Eltee. Ain't much."

"Goofball shit out there, Eltee," said Repatch, slowly and distinctly.

"Repatch, you're sure we're where we were last night?" the Lieutenant asked. He had switched off his penlight, and they were lying next to each other on the ground.

"Roger that, Eltee. I got one end of the 'bush at that crook in that little creek and the other end at the big tree on top of that little knoll. You know the tree. The one with all them vines hangin' down. Same creek, same tree. Look on the map. You'll see where we're at clear as day."

The Lieutenant took a quick look at the map. There was the turn in the creek, and there was the knoll. Repatch was right. The patrol was set up precisely where it had been the night before. *Precisely.* If they had fired that mission, he wouldn't be talking to Repatch right now, because Repatch and every one of the men on that patrol would be dead.

"Okay, Repatch," the Lieutenant whispered. "Cushion, give me Davis."

Cushion handed him the mike and Davis came on.

"What you want me to do, Eltee?"

"Sit tight. We're coming in at first light. Don't do anything until I get back there. Let me know when the shooting stops."

"It's stopped right now, Eltee. They gonna move one more time and drop two, three more rounds down that little 60, and they be finished with their little VC patrol."

"Roger. Out."

The Lieutenant handed the receiver back to Cushion. He crawled over to his depression in the ground and stretched out on his back, waiting.

The radio crackled and Cushion whispered:

"Eltee! Eltee! It's Captain Gardner!"

The Lieutenant crawled back over to the radio and took the receiver.

"Rattail Two," he said resignedly.

"Two, Six. Get your men out of there right now, over."

"Six, Two. Come again, over."

"Two, get your men out of that ambush position. Move them! Move them now!"

"Six, can I ask what's going on? Over."

"Saltlick Six is calling in fire from Div Arty. They're going to put 155 fire on top of your ambush patrol. Do it now! Move them!"

"Two out."

The Lieutenant grabbed Repatch.

"Let's go," he said.

"Righto, Eltee."

"Move. Get them up and let's move."

"Rodge. How far?"

"As far as we can as fast as we can. Saltlick Six is calling in 155s on our position."

"We're gone."

The Lieutenant handed the mike to Cushion and the patrol was up and moving. He followed Repatch into the dark. His head was pouring sweat into his eyes and he rubbed his eyes and they teared up and tears joined the sweat and his chin dripped dirt-black droplets of sweat on his fatigue shirt and the stain spread from his chest across his stomach.

Out of the blackness the distant

BOOOOM . . .

BOOOOM . . .

BOOOOM . . .

BOOOOM . . .

The 155 rounds would be on target in seconds and they were notoriously accurate if fed the right numbers and they had the numbers of the patrol's ambush location *exact*.

They kept moving through the black jungle and they waited.

The explosions, when they came, were deafening. Only a few hundred feet away, they sounded like they were hitting on the other side of that tree. One, two, three, four . . . they hit.

They crouched and waited.

BOOOOM . . .

BOOOOM . . .

BOOOOM . . .

BOOOOM . . .

Somewhere in the distance, four GIs blindly pulled four lanyards and four more rounds sped to their target between a creek and a low knoll in Laos.

It couldn't have been true, but the second four rounds sounded louder than the first group. The Lieutenant covered his ears and tried to forget the sound they made, but he knew he would never forget that sound.

Never.

The radio crackled.

"Fuckin'-A, Eltee, they didn't waste no time. You okay out there?"

It was Sergeant Davis.

The Lieutenant grabbed the receiver from Cushion.

"We're okay. We're okay."

"Rodge, Eltee. Rodge on the okay. Where are you?"

"We ran down a little creek. We're under the creek bank. Jesus fucking Christ, Sarge, they were on target. They had us pinpointed for sure."

"Jeez, Eltee."

"We're all right," said the Lieutenant, more to assure himself than to ask the question.

"Rodge, Eltee."

"Okay, we're going to lay up where we are until first light and come on in. I'm so glad . . ." His voice trailed off and he lowered the mike from his lips and he dropped his chin to his chest.

"Yeah, we see you in a short-short, Eltee. Out."

The Lieutenant sat in the mud along the creek bank for a moment and then slowly roused himself and crawled along the creekbed, checking the men. They were all right.

It was quiet out there now. Repatch and Cushion and Lucky Lemon and Mallick and Moonface and Woodley were tucked up against the muddy bank of their godforsaken little creek in Laos and all was right with the world.

Pop. Pop. Pop. Three more 60mm rounds took flight.

The VC were letting them know that all the 155 rounds in the world weren't going to dislodge them from their holes, from their woods, from their harassing patrols, from their land, from their night . . .

He heard some VC small-arms fire and he heard answering fire from the Battalion and . . .

Then he heard nothing.

It was over. The little war in Laos had lasted about forty-five minutes, and now it was part of the larger history of the war, which was a history of a war made up of thousands of little wars just like the one tonight, a half-dozen little men in black uniforms scurrying around in the dark shooting at a whole bunch of men in green uniforms dug deep into their bunkers shooting back.

Repatch touched his shoulder.

"Davis said they stopped shootin' and they movin' toward the platoon perimeter, sir. He wants to know if you want him to pop some rounds on 'em if they come any closer."

"Tell him to do whatever seems right. Otherwise, tell him to hunker down and sit tight. It'll be light in another couple of hours and we'll be back in time for breakfast."

"Rodge, Eltee."

Repatch crawled back down the creekbed, and the Lieutenant could hear him talking to Sergeant Davis on the radio. Then he reappeared next to the Lieutenant and stood crouched there for a while. Neither man said anything. Repatch drew little circles in the mud with the toe of his boot. The Lieutenant flapped his arms a few times, trying to dry out his fatigue shirt.

"What time you figure they'll be comin' for you, sir?"

"After breakfast sometime."

"They'll be comin' to take you away, won't they, sir?"

"Yeah, Repatch."

"I heard the whole thing, sir. You refused an order from the battalion commander, didn't you, sir?"

"Yeah, I did."

"You refused to put fire on our position, didn't you, sir?"

"Yeah. That's pretty much it."

"Are you gonna want to take anything with you, sir?"

"I don't know. I don't guess so."

"What about those maps, sir? You want me to keep them for you? I can stash them for you, sir. You know. Where nobody's gonna find 'em."

"Sure, Repatch. When we get back, stash them."

Repatch looked over at the Lieutenant. He was staring, just staring into the darkness on the other side of the creek. Repatch had never seen him just sit there and stare like that before.

"Sir, if you'd a fired that mission, them guns woulda rained shit on our ass, right?"

"Yeah."

"So you was right, huh, sir?"

"For what it's worth, yeah. I was right."

"That's all I wanted to know, sir."

The Lieutenant stood there, silent, impassive.

"Will you write to us when you get where you're goin'?" Repatch asked.

"Yeah."

"Sir?"

"Yeah."

"You think the battalion CO is gonna come after you tonight, like he said? And put that fire down himself?"

The Lieutenant turned to look at Repatch. He was grinning, and the sweat streaks on his face made him look like a monkey.

"I don't think we have to worry about that, Repatch. I don't think he could get a chopper at this hour."

"Good," said Repatch. "I'll give Davis and them a ring-a-ling and tell 'em to relax. They was afraid the dude would do what he said, and come on down and shoot them guns himself. They wasn't sure you could stop him."

"I'll start worrying about Halleck in the morning, Dirtball, when the sun comes up. That's when colonels go to war, Repatch."

"When the sun comes up. Rodge, Eltee," said Repatch. "I'll remember that one. I got to tell that one to Davis. He'll fuckin' *love* that one, Eltee."

16

T
he Sergeant Major had been up for two hours when the Colonel came groggily awake and found him on the balcony, yelling at some poor soul on the phone.

"Did I ask you how long it was gonna take, dammit? Then don't start in with your damn complaints to me about how long it's gonna take. Do you think I care about your problems? What do you think God put me in this man's Army for? To wake up every morning wondering what in hell is going wrong for *you* today? What do you think I am? Your personal damn complaint box?"

The Sergeant Major saw the Colonel in the balcony door and stood up. He rolled his eyes and held up his index finger and mouthed, "One moment, sir," and held the phone away from his mouth and yelled:

"You get that shit over here to me by ten hundred hours or I'm going to have your ass pushing a broom around the perimeter of a listening post somewhere outside Dak To, dammit!" He slammed the phone down and turned around.

"Do you want breakfast, sir?" he asked, smiling as if nothing had happened.

"Sure, Sarenmajor." The Colonel was still in his pajamas, a baggy cotton costume the same shade of gray he had insisted his pajamas be all his life, the shade of gray they issued to you at West Point.

"Yes, sir, coming right up. I located the breakfast girl about an hour ago and she's properly schooled, sir."

He picked up the phone and barked something in Vietnamese.

"She'll be up in a minute, sir. Why don't you get yourself a shower, and by the time you're through, breakfast will be here."

The Colonel stood in the balcony door for a moment, a blank look on his face. His large dark eyes were staring across the low rooftops of Saigon into the sunrise, which was typically splendid. The Sergeant Major stood there watching him, then coughed and moved a foot to his right, to break the Colonel's trance.

"Sorry, Top, I guess I lost myself in my thoughts there for a minute."

"Yes, sir. I got the same problem. Too many thoughts and not enough time to think 'em." He chuckled and looked in the direction the Colonel was looking.

"You can't hardly believe where you are when you see a sunrise like they got themselves over here in Vietnam every morning, huh, sir?"

"No, you sure can't, Top. You sure can't." The Colonel turned and headed for the bathroom.

"Breakfast will be ready for you when you are, sir," said the Sergeant Major.

"Righto," said the Colonel.

The Sergeant Major sat back down on his wicker chair on the balcony and dialed the phone.

"Give me MACV headquarters," he barked into the receiver. He waited an instant and barked again:

"Not Mr. MacVee, dammit! MACV headquarters! United States Army, dammit!"

He lit a long cigar while he waited for the call to go through. He was working on a pretty good ash by the time the call went through and someone answered.

"Sergeant Major Bennett here. I'd like a patch through to II Corps HQ at Pleiku, please."

"One moment, Sergeant Major," said a woman's voice. The Sergeant Major puffed on his cigar. Five years of war had come to this: WACs answering the phone at MACV. What in God's name could be next? Dependent housing at the base camps? Day-care centers on the firebases?

The phone crackled and spat static in his ear and a voice said: "II Corps, sir." Very businesslike. Very spec-4.

"This is Sergeant Major Bennett down in Saigon. Who am I speaking to, please?"

"Spec-4 Glaxon, sir," said the voice.

"Glaxon, can you put me through to Sergeant Major Perkins over at the 25th Infantry Division HQ?"

"One moment, Sergeant Major," said the Spec-4.

The phone crackled and spit once or twice as the regular telephone line was patched down to a field phone land-line. He heard the distinctive whir of the field phone ringing.

The voice answering the phone was low and sounded very, very far away, an effect of the patch-through to the direct-current field phone, the Sergeant Major knew.

"Twenty-fifth," said the voice, with no further elaboration.

"Give me Sergeant Major Perkins," commanded Sergeant Major Bennett. He pulled the cigar out of the corner of his mouth and blew smoke at the sunrise. Amazing. At least the WACs hadn't penetrated the division headquarters level out there in the field.

"Wait one," said the voice.

The Sergeant Major puffed contentedly on his cigar. That was the thing about a war. You could get up in the morning and have yourself a stogie and a cup of coffee to get your heart started and there wasn't a damn thing anyone could or would say about it, he thought. No sirree bob. Not in this man's war, anyway.

"Sarenmajor Perkins," growled a voice.

"Slim? It's Ted Bennett. How're they hangin'?"

"Teddy? Damn. Somebody told me you lassoed yourself a club at Cam Ranh Bay. That so?"

"You bet, Slim. I got both the NCO clubs up there. You've got to come down for a visit. I'll treat you to an Omaha steak, right off the CO's plane."

"Shit, I'll take your ass up on that one, Teddy. When can I come down?"

"Not for a while, Slim. I'm . . . I'm . . . off duty for a while, you know what I mean?"

"Sure. Where you at?"

"Saigon for a while."

"Must be nice to be a rich man, Teddy. I always knowed you was going to make out, if they let you keep your stripes long enough."

"I want a little loose information, Slim my good buddy, a little dip into that vat of Texas bear grease that keeps the gears turnin'."

"What can I do you for?"

"I need to know what happened to the weapons platoon out there in the Triple Deuce."

"You ain't asking for much, are you, Teddy? You just want to know about the hottest damn potato I've had my hands on in all my days in this man's Army."

"I need to know, Slim. I do."

"What's up, Teddy?"

"The kid that commanded the platoon? Blue? He's my old battalion commander's son. I owe one here, Slim. A *big* one. The old man pulled me out of a crack deep as the Grand Canyon. I owe my life to him, Slim. I'd never have my clubs right now, wasn't for what he done for me."

There was a long pause punctuated by soft bursts of static as Perkins chewed over what he'd been fed. Finally he cleared his throat and mumbled something and cleared his throat again.

"What'd you say, Slim?" asked the Sergeant Major.

"They're gonna boil that kid alive," said Sergeant Major Perkins.

"I've figured out that much."

"I mean, I don't know what that kid done, or who's behind them charges they filed on him, but I been in the Army thirty-two years and I never seen anything like it. *Never.*"

"What happened to his platoon?"

"Disappeared."

"Reassigned?"

"Disappeared."

"What do you mean, *disappeared?*"

"They'll never find those poor fuckers. They burned their 201s and shit-canned their pay records. It'll take somebody six months of digging in them record warehouses in St. Louis and Indianapolis to even begin to get a handle on where they sent those guys, how they got 'em there, anything else about 'em. They'll be civilians by the time anybody gets to them. It'll be way too late for the kid by then."

"Christ," muttered the Sergeant Major.

"You said it, Teddy."

"You're sure every piece of paper is gone on that platoon, Slim?"

"Hey. You know who you're talking to, Teddy. I know my shit when it comes to my unit, and *this* shit I know forwards and backwards."

"They put you in the middle of it?"

"I didn't see nothing, Teddy, but I had to sign off on the initial release."

"I get you."

"I got a number for you, Teddy."

"What's that?"

"Zero."

"What'd you say?"

"I said zero. They left nothin' behind on this one, friend. Not a single footprint in the dust. They done scorched the earth this time. Nobody will ever prove anything. It was done black, Teddy. They were screaming national security and all kind of shit like that and pulling stuff I've never seen pulled before and I hope I never see pulled again."

"I'm beginning to get your drift, Slim."

"Anything else you want to know?"

"Who was the first sergeant over there at the Triple Deuce?"

"Dude by the name of Connors, Keyson Connors."

"Never heard of him."

"Me neither. He was a ghost when he got here and he's a ghost now he's gone."

"He's out of there?"

"Him and every other son of a bitch that ever saw a piece of paper on the weapons platoon in the Triple Deuce. I'm telling you, Teddy. They ran a damn vacuum cleaner through here and sucked up every scrap of shit they could find. There may as well have not been a weapons platoon over there in the Triple Deuce. They did everything to that poor little platoon but take its tracks."

"The tracks are still there?"

"Yeah, same tracks. That was the one thing I noticed. Everybody gone, all paperwork burned, every swingin' dick disappeared, even their weapons sent south, but they left them tracks behind bigger than shit."

The Sergeant Major thought over what his friend had said, then he blew cigar smoke into the morning air and said:

"Hey, Slim. Let me give you a call when I get back to the Club. I'll send a bird for you and we can get stinkin' and eat some steak and chase some skirt, you hear?"

"You got your own bird?"

"Two of 'em."

"Sign my ass up," said Sergeant Major Perkins.

"Done," said Sergeant Major Bennett. "And thanks, pal. I'll treat you good, don't you worry."

"I got my bags packed, Teddy. Anything to get my ass outta this chickenshit outfit."

"I'll call you," said the Sergeant Major. He hung up the phone and turned to find the Colonel standing in the balcony door dressed in Levi's and a white knit shirt and sneakers. He didn't look like a man forty-five years old. Without the gray hair at his temples and the deep squint lines along either eye, he could have passed for a young company commander rather than a man who'd already had his own Battalion.

"What have you got, Top?"

"Our first break, sir." The Sergeant Major grinned and pointed his cigar behind the Colonel. Breakfast was waiting for them on a table by the balcony doors.

"They left them tracks behind at the Triple Deuce, sir. I talked to the top sergeant up at 25th Infantry Division, an old buddy of mine from Benning, name of Slim Perkins, and he told me they disappeared everything on that platoon but them tracks. Burned 201s and pay records, reassigned everybody that ever set eyes on that platoon, even the first sergeant, and he said the guys in the platoon ... nobody'll ever find them. They're smoke, sir. But not them tracks. They're still up there, big as life."

"And you figure the weapons platoon 113s have got something to tell us?"

"Sir, did you ever know a troop that didn't stash his stuff in every nook and cranny available to him? Those tracks are a damn library of the last few years in their lives, sir. I know it. I can *feel* it."

"Let's eat, Sarenmajor. That's good news. I'm sure you're right."

"What time you got to meet the lawyer, sir?"

"Noon. It's right near here, over at the Continental. He didn't want me coming to his office, and I must say I agree with him. I'd just as soon continue my low profile here in Saigon."

"I know what you mean, sir. We're gonna get ourselves ready for them. I'm gonna bleed them tracks dry of poop, sir. They're going to talk to me in my language, and I don't mean French, sir."

"When are you going, Sarenmajor?" said the Colonel, a forkful of eggs poised before his lips.

"After we go to see the lawyer, sir. I ought to be back sometime this evening."

"Righto," said the Colonel.

Captain Terrence W. Morriss was waiting for them in the lobby of the Continental Hotel, but they didn't see him when they walked in. He was the guy sitting on the wicker sofa reading the morning edition of *Stars and Stripes* with a St. Louis Cardinals cap tilted jauntily on the back of his head. He was dressed almost exactly like the Colonel—a pair of old Levi's and a tennis shirt with HARVARD on the pocket and a pair of old sneakers—but he didn't wear the outfit with quite the aplomb of the older man. When he stood up, an enormous pot belly preceded him across the room, and the tennis shirt, while doing its best to contain the belly, didn't quite make it.

"Sergeant Major! Over here!" Captain Morriss called as the two men headed through the lobby toward the desk.

The Sergeant Major whispered something to the Colonel and

they walked over to Morriss's corner of the lobby, by the windows overlooking the garden.

"I'm Captain Morriss, Lieutenant Blue's lawyer," he said in a low voice, looking over the shoulders of the Sergeant Major and the Colonel.

"I'm Matt's father," said the Colonel. "This is Sergeant Major Bennett."

"Teddy, sir."

"Right. We spoke on the phone. Nice to meet you."

The three men sat down.

"I've got some good news, but I'm afraid I've got some bad news as well," said Captain Morriss.

"Shoot," said the Colonel. "Let's have it."

"They released Lieutenant Blue to my custody last night—" Morriss began.

"They released him?" the Colonel said, leaning forward in his chair. "Last night? What the hell happened? They wouldn't even tell me where he was yesterday. The Sergeant Major told me you were talking about a writ of habeas corpus."

"Yes, sir, I was. I was as surprised as you are at this turn of events. Somebody pretty high up must have issued the order, because they tracked me down at a bar across the street at about ten o'clock and told me to take delivery of the prisoner. They had everybody hopping. The prosecutor was pulled out of a card game and—"

"Yes. Yes. But where is he?" the Colonel asked.

"I'm afraid that's the bad news, sir," said Morriss. "I can't find him."

"You . . . you . . . you . . . can't *find* him? What do you mean, Captain?"

"I checked him into the BOQ with me last night around midnight, but when I got up this morning and looked in on him, he was gone. His bed hadn't been slept in, either. He must have taken off sometime last night."

"Or someone took him off," said the Sergeant Major, extracting a fresh cigar from his shirt pocket and beginning the elaborate process of getting it going.

"What do you mean by that?" Morriss asked.

"I just got off the phone with a buddy of mine up in the 25th," the Sergeant Major said, striking a match on the arm of his chair.

"He said they disappeared the whole weapons platoon. *Poof.* One day they were there, next day they were gone. Maybe somebody decided to disappear the Lieutenant."

The Colonel coughed to clear his throat.

"Sorry, sir, I didn't mean to—"

"That's okay, Sarenmajor," said the Colonel. "We've got to consider all the possibilities, and from the looks of things, that is certainly one of them."

"I feel like a damn fool coming over here this morning without your son, sir, when I had him in my room only last night. I guess I should have made him sleep on the sofa in the next room. I'm . . . I'm sorry, sir. I feel like such a damn fool . . ."

"Knock it off, Captain," said the Colonel. "It's not your fault. If I know that boy, and I think I know him pretty damn well, he'll show up with some kind of elaborate excuse this morning. Maybe you'd better call the BOQ and have them give us a call if he comes in."

"Do you want me to notify the MPs, sir?"

"No! No MPs . . . sir," said the Sergeant Major out of the corner of his mouth, teeth fixed firmly around the freshly shorn end of his cigar. "Last thing we need is a bunch of damn shake-'n'-bake rinky-dink soldier boys playing cop, chasing around Saigon, stirrin' things up."

"I agree, Top," said the Colonel. "That boy of mine can take care of himself. He'll turn up."

"I'm going to call the BOQ," said Captain Morriss. He walked over to the front desk and asked for a phone.

Just then, the Lieutenant and Cathy Joice came down the stairs behind him and headed for the front door. He had a hand on the door when the Colonel called to him.

"Matt," said the Colonel.

The Lieutenant wheeled around, eyes wide and bloodshot, every muscle in his body tightened, on edge. He was holding Cathy with one hand, the other poised on the door, ready to bolt. He did not look like the boy his father had put on a plane the morning he left for Vietnam.

"Over here," said his father.

The Lieutenant swiveled to his left and saw his father. His shoulders dropped and he exhaled a deep breath and took Cathy by the hand and led her to the corner of the lobby.

"Jesus, Dad . . ." He walked into his father's embrace and wrapped his arms around him and rested his head on his father's shoulder.

The older man patted his back and whispered his name.

The Lieutenant raised his head and broke the embrace and reached for Cathy's hand.

"Dad, this is Cathy Joice, she's . . . she's . . . a friend, Dad. You can trust her."

The Colonel took her hand and trained his wide eyes on her.

The Sergeant Major cleared his throat.

"Matt, this is Sarenmajor Bennett. He's . . ."

"I know who he is, Dad. He was with you down in the Delta. Nice to meet you." He shook hands with the Sergeant Major.

"Same here, sir."

The Colonel wrapped his arm around the Lieutenant and led him to the sofa.

"Sit down," he said. "We've got some talking to do."

Captain Morriss walked up as the three men and Cathy Joice sat down.

"Sir . . . he's here! I mean, you're here!"

"Hi, Captain," said the Lieutenant. "Sorry if I gave you a scare. I just had to talk to somebody, and you said—"

"I know what I said," Captain Morriss interrupted. "As long as you're okay, I don't care what you told her."

"I didn't tell her anything," said the Lieutenant.

"He didn't, Terry," said Cathy Joice.

"Whatever."

"Matt," said his father. "Captain Morriss—"

"Terry, sir," said the lawyer.

"Okay, Terry. He says you haven't told him much. We need to know what happened. You've got to tell us everything that happened in the last few weeks preceding your arrest. I can't believe that the officers in your Battalion are so venal and corrupt that they would bring charges against you for no reason.

Something must have happened, Matt. Something must have gone wrong. We've got to know what put this nightmare in motion."

"You've got to be kidding me, right, Dad?" the Lieutenant said. "You're sitting here telling me that you believe the damn *Army* on this? You think I did something wrong?"

"Son, all I know is I've never seen anything like this happen in the Army I grew up in, the Army I've served proudly for more than twenty years."

"Well, this is a different Army, Dad. You wouldn't believe the crap that's going on over here, the way they're fighting this so-called war. It's a shame, Dad. A real shame. Every day, lives are wasted on both sides. And for what? So we can save our honor, some shit like that? So politicians back home won't have to admit that we got into this war for all the wrong reasons, and we're losing this war for all the right reasons. Come on, Dad. Tell me you don't still believe what we're doing over here is right."

"Son, I understand what you're saying, and I know that a lot has happened here in Vietnam that shouldn't happen anywhere, to anybody. But it's the *Army,* son. You're talking about our *Army.* You're talking about the Army in which Army both of your grandfathers served honorably for decades. You're talking about the Army to which I have dedicated my entire life. Don't ask me to believe that the Army has disintegrated to such an extent that this whole business is just wrong."

"That's what I'm asking you to do, Dad. Listen. You've got a choice. Either you accept what I say and you believe in my innocence right here, right now, right from the start . . . or you just continue believing in your almighty Army, in this stupid fucking war. You can't have it both ways, Dad. If you are going to fight me on this, if you're going to try to go down the line with your belief in the Army and the war, you're going to lose me. I'm gone. Because this is a dirty, corrupt little war, and these are dirty, corrupt little charges that have been brought against me by dirty, corrupt little men. This isn't World War II, Dad. God knows. It isn't even Korea. This is fucking Vietnam. This is a piece of shit."

The Colonel sat there for a moment, staring at his son.

The Sergeant Major took the cigar out of his mouth and pulled a notebook out of his satchel.

"Sir, I'm afraid the boy is right. They stuck it to you down in the Delta, when all you was tryin' to do was your job. Now they stuck it to your son. You don't have no choice, sir. It's us against them, same as it was in the Delta. Only thing we got goin' for us is stickin' together."

"I know, Top. I know." The Colonel turned to his son, the Lieutenant. Tears welled up in his eyes as he spoke.

"It makes me so goddamned sad to see this happen to you, son. I just wish you could have grown old in the Army, loving the Army the way I have loved the Army, the way your grandpa loved the Army. That's all I ever wished for you, son. I just wanted you to find your home in the Army the way I did. That's all."

The Lieutenant hugged his father hard, for a long moment, then pulled away.

"I love the Army, Dad, in my own way, in this way: I love my men. I love my platoon. I love being a platoon leader. But they won't let me be the kind of platoon leader you brought me up to be. If I had just gone along and done what I was told, seven men would be dead right now. I couldn't do that, Dad. You wouldn't have wanted me to. Neither would Grandpa. Don't you know I asked myself those questions a thousand times . . . 'What would Dad do? What would Grandpa do?' Don't you know I did what I knew you'd have wanted me to do? If doing my job the way I was brought up to do it means that you get court-martialed here in Vietnam, then fuck it. Let them court-martial me. I did the right thing. I'm proud of what I did. That court-martial is my Silver Star."

"Then tell us what happened, son. I believe you. Tell us." His father sat back and listened.

With four sets of attentive eyes around him, the Lieutenant began his story with the arrival of Lieutenant Colonel Halleck in the Battalion. He was interrupted several times by Captain Morriss, who wanted details about orders he was given and what he did or didn't do to carry them out.

An hour passed before the Lieutenant started describing the incursion into Laos. His father's interest increased measurably when he heard his son describe how his platoon had gone inside the Laotian border and off the operations order map.

"You're sure of your location, son?" he asked. "Absolutely sure?"

"You taught me how to read a map, Dad. Hell, I was first in my class at West Point in map-reading. I know *exactly* where we were. I don't know why they didn't indicate in the ops order that we were going over the border. I know we're not supposed to run operations into Laos, but everyone knows that . . . that it's done. It wouldn't have been a big deal if they said we were sweeping a ways inside Laos, going after one of those base camps over there. It's happened before. It'll happen again. But it became a very big deal—in my eyes, anyway—when I discovered that nobody wanted to admit we were inside Laos."

"You're not saying that this whole thing is a cover-up of an incursion into Laos, are you, son?" the Colonel asked.

"No, I'm not. But I *am* saying that the charges against me are an attempt to cover up something else."

"What's that?" Captain Morriss asked.

"I don't know."

"What do you mean, you don't know?" The Sergeant Major and the Colonel exclaimed nearly together.

"I saw a plane being loaded with some kind of burlap bales one night on a patrol in Laos."

"What kind of plane?" Captain Morriss had his pen and notepad out, and he was scribbling away.

"A DC-3."

"Did it have any markings indicating who it belonged to?"

"None."

"What were they loading into the plane?"

"I don't know, for sure."

"What does any of this have to do with your being charged with desertion in the face of the enemy?" asked the Colonel, looking grim.

"Well, if all I saw was a plane being loaded in the middle of the jungle in Laos, it wouldn't have much to do with anything. But it was the middle of the night, and the men doing the loading were Americans, and they were armed, and when I called out to them, they fired on my patrol and they killed one of my men, Corporal

Lester G. Strosher. It was when I handed in my after-action report, my report of casualty due to friendly fire telling how Strosher got killed, that's when all hell broke loose."

The faces around him looked wan and drawn. Even the face of Captain Morriss, a fleshy piece of work if there ever was one, had lost a pound or two. Nobody said anything for one minute, two minutes. Then the Sergeant Major pulled the cigar out of his mouth and spoke.

"Lieutenant Blue, what you're telling us is that you lost a man in a firefight with a bunch of American soldiers?"

"I don't know if they were soldiers, Sarenmajor," said the Lieutenant. "They were dressed in Levi's and camouflage T-shirts and boots, and they were carrying Kalashnikovs."

"Then how do you know they were Americans?"

"Strosher was hit by three rounds from a Kalashnikov. But the man firing it was an American. I know he was. I could see his face."

"You are absolutely certain of that?" Captain Morriss studied the Lieutenant's face for any signs of uncertainty. He found none.

"Absolutely."

"How can you be so sure?" Captain Morriss asked.

"The grass strip the DC-3 was sitting on was lit with cans of diesel down both sides of the strip, so there was enough light to see their faces. We were only a hundred feet away, and before I called out to the men loading the plane, I had a close look at them and at the men guarding the plane through my binoculars. They were Americans, sir. They weren't Vietnamese, and they weren't Russians, and they weren't Chinese. They were Americans."

"Damn." The Sergeant Major took the cigar out of his mouth and studied its ash. "I knew there was some shit going on inside this thing. I *knew* it. I fucking *knew* it. Sorry, ma'am."

The Sergeant Major nodded in the direction of Cathy Joice.

"Forget it," she said.

The Colonel pulled a toothpick from his pocket and started sucking on it.

Captain Morriss scribbled madly in his notebook.

Cathy Joice looked at the Lieutenant quizzically.

"Tell us more about what happened when you handed in your, uh, report," she said.

The Lieutenant described the meeting with Lieutenant Colonel Halleck, the battalion commander, and Colonel Testor, the brigade commander, in the bunker at the battalion base camp. When he was finished, he sat back on the wicker sofa and said:

"Whew. I haven't even thought about that since it happened. I guess your mind has a way of shutting stuff out, doesn't it? Weird."

"If you're lucky, it does," said his father.

"Tell me something, Matt," said Captain Morriss. "When it became clear to you that this after-action report of yours was going to cause you big trouble, why didn't you just knuckle under and do what they said? Why didn't you just change the report and forget about it?"

"That would have been lying," said the Lieutenant, looking directly at Morriss. "And worse, it would have been denying that Strosher died the way he died. He was shot by an American, goddammit! I told the Colonel . . . I told both of them. I've seen some strange shit in this war, and I've had some strange shit happen to me and to my men. But nothing prepared me for having one of my men killed by another American in cold blood. Strosher was a good troop, and goddamn if I'm going to have someone tell me to write Strosher off and forget him. Goddamn if I'm going to do that, no matter what Halleck and Testor say, no matter what anyone says. If telling the truth about how Strosher got shot means that I'm going to take a lot of heat, then fuck it. I'll take the heat. Strosher took heat for me when he was alive. And he'd do the same for me if he was in my place. You taught me that, Dad. That's what a platoon is. . . was. You stick together no matter what. I know he would do the same for me. I know it."

Nobody looked at him and nobody said anything for a moment, and then Captain Morriss spoke up.

"I hope you understand I wasn't advocating that you change the report. I simply had to ask the question, because if this becomes an element in our defense, which I'm sure it will, you are certain to be asked the same question somewhere along the line, and I have to know the answers to every question you might be asked, before they ask you."

"I understand, sir," said the Lieutenant.

"Cut the 'sir' crap," said Captain Morriss.

"Okay."

"I've got a question," said the Colonel, looking very grave. "I want to know what we're going to do with this information. It seems to me that unless we can tie this business down so there is no question whatsoever of the truth of what Matt says, then we're right back where we started. It's going to be Matt's word against the word of Colonel Testor or Lieutenant Colonel Halleck, and we all know how courts-martial tend to consider the word of the accused. Very, very skeptically. The natural tendency of any officer in the Army is to take the dimmest of views of any fellow officer accused of a crime. If Matt's going to beat this thing, we're going to have to go in there with an airtight defense. And I mean *airtight*."

"You've got a very good point, sir," said Captain Morriss. "I'm glad to see that someone has the same ideas I have about Army courts-martial."

"Well, I've sat on a few of them in my day," said the Colonel, "and I've convened a few. And I wouldn't describe either experience as a completely pleasant one."

"Exactly my point, sir," said the lawyer. "Now. Since they have apparently 'disappeared' the Lieutenant's platoon, in the marvelous word of the Sergeant Major here, we don't have witness one who can attest to the facts surrounding this incident on the patrol as the Lieutenant knows them."

"We've got one witness," said the Lieutenant. Every eye turned to him.

"Repatch."

"Who is Repatch?" Captain Morriss asked.

"One of the guys in my platoon. He walked point the night the patrol ran into the DC-3."

"But the Sarenmajor says they reassigned every man in your platoon, and he's been told they even went so far as to destroy their personnel records," said the Colonel.

"Well, they missed one, Dad. I saw Repatch last night . . . er . . . this morning. He's right here in Saigon."

"Where is he now?"

"I don't know."

"You don't know?"

"Nope."

"How can you not know the whereabouts of someone as important to you as this man Repatch is?" asked his father.

"He comes and goes," said the Lieutenant. "He's kind of a ghost."

"I'll say he is," said Captain Morriss. "I have a copy of your platoon roster I was able to get from MACV before they deep-sixed your records. His name is nowhere on the list."

"It wouldn't be," said the Lieutenant. "Repatch isn't his real name. His real name is Fish."

"There's a Fish, all right," said Morriss.

"That's him."

"A Fish who rotated home over a month ago, according to MACV records."

"What? Let me see that."

The Lieutenant studied the platoon roster Morriss handed him.

"You're right. He's supposed to be gone. But he's here. I saw him last night. Cathy saw him."

"When was the last time you had a look at a company morning report, son?" the Colonel asked.

"I don't think I've seen a morning report since I've been over here."

"How did you keep track of your platoon?"

"In my pocket notebook, the way they taught us at Benning."

"So you've never seen an *official* roster for your platoon."

"Never."

"That must account for the discrepancy. The situation with personnel over here is rather fluid. What I'm saying is, anything can happen in a war, especially *this* war. About this war, I'd believe anything."

"Dad, this guy Repatch, you'd believe almost anything when it came to him, and you would too, if you saw him. They could have missed him. Hell, *I* missed him half the time. He lived in his own little world. All he wanted to do was walk point, which I was only too happy to have him do. He was one of those guys, the way to get the best out of him was to let him be."

"What's he doing in Saigon, son?"

The Lieutenant chuckled, then looked up, embarrassed. This wasn't the time or the place to be laughing.

"I don't know. He showed up last night, right when we needed him. We were in a kind of sticky situation down in South Saigon when out of nowhere here's Repatch and he extracts us from the trouble we were in and as quick as he was there, he was gone."

"How the hell did he get from the 25th Division down here?" asked the Sergeant Major, who had evidently recognized in Repatch a type he knew only too well.

"He said he walked out of the battalion logger and caught a ride from Dak To."

The Sergeant Major laughed out loud.

"This is a troop I want to meet," he said, pulling happily on his cigar.

"When was this?" asked his father.

"I don't know exactly. Maybe a week ago?"

"And where has he been all this time?"

"He told me he spent last week up at Long Binh, waiting for me."

"Where was he at Long Binh?"

"I don't know for sure, but if I know Repatch, he was holed up in Bien Hoa at night, and he was probably right outside the wire of the stockade during the day."

"How could that be?"

"If he didn't want them to see him, they wouldn't see him."

"You think we can find this guy?" Captain Morriss asked.

"My guess is he'll find us," said the Lieutenant.

"And you say he was a witness to the incident with the DC-3, to the death of your man Strosher?" Captain Morriss looked up from his notes, his brow furrowed.

"Yeah. He saw the whole thing."

"So we're not out of the woods on the DC-3 thing yet, but we're not trapped in the woods without a map, either," said Captain Morriss.

"We've got Repatch. He saw everything I saw. He looked through the binoculars, too. There isn't anyone I want here to testify for me more than Repatch. He's the best witness we could have, in my estimation," said the Lieutenant.

"We've got him, but we don't have him," said the Colonel.

"We've got to find him, because he's the only witness we've got at this point," said Captain Morriss. "And there's something important we haven't discussed yet. We're in a combat zone. The jury on this court-martial is likely to begin with a presumption that you're guilty, that the charges against you are correct, before we even start. From what you've told us about the night in question, it's going to be your word against theirs when it comes to proving where you were and why you refused to call in that fire mission. So we're not only going to have to try to prove that the prosecution's version of the events of that night is false; we're going to have to attack the reason the charges were made in the first place. It sounds to me like they tried to kill you out there, and when that failed, they decided to bring these charges against you to discredit you, to hush you up, so the information you reported will never get out. Is that the way you see it, Lieutenant Blue?"

"Yes, sir. That's it in a nutshell."

"Then we've got our work cut out for us. Let's go."

17

The next morning the phone in the BOQ rang at 6:00 A.M. Captain Terrence W. Morriss groped in the dark and knocked the phone to the floor. He retrieved the receiver from beneath the bed and mumbled, "Captain Morriss, sir."

"Are you the Captain Morriss who's the goddamned lawyer?" asked a voice that sounded like a Mississippi farmhand with a bad cigarette habit.

"Yes, sir, I am," said the Captain, sitting up in bed, reaching for the light switch.

"This is General Blue. Get somebody out here to this goddamned airbase and pick me up."

"General Blue?" Morriss found the switch and rubbed the sleep from his eyes with one hand and juggled the phone receiver with the other.

"That's what I said, goddammit. Now get your ass or somebody's

ass out here. I'll be standing outside of the door in the main
terminal."

"Yes . . . yes, sir," Morriss stammered. "I'll be there in twenty
minutes, sir."

"Did they let that boy out of Long Binh?" the General asked,
gruffness slipping from his voice a point or two.

"Yes, sir. On Monday night."

"Good. Now get out here, goddammit. It's hot as hell and I'm
sweating through my goddamned suit."

"Yes, sir."

"Captain?"

"Yes, sir?"

"When is the goddamned court-martial?"

"It starts tomorrow morning, sir."

"Twenty goddamned minutes it's going to take you?"

"Yes, sir. Right away, sir." He hung up the phone before the
General could come up with something else to yell at him about.

Morriss struggled out of bed and into the bathroom, ran some
water in the sink, dipped his face, lathered up and shaved, and
threw his khakis on.

He had never chauffeured a four-star general before. He wasn't
even sure where he could get a jeep.

Twenty minutes. They never taught you at Harvard how to get
shaved and dressed and five miles down the road in twenty minutes
when you didn't even have a car. He'd have to remember this lesson
if he ever taught a class in law school. Those young kids sitting out
there waiting to be lawyers just wouldn't believe it . . .

The Colonel was standing in front of his hotel in downtown
Saigon when Captain Morriss pulled up in the jeep he had borrowed.
The jeep had seen better days. It was muddy and it was heaving and
bucking and running on three of its four cylinders. The backseat
cushion was torn, and the ones on the front seats were thin from the
wear and tear of ferrying officers around Saigon from one cocktail
party to another, which was what the jeep had been doing for the
last five years.

"I'm glad I reached you this morning, sir," said Morriss. "I figured
you'd want to come along."

The Colonel climbed in. He was still in civvies, and he was carrying a briefcase.

"Thanks, Terry. I'm glad you called. Let's go."

Captain Morriss pulled away from the hotel and beeped his way into traffic. In a few minutes they were on the outskirts of Saigon, heading for the airport. The MP at the gate stopped them and checked the Colonel's identification, saluted when he saw his rank, and signaled them through.

The General was standing at the curb in front of the main terminal at Tan Son Nhut. He was wearing a light blue seersucker suit, a panama hat with a navy and red striped hatband, and shiny brown shoes. He was shorter than Morriss would have guessed from hearing his voice on the phone, but he made up for any lack of physical stature with the scowl on his face, which was practiced and profound. His lips turned down at the corners and his large eyes squinted into the morning sun. As the jeep coasted to a halt, his eyes opened wide for an instant, then squinted again. He stood at the curb, immobile, a fearful, squat statue of doom. Captain Morriss imagined him on a beachhead in Italy, squinting into the sun as a million men under his command came ashore and readied themselves to fight and if necessary to die for him. He shuddered.

The jeep stopped and the Colonel climbed out. He and the General stood there looking at each other for a long moment, then the Colonel reached for the General, but the General looked away and the Colonel stopped and said softly, "Nobody told me you were coming back, Dad."

"That's because I didn't tell anybody," the General growled. "What took you so goddamned long, Captain?"

Captain Morriss jumped out of the jeep, put on his cap, and stood at attention as militarily as he could.

"I stopped to pick up your son, sir," he said.

The General grunted and reached down for his suitcase.

"Wait a minute, Dad."

The General straightened up and stared stonily across the runways of Tan Son Nhut. C-130s followed each other on and off of the runways like great green ducks landing on and taking off from a huge pond.

"I'm glad you're here, Dad," said the Colonel. He looked straight at his father, who was scowling into the early sun.

"It means a lot to me, and it will mean a lot to Matt. I know you arranged for his release from Long Binh. I want to thank you, Dad. And I know Matt thanks you."

His father half-turned and glanced at the Colonel, then looked away.

"I want to thank you, Dad," said the Colonel again, his voice even, unwavering. He took a step toward his father and the old man half-turned and the Colonel folded his arms around his father and hugged him hard and didn't let him go.

Slowly the General's arms lifted and he held his son and patted his back gently.

He cleared his throat.

"What does a man have to do to get a goddamned drink around here, goddammit? It may be breakfast time for you, but it's cocktail hour for me, goddammit!"

The Colonel gave one last squeeze around his father's shoulders and let go and stepped back. Tears were forming in his eyes and he resisted the impulse to reach up and wipe them.

The General dug in his back pocket and pulled out a handkerchief and handed it to his son. He watched him wipe his eyes, and slowly a warm smile crept onto his lips.

"You're the lawyer," said the General, turning to Captain Morriss.

"Yes, sir."

"Drive this goddamned thing to the nearest officers' club, son. We three have got some things to talk over."

"Yes, sir," said Morriss, climbing back behind the wheel. The Colonel threw the General's suitcase in the back and vaulted into the backseat as the General eased himself into the passenger seat. He slapped the top of the windshield with his palm and nodded. It was a slap he'd made maybe ten thousand times during the war, riding in jeeps from North Africa to Sicily to Italy to France to Germany. He'd slap the windshield and his driver, whom he called "Bull," would hit the gas and the jeep would jerk forward, heading down the never-ending rutted road of World War II.

"Let's go, Captain. We're not sitting in this goddamned vehicle as decoration."

"Yes, sir," said Morriss. This guy ought to teach procedure to first-year students at Harvard Law, Captain Morriss thought. They would *love* him up there.

The General turned around in his seat to address his son.

"How's the boy?" he asked.

"He's doing about as well as can be expected, Dad," the Colonel said.

"Well, he's going to be doing one hell of a lot better than that from now on, goddammit," the General growled. "I didn't fly all those goddamned hours on that goddamned plane to get to this godforsaken hellhole to preside over a goddamned wake. When those sons of bitches decided they'd court-martial a man by the name of Matthew Nelson Blue, they bit off one hell of a lot more than they could chew, goddammit. When we're through with them, there's going to be a few sons of bitches choking on those goddamned charges they filed. They didn't know what circle of hell they stuck a stick into when they decided to mess with that boy of ours, goddammit. Nobody puts it to a Blue and gets away with it."

He took a deep, wheezing breath and turned around and looked through the windshield across the brown fields of Vietnam.

"Nobody, goddammit," he muttered. "You got that?"

"Yes, sir," said Captain Morriss.

"Yes, Dad," said the Colonel.

The sun slipped behind a cloud and the rice fields were plunged into dull gray light and then the sun peeked around the edge of the cloud and illuminated a row of shacks with a soft light that made them look rose-hued and golden and in the distance thunder sounded and at the edge of the field it began to rain and the rain spattered the jeep. The General tugged on his panama, pulling it over his eyes, and he reached up and held onto the windshield and shouted:

"Drive this goddamned thing, Captain, goddammit! I want a drink sometime before taps today, you hear me, goddammit!"

"Yes, sir!" Morriss yelled into the wind and rain and mud that was spattering the windshield.

The General was back in Vietnam, but this time he hadn't come on a Pentagon plane so nobody knew he was there.

The General squinted and wiped rain from his face and grinned widely at his son.

The jeep wheeled around a curve, throwing mud in a brown arc, and they were gone down the road in the thunder and the rain.

18

I t was the first thing you noticed: the courtroom was not air-conditioned and inside the air was a hot, still, stale, humid, lifeless gas that must have been ninety degrees at ankle level, ninety-five around your neck, one hundred stifling degrees at your face.

The second thing you noticed was the absence of press—no TV cameras, no reporters standing around, notebooks in hand. No microphones. Nothing. Cathy Joice and her crew had been turned around at the Tan Son Nhut complex gate. Nobody else who could wield a pencil in Saigon, it seemed, even knew the court-martial of Lieutenant Blue was taking place. The Army had accomplished what it had set out to accomplish: In seven days, they had the Lieutenant on trial for desertion in the face of the enemy, and other than Cathy Joice, nobody knew about it.

Nobody.

The court was a small Quonset hut on a street in the American military complex between the MACV compound and Tan Son Nhut, and not only wasn't it air-conditioned, but there were only three dormer-style windows jutting from the gently curving sides of the Quonset hut, and one of them didn't open. Circulation in the hut was about that of a walk-in closet, although the hut wasn't as luxurious.

The court-martial of Lieutenant Matthew Nelson Blue IV was to take place in what had to be one of two or three non-air-conditioned places in Saigon. Captain Morriss's theory was simple. The prosecution, which had lost its team leader the day before the court-martial, hoped the oppressive heat of the courtroom would discourage any lengthy questioning of their witnesses and further discourage any delaying tactics by the defense. Just walking into the room made you realize that every moment spent under its green, peeling, damp corrugated-steel ceiling would not be tallied in the defendant's column. Captain Morriss was about to file an official protest with the MACV court-martial convening authority but the General stopped him.

"That's precisely what they're goddamned waiting for," the General rasped between bites of his breakfast at the Caravelle. They want to goddamn sweat, we'll goddamn sweat with them. They are the ones who'll get goddamned flustered. Did you see the goddamned prosecutor? What in God's name was that?"

"Captain Alvin Z. Dupuy," said Captain Morriss. "They had a colonel they flew over from Hawaii to head up the prosecution team, but he spent the night out on the town in Saigon about a week ago, and he hasn't been the same since."

"This Dupuy is all they've got?"

"Dupuy and a major by the name of Thompson, Harold Thompson. But Dupuy will be running things. He ran the 32 investigation, and he's the only man they've got who really knows the case. Thompson is just window-dressing. They want the court to know the command feels this case is very, very important."

"What in hell is Dupuy's goddamned problem? I have never seen an Army officer with a face quite like his. There is a softness around his eyes and his chin . . ." the General's voice dropped off. He couldn't find the words to describe what he saw in Dupuy—or what he didn't see.

"Then you've never seen an Army officer with a trust fund approximately the size of the NATO budget, sir," said Morriss.

"So that's it," the General said, digging into his eggs.

They finished breakfast and met the Colonel and the Sergeant Major and the Lieutenant in front of the Continental. Captain Morriss had followed instructions from the General and found and exercised a regulation that permitted the defense team in any general court-martial the number of Army vehicles necessary to transport the team to and from court. In the case of Lieutenant Blue's team, it was two air-conditioned staff cars driven by two spec-4's supplied by the Sergeant Major. He didn't want drivers from MACV overhearing their conversations on the way to and from court, reporting back to the prosecution.

The Lieutenant looked straight ahead as they walked into the court. He wanted the defendant looking as much like a defendant as possible. In the military, especially in the Army, when you were about to be court-martialed it made sense to act contrite, even if your innocence boiled inside you like oil in a deep-fat fryer. If you were a lieutenant, the idea was to act the way a lieutenant was supposed to act in such a circumstance: scared out of your wits.

One of the peculiarities of the system of military justice was the presence of rank in the courtroom. Almost invariably the defendant would be the lowest-ranking man in the room, and it was expected that he behave that way. The court-martial of Lieutenant Blue was no different.

Inside the Quonset hut, the court was arranged by rank. On a raised platform at the end of the room were tables to the left and right for the court and for the military judge. The table for the court sat seven. The table for the judge was smaller, and it had been draped with a forest green cloth. An armless wooden chair for the witnesses sat on the platform exactly between the judge and the members of the court. In front of the platform were the tables for the prosecution, on the right, and for the defense, on the left. A court reporter sat at his stenotype machine between the tables for the court and the judge. An old oak lectern stood at the foot of the platform between the tables for the defense and prosecution.

The court sat by rank, left to right, and cards with the names and ranks of the members of the court stenciled in black letters sat on the table before the appropriate chairs.

The military judge, Colonel Charles Kelly, had his name and rank on his table, and he had brought his own. It was of hand-carved wood, and it was about twice the size of every other name card in the court.

"Trouble," whispered the Lieutenant to Captain Morriss after they sat down.

"What trouble?"

"The judge. The colonel. Only assholes have those wooden name plates."

"Yeah? Well, I think for once you're right when it comes to Kelly. He's one of the bigger assholes they've got."

The Lieutenant turned and looked behind him. The Quonset hut had seats for about forty people, but most of the chairs were empty. The General and the Colonel sat directly behind him with the Sergeant Major. They were the only people in the room.

It wasn't much of a crowd.

The Army had set out to court-martial the Lieutenant in virtual secrecy, and by the looks of things, they were well on their way to accomplishing just that.

An MP appeared in a door at the far end of the Quonset hut and announced in a loud but high-pitched voice:

"All rise!"

The members of the court filed in, followed by Colonel Kelly, the military judge. He wasn't wearing traditional judge's robes. In the Army, in the tropical heat of Vietnam, khakis were considered traditional enough.

"This court will come to order," said Colonel Kelly. He was a florid-faced man with a salt-and-pepper crewcut, broad shoulders, thick arms, and huge, meaty hands. He wore a pair of half-glasses over which he peered like an all-state fullback playing bookkeeper.

"Before we begin, I have something to say to both sides in this case."

The Judge peered over his half-glasses as he read from a document before him.

"I have been informed by the court-martial convening authority, Commander-in-Chief MACV, that the case before this court today involves matters of national security. For this reason, all those present in this court are ordered as of now that they are not to speak to any members of the press. If anyone is found to have contacted the press, or have been contacted by the press, you will be held in contempt of court, and I will personally see to it that your punishment is commensurate with the national security aspects of your crime. This is a combat zone, gentlemen. Rules of procedure are different when the enemy threatens. Do I make myself clear?"

The Judge peered over his glasses.

"Do I make myself understood to all those present in this court?"

Morriss stood up.

"Yes, Your Honor. The defense understands and respects your order."

"Can he do that?" whispered the Lieutenant when Morriss sat down.

"You heard him," said Morriss. "This is *Vietnam,* my man. They can do anything here. Any fucking thing. That much ought to be clear to you by now."

"Yeah. It's clear enough," said the Lieutenant. He turned around. They could court-martial him and hang him and the only people who would know it happened were sitting right behind him: the General, the Colonel, and the Sergeant Major. He was scared.

He nodded to the prosecution table.

Captain Dupuy stood and read from a sheet of paper.

"This general court-martial has been convened pursuant to Court-Martial Convening Order number 779-A issued by the Court-Martial Convening Authority, Headquarters, Military Assistance Command Vietnam. A copy of this order has been given to the members of the court, to the military judge, to the defense counsel, and to the defendant."

Dupuy took a deep breath, looked meaningfully at the judge, and announced, "The prosecution is ready with its case against Matthew Nelson Blue, Second Lieutenant, United States Army,

Fourth Division, Second of the 22nd Infantry. The defendant is present in court along with his defense counsel, Your Honor."

Dupuy sat down.

Colonel Kelly peered over his spectacles at Lieutenant Blue, then at the court, then at Dupuy.

"I will now swear the members of the court."

He turned to the seven officers on the court and swore each one individually. Then he swore in Dupuy, Major Thompson, and Captain Morriss. When he was finished, Dupuy stood to swear in the judge. Dupuy sat down.

Colonel Kelly turned to Dupuy.

"Does the prosecution have a preemptory challenge or a challenge for cause?"

"No, sir, we do not," said Dupuy, half-rising from his chair. He sat down and looked over at the defense table.

"Does the defense have a preemptory challenge or any challenges for cause?"

Captain Morriss whispered to Lieutenant Blue, "Recognize anybody? Anybody from your unit, from Benning or West Point or anywhere else?"

The Lieutenant looked them over. The panel consisted of one lieutenant colonel, three majors, two captains, and a first lieutenant. All were white. All wore khakis. All had gotten recent haircuts. Three of them had burrs, one was almost bald, and the rest had white sidewalls.

Every last one of them looked as if he couldn't wait to put that lily-livered little deserter on the gallows and personally watch him hang.

"Nobody. Never seen any of them before."

"Anybody you want to preemptorily challenge?" Captain Morriss asked. "We can kick one of them off the court for no reason. Anybody you don't like the looks of?"

"I don't like the looks of any of them," said the Lieutenant.

"Then let's leave them up there to sweat it out in this hole with the rest of us."

"Okay by me."

Captain Morriss looked up at the judge.

"No challenges, Your Honor," he said.

Colonel Kelly nodded at the defense table.

"The accused will rise."

Lieutenant Blue and Captain Morriss stood.

"Lieutenant Blue, we are gathered here today to try you by general court-martial. You are charged with violating Article 122 of the United States Code of Military Justice. How do you plead to the charge and to the specification?"

"I plead not guilty to the charge and not guilty to the specification, Your Honor," the Lieutenant said without hesitation.

The judge nodded, and Lieutenant Blue and Captain Morriss took their seats.

"The prosecution and the defense may now make opening statements," said the judge. "Whether they choose to make statements or not, no conclusions will be drawn from their choice. Is that clear?"

The members of the court nodded in unison.

"Does the prosecution have an opening statement?"

"We do, Your Honor," said Dupuy, rising with a sheaf of papers in hand. He approached the lectern and spread the papers on its tilted surface.

"This ought to be good," Morriss whispered to the Lieutenant.

"Gentlemen, the charges in this court-martial are indeed profound, but the facts of the case are not." Dupuy faced the seven officers of the court and spoke slowly, seeming to choose his words one by one.

"They are very simple facts because what the defendant did was very simple. He was given a direct order to engage the enemy, to place fire on an enemy position, in this case with the four-point-two mortars of his weapons platoon, and he refused this order, thus deserting the field of battle in the face of the enemy. The prosecution will present witnesses testifying to these facts as I have briefly outlined them to you. When the prosecution is finished, these profound charges against this Lieutenant in the United States Army will be proven without a shadow of doubt. Of this you can be sure."

Dupuy gathered his papers and sat down.

"Is that all?" the Lieutenant whispered.

"I guess so," Morriss whispered back.

"Then why did he bring all those papers with him to the lectern?"

"Your guess is as good as mine. He wanted some company up there. Who knows?"

"Does the defense have an opening statement?" the judge asked.

Captain Morriss stood.

"The defense will reserve its opening statement until it begins to present its case, Your Honor."

"The prosecution may call its first witness," said the judge.

Dupuy stood up.

"The prosecution calls Lieutenant Colonel Henson W. Halleck."

The MP opened the door behind the judge, and Lieutenant Colonel Halleck entered and took the witness chair.

"The witness will be sworn," said Colonel Kelly.

Dupuy swore him in and stood at the lectern, facing the witness. The surface of the lectern was covered with three-by-five cards, and more of them were banded together with a rubber band and held in Dupuy's left hand.

"State your name please, sir."

"Henson W. Halleck."

"And your rank and the rest, please, sir," said Dupuy, glancing at the lectern.

"Henson W. Halleck, Lieutenant Colonel, United States Army, Infantry, 25th Division, Second of the 22nd."

"Do you know the accused?"

"Yes. I'm the man who brought the charge against him."

"How long have you known the accused?"

"Let me see ... for two months at Fort Benning, and for approximately a month here. Three months."

"You served with the accused at Fort Benning?" Dupuy seemed unprepared for this news.

"I taught him tactics. He was my student."

"So you had knowledge of the accused before taking command of the Second of the 22nd."

"Yes, I did."

"What kind of student did you find him?"

"Your Honor, I object," said Captain Morriss, rising from his chair. "This line of questioning is going nowhere fast. Let's get on with the facts of the case."

"Where are you going with this line of questioning?" the judge asked Dupuy.

"Your Honor, I'm simply establishing Lieutenant Colonel Halleck's familiarity with—"

"Colonel Halleck does not have to have been familiar with the defendant previously in order to have knowledge of the facts of the case. I'll uphold the objection. Ask your next question."

"Lieutenant Colonel Halleck, where were you on the night of October 13, 1969?"

"I was in command of my Battalion, the Triple Deuce."

"By the Triple Deuce, you mean the Second of the 22nd."

"Yes."

"And where was the Battalion located on that night?"

"The Battalion was making a sweep of enemy territory in the vicinity of Dak Sut in II Corps. We were the strike Battalion on Operation Iron Fist One."

"The Battalion was engaged in combat, in other words."

"When you're making a sweep, you're engaged in combat. The answer is yes."

"And how long had the Battalion been on the sweep, sir?"

"October 13 was the second night of Iron Fist One."

"Two days, then."

"Two days. Yes."

"And during the course of the first day of the sweep, did you have occasion to personally issue any orders to Lieutenant Blue?"

"Not the first day, no," said Lieutenant Colonel Halleck. He paused to take a sip of water from a glass on the table next to him.

"Hey, what's going on here?" the Lieutenant whispered to Captain Morriss. "I thought he'd call some other witnesses before Halleck. Captain Gardner, maybe. The XO. Somebody who was standing there in his bunker when he was talking to me on the radio."

"Dupuy is pretty confident he's got you cold," Morriss whispered back. "He's not wasting any time. He's going with his number-one boy. He's going right for the jugular."

"I'll say he is."

"Correction," Lieutenant Colonel Halleck continued. "I issued orders through his company commander, Captain Gardner, that would have involved Lieutenant Blue."

"So you issued no direct orders personally the first day. Did you issue any direct orders the second day?"

"Not during the day, no."

"But you issued orders to Captain Gardner that would have been passed on to Lieutenant Blue?"

"Yes. The second day of Iron Fist One was just like the first."

"I'll fucking say it was," whispered the Lieutenant to Captain Morriss. He shushed the Lieutenant under his breath.

"When did you issue your first direct order to Lieutenant Blue, Colonel?"

"When I gave him the order he refused."

"So the first verbal order you issued to this Lieutenant on that combat mission was the order he is charged with having refused, thus deserting his mission in the face of the enemy?"

"Yes. The first order. He disobeyed the first order I gave him and deserted the field of battle."

"Have many of the orders you have issued in combat have been disobeyed, Lieutenant Colonel Halleck?"

"None."

"Other than by Lieutenant Blue?"

"Other than by Lieutenant Blue."

"To the best of your knowledge, has anyone else under your command deserted his mission in the face of the enemy?"

"No. No one."

"Objection," said Morriss in a loud voice.

"What could he possibly object to, Your Honor?" asked the prosecutor.

"We're here to try Lieutenant Blue, not to hear about Lieutenant Colonel Halleck's illustrious career of giving orders to others."

"I am simply trying to establish the Colonel's experience as a battalion commander, Your Honor."

"A little less sarcasm from you, Captain Morriss. And a little more attention to facts bearing directly on this case from you, Captain Dupuy." The judge squinted over his spectacles at both men.

"Yes, sir," said Morriss. He sat down.

"Yes, sir," said Dupuy, glancing at the three-by-five cards on the lectern. He unwrapped the rubber band around the cards in his hand and shuffled through them. Then he looked up at the witness.

"Lieutenant Colonel Halleck, I want you to set the stage for the events which transpired on the night of October 13 of this year. I want you to tell the court the nature of your mission in conducting the sweep known as Iron Fist One."

"Intelligence had made the division aware of a large enemy force operating to the west of us as a screen for shipments down the Ho Chi Minh Trail. An NVA Battalion—reinforced—was suspected to be in the area. Our mission was to sweep the area, to find and engage the enemy unit if possible. If that was not possible, our mission was to deny him access to the territory in which he had been operating pretty much with impunity. Our mission was considered vital to the United States mission in Vietnam, in that shipments down the Ho Chi Minh Trail had picked up in recent months, and another offensive of the Tet Offensive variety was suspected to be in the offing."

"Thus, when your unit engaged in such a sweep of this territory, its mission was not merely protective of itself or of its parent unit, but in fact protective of our nation's overall objective in Vietnam. Was that the case, Lieutenant Colonel Halleck?"

"Yes, that was the case. I personally considered Operation Iron Fist One the most important mission I had ever had the privilege to be associated with."

"Would you say that the morale of the men in undertaking this mission was good?"

"The men's morale was excellent. The Triple Deuce is known as a Communist-hating bunch of street fighters, and we were ready to take the fight to the enemy's streets."

"Oh, Jesus," muttered the Lieutenant, looking down at the table.

Captain Morriss touched his hand and he shut up.

"Lieutenant Colonel Halleck, tell us the circumstances that preceded the order you issued to Lieutenant Blue."

"The Triple Deuce was well established in a night defensive perimeter west of Dak Sut, directly in the middle of the enemy area of operation. This was our second night in the perimeter, and the enemy had had time to pinpoint our location and we were beginning to experience some enemy feelers."

"Feelers?"

"The enemy was testing our resolve, Captain Dupuy. The enemy was hitting us and pulling back, hitting us and pulling back. It is a common enemy tactic, one they use to test our readiness and to discourage us from further operations and to lower morale among the troops. I was determined that the enemy's goals not be realized. I was determined that these enemy feelers would be repelled with great dispatch, in order to discourage him from mounting a larger strike against our NDP."

"How would you characterize these enemy . . . er . . . feelers, sir?"

"Very disciplined. Very determined. Well planned. Well executed. I took them very seriously."

"And what combat intensity would you say the enemy employed, sir?"

"They were hitting us with several small units, with everything those units had. We were hitting them back, of course, but they were employing a typical enemy pattern. Hit. Move. Hit again. Move again. Hit harder. Move. Hit harder still."

"Were you concerned for the safety of your Battalion, sir?"

"Not for its overall safety, no sir. We were well established, expertly dug in. There was nothing on God's green earth that could have dislodged us from that NDP. Nothing human, that is."

A few titters could be heard at the back of the room, and the judge gaveled them down and gave the offenders a stern look over his spectacles.

"You were determined, at any rate, to deal the enemy a punishing blow for this hit-and-run behavior, were you not, Lieutenant Colonel Halleck?"

"Yes, I was."

"And in order to deal the enemy this crushing blow, you decided to employ the firepower of Lieutenant Blue's weapons platoon."

"Yes, I did."

"You had employed the weapons platoon in combat previous to October 13, is that not correct, sir?"

"Yes, I had."

"And so when you gave Captain Gardner an order to contact his weapons platoon and direct fire on the enemy, you expected that fire to be forthcoming immediately, did you not, sir?"

"I did."

"And what happened?"

"Captain Gardner reported to me that Lieutenant Blue was refusing to fire his weapons as ordered."

"And what did you do?"

"I got on the radio and ordered Lieutenant Blue to fire his weapons on the target specified, and he refused."

"He refused several times, did he not?"

"Several times."

"And the last time he refused he implied that if you wanted fire from his mortars you would have to come to his platoon and fire them yourself?"

"He didn't imply it. He said it to me directly. I have a very distinct memory of his challenge."

"And you threatened him?"

"I told him to fire the weapons or there would be hell to pay. Yes."

"And he refused to fire the weapons?"

"Yes."

"And your Battalion continued to draw periodic but intense fire from the enemy?"

"It did."

"And what did you do?"

"I got on the horn to Div Arty . . ."

"Div Arty, sir?"

"Division Artillery. I called them on the radio and ordered 155 howitzer fire on the objective."

"And you received such fire from . . . Div Arty, sir?"

"Immediately."

"And this fire silenced the enemy?"

"Eventually. Yes, it did."

"So if Lieutenant Blue had fired his four-point-two-inch mortars as ordered, you would have been able to silence the enemy much earlier than you were able to, making use of . . . Div Arty?"

"That is so."

"Would you say that Lieutenant Blue's refusal of your order constituted desertion in the face of the enemy, sir?"

"Objection," Captain Morriss interrupted. "Asking for a legal opinion the Colonel is not expertly qualified to give."

"Sustained," said Colonel Kelly.

"I will rephrase the question," Dupuy said. "When Lieutenant Blue refused your order, it had the effect of withdrawing the weapons platoon from your use in a combat situation, or, as it were, in the face of the enemy, sir?"

"It did."

"That is all I have. Thank you, Lieutenant Colonel Halleck. You have been very forthcoming."

"Your witness, Captain Morriss," said the judge.

"The defense has no questions at this time, but reserves the right to call Lieutenant Colonel Halleck at a later time."

"Granted. Next witness."

Dupuy started shuffling through his papers, looking for something.

"What are you doing?" the Lieutenant asked Captain Morriss in a voice that was not quite a whisper.

"Ssshh. I want to see what else he's got. I think he just shot his wad. I'm thinking our boy Dupuy is so confident of the facts as Halleck gave them that all he's going to do now is a lot of backing and filling."

"So it's okay, the way you're doing it?"

"It's a tactic. There are risks. The court might think we don't have anything to ask, but they won't think that for long. I'll eat Halleck for lunch when the time comes."

The Lieutenant turned to look at his father and grandfather. The Colonel looked worried. The General had a look on his face the Lieutenant had never seen before. It was a look of such utter hatred and contempt that the Lieutenant was surprised paint wasn't peeling from the walls.

"Don't worry," the Lieutenant whispered.

The General didn't even flicker an eye.

"The prosecution calls Captain Henry G. Gardner to the stand."

The MP opened the door and Goose Gardner emerged and took the witness chair. Dupuy swore him in and got his particulars.

"Captain Gardner, you are—*were*—Lieutenant Blue's company commander. Is that correct?"

"Yes. I commanded headquarters and headquarters company, Second of the 22nd."

"You were present in the command bunker on the night of October 13. Is that correct?"

"Yes."

"Your presence was requested when?"

"After I had contacted Lieutenant Blue by radio."

"After Lieutenant Blue had refused your order, is that more accurate?"

"After he had refused the order, yes."

"And you heard the conversation Lieutenant Colonel Halleck had with Lieutenant Blue on the radio?"

"Yes, I did."

"Was his recollection of that conversation accurate?"

"As far as it went."

"What do you mean, Captain?"

"I mean exactly that. As far as it went."

"Elaborate, please."

"His recollection was accurate as to his end of the conversation. I did not hear Lieutenant Blue's end, so I cannot testify as to the accuracy of his recollection of what Lieutenant Blue said."

"All right, Goose!" the Lieutenant whispered.

"Shut up," whispered Captain Morriss.

"Was your company taking enemy fire on the night of October 13, Captain?"

"Yes."

"Did your company continue to take fire from the enemy after

349

Lieutenant Blue refused to place mortar fire on the objective you gave him?"

"Yes, but—"

"A simple yes or no will suffice, Captain."

"Objection," said Captain Morriss. "He's treating Captain Gardner like a hostile witness when the witness has not been declared hostile."

"Overruled."

"Your Honor, Captain Gardner wanted to answer the last question in his own way, and the prosecution cut him off. I respectfully submit that the witness is a witness for the prosecution, and he should be allowed to answer the questions as Lieutenant Colonel Halleck did, at whatever length he desires."

"The prosecution can elicit from its witness what it wants to elicit, Captain Morriss. You'll have your chance to let the witness run off at the mouth if that's what you want him to do. Go ahead, Captain Dupuy."

Morriss sat down.

"What was that all about?" asked the Lieutenant.

"I just wanted to plant the notion in the minds of the court that the prosecution is afraid of its own witness."

"Captain Gardner, one last question. What did Lieutenant Blue say to you the next morning, when you and Lieutenant Colonel Halleck flew to Firebase Zulu-Foxtrot?"

"I'm not sure what you mean."

"I mean, when you asked him why he refused to execute the fire mission."

"He said, 'Can't get no satisfaction,' I believe."

"What?"

" 'Can't get no satisfaction.' That's all he said. It's a—"

"That is all, Captain. Thank you."

Morriss jumped to his feet before the judge could say, "Your witness."

"What were you just trying to say, Captain Gardner, when Captain Dupuy so rudely cut you off?"

"I was trying to say that 'Can't get no satisfaction' is a rock-and-roll lyric by the Rolling Stones, I believe."

"And in your estimation was Lieutenant Blue being sarcastic?"

"It was a running joke in the company, sir. The words refer to the fact that in life in general but in war in particular, and in *this* war even more particularly, it is very difficult to get any satisfaction from your daily life. It was an assessment of the way life is, sir. A very bleak, very black reading of the moment."

"And the other time you were cut off, Captain?"

"I was trying to say that we were not taking very heavy fire. It was typical VC harassing fire. Small arms and a 60-millimeter mortar. We were very well dug in. We had no casualties as a result of that fire or any other enemy harassment fire on that night or any other night."

"Thank you for elaborating further on your answer to the prosecution's question, Captain. Now. I'd like to take you back to the events of October 13. When you called Lieutenant Blue on the radio with your fire mission, from whom did you get your intended target?"

"From Lieutenant Colonel Halleck."

"And in what form was the target specified?"

"It was a set of grid coordinates from a map."

"And from these grid coordinates, Lieutenant Blue could pinpoint the target and calculate the direction and elevation for his weapons and place accurate fire on the target. Is that the way it works, Captain Gardner?"

"Generally. Some targets are preset. Others have to be acquired by specification of grid coordinates from the map and then adjustment of fire from observation on the ground."

"Adjustment?"

"You observe the explosions of the rounds, and if they're off target you adjust them accordingly, like 'left fifty, add fifty' would change azimuth left fifty meters and raise elevation fifty meters, and those instructions would result in a new sighting of the weapon and new rounds would be fired, and they too would be adjusted if they were not yet on target. Mortar fire, or artillery fire in general, is a kind of trial-and-error thing."

"So mortar fire is not always accurate."

"Not immediately, no."

"Would you direct fire close to your own position?"

"I don't know what you mean by 'close.' "

"Fifty meters."

"No."

"A hundred meters."

"No."

"How close would you come with mortar fire?"

"Not less than two hundred meters. Inside two hundred you're taking chances you shouldn't be taking."

"So if fire was to be called in within two hundred meters of friendly forces, and Lieutenant Blue were to notice that this was the case, it would be incumbent upon him to notify you of this fact and of the danger to the friendly forces."

"Yes. The weapons platoon leader has a map, and all friendly positions are marked on the map and those positions define zones within which mortar fire cannot be called."

"Did Lieutenant Blue make such a notification to you on the night of October 13?"

"He did."

"What did he say?"

"He said we were calling in fire on his ambush patrol."

"Were you aware of this fact before he pointed it out to you?"

"No, I was not."

"Did you have the location of his ambush patrol marked on your map?"

"Yes, I did. Lieutenant Blue had called in their position earlier in the evening, immediately after they were established."

"What were those grid coordinates, Captain?"

Captain Gardner pulled a notebook from his pocket.

"I wrote them down that night in this notebook. The coordinates of the ambush patrol were 72548869."

"If you had the coordinates of the ambush patrol, why did you not take notice of the fact that you were ordering fire on a friendly position?"

Captain Gardner shifted nervously in the witness chair.

"Because we were using different maps."

"Different maps? That's kind of like an orchestra trying to play together from different scores of music, isn't it?"

"Yes."

"But far more dangerous, Captain Gardner. How did this come about, that you and your weapons platoon leader were using different maps?"

"To this day, I am not entirely sure."

"But it was clear to you at the time that this was indeed the case. You *were indeed* using different maps."

"Yes. That was clear to me."

"Explain to us the effect this had."

"When I called in the target grid coordinates, I called them in from one map. But when Lieutenant Blue had called in the grid coordinates of his ambush patrol, he had called them off another map. I plotted them on our map, which was different from his, so the grid coordinates of the target and the grid coordinates of his ambush patrol were different. The effect was, it didn't look like we were calling in fire on his patrol."

"But, in fact, you were directing fire on top of him and his men, were you not, Captain?"

"That is what Lieutenant Blue said."

"And did you believe him?"

"At the time, I didn't know what to believe. I couldn't understand then, and I can't understand now, how we ever had a mix-up of maps in the first place. What he said sounded right, but I could not establish absolutely that he was right, that the location of his patrol and the location of our target were in fact the same place on the ground."

"But did you believe Lieutenant Blue at the time?"

"I had no choice but to believe him, sir. It is his job to be scrupulous about pinpointing friendly forces and avoiding them when firing his weapons. There is nothing worse in this business, in my opinion, than hitting your own men with friendly fire, than taking casualties from friendly fire. Nothing worse. Because it's such a waste."

"Objection. The witness is editorializing, sir," Dupuy said.

"Sustained. Confine your answers to the facts, Captain," Colonel Kelly ordered.

"Yes, sir."

"What happened when you reported to Lieutenant Colonel Halleck what Lieutenant Blue had said?"

"About the ambush patrol being in the location of our target?"

"Yes."

"He became enraged."

"And what else?"

"He ordered me over to the command bunker."

"And you went."

"Yes."

"Did you attempt to explain further what Lieutenant Blue had said about his ambush patrol?"

"Yes, I did, but I was not successful."

"Why was that?"

"For one, because I didn't completely understand the problem myself. And second, because I did not have the map Lieutenant Blue had, so I could point out, on the map, specifically what he was saying over the radio."

"You believed Lieutenant Blue, however."

"Yes, as I said, I had to."

"Had Lieutenant Blue ever steered you wrong about such a grave matter previously?"

"Never."

"He was, as you said, scrupulous in his pinpointing of friendly forces on his map?"

"Lieutenant Blue is the best map reader I have ever seen. On occasion, I would lose track of exactly where we were on an operation, and I could always call him and get accurate grid coordinates, because he always had us on the map to within a foot of where we were on the ground."

"You trusted his expertise in these matters."

"Absolutely."

"However, Lieutenant Colonel Halleck did not."

"I couldn't say, sir."

"Never mind. Would you say, however, that Lieutenant Colonel Halleck disagreed with what Lieutenant Blue said about the position of his ambush patrol?"

"That would be putting it mildly."

"In your opinion as a company commander—as the commander immediately over the weapons platoon leader—was Lieutenant Blue justified in his actions?"

"Objection," said Captain Dupuy. "Calls for expert opinion the witness is not qualified to give."

"Your Honor, I am not asking for a legal analysis from Captain Gardner. I am asking him, as a company commander, as the man responsible for the weapons platoon as well as for the lives of a hundred and sixty other soldiers, and based on his understanding of the facts surrounding the incident, was Lieutenant Blue justified? Certainly his position gives him the qualifications to make such a judgment, or the Army may as well not put company commanders in charge of units such as weapons platoons."

"Overruled. Answer the question."

"In my opinion, yes, he was justified."

"Thank you. That is all."

Morriss sat down and folded his hands on the table in front of himself. Dupuy shuffled through the papers on his desk.

"Anything in rebuttal, counselor?" asked the judge.

"No, Your Honor," said Captain Dupuy, not looking up at the judge.

"Call your next witness."

"Your Honor, the prosecution requests a brief recess at this time."

The judge looked at his watch.

"It's late. The court will be in recess until ten hundred hours tomorrow."

He banged the gavel, and everyone rose to his feet, and the judge and the court filed out the back door.

"What do you think, Dad?" the Lieutenant asked. He was wearing a tan suit and a blue shirt and a dark tie and loafers. He squinted at the backs of the court as they went out the door.

"I've been watching the men on the court. I think they bought Colonel Halleck, lock, stock, and barrel. I think they take Captain Gardner for a typical HHQ commander, not up to par, not strac enough to command a line company. It didn't help that he had a hard time understanding the map stuff. I don't know. You guys have a ways to go if you're going to turn that bunch around to your way of thinking."

"How about it, General?" Captain Morriss asked.

"They came in here ready to ship your ass out of here in goddamned chains, and nothing they've heard has changed that attitude. You can forget the goddamned Constitution and the presumption of innocence when you start dealing with courts of law in the military, and you can sure as hell throw the goddamned Constitution out the window in a courtroom in a combat zone in a war. Don't count on their goddamned love of country and justice and all that crap. They love their own asses first and every ass above them second, and you're going to have to get them to forget their love of their own asses and their superiors' asses if you're going to walk out of this goddamned courtroom with your life and your honor intact. You have got to get their goddamned *emotions* going your way. Forget their heads. Go for their goddamned *guts*. Put them in your goddamned position and see how they like it. Put them where you were that night and make them see it your way and make them want to have acted the way you acted. That's your ticket out the front door."

"Your grandfather is as right as rain, son," said the Colonel. "He knows more about the men on this court than they know about themselves. You've got to move them, *physically* move them to that armored personnel carrier you were sitting in. Move them out in the dark to the spot in the woods where your patrol sat, knowing nothing of the situation back at Battalion. Get them the hell out of this courtroom and out in the boonies and they'll go along with you because they won't have any choice. They'll be too scared to do anything else."

"That's what we're going to do, Dad."

"I sure as hell hope so, boy," said the General, "because if you don't, you're going on a long goddamned trip that'll end up at the end of a goddamned rope about two hundred feet from that set of quarters where you picked up Wendy Williams for your first date."

"How'd you know about that, Grandpa? Jesus, that was years ago."

"Never mind how I know what the hell I'm talking about. You don't want to know. Just dig a hole this afternoon and pull every goddamned one of those sons of bitches down in it with you, boy. Dig it for me. Dig it for your mom. Dig it for your dad. Dig it for your brother and your sister. Dig it for the memory of your grandmother. Dig that goddamned hole like your life depended on it, boy. Because it does."

S E V E N

☆

══════════

Maybe Never Again

Firebase Zulu-Foxtrot
Day Seven

The sun was rising over the tree east of the perimeter when he heard them coming.

Thwap-thwap-thwap-thwap . . . one chopper.

Farther off in the distance . . .

Thwap-thwap-thwap-thwap . . . another.

Behind the second . . .

Thwap-thwap-thwap-thwap . . . a third.

"You see 'em yet, Eltee?" Repatch was standing on the ramp of the Lieutenant's track, shading his eyes against the sun. The Lieutenant was sitting on top of the track, his feet dangling through the commander's cupola.

His track.

His commander's cupola.

His .50-caliber machine gun.

His platoon, the weapons platoon.

"I got 'em now, Eltee, over yo' shoulder, comin' outta the sun." Dirtball pointed a grimy finger.

Thwap-thwap-thwap-thwap . . . they came out of the sun, a chorus of angry rotors pounding the chill from the morning air, beating back the mist, grinding through the air above the jungle treetops, three of them . . .

Thwap-thwap-thwap-thwap . . .

Pushing back the night with the dirty sound of Americans at war.

The lead chopper put down inside the west edge of the platoon perimeter, the second and third choppers settling into the dust behind.

They kept their engines on, three sets of rotors twirling lazily, whipping dust across the weapons platoon, ruffling the treeline . . .

Whoosh-whoosh-whoosh-whoosh . . .

Waiting.

Two figures emerged from the first chopper, bent over at the waist, left hands on their heads, holding caps against the wind.

"You see who it is, Dirtball?" called Repatch.

"Halleck and Testor is what I see, man."

"Both of 'em. They're serious, Eltee," said Repatch. He looked up. The Lieutenant was still sitting there. He was looking the other way, to the east, where the rest of the weapons platoon had pulled itself into a ragged line, standing at attention. One of the men— who was it?—he couldn't make out the man's face through the dust—one of them had dug up the weapons platoon guidon and hung the frayed flag from a PRC-25 antenna. The guidon whipped stiffly in the wind from the choppers.

The second and third choppers each emptied a squad of MPs, fatigue-clad, wearing shiny black helmet liners and the distinctive black MP armbands.

"Get down from there, Lieutenant."

It was Lieutenant Colonel Halleck. He called to the Lieutenant on the run.

The Lieutenant slid into the commander's cupola and crept out the back of the track. He was standing next to Repatch and Dirtball when Halleck and Testor reached the track.

"Lieutenant Matthew Nelson Blue the fourth, it is my duty to place you under arrest," said Lieutenant Colonel Halleck. He was standing about ten feet from the back of the track. Next to him stood Colonel Testor, the brigade commander.

The Lieutenant stared at him for a moment. He didn't move a muscle. He didn't say anything. He just stood there staring.

"The charge is desertion in the face of the enemy, Lieutenant," said Colonel Testor.

"The Eltee, he didn't desert nothin'," said Dirtball.

"Why is this man out of uniform?" said Lieutenant Colonel Halleck, pointing at Dirtball, who stood on the ramp of the track in a pair of OD drawers and an OD T-shirt.

"Get that man in uniform," said Lieutenant Colonel Halleck, his finger trembling.

Testor took a step forward. He looked around. The ragged line of troops had broken and re-formed around the Lieutenant's track. Four men stood between Colonel Testor and the Lieutenant. Each of the men carried his weapon.

Moonface had his '60 resting across his shoulders.

The butt of Mallick's M-79 grenade launcher was rested on his hip, its muzzle pointing directly at the two colonels.

Lucky Lemon had another '60 standing on the ground between his legs.

Whoopie Cushion Ridgely danced nervously to one side, snapping the slide on his M-16, hollow metallic chops breaking the silence.

"Get your helmet, Lieutenant," said Colonel Testor. "Let's go."

Testor had taken over from Halleck, who hung back a step. Testor signaled the MPs, and seven of them moved forward, their right hands on their holstered .45s.

The Lieutenant didn't move.

"All right. Let's go," said Colonel Testor. He took another step.

Whoopie Cushion yelped. Moonface growled.

"Get these men back," said Testor.

The Lieutenant looked to his left and his right. All of them were on line now, facing Halleck and Testor and the two squads of MPs.

"Back to your holes, men," said the Lieutenant. "I don't want any trouble."

One by one they scooted backward through the dust.

"You doin' a wrong thing," said Sergeant Davis, who stopped next to the Lieutenant. "This is a good Lieutenant. Every man here tell you the same thing. This is a *good* Lieutenant. None better."

"Move on, Sergeant," said Colonel Testor.

Sergeant Davis didn't move.

"Go on, Sarge. Get them back on the perimeter," said the Lieutenant. He gave Davis a gentle push away from the track.

"I'll be seeing you later, sir," he said.

Dirtball was on top of the track, next to the antenna. The Lieutenant looked around. Repatch, who had been standing next to him an instant before, was gone.

The Lieutenant reached inside the track for his cap. He looked up. The photo of Dirtball's girlfriend stared at him from the firewall. His poncho liner was still bunched up on his air mattress. His typewriter grinned at him from the side bench. If you closed your eyes and squinted real hard so that everything became a blur, the inside of the track looked like a boy's bedroom, cluttered with the remnants of a worshipful youth. It was messy and dirty the way boys are.

The way war is.

It was *his* track, and he knew he was looking at it for the last time. He stuck his cap on his head and flopped the cover over the dusty Olivetti. He looked up through the commander's cupola at Dirtball.

"You can have the Olivetti, Dirtball. Distribute the rest of this shit to whoever needs it."

Dirtball looked down.

"Will do, sir."

The Lieutenant crept down the ramp and walked between the two lines of MPs who were waiting outside. They did an about-face, and marched him to the first chopper.

The blades turned faster.

Whoosh-whoosh-whoosh-whoosh . . . thwap-thwap-thwap-thwap . . .

Two MPs followed the Lieutenant into the chopper and the bird lifted off and tilted forward and rose over the jungle treetops and was gone.

19

I think I've lost my objectivity," said Cathy Joice.

"I do too," said the Lieutenant.

The first day of the court-martial was over, and they were sitting in bed, looking out the balcony doors of Cathy's hotel room. A room-service supper tray lay between them and they were picking at dessert and sipping lukewarm coffee.

"What are you going to do about it?" the Lieutenant asked.

"About what?"

"About your lost objectivity."

"I'm going to look for it. It's got to be around here somewhere. I put it down just the other day."

The Lieutenant smiled, but his smile didn't last long.

"You're worried, aren't you?" she said, taking his hand in hers.

The Lieutenant didn't look at her. He just kept staring out the balcony doors.

"What are you feeling, Matt?"

"Nothing. I'm feeling absolutely nothing."

"I don't believe you."

"Believe it. I think I've finally reached that Zen state they write about in books, you know, where your mind is absolutely blank and you're not thinking and you're not feeling, you're just *there*. You just *be*."

"You mean to tell me you don't care if they find you guilty?"

"Whatever is going to happen is going to happen. What can I do? I lost my knack for having an effect on my life the day my feet touched ground at Tan Son Nhut."

"Come on, Matt, you're being ridiculous."

"You think so?" He turned to look at her. "Ridiculous? All I've done is my job, and they're going to fucking court-martial me for desertion in the face of the enemy and I'm being ridiculous because I've got myself to this point where I don't care what they do anymore, they can just fucking do it to me, they did it to me before, they did it to me at West Point and they did it to me when I got sick of getting guys in my platoon killed for absolutely fucking nothing, and they're doing it to me with this fucking court-martial, and I know there's nothing I can do about it, and you say I'm being ridiculous? Is that what being ridiculous is? Taking a look at your life and realizing it's not yours anymore, it belongs to somebody else, it belongs to the assholes, which is probably where it belonged anyway? That's being ridiculous?"

"Yes."

"You're probably right."

"I know I'm right." She rested her head on his shoulder.

"Yeah, well, you may be right, but I know where your objectivity went." A smile cracked on his tight lips. Not much of a smile, but a smile nevertheless.

"You do?"

"Right here!"

The Lieutenant laughed and pushed her back on the pillow and shoved the tray to the bottom of the bed and wrapped his arms around her and pulled her down on the bed and draped his body over hers.

"I think I found it," he said.

"Where?"

"Right here." His hand found the valley between her breasts and rested there.

"It's hiding under this bow. You see this bow?"

She looked down.

"Which one?"

"The big bow in the middle. The one holding these two pieces of lace together."

"Oh. *That* bow."

"It's right under this bow is where it is."

"What?"

"Your objectivity."

"Oh. Right. My objectivity."

"You want me to get it for you?"

"Sure. I've been looking *everywhere* for it. For *days* I've been looking for my poor lost objectivity."

"I'm going to have to untie this big bow right here if I'm going to get to it."

"That's okay."

"But if I untie this big bow, then your nightgown is going to come off."

"That's okay, too."

"Anything for your objectivity, right?"

"Anything."

He untied the bow and she giggled and he buried his face between her breasts and he pursed his lips and blew hard and he made a noise like a motorboat a *bbbbbbbbrrrrbbbbbbbbtttt* sound and she threw her head back and screamed:

"Okay! Okay! You found it!"

He looked up.

"Found what?"

"My lost objectivity! You found it, okay!"

"No I didn't. But I found something else."

She looked at him warily.

"What?"

"A microphone! You've been taping everything I said!"

He buried his face again and *bbbbbbbbrrrrbbbbbtttted* and her breasts quivered and she giggled and he pulled her over on top of him and yanked the sheet over them and kissed her and kissed her and kissed her . . .

In the morning, Cathy was up, into the shower, and out of the room before the Lieutenant's feet hit the floor. She found the Colonel and the Sergeant Major in the hotel lobby, waiting for Captain Morriss.

"Colonel Blue? Can I have a word with you and the Sergeant Major?" she asked. She was wearing a tan suit and a white blouse and chocolate brown pumps. She had pulled her hair back into a ponytail, and her face was creased with worry lines.

The Colonel stood up to greet her.

"What's on your mind, Cathy?" he asked.

"I'm concerned about your son, sir," Cathy said.

"So am I," said the Colonel. "I didn't like the looks on the faces of that court yesterday."

"I've got an idea, and I wondered what you and the Sergeant Major might think of it."

"Shoot," said the Colonel. They sat down in a corner of the lobby.

"I know a man here in Saigon who might be able to help Matt," she began. "He's an old friend of my father's, and I've used him as a source in some of the reporting I've done here. He has always proved to be scrupulously accurate and reliable."

"Who is he?" the Colonel asked.

"He's called Ba Tam, and he owns a restaurant on the waterfront. But that's not all he owns. He is a large landowner in the Song Cai Valley."

"Where is that?" asked the Colonel.

"It's up in II Corps," said the Sergeant Major. "I know who she's talking about."

"You know this man, Sarenmajor?"

"No, sir, but I've heard of him. He's a big man up in II Corps. He ain't such a small fry down here, either."

"How do you know of him, Sarenmajor?"

"I've ... uh ... done some business with his partner in the restaurant, sir. A man called Cam Tho."

Cathy Joice interrupted them.

"I think Ba Tam may be able to find out something about what happened to Matt in Laos. He has many relatives in that area. If anyone can help you prove that what Matt says he saw actually took place, it's Ba Tam."

"Just a minute, Cathy," said the Colonel. He turned to the Sergeant Major.

"This man Cam Tho, the business you've had with him—is it black-market business?"

The Sergeant Major shifted nervously in his chair.

"Yes, sir."

"I don't like it."

"Listen, sir, this ain't something I'm proud of, necessarily, but as long as there have been wars, there's been a black market associated with wars. Liquor, cigarettes, shoes, you name it ..."

"Weapons."

"And weapons, yes, sir, but I don't have nothing to do with weapons, sir. You'll have to take my word on it, sir. I've never sold a weapon to anybody. On my honor."

The Colonel studied the Sergeant Major for a long moment and said, "Go ahead. Tell me about it."

"I trade some liquor with this gentleman, uh, Cam Tho. That is all, sir. He's a partner of this man Ba Tam in the restaurant here in Saigon, and he is an upstanding member of their community here, sir. Honest to God. It's just that ... well, I've got a few things he needs, and he's got a few things I need. You know how it is, sir. We did the same thing in the Battalion. What you don't got, you scrounge. Well, he scrounges from me, and I scrounge from him. It works out. That's what a black market is, sir. Kind of an organized system of scrounging."

"I still don't like it," the Colonel said. But his voice showed weariness, resignation, not finality. He was giving in, and the Sergeant Major knew it.

"I don't see what difference it makes what either man does for a living," said Cathy Joice. "If Ba Tam can help Matt, that's all that counts."

The Sergeant Major nodded.

"Sir, we're up against it with your son. All I'm saying is, if Cathy can get us in to meet this gentleman, we'll find out what he knows."

"He might know about DC-3s on grass strips in the middle of the night in Laos?" The Colonel looked Cathy Joice in the eye, waiting for her answer.

"I don't know what he knows," she said. "He may know something. He may not. He may be able to help us, he may not. Either way, you don't have much choice at this point. I don't think the court-martial is going at all well for Matt. Ba Tam may be all that stands between him and conviction. You owe it to Matt to at least listen to him."

The Colonel walked away from the Sergeant Major and Cathy Joice and stood in the window overlooking the hotel garden. He watched some pigeons feeding under a palm tree for a moment, then he turned and walked back.

"Okay. But this goes against my better judgment," he said.

"It's not like Ba Tam has a disease and you're going to catch it, sir," Cathy said. "Ba Tam is an old friend of my father's. There is nothing wrong with turning to someone you don't know when you're in need."

"Where is he?"

"Down by the ferry, sir," Cathy said. "His restaurant is on the waterfront."

"Let's get down there and get it over with."

"Let me leave a note for Matt at the desk," said Cathy. She hurriedly scribbled a note and handed it to the desk clerk and returned. The Colonel and the Sergeant Major stood.

Cathy Joice led the way out the door of the Continental. Silently she prayed that her father's old friend could help them.

Restaurant Viet-Français was an old covered pier that stood on pilings sunk deep into the black mud of the Saigon River. Popular with American civilian officials stationed in Saigon, it was a throwback to French colonial days, serving traditional French dishes, upper-crust Vietnamese fare, and the tasty mix of the two cuisines that was peculiar to Saigon eating establishments.

It wasn't yet noon, and the restaurant was closed, but through the windows, Cathy Joice, the Sergeant Major, and the Colonel could see waiters scurrying this way and that, making preparations for lunch. The Sergeant Major banged on the door and one of the waiters came to the door and waved his hands, indicating that the restaurant was closed.

The Sergeant Major tried the door. It was locked. The waiter shook his head and tapped his watch.

"Mr. Ba Tam. We want to see Ba Tam," Cathy yelled through the closed door.

The waiter nodded and ran toward the back of the restaurant. In a moment he returned and unlocked the door. He led them through the front room, down a hall, through a back room that overlooked the river through sliding glass doors, and through swinging doors into the kitchen. They turned left and passed through another narrow hall, and the waiter knocked on a door.

Someone in the room said something in Vietnamese, and the waiter opened the door. A wisp of a man wearing an expensively cut western-style suit was standing behind a large desk.

"Come in, Miss Cathy," the man said in near-perfect English, with a smile, revealing two rows of yellow teeth. "It good to see you again. How is your father?"

His hair was white and cropped close to the skull and his fingers were long and so were his fingernails. That was what you noticed about him first, the yellow teeth, the long nails. Then you noticed his face, which was deeply lined and dark, and his eyes, which were steely gray within their thin slits.

"He is very well, Ba Tam. Let me introduce you to my friends. Ba Tam, this is Colonel Blue and this is Sergeant Major Bennett."

The Colonel reached across the desk to take the man's hand. The little man bowed slightly as he shook hands, and grinned widely.

"Always happy to meet friend of Miss Cathy," said the little man.

"Colonel Blue isn't just a friend, exactly, Ba Tam," said Cathy. "He is a man in need of help."

"Ah yes," said the little man.

"Please, sit," he said, indicating armchairs upholstered in red leather. "It is pleasure to make your acquaintance."

"It is nice to meet you, Mr. Tam," said the Colonel, realizing they were going through some kind of elaborate Oriental rite.

"Ba Tam, please."

The Colonel nodded his assent, watching the little man with mounting interest.

"What is nature of visit, Miss Cathy?" asked the little man with another yellow smile.

"The Colonel is a man who means a great deal to me, Ba Tam, as I have told you." Cathy Joice sat forward in her chair and placed both palms on the desk in what the Colonel took to be a gesture of supplication.

The little man nodded and smiled.

"His son, Lieutenant Blue, means a great deal to me."

"I can see, Miss Cathy," said the little man. He wasn't smiling now.

"Colonel Blue has a problem, Ba Tam."

"And what is problem, please?"

"It concerns his son, Lieutenant Matthew Blue, who is named for his father and for his grandfather. He has been charged with a very severe offense by the military authorities in Vietnam."

"And what is offense, please?"

"Desertion in the face of the enemy, Ba Tam."

"Very serious."

"He is not guilty of this offense, Ba Tam. He is facing this charge because the American authorities seek to cover up something else, something Lieutenant Blue witnessed." Cathy's voice was steady and low, and her eyes never left the little man's eyes.

"This happened before, I know," the little man said. His palms were flat on the desk before him, and not a muscle in his body moved.

"Lieutenant Blue saw a plane being loaded with burlap bales in Laos, Ba Tam. A couple of weeks ago. Near Thac Hiet."

"Yes?"

"He and his patrol came upon an airplane being loaded with these bundles in the jungle, in the middle of the night. The men doing the loading were Americans, Ba Tam. There was some trouble, and a man was killed. One of Lieutenant Blue's men."

"Very, very serious," the little man said gravely.

"Yes, it is," said Cathy.

"What I can do for you, Miss Cathy?"

"Lieutenant Blue does not know what those men were loading in the plane in Laos. All he knows is what I have told you. Enough value was placed on the shipment that the men loading the plane killed one of Lieutenant Blue's men in a firefight. We need some evidence. We would like you to tell us what you know about American airplanes in Laos, Ba Tam."

"I know nothing of airplanes in Laos, Miss Cathy. You ask me many questions in past, and I answer you truthfully. I answer you truthfully today."

"Then we would like you to find out for us what you can. What were they loading? Why would they kill another American?"

"I will do for you with pleasure," the little man said.

"That's what I hoped you would say, Ba Tam."

"For Lieutenant Blue, you would do anything, is not so?"

"Yes, it is so."

"For you, for your family, I will do all I can do," said the wizened little man. He stood up.

Cathy stood, followed by the Sergeant Major and the Colonel.

"You have very good Sergeant, Colonel Blue," said the little man. "Cam Tho tells me many good things about your Sergeant."

"I know I do, Ba Tam," said the Colonel.

"Man like this does not come every day, Colonel Blue," said the little man.

"I know," said the Colonel.

"Also true of Miss Cathy."

"I know."

"Because she asks me, I do this thing for you. I ask many questions. I have answers for you by nightfall."

"Thank you, Ba Tam," said the Colonel.

The little man proffered his hand and the Colonel shook it.

"Where do you stay, Miss Cathy?"

"At the Continental, Ba Tam. I am in the same room as before."

"Thanks, Ba Tam," said the Sergeant Major.

The little man waved his hand before his face and smiled a yellow smile and his eyes twinkled within their narrow slits.

"You hear from Ba Tam tonight, then."

"Yes," said Cathy. "I will wait for your call."

The door opened behind them and the waiter appeared and escorted them from the deep reaches of the restaurant to the street entrance.

"That was really something," said the Colonel.

"He is an interesting man," said the Sergeant Major.

"My father would say that was an understatement," said Cathy.

The Sergeant Major extracted a fresh cigar from his shirt pocket and started to light it.

"You know something, sir? You come over here with a unit like our Battalion and you get out in those boonies and you start fighting the enemy and you chase him this way and you chase him that way and you get into your night loggers and you chase him again and it's easy to lose track of the idea that we're fighting this war over here for people like Ba Tam. You know what I mean? That man *is* Vietnam, the way he looks at you, the way he talks to you. You know, sir?"

"I know exactly what you mean," said the Colonel.

They started walking back to the hotel. Around them, the city of Saigon bustled its way through another hot day. Auto taxis barked at bike-taxis. Old women hung out laundry. Shopkeepers stood in their doorways, beckoning to passersby with wide smiles. Within the wet darkness of the bars, girls could be seen in tight *ao dai*s, also beckoning. Diesel exhaust hung thickly in the air, Saigon perfume. The sun glowed dimly through the diesel fumes and the heat came from the pavement and from the sun and from the walls of the buildings and from the passing taxis and from the yelping and nattering of the taxi drivers and the washerwomen and the B-girls.

Saigon was the reason they were fighting the war, and it was the reason Cathy Joice was reporting the war, and still it was forever foreign to them, more foreign than ever right now on this street on this morning.

"You know something?" the Colonel asked as they pushed their way through the street fog, through the human detritus of Saigon, of the war.

"What's that, sir?" Cathy asked.

"That little man back there, Ba Tam? He was really something."

"Yes. You're right about that."

"And you know what else? That little Vietnamese man reminded me very, very much of my father."

Cathy Joice said nothing and the Sergeant Major said nothing and the Colonel said nothing and they shouldered their way through the smoky battlefield that was the morning streets of Saigon.

20

When the court convened the next morning, the Lieutenant was even more frightened than he was the day before. He had spent the morning mulling over what his father and grandfather had said, and they were right. Morriss could make all the legal points he wanted to make and those seven officers could sit up there and happily find him guilty and send him to Leavenworth for the rest of his life or, worse, send him there and have him hanged for a crime that was the moral equivalent of treason. He hoped Morriss had a few tricks up his sleeve. He hoped he would eat Lieutenant Colonel Halleck alive, but, more important, he hoped Morriss would make the members of the court *want* to see Halleck chewed up and spat out like so much gristle.

The MP opened the rear door to the court and called:

"All rise!"

The judge and the members of the court filed in.

"The court is now in session. All persons previously sworn remain sworn and are present. Proceed, Captain Dupuy." The judge didn't waste a moment. He pulled his half-glasses out of his shirt pocket, propped them on the end of his nose, and gazed over the room.

The Lieutenant turned around and stole a glance.

The court's spectator section was just as empty as it had been yesterday. He was being court-martialed in a vacuum.

"The prosecution calls Colonel James Franklin Testor."

The back door opened and the commander of the Third Brigade of the 25th Infantry Division walked in and took the oath. Dupuy got him identified and approached the lectern.

"What in hell is he doing here?" the Lieutenant asked in a whisper.

"I don't know. Dupuy is either very stupid or he's got something. We'll see."

"Colonel Testor, how long have you commanded the Third Brigade of the 25th Infantry Division?"

"Nine months and six days," Testor said with a thin smile.

"And how long have you served your country in Vietnam?"

"This is my third tour. Two years, nine months, and six days." He smiled again.

"Would you consider yourself an expert when it comes to combat operations, Colonel?"

"Yes, I would."

Behind him the Lieutenant heard his grandfather cough, nearly choking. He pulled out a handkerchief and spat in it and put it back in his pocket.

"As the commander of the Third Brigade of the 25th Infantry Division, you command more than Infantry soldiers, do you not, Colonel?"

"Yes, I command helicopter crews and various administrative units and medical personnel and even an Air Defense Artillery Platoon." He sat back in the witness chair and relaxed. He was enjoying himself.

"Previous to the Third Brigade of the 25th Division, you commanded a Battalion in combat, did you not?"

"Yes. The First of the 45th. In the Central Highlands."

"And you commanded what? A company also?"

"Yes, but not in combat."

"But in Korea you had a command, did you not?"

"Yes. I was a platoon leader."

"What kind of platoon leader were you, sir?"

"I was in command of a weapons platoon."

"Oh-oh," Morriss whispered. "Oh-oh."

"How long during the Korean war were you in command of your weapons platoon, sir?"

"For two years."

"So you had occasion to bring the firepower of the weapons platoon to bear in numerous combat situations over the course of two years, did you not, sir?"

"Yes, I did."

"In all of your lifetime of experience as an Army officer, sir, in all your years commanding weapons platoons and battalions and brigades, did you ever come across a situation similar to the one at issue in this court, sir?"

Morriss was out of his chair and around the front of the table and practically in Colonel Testor's face.

"I object, Your Honor! I object! Irrelevant! Immaterial! Without basis in law! Irresponsible! The prosecution is trying to sway this court with irrelevancies and innuendo! The prosecution should stick to the facts of the case! Objection! Objection!"

"Your Honor! Your Honor!" Dupuy was yelling.

The judge pointed the handle of his gavel first at Morriss and then at Dupuy.

"Sit down. Both of you. I'll not have this kind of behavior in my court."

Morriss immediately took his seat. Dupuy took his time, a hurt look on his face, as though somehow his noble effort to let this great man have his say had been thwarted. In truth, he had gotten what he wanted, and he knew it. All he wanted was the legitimacy that the man would bring to his case. All he wanted was that identification . . .

Weapons platoon leader.

From there, his question answered itself in Colonel Testor's smug silence.

Of course he'd never come across such nonsense, his silence implied. Why, if he had, he'd have tried the man and had him shot! All of it was on the brigade commander's face, and the members of the court could not help but see it.

"I'm going to uphold the objection, Captain Dupuy," Colonel Kelly said. "There is no place in this courtroom for the kind of grandstanding you were attempting. I told you before this trial began that we would be going by the book, and I meant it. And that means no irrelevant, immaterial grandstanding from you or from any of your witnesses. Do I make myself understood?"

"Yes, sir," said Dupuy, still trying to look as wronged as he could look.

"Now. Continue your questioning of Colonel Testor in a new line."

"Colonel Testor, you are familiar with the operation known as Iron Fist One."

"Yes, I am."

"And you are familiar with the territory west of Dak Sut, Vietnam."

"Very. I spent both my other tours in II Corps. This makes my third year in that area."

"Would you say that Operation Iron Fist One was essential to the Army's mission . . . to the war mission, sir?"

"Absolutely. Without periodic sweeps like Iron Fist One, the NVA have free run of the Ho Chi Minh Trail. It is my job, and that of my brigade, to deny the enemy such freedom. We have accomplished this in the past, and we accomplished our mission with Iron Fist One."

"You are familiar with the charges in this case?"

"Yes, I am. Lieutenant Colonel Halleck reported the refusal of Lieutenant Blue to fire his weapons the night it happened. The next day I processed the charges filed by Lieutenant Colonel Halleck. I am *very* familiar with the charges."

"Have you ever had occasion to doubt the word of Lieutenant Colonel Halleck in the past?"

"No, I have not."

"And do you doubt his word in this instance, the matter of the charges he has brought against Lieutenant Blue?" Dupuy pointed an accusing finger at the defendant.

"No, I do not. The charges are in accordance with what Lieutenant Colonel Halleck reported to me the night of the incident."

"No further questions, Your Honor," Dupuy said with a self-indulgent little smile. "Your witness, Captain Morriss."

Morriss sat there staring at the brigade commander with a look of utter contempt on his face.

"Captain Morriss. Do you have any questions of this witness?"

"No, sir. No questions."

"Colonel Testor, you are excused. Thank you," said the judge.

Colonel Testor stood and made a show of straightening his uniform before he walked off. He was almost to the door when the Lieutenant thought of something.

The Lieutenant tugged at Morriss's shirt sleeve.

"Ask him what kind of weapons platoon he had," he whispered.

"Are there more than one?"

"I think there used to be. Ask him. Go ahead. We've got nothing to lose with this guy."

"One moment, Your Honor. I have a question for the witness."

"Go ahead," said the judge, looking sternly over his glasses.

Colonel Testor looked perturbed and slowly returned to the witness chair.

"How long ago did you command your weapons platoon, sir?"

"Let me see . . . almost twenty years ago. Yes. That is correct."

"And what kind of weapons platoon was it, sir?"

"Come again?"

"What kind of weapons platoon did you command, sir?"

"It was a quad-fifties platoon, as I recall."

"A what, sir?"

"A quad-fifties platoon."

"What kind of weapon would that be, sir? Could you describe it for the court?"

"We had braces of four .50-caliber machine guns mounted on truck beds. Three of them."

"So your weapons platoon was *not* a mortar platoon. Is that right, sir?"

"Yes. That is correct."

"And as a platoon leader, you had no experience whatsoever with mortars."

"Yes, but—"

"That's all I wanted to know, sir. No further questions."

Captain Morriss sat down and Colonel Testor looked quizzically at Captain Dupuy and then at the judge.

Dupuy didn't even look up from his desk. At least part of his gambit with Colonel Testor had been foiled.

The judge peered at Colonel Testor over his spectacles and said, "You may go now, sir. You are finished."

Colonel Testor stood up and stalked out of the room.

Dupuy rose slowly from his chair.

"The prosecution rests, Your Honor."

The judge looked startled.

"Is the defense prepared at this time?" The judge glanced at his watch, giving Morriss an opening.

"If it please the court, Your Honor, the defense would like the balance of the day to prepare, sir."

"Granted. Court will convene tomorrow at ten hundred hours." Colonel Kelly banged the gavel and led the court from the room.

Captain Morriss, the Lieutenant, and the Colonel worked long into the night, preparing for the next day. Morriss studied his opening statement. He had written it out in longhand two days previously, but after hearing the prosecution's case, he felt it needed extensive revision. He sat alone in a room at the Caravelle, tightening its focus and expanding on the one new theme he would introduce to the case.

The Colonel and the Sergeant Major met afterwards in their suite and pored over the evidence the Sergeant Major had unearthed during the day. Captain Morriss and the Lieutenant joined them at midnight. It wasn't much, but any evidence at all favorable to the defendant was useful in a capital case.

It was almost 1:00 A.M. when the Lieutenant knocked on the door of Room 306 at the Continental Hotel. Cathy Joice answered the door fully dressed.

"I didn't think you were coming," she said, wrapping her arms around his neck.

"Then what are you doing still awake, still dressed?"

"Your grandfather and I had a visitor."

"Who? What about?"

"A Vietnamese man by the name of Ba Tam. Your father, the Sergeant Major, and I met with him this morning. He's a big landowner in the Song Cai Valley—"

"That's up in II Corps!"

"You're right. Ba Tam, it seems, is quite familiar with your brigade commander, Colonel Testor, whose three tours in II Corps were not exactly arranged by chance."

"Where are they, the General and this man . . ."

"Ba Tam."

"Yeah. Where'd they go?"

"They seem to have a few mutual friends, so they have gone back to Ba Tam's restaurant on the waterfront to talk things over. You didn't tell me your grandfather was in the CIA."

"Oh. Yeah. I didn't know myself until a couple of years ago."

"So was my father."

"No kidding?"

"He and Mom always said he worked for the State Department, but when I grew up, it didn't take me long to draw my own conclusions."

"I know what you mean. Where did your father work?"

"In embassies all over the world. I guess I lived in six—no, seven—different countries when I was growing up."

"Me too."

Cathy nuzzled against the Lieutenant's shoulder and closed her eyes.

"When are we going to know what your friend Ba Tam found out?" Lieutenant Blue asked.

"Tomorrow morning. I'm worried, Matt. Everyone was talking after court today. Nobody would bet that you will win the case. Not a single reporter. They're thinking about starting a pool tomorrow, picking the date you will hang. A pool is the only way they think they can gamble on your case, and you know reporters are inveterate gamblers."

"Tell someone you'd like to place a bet on me, because that someone is going to make out like a bandit," said the Lieutenant, looking straight in her eyes.

She threw her arms around him and held her breath, then whispered rapidly in his ear before he could pull away, "I hope so, Matt Blue, because I love you very, very much and I couldn't stand it if they took you away from me. I would die. Really I would."

The Lieutenant unwrapped her arms and stepped back from her. She was wearing a straight tan skirt and a light silk blouse, very plain, very businesslike, but her workaday clothes could do little to disguise the fact that she was the sexiest woman he had ever seen in his life. He reached down and scooped her into his arms and walked across the room and lowered her onto the bed. Then he undressed her and undressed himself and yanked back the covers and climbed into bed next to her and pulled the covers all the way over them and said:

"There. Now we're safe. No one will ever find us in here and we can do whatever we want."

"You sound like a kid, Matt," she giggled as she buried her face in the hairs on his chest.

"Well, I'm not a kid, Cathy. I'm a full-grown man and a Lieutenant in the United States Army, and I'm head over heels in love with someone I barely even know. What do you think about that?"

"What do I think about that? I think you should prove it, tough guy."

So he did.

"Gentlemen," Captain Morriss began, standing in front of the defense desk without notes, not a scrap of paper in front of him, leaning on his right elbow, which was resting on the top edge of the lectern. "Gentlemen, my name is Captain Terrence W. Morriss, and I am the lawyer for the accused in this case. I have been in the

Army for just over one year and I am not a combat veteran, but gentlemen, I know baloney when I see it and when I smell it, and that is exactly what I see and what I smell in the case the prosecution has presented to this court: baloney."

Morriss shifted his weight to both feet and stood erect, hands on hips. With his pot belly and his ill-fitting khakis, he looked like a tan fireplug.

"The prosecution described the charges against Lieutenant Blue as profound. They are. And the prosecution described this case as simple. It is not. A capital case that is simple is an oxymoron, gentlemen, a contradiction in terms. The charge against Lieutenant Blue is profound, and this case is profoundly complicated. Pay close attention to what I say, gentlemen, because I am going to outline the defense case for you, then you can sit back and listen to it unfold in the words of the men who were there, the men who were responsible for the mission of the Second of the 22nd Infantry, the men who were responsible for bringing these profound charges against Lieutenant Blue, the men who, gentlemen, and this is key, have a great deal—*a very great deal*—of explaining to do. Once they have explained themselves, gentlemen, you will be convinced of the innocence of this defendant and of the great injustice that has been done to him."

Morriss paused and looked at each member of the court in turn, assuring himself that he had their undivided attention. He had them, all right. Something in his manner had told them this was no ordinary Army lawyer. He continued, speaking slowly and deliberately:

"First, the defense will prove to you beyond a reasonable doubt—and that is the standard of proof, gentlemen, a reasonable doubt—that the order Lieutenant Blue refused was an illegal order, and that if he had obeyed that order, seven American soldiers would be dead on the ground, the victims of mortar fire from their own platoon."

He paused and cleared his throat.

"Second, the defense will prove a motive for the charges brought against Lieutenant Blue. I know that defense proof of motive is highly unusual—extremely rare, in fact—and totally uncalled for in most cases, but what we have here in this room is a highly unusual case and an extremely rare charge. It is a capital charge, as you know. And motive bears upon the facts of this case in a highly unusual but crucial way. We will prove motive behind the charges against Lieutenant Blue, gentlemen. When you understand motive, you will understand the innocence of the defendant."

One or two of the members of the court perked up at the mention of motive. Morriss took note of their interest and continued:

"Third, the defense will show that the so-called mission that the Second of the 22nd was engaged in was a false one, that the true tactical intent of the so-called sweep called Operation Iron Fist One was something else entirely, and that Lieutenant Blue, in carrying out his mission, had come across the true intent of Iron Fist One. This last fact, not any other fact or set of facts that have been presented to this court, was the reason that the capital charge of desertion in the face of the enemy was brought against him."

Morriss paused and looked each member of the court in the eye, then took a step backward and dropped his voice in tone and volume.

"The prosecution insists that this case is a simple one. Maybe they are right. The wrong man has been charged here, gentlemen, and that is a very simple thing to understand. You will understand the truth of what I say when I am finished. And you will find this man . . ."

Morriss turned around and walked to the Lieutenant's side and placed his hand on his shoulder.

". . . You will find this man innocent of the charge and the specification against him."

Morriss walked from behind the defense table. "The defense calls Specialist Fourth Class James Fish."

"Call the witness," said the judge.

The MP opened the door and Repatch appeared in a set of brand-new khakis that he had bought that morning at the Tan Son Nhut quartermaster store. His hair was slicked back, and brand-new Spec-4 chevrons gleamed on his collar.

Captain Morriss swore in the witness.

"Specialist Fish, you are and you were a member of the weapons platoon, Second of the 22nd Infantry, are you not?"

"Yes, sir. I sure am."

"You were a member when Lieutenant Blue was the platoon leader?"

"Yes, sir. And before that and after that."

"What happened to the others who served in the weapons platoon with you under Lieutenant Blue?"

"They was shipped out the morning after they came and took the Lieutenant away," Repatch said without emotion.

"Do you know why they were shipped out?"

"I figured they didn't want them around no more, because of the Lieutenant and all."

"Was the entire platoon reassigned before, when your previous platoon leader left?"

"No, sir. This is the first time this reassignin' thing has happened. I been there through three platoon leaders, and they never done this before."

"But you were not shipped out with the others?"

"No, sir."

"May I ask why not?"

"Because I wasn't there, sir. They can't ship you out if they can't find you, know what I mean?"

"You weren't there?"

"No, sir."

"Where were you, Specialist?"

"I was ghostin', sir."

"Ghosting?"

"Makin' myself scarce, sir."

"Why did you make yourself scarce, Specialist Fish?"

" 'Cause I didn't want to leave the platoon, sir. It's my platoon. It's the only platoon I got. I didn't want them to take me away from my platoon. It's kinda like my house ... my home, the platoon. Sir."

"So you hid out, then you reappeared ..."

"Yes, sir."

". . . As Specialist Fish."

"Yes, sir. But I was Fish before, too, sir, but they didn't call me that."

"What did they call you?"

"Repatch, sir."

"That was your name?"

"Then. Now it's Fish."

"So you stayed on."

"Yes, sir. To wait for the Eltee. Then I heard they had him down in Long Binh, so I came down here to wait for him."

"You were waiting for the Lieutenant for what reason, Specialist?"

"Because he saved my life, sir. And because he was one hell of a good platoon leader. You don't get good lieutenants all the time, sir. Hardly ever. When you get one, you want to hang on to him, sir. Good Eltees can make your life a little better, and they can keep dudes from gettin' themselves shot, too."

Dupuy was rummaging through his papers, looking bewildered. The members of the court were sitting forward on their chairs, paying very close attention. Each one of them, it seemed, had come in contact with a ghost like Repatch, but none had ever heard him describe his methodology. They were fascinated.

"Specialist Fish, you are familiar with the events of the night of October 13, are you not?"

"Yes, sir. I was right in the middle of 'em."

"Where were you?"

"I was out on the ambush patrol that was ordered up."

"And what was your position on the patrol?"

"I was walkin' point. That's what I do, sir. I walk point. It's my job."

The members of the court shifted nervously in their chairs. This guy was one for the books.

"What was your location on patrol that night?"

"We was the same place we was at the night before, 'tween a creek and a little knoll maybe two kliks from the platoon. The Eltee, he told me to take us out to the same place as the night before, so I done like he said. My experience with the Eltee is like, if you do pretty much what he says, you gonna keep your shit together, sir." Repatch glanced at the judge. "Sorry, sir."

"Do you recall the grid coordinates of your position, Specialist Fish?"

"No, sir. Not them numbers."

"Would you be able to find your position on a map?"

"I could find that spot in my sleep, sir."

Morriss turned to the defense table and pulled two maps from an envelope.

"Your Honor, I would like to introduce these maps as defense exhibits A and B."

"Without objection, it is so ordered."

Morriss reached behind the defense table and pulled out a bulletin board and an easel and set them up on the left side of the room, directly in front of the seven members of the court. He unfolded the maps and pinned them to the bulletin board.

"Specialist, could you point to your ambush position on either of these maps?"

"Yes, sir. On both of 'em."

"Do so." Morriss handed Repatch a pointer. Repatch whipped the pointer back and forth in the air once or twice, making a sharp *whoooooosh*. He grinned widely and walked to the easel and pointed to the ambush position near the edges of both maps.

"Right there is where we was at, sir. 'Tween the creek and the knoll, like I said. See, this little blue line is the creek"—he jabbed the map with the pointer—"and this here little brown thing looks like a buncha coffee rings inside a' one another, that's the knoll, sir."

"Would you mark the patrol's position with these red pushpins, please?"

"Glad to."

Repatch pinned both maps and sat down. He was still holding the pointer, twirling it between his fingers and smiling.

"Do you know why the ambush position is on both maps, Specialist?"

"Yes, sir. Because they overlap, those two maps do. The ambush was on the south edge of the one map and the north edge of the other map, right where they overlapped, right where I pinned it, sir."

"Can you read for me the grid coordinates of the ambush position from each map?"

"Glad to, sir." Repatch walked to the board and read the numbers.

"This here one, map 24-Lima, is the map we was usin', me and the Eltee."

"The Eltee?"

"The Lieutenant, sir. He was leadin' the patrol and I was walkin' point, so we was in close contact about where the hell we was at that night. Anyways, we was usin' 24-Lima, and our ambush was set up at grid 72548869. I remember them numbers now. Right there where I pinned it, that's what the numbers would be."

"Do the members of the court want to inspect the map?" Morriss asked when he noticed the entire court leaning forward to see the map. They shook their heads. They could see well enough.

"This here map is 22-Lima, and we was on this one, too, but we didn't know it. Lemme see . . . on 22-Lima we was at . . ." Repatch dropped on one knee and poked the map with his finger and counted. ". . . seven . . . two . . . five . . . four . . . Hey, them numbers is the same! . . . one . . . one . . . one . . . eight. Yeah, there we was. You can see we was on the same vertical line from one map to the other, the seven line. But on the one map, we was on the eight line crossways . . ."

"Horizontally."

"That's what I said, sir, crossways. And on the other one here, we was on the one line crossways."

"You seem to know a great deal about map reading, Specialist. Did you go to an Army school to learn how to read a map?"

"No, sir."

"How did you learn then?"

"Sir, if you was gonna walk point through these weird boonies over here in the 'Nam, you'd get real familiar with maps real fast, or you wouldn't be walkin' point for very long."

"How long have you been walking point, Specialist Fish?"

"I'm on my third year walkin' point, sir."

Morriss stared at Repatch in amazement, then turned to the

defense table and shuffled some papers. He returned to his spot next to the lectern.

"Are you familiar with the charges Lieutenant Blue is facing?"

"Yes, sir."

"Are you familiar with the circumstances surrounding the facts of this case?"

"Sir, like I said, I was there."

"Tell us what happened, Specialist Fish. Tell us in your own words, and take your time."

"Battalion, somebody up there, called in a fire mission and they called it in on our position, see. The Eltee, he refused the order because if he'd obeyed the order, them mortars woulda killed all of us on the patrol, sir, because the weapons platoon, we place some accurate fire when we get a fire mission, and if the Eltee woulda shot them mortars, he woulda hit what he was shootin' at, and what he was ordered to shoot at was us. That's what I mean. He saved my life and he saved the lives of the rest of the patrol, too, sir."

"What is your understanding of how this mixup came about, Specialist?"

"It's real simple, sir." Repatch stood up and walked over to the board with the pointer.

"The Eltee, he called in these coordinates offa this here map"—he pointed to map 24-Lima—"and Battalion, they plotted 'em on this here map"—he pointed to map 22-Lima—"and they thought we was here"—he pointed to the top of map 22-Lima—"when we was really down here." He pointed to the bottom of the same map.

"They was usin' the wrong map, Battalion was. You look close, sir, the battalion NDP wasn't even *on* 22-Lima. It was on 24-Lima, sir. See here, right here in this clearin'?" Repatch poked the map with his pointer. "That's where the battalion NDP was at. You could always find the battalion NDP, sir. All you had to do was look for a clearin', and there they was, bigger'n—well, that's where they'd be at, sir. The Eltee, he knew where Battalion was at and where we was at and where he was at, but Battalion, they didn't know where none of us was at. Not a soul of us. And if it wasn't for the Eltee refusin' that order, sir, that's all we'd be—me and Davis and Whoopie Cushion and Mallick and Moonface and Lucky Lemon and Simpleton and Woodley and the Eltee—all of us would be souls, not bodies, sir. 'Cept the Eltee prevented us takin' early retirement and becomin' souls, sir, which is why I been waitin' for him to come back to the weapons platoon where he belongs. Sir."

"With the help of your testimony, Specialist, that is exactly what will happen. Thank you . . ."

"Objection. He's making a speech, sir." Dupuy was on his feet, red-faced.

"Withdraw my last comment, sir. Sorry." Morriss turned around to the defense table and grinned.

"Objection. Sir! He's laughing at my objection! He is grandstanding, sir! He is playing to the gallery, sir!"

"Captain Morriss?"

"Yes, sir."

"Keep your attention centered on the matters at hand. Understood?"

"Yes, sir."

"Are you finished with the witness?"

"Yes, sir."

"You may cross-examine," the judge told Dupuy.

Dupuy walked up to the lectern laden with paperwork. Methodically he laid the papers on the lectern. Then he turned to Repatch.

"Specialist Fish . . . that is your name, isn't it?"

"Yes, sir. Fish. And Repatch. I like 'em both, sir. You can call me Spec-4 Fish, or you can call me Repatch. I'll be happy both ways. Sir."

"How long have you held your present rank, Fish?"

"Off and on, sir, I'd say about five years."

"And you have been in the Army . . . ?"

"About seven years."

"So you have been busted?"

"Many times, sir. You're not an enlisted man, but if you was, sir, you'd know that if you stay in this man's Army, you're gonna go up and down in rank a few times. It just seems to happen that way, sir. Happened to me, anyways."

One or two of the members of the court stifled a smile.

"So even though you've been busted up and down a few times, as you said, you consider yourself qualified to testify about these matters regarding map positions and so on."

"Yes, sir."

"And you have not been to school to learn map reading?"

"No, sir."

"And you still insist you are expert enough to swear that your understanding of these matters is a correct one?"

Repatch stared at Dupuy for a moment, then he leaned back in his chair and took a deep breath and leaned forward and looked directly in Dupuy's eyes.

"Sir. I done told you the way it is. You do what you got to do. You learn what you got to learn. You want to walk point, which is what I want to do and which is what I *do,* then you learn this stuff about grids and verticals and such. Either that or the only thing you're gonna be expert at sure ain't on this earth. And me, I'm still here, and on what you're askin' me about, sir, just stayin' alive makes you 'bout as expert as you can ever be. Sir."

Dupuy shuffled his papers on the lectern and said, without looking up, "No further questions at this time, Your Honor."

"Call your next witness."

"The defense calls Lieutenant Colonel Henson W. Halleck for the purpose of cross-examination."

"Call Lieutenant Colonel Halleck."

There was a wait of several minutes, during which Morris removed the pins Repatch had stuck in the maps, and removed map 24-Lima from the bulletin board. Finally, Halleck came through the back door, spit-shined and starched and shaved and stern.

Dupuy reminded him he was sworn.

Morriss walked up to Halleck and handed him the pointer and turned around and walked back to the defense table. Then he turned and shot questions at Halleck one after the other, rapid-fire.

"Lieutenant Colonel Halleck, this is a copy of a map you were using on the night of October 13 is it not?"

"Yes, it is."

"Can you find for us the grid coordinates 72548869 on this map, sir?"

"Yes."

"Please do so, sir."

Halleck stood up and pointed to a spot near the top of the map.

"Would you please place one red pushpin on that spot, sir?"

Halleck pinned the spot and sat down.

"I am going to show you another map, sir." Morriss pinned 24-Lima to the board.

"Can you find grid coordinates 72548869 on this map, sir?"

Halleck looked disgusted as he walked to the map and pointed to the ambush patrol's location near the top of the map.

"Pin the spot, please, sir."

Halleck picked up a pin and stuck it in the map.

"When you ordered a fire mission on the night of October 13, you did so by specifying a set of grid coordinates. Could you recall those coordinates for us and find them on the left-hand map, map 22-Lima?"

Halleck approached the map.

"I ordered fire on grid 72541118 . . . here." He pointed to the bottom of 22-Lima.

"And Lieutenant Blue's patrol coordinates were . . ."

"Here." Halleck pointed to the pin at the top of 22-Lima.

"Colonel, will you find the terrain feature designated by 72541118 on map 24-Lima for us, please?"

"What?"

"72541118 denotes a spot between a stream and a knoll, does it not, sir? On map 22-Lima, sir."

"Yes, it does."

"Please find those terrain features on map 24-Lima."

Halleck studied map 24-Lima. After a moment he pointed to a spot near the top of the map.

"Here is a stream and knoll similar to the ones on 22-Lima."

"Read the coordinates for us, please sir."

"7254886 . . . 8 or 9. Could be either."

"Coordinates 72548869 could be an accurate reading?"

"Yes, it could."

"What were the grid coordinates of the weapons platoon ambush patrol?"

"I don't recall."

"I will read them to you from Captain Gardner's testimony, if you'd like. He kept the coordinates written down in a notebook. Would you accept his recollection, based on the notebook he kept on October 13?"

"Yes."

"Captain Gardner said the coordinates were—and here I am reading from his testimony—quote, 72548869, unquote."

Halleck glanced at Dupuy and at the judge. Then he looked back at Morriss.

"Did not Lieutenant Blue tell you on the night of October 13 that your fire mission would place fire from his own mortars on his ambush patrol, Colonel?"

"He may have. I don't recall exactly."

"You don't recall exactly. Is it not true that the fire mission coordinates you gave him, 72541118 on map 22-Lima, denote the same physical location on the ground as that found at coordinates 72548869 on map 24-Lima? Sir."

Halleck looked at Morriss for what seemed like a very long time.

"Yes." He grunted the word as though it had been torn from his throat with a pair of Vise-Grips.

"Did you or did you not proceed to call in 155-millimeter howitzer fire on grid coordinates 72541118 on map 22-Lima which are also coordinates 72548869 on map 24-Lima, the weapons platoon ambush patrol's location?"

Again a wait.

"Yes."

"Who gave you the order to call in the one-five-five fire?"

"Colonel Testor, the brigade commander, gave that order."

"Colonel Testor gave the order. Does Colonel Testor usually direct you to call in fire from the one-five-five battery, Lieutenant Colonel Halleck?"

"I believe that was the first time."

"The first time. And how many one-five-five rounds were put on that location?"

"Eight."

"Do you know why no one was killed by your 155-millimeter howitzer fire, Colonel?"

"No."

"Well, stick around, sir, and you'll find out. No further questions."

"Prosecution redirect? Or recross?" The judge looked at Dupuy, who was looking at Halleck.

"Not at this time, Your Honor."

"The defense recalls Captain Henry G. Gardner to the stand."

Captain Gardner entered the court through the rear door and stood in front of the witness chair. Dupuy reminded him he was under oath.

"Captain Gardner, were you present when Lieutenant Colonel Halleck received his orders from Colonel Testor, the brigade commander, to call in one-five-five howitzer fire from Division Artillery?"

"Yes, sir. I was present."

"You heard the radio transmission from Colonel Testor?"

"Yes, sir. I heard it."

"You heard him call for one-five-five fire, and you heard him call in this 155-millimeter howitzer fire on the same grid coordinates that Lieutenant Blue had just refused to train his mortars on. Is that correct?"

"Yes, sir."

"And what did you do, Captain?"

"Sir, I left the command bunker and returned to my company and got on the radio and called Lieutenant Blue and told him that Lieutenant Colonel Halleck had called in one-five-fives on his ambush position and I told Lieutenant Blue to move his men."

"Did Lieutenant Blue move his men from their ambush patrol location?"

"Yes, sir."

"How do you know he did?"

"Because he radioed me and told me he had moved down the creek. The one-five-fives hit right, where they had been."

"So the one-five-fives missed the ambush patrol because you had warned Lieutenant Blue they were coming and he moved the patrol."

"Yes, sir."

"Did Lieutenant Colonel Halleck tell you to warn Lieutenant Blue?"

"No, sir."

"Did Colonel Testor?"

"No, sir."

"Did either man know you warned Lieutenant Blue to move his patrol?"

"No, sir. I never told either of them."

"So, as far as both commanders were concerned, things were just the way they were moments before, when Lieutenant Blue refused his order to fire his mortars because the fire mission would have hit his ambush patrol?"

"Yes, sir."

"Thank you, Captain Gardner. Your witness."

"Captain Gardner, did you personally see where the one-five-five rounds hit?"

"No, sir."

"Then all you've got to go on with this testimony is the word of Lieutenant Blue?"

"I guess so, sir."

"That is what I figured. No further questions."

"The witness is dismissed," said Colonel Kelly. "Call your next witness, Captain Morriss."

"Defense calls Colonel James Franklin Testor, Your Honor."

Morriss was proceeding without hesitation, seemingly without caution. He was not building his case brick by brick, the way they taught you at Harvard Law. He was hammering it together wall by wall, throwing up a stockade around the prosecution's errant charges. He was doing what he had said he'd do. First he'd attacked the facts of the case; now he was going after the reason the charges had been brought. Within an hour or two, if things went right, he would have corralled the prosecution and squeezed it dry. Every eye in the place was on the back door, waiting for the next piece of wall Morriss would raise.

Testor walked in like a football coach on his way to the locker room to lecture the team at halftime. Unaware of Halleck's testimony and Repatch's colorful memories, Testor was ready to do battle for the forces of right and might and justice and honor.

Dupuy reminded Colonel Testor that he was sworn, and Morriss extracted his particulars. Then the potbellied defense attorney reached into his briefcase and pulled out a sheaf of carbons. He approached the judge and laid them on the table.

"Defense would like to mark these carbons as exhibit C, Your Honor."

"Without objection, so ordered."

Dupuy looked confused.

The Lieutenant looked back at his father and grandfather. His father had allowed himself the beginnings of a minor smile. The General's scowl was, if anything, more grim than the day before.

"Colonel Testor, are you familiar with this report?"

Morriss handed the sheaf of carbons to Testor.

"I am."

"Can you tell us what it is?"

"I cannot."

"Why, Colonel?"

"Because this report is classified."

Morriss reached for the carbons and Testor handed them over. He looked at each page, turning it over slowly, making a show of the process.

"Colonel, I cannot find a classification on this report. Did you see one? Where did you see it?"

"The classification is not there because that is a copy."

"Colonel, because there is no classification stamped on this report, nothing that certifies it Top Secret or 'Eyes Only,' I am going to ask the question again. What does this report say?"

"I cannot answer. The report is classified."

"Your Honor, I want the witness directed to answer." Morriss walked over to the judge's table and laid the report in front of him.

"Will both counsels please approach the bench?"

Dupuy joined them.

"Where did you get this?" the judge asked.

"Your Honor, I got it from Lieutenant Blue's track. It is a copy of an after-action report he wrote, a report of casualty due to friendly fire."

"Your Honor, I fail to see the relevance of this report."

"Your Honor, I will show relevance of the report. We have already received new testimony that Colonel Testor ordered Lieutenant Colonel Halleck to call for one-five-five fire. The relevance of this witness and of this exhibit goes to the issue of the reason charges were brought against Lieutenant Blue, Your Honor. This is an essential element of my case."

"Sit down," said the judge. He quickly read the report.

"I'll allow the exhibit, and I'll allow the questions of the witness and I'll direct the witness to answer."

"Colonel Testor, do you want me to repeat my question?"

"No."

"Then answer the question, please, sir."

"The report is a report of casualty due to friendly fire written by Lieutenant Blue dated October 13."

"What does it say, sir?"

"You know what it says."

"Do you want to read it into the record, or should I, sir?"

"You do it."

Morriss read the Lieutenant's report about the death of Strosher into the record. When he was finished, he looked up at Colonel Testor.

"Did you classify this report, sir?"

"I did."

"Why?"

"Because I did not want it getting into the wrong hands."

"Hands such as mine?"

"Exactly."

"Did you have a conversation with Lieutenant Blue about this report?"

"I did."

"Was anyone else present?"

"Lieutenant Colonel Halleck."

"What was the nature of the conversation and where did it take place, sir?"

"It took place on the afternoon of October 13 in Lieutenant Colonel Halleck's command bunker. I told Lieutenant Blue to change his report or withdraw it."

"Why was that, sir?"

"Because I did not believe it."

"Is it your job to pass judgment on such a report, or is it your job to examine the report and pass it up the chain of command to your superiors, as required by Army regulations?"

"Both."

"We already know your judgment of the report. Did you pass the report on to Major General Cardozo?"

"No."

"Why not, sir?"

"Because the report was false."

"Do you have any evidence as to the falsehood of Lieutenant Blue's after-action report describing the circumstances of the death of Corporal Lester G. Strosher?"

"No."

"Were you on patrol with him when they came upon the DC-3 being loaded with burlap bales in the middle of the night in the middle of the jungle?"

"Judge, he's being insubordinate," said Colonel Testor.

"Answer the question, sir. You may consider the questions of the defense as insubordinate, but I assure you he is only doing his job."

"I wasn't in the damn jungle with him, no." Testor was red-faced, seething.

"Did you see the body of Corporal Strosher?"

"No."

"But you heard about his death, did you not? His death was reported to you through channels other than this report."

"Yes."

"You do not believe Lieutenant Blue's report, but you believe Corporal Strosher to be dead?"

"That is correct."

"How did Corporal Strosher die?"

"I think he got shot by some VC, and Lieutenant Blue was scared he would get in trouble for losing a man to a lesser force than his own, and he made the whole thing up. That's what I think."

"Do you have any evidence to that effect, Colonel Testor, or is that a guess?"

Testor stared at Morriss for a long moment.

"It is my opinion."

"Absent evidence to the contrary, what does the Army say you are to do with such a report of casualty due to friendly fire?"

"Send it up."

"But you did not send it up."

"No, I did not."

"Did you discuss the report with Major General Cardozo?"

"No."

"Oh. You didn't discuss it with General Cardozo. Why not, Colonel?"

"Because the report was and is a crock."

"So General Cardozo never got the report."

Testor looked momentarily confused, then he brightened.

"No. He didn't. I told him I had a false report, and he told me to classify the report and hang on to it."

"Was that the normal manner in which you handled such a report in your brigade?"

"Yes."

"Thank you, Colonel. No further questions."

Morriss sat down.

"Cross-examine, Captain Dupuy?"

Dupuy stood up.

"Colonel Testor, in all your long years in the Army, did you ever see anything as fantastic as Lieutenant Blue's report of casualty due to friendly fire?"

"No."

"Did you ever know an American soldier to carry a Kalashnikov rifle like the one Corporal Strosher was shot with?"

"No."

"So you had good reason to doubt the validity of this report, sir?"

"Yes."

"That is all, sir."

"Redirect?" asked the judge.

Morriss stood up.

"In all your years in the Army, sir, were you ever in Laos?"

"No."

"Are you familiar with either of the maps on the board in front of you, sir?"

"I am familiar with the one on the left, map 22-Lima."

"And what does the map show, sir?"

"It shows the area of operations of Operation Iron Fist One, which I had the privilege to command."

"And what area does the map describe, sir?"

"An area of enemy-held territory to the west of Dak Sut, Vietnam."

"That wouldn't be Laos to the west of Dak Sut, would it Colonel?"

"Not to my knowledge. Iron Fist One skirted the border with Laos, but we did not cross into neutral territory."

"You are sure of this?"

"I am certain."

"That is all I have, Your Honor."

"The witness is excused," said Colonel Kelly. "Do you have another witness, Captain Morriss?"

"I have several witnesses, Your Honor, but I will be exceedingly brief with each of them."

"Will you be finished with your witnesses by fifteen hundred hours?"

"I hope to be, Your Honor."

"Call your next witness."

"The defense recalls Specialist Fish, Your Honor."

"Call Spec-4 Fish," said the judge.

Repatch came through the back door and took the witness chair.

"Specialist Fish, you are reminded that you are still under oath," Morriss said.

"Yes, sir," said Repatch.

"Specialist, I would like to question you now about the events of the night of October 12, 1969. Did you go out on the ambush patrol led by Lieutenant Blue that night?"

"Yes, sir. I walked point, sir."

"So you were present when the patrol came upon the DC-3 being loaded with burlap bales in the clearing that night?"

"Yes, sir. I was the first one who seen it."

"And you were there when Strosher was killed?"

"Yes, sir. I was right there. I seen the whole thing."

"The man who killed Strosher, was he an American?"

"Yes, sir, I had a look at 'im through the Eltee's glasses, and he sure wasn't no VC."

"Lieutenant Blue's after-action report states that the airplane was being loaded with burlap bales. Did you get a good look at what they were loading on the plane, Specialist?"

"Yes, sir."

"Do you know what was in those burlap bales, Specialist?"

"They was loadin' smack on that plane."

"Smack?"

"Heroin, sir. I seen them bales a' opium and heroin before, and that's what they was, sir."

"Where did you see the bales before, Specialist?"

"In a opium den over near the zoo, sir."

"Do you know of any other evidence that the airplane was being loaded with drugs?"

"Yes, sir." Repatch sat forward in the witness chair and reached behind him and pulled a pint bottle from his hip pocket. He handed the bottle to Captain Morriss.

"Bottle's fulla smack, sir. I sneaked back to that clearin' and filled it up with the smack that spilled out when Moonface hit one a' them bales with his '60."

Morriss took the bottle to the judge's table.

"Sir, the defense would like to mark this bottle defense exhibit D."

"Objection!" Dupuy was on his feet, waving his hand over his head. "There has been no evidence supplied by the defense that the contents of that bottle actually came from where the witness says it came from."

The judge turned to Captain Morriss.

"Captain?"

"May I ask a few more questions of the witness before you rule on the prosecution motion, Your Honor?"

"A very few, Captain Morriss. This is highly irregular."

"Why did you return to the clearing and fill this bottle with the heroin that spilled from one of the burlap bales, Specialist?"

"I done it for the Eltee, sir. I knowed he was gonna get in some bad trouble, 'cause a' Strosher getting it and all. I snuck back and got that smack so's he could prove what happened is what happened. Who's gonna believe you, sir, when you say you seen a plane gettin' loaded fulla smack in the middle of the night in Laos, sir?"

"You are sure the clearing you came upon was in Laos?"

"Yes, sir." Repatch stood up and walked over to map 24-Lima and pointed to a spot on the map.

"It was right there, sir, and that ain't Vietnam, sir, that's Laos."

"Captain Morriss, do you have any further testimony regarding this evidence?"

"No, sir."

"Then I'm compelled to rule the evidence inadmissible."

The judge struck his gavel, and Morriss shrugged his shoulders. Dupuy was grinning.

"Your witness," said Morriss.

Dupuy stood behind the prosecution table and questioned Repatch in a bored, you-don't-say voice.

"Regarding the so-called evidence you tried to present, Specialist, you say the bottle contains heroin. How do you know this, Specialist Fish?"

"It's heroin, sir. Them guys wasn't loading bales a' sugar in that plane in Laos, and they sure wasn't bales a' Johnson's Baby Powder, sir."

"Have the contents of the bottle been tested by a chemist?"

"No, sir."

"Then you expect us to take your word that, one, you filled the bottle with powder in the middle of the night in a clearing in Laos, and, two, that the powder you put in the bottle is, in fact, heroin. You expect us to believe this with absolutely no concrete evidence that what you say is true?"

"Yes, sir."

"This is fantastic, Specialist Fish. You waltz in here with a *whiskey bottle* and you tell us that it contains not whiskey, but *heroin,* and you tell us further that you filled it with this *heroin* in the middle of the night in some field in *Laos,* and you just sit there and figure that we're going to take your *word* that this is true. *Fantastic,* Specialist. *Incredible . . ."*

"Objection, Your Honor," said Captain Morriss. "If counsel has a question of the witness, he should ask it. You've already ruled the bottle of heroin inadmissible. We've had enough sarcastic speeches for one day."

"I have no further questions of this witness, Your Honor."

"Redirect, Captain Morriss?"

"No, sir."

"Call your next witness."

"The defense calls Major General Lawrence Cardozo."

"Call General Cardozo," said the judge.

Major General Cardozo entered and was sworn in as a witness by Captain Dupuy.

"I have just one question for you, sir. Did you give the order to mount Operation Iron Fist One, the sweep of enemy territory to the west of Dak Sut, Vietnam?"

"No, sir, I did not."

"Your witness," said Morriss.

Dupuy waved his hand without looking up from his papers.

"No questions."

"You are excused, General Cardozo. Thank you."

"Sir, the defense calls Lieutenant General Wesley Kramm."

"Call General Kramm," said the judge.

After a wait of five minutes, the back door opened and Lieutenant General Wesley Kramm entered. He was tall and distinguished looking, and he wore the starched fatigues of the Vietnam war high command, signaling that his testimony had necessitated a return from "the front."

Dupuy swore him in. Morriss established that Kramm was II Corps commander. He leaned on the lectern and asked his question laconically.

"Did you give the order to mount Operation Iron Fist One, sir?"

"No, I did not."

"Thank you, sir. That is all I have for you. Your witness," said Morriss to Dupuy.

"I have no questions for General Kramm, and I must add that I fail to see where this line of questioning of these witnesses is going," said Dupuy.

"Do you want to make an objection, counselor?" the judge asked.

"No, sir. I merely wanted to register my bewilderment that this court has allowed this obvious disruption of the command structure in the United States Army in Vietnam."

"Your bewilderment is noted, counselor. Absent any objection, call your next witness, Captain Morriss."

"The defense calls General Paul Fleming, sir."

The back door opened before the judge could order the witness called, and General Paul Fleming, a man who closely resembled a pit bull terrier, strode into the room. He, too, was starched and pressed in the Vietnam high command manner, and he stood stiffly in front of the witness chair as he was sworn in by Captain Dupuy.

"General, you are commander of MACV, is that correct?" Morriss asked.

"That is correct," said General Fleming in a voice that boomed through the Quonset hut like rolling thunder.

"I will ask you one question, sir . . ."

"Shoot," said General Fleming, smiling widely.

"Did you give the order to mount Operation Iron Fist One?"

"No, I did not. Anything else you want to know?" he asked.

"Thank you, General," Morriss said. "Your answer has been sufficient for my purposes. Your witness." He sat down.

"I have no questions for General Fleming, but want the record to show that General Fleming has been kept waiting in his staff car outside this room for two hours so that he could answer the momentous questions of the defense in this case."

"I'm sure the record will reflect your remarks, counselor," said the judge.

"Your Honor, I would like the record to reflect the prosecution's characterization of my question of General Fleming as, quote, momentous, unquote."

"The entire comment of Captain Dupuy's has been accurately noted, I am certain," the judge said. "Do you have further witnesses?"

"Yes, sir, but due to the lateness of the hour, the defense would like to wait until tomorrow's session to call its final witnesses."

"Defense request granted. Court will recess until ten hundred hours tomorrow." The judge and the court stood, and all filed out the back door.

The Lieutenant followed Captain Morriss from the court, and they were followed closely by the Colonel, the General, and the Sergeant Major.

They got in the staff cars and drove into Saigon. Alone together in the backseat of the first car, the Lieutenant badgered Captain Morriss.

"What do you mean, one more witness? You mean me, don't you?"

"No, Matt. I don't mean you."

"I want to take the stand, damn it. My life is at stake. My integrity has been assaulted. The name of the Blue family has been dragged through the dirt in that courtroom, and I want to defend myself and my family name."

"*I* will defend you, Lieutenant Blue. That is what a defense attorney is for. That is why I am here. That is why the Army pays me the grand sum of $640 a month. To defend you. It is not necessary for you to defend yourself. And so long as I am your attorney, you will not take the stand in your own defense. That way has been the path to one courtroom disaster after another."

"But I won't screw up on the stand! I want to stick it to them! I want them to regret the day they decided to ruin me and my reputation!"

"I will stick it to them with tomorrow, Matt. You will sit at the defense table and watch. Back in the Triple Deuce you were in command of your platoon. But within the lovely confines of Quonset hut 648, *I* am the commander. You will do what I say and then you will thank me later over a beer at the Continental, and you can shoot your damn mouth off all you want."

"Yes, sir," said a chastened Lieutenant Blue, recognizing the voice of reason at last.

21

T he chopper came in low, brushing the roof of the jungle with its rotors. The sun was setting, and there was just enough light to make out the breaks in the jungle below.

"That's where it's at!" Repatch yelled over the roar of the Huey. "Down there! See it?"

Danny Jannick leaned out the door of the chopper and squinted against the wind.

"Yeah. That long grassy spot, right?"

"You got it!"

Repatch tapped the pilot's shoulder and pointed to the ground. He nodded, and the Huey started down.

Jannick poked his head back in the chopper and signaled the cameraman. He tightened his seat belt, leaned out over the edge of the chopper's door, pointed his camera toward the ground, and started filming.

"Keep it running until we set down, Tommy!" yelled Cathy Joice to her cameraman.

"Right!" he yelled back.

The chopper headed for the grassy strip and settled down with a soft *whoosh-whoosh-whoosh-whoosh* of its rotors. Repatch and Jannick jumped out, followed by the cameraman and Cathy Joice. Repatch walked around to the pilot's side of the chopper.

"Wait here. If there's anything out there, it shouldn't take long to find it, man. Thirty minutes. That's all."

"It better be thirty minutes," said the pilot, a warrant officer who didn't look a day over nineteen. "It's getting dark. We've got to get up and out of here if we're going to find our way back to Pleiku."

"Sure. Gotchew."

Cathy Joice was standing in front of her cameraman with a mike in her hand.

"We are approximately ten kilometers inside the Laotian border, on the grass strip mentioned in testimony at the court-martial of Lieutenant Blue." She paused, then said, "Cut. Give me a minute, Tommy. I'm out of breath."

"Take your time," said the cameraman.

She held the mike and started again.

"This is the makeshift Laotian airstrip that has figured prominently in the defense strategy of Lieutenant Matthew Nelson Blue the fourth, who is defending himself against Army charges of desertion in the face of the enemy. At this moment we are more than ten kilometers inside the border of Laos. We have come here with Specialist Fish to attempt to locate physical evidence of the heroin shipment that the defense insists was lifted off this very strip on an unmarked DC-3 aircraft."

Repatch stepped in front of the camera and grabbed her by the arm.

"C'mon. We ain't got much time."

"Roll it, Tommy," she said as she followed Repatch on the run.

Repatch headed for the treeline at the end of the grassy strip. When he reached the trees, he slowed down. Both he and Jannick started combing the woods, moving aside bushes and low-hanging branches.

Cathy and her cameraman followed close behind.

"See anything?" Repatch called.

"Nothing so far," said Jannick.

"Over here," Repatch called. "That plane banked to the right when it got up in the air a bit."

He led them farther into the woods. Cathy Joice and her cameraman were falling behind, and it was getting darker and darker as the sun dropped lower on the horizon.

"Jesus!"

"What's that?" Cathy called.

"I tripped," Jannick called back.

"Where are you?" Repatch shouted.

"Over here," Jannick replied.

Repatch struggled through the undergrowth until he reached Jannick, who was sitting down with a wide smile on his face.

"Bingo," said Danny Jannick, grinning widely.

"Jannick. You done it."

"I tripped on the fucker," said Jannick, standing up. He had been sitting on a bale wrapped in burlap.

"Over here!" Jannick called.

Cathy and her cameraman appeared out of the trees, the camera still running.

"Get a close shot, then back up and get me full length," said Cathy.

The cameraman went in tight, then backed away.

Cathy took the mike and approached Jannick.

"Tell us what happened," she said, sticking the mike in his face.

"I tripped on it," said Jannick, pointing to the burlap-wrapped bale.

"Is this one of the bales you saw them loading on the DC-3 that night, Specialist Fish?"

"Yes, ma'am. It's one of 'em, all right. That right there is fifty pounds a' smack." Repatch took his knife and cut into the bale. He stuck his finger in the bale and pulled it out. His finger was covered with white dust.

Cathy's cameraman zoomed tight on Repatch's finger, and she said, "Let's get back in that chopper and get out of here."

"I'm right behind you," said Danny Jannick.

Repatch shouldered the bale and they crashed through the woods and exited the treeline. The chopper's blades started turning, *shoop-shoop-shoop-shoop,* and they climbed on board. The chopper picked up and tilted and they were gone over the treetops, headed east into the night.

The court-martial was gaveled to order the next morning at 10 A.M.

"Call your next witness, Captain Morriss," said Colonel Kelly with a nod at the defense table.

"Sir, the defense recalls Specialist Fish."

"Call Specialist Fish."

Repatch appeared in the back door and took the stand.

"You are reminded you are still under oath," Dupuy said.

"Yes, sir," Repatch said dutifully.

"Specialist, yesterday you had evidence you tried to introduce to this court, which was disallowed. Do you recall this evidence?"

"Yes, sir. I had me a pint bottle fulla smack."

"Heroin."

"Yes, sir. Heroin. Same difference."

"And you said you had scooped up the heroin from the site of the grass airstrip where you and Lieutenant Blue witnessed a DC-3 being loaded with bales of heroin. Is that correct?"

"Yes, sir."

"Your Honor . . ." Dupuy was on his feet. "I object, Your Honor. This is old news. We went over this yesterday, and Your Honor disallowed the evidence. I see no reason we should be subjected to this nonsense any further."

"Your Honor, the defense has new evidence to present, if Captain Dupuy will allow us the courtesy of the time in which to present it."

"Go ahead, Captain," said the judge.

"Do you have new evidence today?" Morriss asked.

"Yes, sir," Repatch said. "I got to get it."

He stood up and walked out the back door and returned a moment later with the bale of heroin. An audible stir in the court greeted the sight of Repatch carrying a burlap-wrapped bale the size of a milk crate. Repatch put the bale down in front of his chair and took his seat.

"Your Honor, this is another case of grandstanding," said Dupuy, jumping to his feet. "We don't know where this so-called bale came from. This is a defense trick, Your Honor. I object."

The judge turned to Captain Morriss.

"Captain?" he asked.

"Your Honor, we're not finished. If the court please . . ."

"Go on."

"Specialist Fish, where did you get this . . . this bale?"

"I got it up in Laos in the boonies, sir."

"When?"

"Yesterday afternoon."

"How did this come about?"

"I flew up there and went out in the boonies where that grass strip was, and we found it at the end of the strip in the woods. It fell outta the plane when it was takin' off, sir."

"Do we have to take your word for this, Specialist?"

"No, sir."

"Why not?"

" 'Cause I got a movie of the whole thing!"

"Your Honor! Your Honor! Objection!" Dupuy was on his feet, shouting.

"Your Honor," said Captain Morriss. "The defense has an explanation."

"I hope so," the judge said. "Proceed."

"Your Honor, the witness was accompanied on his helicopter trip into Laos yesterday by a television news crew and a print reporter. Film of the entire trip exists and is available today, along with testimony of all three individuals who accompanied Specialist Fish. They are prepared to testify, and we are prepared to show film of the discovery of this evidence."

The judge removed his glasses and stared balefully at Captain Morriss.

"This was a violation of the order I read on the first day of this court-martial, was it not?"

"Yes, Your Honor, it was. But if it please the court . . ."

"Nothing would please the court more right now than finding you in contempt, which is what I'm going to do . . ."

"Your Honor, under the circumstances, we had no other choice. Filming the acquisition of this evidence was the only way the defense could confirm its validity. Yesterday, the court refused to allow the introduction of the bottle of heroin. This evidence is absolutely essential to the defense if we're to get a fair trial, Your Honor. It goes to the heart of our case. Indeed, without the film showing the acquisition of this evidence, Your Honor, we don't have a case."

"You may not have a career when this is over, Captain," said the judge.

"I realize that fact, Your Honor."

"None of this material has been reported in the press or gone out over the air?"

"No, sir. To that extent, we have adhered to your order."

"Will you continue your objection, counselor?" the judge asked Dupuy.

"My objection stands, Your Honor. This is highly irregular and prejudicial, and smacks of the kind of grandstanding the defense counsel is known for."

"Then we will see the film and hear from the witnesses," said the judge, "and I will reserve my ruling on both the objection and the contempt citation until we have taken this additional testimony. Proceed, Captain."

Morriss gave a signal, and two GIs emerged from the back door and set up a movie screen and a 16mm film projector. Morriss gave another signal and the lights in the Quonset hut were turned off, and one of the GIs switched on the projector. It flickered a couple of times and the image of Cathy Joice appeared on the screen.

"We are in Pleiku, Vietnam," she said, pointing to a sign behind her that read PLEIKU in big letters. "We've stopped at the airstrip here to refuel. We're on our way to Laos with Specialist Fish to look for evidence that a heroin shipment, which he says he and Lieutenant Matthew Blue witnessed, actually took place."

Repatch appeared on the screen. "We got to go," he said.

The camera pulled back, showing the helicopter, which could be heard starting up, its engine beginning the high-pitched whine preceding the rotors turning.

The next image was of Cathy Joice in the chopper aloft. She was screaming into her mike over the roar of the chopper.

"We just crossed over into Laos! We're dropping down to treetop level! Nobody knows what's out there! We don't know if we'll encounter enemy fire!"

The camera panned out the door to show jungle rushing by below.

Then the screen showed the footage from the grass airstrip in the jungle, including the discovery of the bale of heroin. The screen then showed Cathy Joice standing on the tarmac at Pleiku again. It was night, and she was illuminated by a light over a hangar door.

"We're back in Pleiku now," she said. "It is worth noting, for the purposes of the trial as well as for my editors back in Kansas City, that the piece of film you have just seen is seamless. We have used one can of film, and there are no splices. What you have seen was shot in Pleiku, Laos, and back in Pleiku again, which is where I am right now. You have just watched the discovery of a shocking piece of evidence, a fifty-five-pound bale of heroin found in the jungle at the end of a grassy strip in Laos. The pilot and copilot of the helicopter can testify as to where we went today. Gentlemen . . ."

Two young flyboys appeared next to her.

"Did you fly us into Laos today?"

"Yeah," said the pilot.

"It was Laos," said the copilot. "I've got the whole route plotted on our map."

"Thank you," Cathy said.

The flyboys walked away.

"By the time this film is shown, I am certain that tests on the bale will have proven its contents are indeed heroin. But as for me, I need no more proof than what I've already seen today, shocking evidence of apparent complicity of the United States Government in the heroin trade in Southeast Asia."

The screen went blank and the lights came on.

Repatch was still sitting there, waiting.

"Specialist Fish," said Captain Morriss, who had stood up and walked around in front of the defense table.

"Specialist, was that a film of the journey you took yesterday in search of this bale of heroin?"

"Yes, sir. Sure was."

"Your Honor, I would at this time like to introduce into evidence a report from the Criminal Investigation Division lab attesting to the contents of the bale. The report states the contents of the bale are indeed heroin, approximately ninety-two percent strength."

Morriss handed the report to the judge.

The judge looked over at Captain Dupuy.

"Captain, without further testimony I am inclined to admit this report and to admit the burlap bale as evidence."

Dupuy shrugged.

"The prosecution would like its objection noted for the record."

"So noted," said the judge. "Report is marked defense exhibit E."

"Specialist, I have one final question for you," Morriss said. "Lieutenant Blue and you witnessed bales like this one"—he pointed to the bale at Repatch's feet—"being loaded on a DC-3 on the night of October 12. You have testified that it was during the loading of these bales that Corporal Strosher was killed. Is it still your testimony that the man who killed Corporal Strosher was an American?"

"Yes, sir. He was."

"No further questions. Your witness."

Dupuy stood up as though he was planning to ask some questions, but then he sat down.

"The prosecution has nothing further for this witness, Your Honor."

"You are excused," said the judge.

Repatch exited out the back door. The bale of heroin still sat where it was, at the front of the courtroom, now evidence in the court-martial.

"Do you have any further witnesses, Captain Morriss?" the judge asked.

"Sir, the defense calls Mr. Jacob Rousseau to the stand."

"Call Mr. Rousseau," said the judge.

Jake Rousseau strode to the witness chair and was sworn in by Captain Dupuy. He sat down. His hulking figure seemed to fill the front of the court, and the officers on the court leaned forward for a better look.

"Mr. Rousseau, you are the Central Intelligence Agency station chief in Vietnam, are you not?"

"I am Deputy Director of the Agency for International Development," said Rousseau.

"Do you deny that in fact you are CIA Saigon station chief, sir?"

"I have answered your question. I'm Deputy Director of AID."

"Mr. Rousseau, is it United States policy in Vietnam to aid Meo tribesmen in Laos in the harvesting and marketing of their opium crop?"

"Not to my knowledge."

"Are you aware that the Central Intelligence Agency has in fact been involved in the opium and heroin trade in Laos for five years?"

"No, I am not."

"Do you deny CIA involvement in the Laotian opium and heroin trade, sir?"

"AID has nothing to do with Laos. That's all I can testify to."

"Are you aware that Lieutenant Blue . . ." Morriss walked behind his client and placed his hands on the Lieutenant's shoulders. "Are you aware, sir, that Lieutenant Blue and his patrol witnessed a heroin shipment from a makeshift airfield inside Laos?"

"I've heard the allegation. I don't believe it."

"I direct your attention to the burlap bale on the floor beside you, sir. A CID lab test confirms that this fifty-five-pound bale contains pure heroin. The bale was found in the trees at the end of the grass airstrip where Lieutenant Blue witnessed the loading and takeoff of a DC-3 full of bales exactly like this one. Is it still your testimony that you do not believe Lieutenant Blue and his men witnessed the heroin shipment, sir?"

"I don't believe it."

Captain Morriss looked at the witness for a moment, then shook his head slowly.

"Your witness," he said.

Captain Dupuy stood up.

"Mr. Rousseau, can you think of any reason you should have been called here today as a witness?"

"No, sir, I cannot."

"You said you are the Deputy Director of AID. In that position, did you have any knowledge at all of this fantastic scenario the defense has laid out to this court, this nonsense about heroin trafficking and the like?"

"I have no such knowledge."

"Do you know of any other agency of the United States government that might possibly have engaged in such fantastic behavior?"

"No, sir, I do not."

"Thank you, Mr. Rousseau, for your forthright and honest testimony."

"Redirect, Captain Morriss?" the judge asked.

"No, sir."

"You are excused, sir," the judge said.

Rousseau stood up and looked over the courtroom for a moment, his eyes finally finding those of the General. He smiled briefly and left the stand and walked out the back door.

"Captain Morriss, call your next witness."

"Sir, the defense has one final witness who does not appear on the defense list of witnesses. I ask permission of the court to call this witness, despite the fact that his name was not supplied to the prosecution beforehand."

"Does the prosecution have any objection?"

"Sir, the prosecution objects most vehemently to this tactic."

"Captain Morriss, can you supply the court with an explanation for your failure to include this witness on your list?"

"Sir, this witness did not become available to the defense until this morning. I recognize that my request is extraordinary, but this witness is essential to our case, Your Honor."

"This is your final witness, Captain Morriss?"

"Yes, sir, he is."

"I'm going to allow the witness," the judge said.

"Sir, I want the prosecution objection to this witness noted for the record," said Captain Dupuy.

"So noted," said the judge.

"Sir, the defense calls Mr. Ba Tam to the stand."

"Call Mr. Ba Tam," the judge ordered.

The back door opened, and the stooped figure of Ba Tam appeared. He paused at the door and looked around the room. Then he lowered his head and scooted across the floor and stood in front of the witness chair. He was wearing a sharply cut Western-style suit and black shoes. His hair was white and his eyes were sunk deeply within squinty slits. He was bent over, and his shoulders slouched forward like a peasant's. He looked very old and very small on the platform in front of the court and the judge.

"Do you swear to tell the truth, the whole truth, and nothing but the truth, so help you God?" Captain Dupuy asked.

"Yes, sir, I do," Ba Tam said quietly.

"Be seated."

Ba Tam sat down.

"Mr. Tam," Captain Morriss began, "you have sworn to tell the truth, the whole truth, and nothing but the truth, in an American military court of law. Are you aware of the gravity of the oath you have taken?"

"Yes, sir. I am aware." Ba Tam's deeply lined face was impassive and his voice was level and almost accentless.

"Mr. Tam, the oath you have taken is a grave one for two reasons. The first reason is that you are under penalty of perjury if you do not tell the whole truth. If you are found to have lied to this court, you could go to prison for a very long time. That is the way of American justice. Our system demands of you absolute adherence to its judicial rules, and the rule of law has one absolute above all others, and that is the requirement to tell the truth, the whole truth, and nothing but the truth. Do you understand what I have said?"

"Yes, sir, I understand this."

"The second reason your commitment to tell the truth to this court is a grave one is the fact that a young man's life is on the line in this case. He has been charged with desertion in the face of the enemy, and under our system of military law, he can be hanged by the neck until dead if he is found guilty. Therefore, the questions I will ask you must be answered completely truthfully, because your failure to do so may jeopardize the life of this man." Morriss pointed to the Lieutenant.

"I understand this requirement for truth," said Ba Tam.

"I will begin again," said Captain Morriss. He walked around in front of the lectern so that he was only a couple of feet from the witness. He wanted the intimacy of close contact. He wanted the members of the court to watch very, very closely, and to listen even more closely.

"Your name is Ba Tam, and you own a business called the Restaurant Viet-Français on the waterfront in downtown Saigon. Is this correct?"

"Yes, sir, this is part correct," said the witness. "My name is Ba Tam. But I am not owner of Restaurant Viet-Français."

"Who owns the Restaurant Viet-Français, Mr. Tam?"

"People's Revolutionary Government owns Restaurant Viet-Français, sir. I operate restaurant for People's Revolutionary Government, sir."

"Can you tell this court who, in fact, you are, Ba Tam?"

"Yes, sir. I am general of the People's Home Guard for Song Cai Valley, and for Ya Krong Bolah Valley, sir. I am Province Leader for the People's Revolutionary Government. I am VC general, sir."

Dupuy jumped to his feet screaming, "Arrest him! Arrest him! Objection! Arrest him! Objection!" Several members of the court stood up and started to move away, as if they were afraid the witness would pull a pistol from his suit jacket and start shooting up the court. The judge banged his gavel and shouted:

"Order! Order! There will be order in this court!"

Dupuy remained on his feet, a look of stark terror in his eyes, which were staring at the witness. Morriss remained standing. The members of the court who had moved away from their table eased themselves into their chairs and kept their eyes locked on the witness.

Only Mr. Tam had remained calm throughout the ruckus. He was an old man and he had seen his share of mad behavior on the part of his enemies. They had come and gone over the years, and he had simply exchanged one enemy for another while he continued to run the Restaurant Viet-Français on the waterfront. His face was expressionless. He seemed to be listening to an inner voice that assured him that these enemies, too, would go the way of the French and the others. All you had to do was sit there and wait, so he just sat there at the front of the room, waiting, with his hands folded in his lap and his feet dangling in the air, for his legs were too short to reach the floor.

"This is a court of law and as such it is not a battlefield and the rules observed here are not the rules of engagement, they are the rules of the United States Code of Military Justice. If anyone has any doubts that I mean what I say, they will leave the court immediately."

He waited for a moment, then he gaveled the court to order.

"Proceed, counselor," he instructed Captain Morriss.

"Thank you, sir," said Morriss. He regained his position close to the witness and said:

"Mr. Tam, you have made a serious admission to this American court of law. You have told this court that you are a Vietcong general and that you are a Province Commissar in the Vietcong government in exile. Judging by the behavior in this room when you admitted your true identity, it is obvious that you have put yourself in great jeopardy. You must have a very good reason for having done so. Will you please tell the court what that reason is?"

"Sir, what is said about opium trade in Laos true." He pointed to the bale of heroin.

"You have information about opium and heroin shipments being made from Laos?"

"Yes, sir. My province on border with Laos. People's Revolutionary Guard tries many years to stop opium trade."

"So you are saying that you have something of a selfish motive for coming forth with your admission, Mr. Tam, are you not?"

"Yes, is in interest of my nation, the nation of Vietnam." Mr. Tam looked around the room with steely gray eyes, then he turned his gaze on Captain Morriss.

"Go on, sir."

"Yes, sir. Every year, in October, American high command has made operation similar to Operation Iron Fist One. Last year, 1968, was Force Field. In 1967, operation was Short Strike. In 1966, Body

Blow. In 1965, operation was Bold Bayonet. Each year at same time, same operation. This is why I come here to this court: to tell truth of Operation Iron Fist One. This man, Lieutenant Blue, he discovers truth of the operation, but he does not know that he knows this truth. I am here to tell truth, Captain. You have asked me for truth, and I will tell truth."

"We are listening," said Captain Morriss, and it was true. The courtroom was rapt. Not an eye wavered from the face of the slight gray man seated in front of them. Not a single ear was inattentive to the sound of his voice, the calm tones of learning and academia brought home to the reality of a Quonset hut outside Saigon.

"American Colonel Testor makes Iron Fist operation to stop People's Home Guard from making war against opium traders. This American colonel has made such operations before, sir. Many tons of opium, much heroin, leave Laos every year at this time. This American Lieutenant sees American airplane being loaded with opium and heroin. Men he sees are American mercenaries, work for American Central Intelligence Agency. Because he sees this, American Colonel Testor demands Lieutenant Blue make no report about death of his soldier. Lieutenant Blue see something he should not see. Make report he should not make. Lieutenant Blue has much courage to make report. This is reason for trial, sir. Not for desertion."

"Mr. Tam, you seem to have a sophisticated understanding of these proceedings, and of the matters about which you are testifying. Can you tell this court why this is so, and why this court should believe you?"

"Yes, sir. I am general of People's Army in Song Cai Valley, sir. This is my job, to know American movements, to know American strategy. My soldiers fight soldiers of American Colonel Testor many months. We know purpose of Operation Iron Fist. We know Americans support opium trade in Laos. We know why Meo peoples make war against us. American government makes war against people of Vietnam, sir. People of Vietnam must defend against war. This is why I come today. American Colonel Testor must not succeed to protect opium traders."

"So despite the fact that you are an avowed enemy of the

421

American Army, you are asking us to believe you because of your motive in coming forward, because you have a vested interest in stopping the opium trade in Laos."

"Yes, sir."

"You are a VC general?"

"Yes, sir."

"And you expect this court to believe a VC general?"

"Yes sir. Sir, there is much I admire about United States of America. I graduated in United States from Princeton University. My family sent me to United States to learn great principles of democracy. I admire system of American education. American courts of justice I admire. American Constitution and Bill of Rights, yes. American wars against movements of national independence, no. I must fight against American support of criminal opium trade. I am here as man educated by America. I proudly say my belief in innocence of Lieutenant Blue, my belief in rightness of my cause, cause of people of Vietnam."

Captain Morriss stood before Mr. Tam for a long moment, then turned and walked behind the defense table and stood next to his client and said:

"Thank you for your testimony, Mr. Tam. I have no further questions for you. Your Honor, the defense rests its case."

Colonel Kelly took a moment to gather himself, then he turned to Captain Dupuy.

"Does the prosecution have any questions for this witness?"

"Yes, sir," said Captain Dupuy. He walked to the lectern and faced Mr. Tam.

"So you come into this court and you admit that you're a VC general and a VC commissar, and you tell us this fantastic story about opium in Laos and American involvement in the opium trade, and you expect us to believe a goddamn VC general?"

"Yes, sir," said Mr. Tam.

"Why should this court believe you, a VC general?" Dupuy asked sarcastically.

"Sir, you should believe because I must know these things I say because my soldiers fight against Operation Iron Fist One. Vietnam *my* country, sir. You invade *my* country. I am at war with American

Colonel Testor because these reasons. You should believe me because I am your enemy, sir."

Dupuy leaned over, and Major Thompson whispered something to him. Then he stood up with a smile on his face.

"Mr. Tam, it has come to my attention that you have faced charges of black marketeering in the past. Is this true?"

"Yes, sir. Is true."

"So not only are you a VC general and a VC commissar, you are a black marketeer. What do you have to say for yourself now, Mr. Tam?"

"Sir, black market is economy of war. When you end war, you end black market. Until war ends, I will proudly continue in black market. It is way of war, sir, and I am warrior."

Dupuy sat down. Nothing he said could penetrate the armor of pride on the face of Mr. Ba Tam.

"Do you have any further questions, Mr. Dupuy?" the judge asked.

"No, sir," Dupuy said.

"You are excused," said the judge to Mr. Tam.

Ba Tam strode to the first row and took the seat next to the Sergeant Major.

The judge shuffled papers for a moment, then said, "Captain Dupuy, does the prosecution have any closing statement?"

"Yes, sir," said Captain Dupuy. He carried a sheaf of papers to the lectern and addressed the court.

"The issue before you today, gentlemen, is a simple one. Did this man, Lieutenant Blue, desert his post in the face of the enemy when he refused the order for a fire mission? You have heard succinct testimony that he did. You have heard from his company commander on this question. Captain Gardner testified that he gave the order and Lieutenant Blue refused it. You have heard from his battalion commander. Lieutenant Colonel Halleck testified that he, too, ordered the fire mission, and Lieutenant Blue refused his order. The defense has tried and failed to muddy these waters, gentlemen. The testimony of these witnesses has gone unrefuted. This man was given two direct orders for fire missions, and he refused both orders. He removed himself and his mortars from the field of battle in the face of an attack on his Battalion. When he refused two orders to place fire on the enemy, he deserted his post in the face of that enemy. That is the allegation, that is the truth. The fantastic story the defense has propagated about opium and heroin in Laos has nothing to do with this case, gentlemen. The incredible testimony given by the last defense witness, this self-described Vietcong General Tam, has nothing to do with this case. This so-called evidence"—Dupuy pointed to the burlap bale of heroin—"has nothing to do with this case. There is only one question you have to answer in order to bring a guilty verdict in this case. Did Lieutenant Blue refuse two direct orders to fire a mission with his four-point-two-inch mortars? The answer is yes. He refused that order. He is guilty of desertion in the face of the enemy, gentlemen. The prosecution asks you to ignore the smokescreen the defense has thrown up and return a verdict of guilty against the defendant."

Dupuy gathered his papers and sat down.

"Does the defense have a closing statement?" the judge asked.

"Yes, sir," said Morriss. He walked to the front of the court and leaned against the defense table.

"This is not a simple case, gentlemen, as the prosecution said in its closing statement. This case is very complicated. It is complicated in its facts, and it is complicated further by the motive behind the case."

Morriss took a breath and paced the floor in front of the jury.

"The defense has presented this one piece of evidence: Lieutenant Blue indeed refused the order to fire his mortars, because had he done so, he would have been calling in fire on his own position. We presented evidence that there was confusion involving the maps used to plot the position of Lieutenant Blue's patrol, and the position against which the fire mission was to be fired. Lieutenant Blue was using map 24-Lima. Lieutenant Colonel Halleck was using map 22-Lima. This confusion was not Lieutenant Blue's fault. The fire mission he was called for from the weapons platoon would have wiped out Lieutenant Blue's patrol. Seven men would have died. The evidence that this was true is clear. When Colonel Testor, the brigade commander, called for one-five-five fire on the same position, the shells landed right where Lieutenant Blue's patrol had been. You heard testimony to this effect from a member of Lieutenant Blue's patrol. Now, gentleman. One of two things is true. Either that fire mission was ordered on Lieutenant Blue's position by mistake, or it was ordered on purpose. Either way, the evidence we have presented shows Lieutenant Blue was within his rights in refusing the order. He knew that firing the mission that Lieutenant Colonel Halleck called for would have killed himself and his men. And he knew something else, something truly shocking. Colonel James Franklin Testor had a motive for ordering that fire mission. He had a motive for wanting this lieutenant dead. Lieutenant Blue had written an after-action report that very day describing the death of one of his men, Corporal Strosher, by friendly fire. Lieutenant Blue had stumbled on an aircraft being loaded in the jungle. We have produced one of the bales that was loaded on the aircraft. It contains heroin. We have produced testimony from Specialist Fish, a member of the patrol, describing the aircraft and the heroin. We have produced a CID report proving that the bale contains heroin. We have produced Lieutenant Blue's after-action report exposing in detail the shipment by night of these bales from the Laotian jungle. We took the extraordinary step of producing a witness, Ba Tam, an enemy general, who described the real reason behind Operation Iron Fist One. Taken together, gentlemen, this evidence and testimony say one thing only: the wrong man is on trial here. Lieutenant Blue refused an order, yes. An *illegal* order. He did not desert the field of battle in the face of the enemy, gentlemen, unless you consider that his real enemy that night was his own brigade commander, Colonel James Franklin Testor, the man who ordered Operation Iron Fist One. No other commander in Vietnam ordered Iron Fist One. You heard each of their testimonies. Thus, under these circumstances, Lieutenant Blue is guilty of only one thing, gentlemen, and that is protecting his own men from the fire mission ordered by Colonel Testor. When Colonel Testor first ordered the fire mission on Lieutenant Blue's position, Lieutenant Blue refused both orders to fire the mission. When Lieutenant Blue refused to place fire on his own position, Colonel Testor called for one-five-five fire on Lieutenant Blue's position. Only the warning of Captain Gardner saved those men's lives. Lieutenant Blue is innocent, gentlemen. The prosecution must prove its case beyond a reasonable doubt, and there are so many reasonable doubts in this case . . . in fact, gentlemen, that is all we've heard in this courtroom. One reasonable doubt after another regarding the facts of the prosecution's case, one reasonable doubt after another. Lieutenant Blue filed his after-action report about Corporal Strosher and they tried to silence Lieutenant Blue forever with his own mortars, and when that didn't work, they tried to silence him forever with one-five-five rounds, and when that didn't work, they tried to silence him forever by bringing these charges against him, by discrediting him as an officer and as a man, and by charging him with an offense punishable by death. Well, gentlemen, it didn't work. He survived rifle fire from American heroin traders. He survived artillery fire from his own brigade commander. You have listened to the evidence, gentlemen. Now listen to your conscience and reject these bogus charges and return to this man his dignity and find him innocent. Thank you."

Morriss returned to the defense table and sat down.

The Lieutenant whispered, "Thanks, Terry. Jesus. Thanks."

"I will now instruct the jury," the judge said. He turned to the members of the court.

"Gentlemen, you are instructed to consider the evidence and only the evidence as you make your decision as to the guilt or innocence of the accused. You may not allow prejudice of any kind to invade the jury room. You will be reminded at all times that the accused is innocent until proven guilty by the prosecution beyond a shadow of a doubt. The accused is not required to prove anything. The burden of proof has been on the shoulders of the prosecution, and there it shall remain as you make your deliberations. Matters of law will be the province of this court, and if you have questions regarding the legalities of the actions of the accused or of anyone involved in the testimony in this case, you will direct your questions to me, to the military judge, and you will follow my rulings. Have I made myself clear?"

Seven heads nodded their assent.

"You may retire to reach your verdict."

"All rise!" squeaked the MP.

The members of the court filed out the back door. The Lieutenant and Captain Morriss and the Colonel and the General and the Sergeant Major and Mr. Tam remained seated. No one spoke.

The jury came in at 6 P.M.

"All rise," said the MP in a tired, high-pitched voice.

The members of the court filed in, followed by Colonel Kelly.

"Be seated, please," he said.

"Sir, have you reached a verdict?" the judge asked the jury foreman.

"We have, sir."

"Captain Morriss, will you and the defendant please stand?" the judge instructed.

The Lieutenant and the Captain stood, and behind him the Lieutenant could hear the scrape of chairs. He turned around. The Colonel and the General and the Sergeant Major and Ba Tam were standing, and behind them, Repatch stood stiffly at attention in his new khakis, eyes straight to the front. The judge considered this minor departure from normal courtroom procedure and decided against gaveling it down.

"Read your verdict."

"Sir, the verdict of this court, by secret ballot, all seven members voting, to both charge and specification, is not guilty."

The Lieutenant turned to Captain Morriss and shook his hand violently. Captain Morriss's face reddened and he collapsed on his chair.

First the Colonel, then the General shook the Lieutenant's hand and threw their arms around him. The Sergeant Major waited his turn, and when it came, he saluted the Lieutenant. Repatch hung back, and when he caught the Lieutenant's eye he flashed the thumbs-up sign, grinning his gap-toothed grin. Ba Tam bowed at the waist and said:

"Thank you, sir. The people of Vietnam thank you."

Captain Dupuy walked over and shook hands with Captain Morriss.

"Harvard beats Tulane. Is that tomorrow's headline?"

"Right," said Morriss. "If only."

The Lieutenant led the way out the door of the Quonset hut into the dusty tan wasteland of the Tan Son Nhut MACV complex. A thousand Vietnamese civilians had gathered in front of the Quonset hut, and with one voice they began shouting his name:

"Looo-ten-ut Bloo . . . Looo-ten-ut Bloo . . . Looo-ten-ut Bloo . . ."

"What . . . what's going on?" the Lieutenant asked.

He looked at the mass of Vietnamese shouting his name. The Quonset huts and warehouses and Butler buildings and motor pools were washed in the soft red glow of the tropical sunset. He didn't know what to think. Just then, he felt someone grab his elbow. He turned to find Captain Morriss.

They pushed through the crowd of Vietnamese to the edge of the sidewalk. A staff car pulled up, doors open, waiting. A jeep followed behind, driven by a Spec-4. The Sergeant Major stood next to the driver, his hand on the jeep windshield, whispering. Then the Spec-4 stepped out of the jeep and Repatch climbed in behind the wheel.

The Lieutenant stood at the curb, awash in the sound of his own name, then he turned to his grandfather.

"Grandpa, what's going to happen to Ba Tam?"

The General pointed to the slight, stooped figure of Ba Tam. He had elbowed his way past the General, past the staff car, and with head bent forward, he walked into the chanting mass of Vietnamese.

"I don't think you have to worry about that fine old gentleman, boy," said the General.

"Where is he going, Dad?" the Lieutenant asked his father, who had moved to the other side of him.

"Mr. Tam is going home, son. That's where he's going. Mr. Tam is going home to Vietnam."

"Mr. Tam, he'll be all right?"

His father nodded.

"Don't you worry about Ba Tam, my boy," said the General. "I have a strong suspicion he arranged this demonstration . . . for you and for himself. Take a look."

The Lieutenant stepped up on the staff car's bumper and looked at the crowd before him, stretching across the road into a field leading to one of the runways. Ba Tam was nowhere to be seen. The crowd had absorbed him. He was gone.

"What is going to happen now, Dad?"

"Everybody will go back to the job of trying to win this goddamn war in Vietnam. But you know what is clear to me now, after everything that has come out in your case?" He took a deep breath and looked at his son and a tear crept into the corner of his eye.

"Nobody is going to win this war, my boy. I think that's just the way God meant it to be. No winners. Not this time. Maybe never again."

He wrapped one arm around his son and they pushed their way through the crowd and climbed in the staff car and drove through the dusty warehouses and Quonset huts and Butler buildings of the Tan Son Nhut MACV complex, heading toward Saigon.

Firebase Zulu-Foxtrot
Epilogue

Cathy Joice took a deep breath and looked straight into the lens. She was dressed in blue slacks and an old chambray shirt with the sleeves rolled up to her elbows. She held the mike like a torch, and it seemed to infect her eyes, giving them an eerie, threatening look. The world outside was bright and adoring, but behind her eyes loomed a storm that cast a shadow over every word she spoke.

"This is where it happened," she began, speaking softly, slowly, coming on to the camera like a professional, which was what she was.

"This is the place where Americans fired their weapons purposely at other Americans, leaving one man dead in the tall grass right here."

She pointed to a spot in the grass at her feet, and the camera followed her hand.

"His name was Lester Strosher, and he was a corporal in the

United States Army. His enlistment papers say he was eighteen. The last nine months were his first time away from his home in Techute, Alabama. The men in his platoon teased him for his youth. He wasn't eighteen. He was sixteen. He had lied about his age to get into the United States Army, to come to this place so far away from his home and die for his country."

She took a breath and half-turned to her left.

"Over there was the DC-3, the World War II–vintage plane that was loading the heroin."

She half-turned to her right and pointed to the jungle and the camera followed her finger.

"And over here, in the woodline, were Lieutenant Blue and his men, seven young American soldiers outside the wire of their platoon NDP, their night defensive perimeter, out on a patrol ordered by their battalion and brigade commanders."

When the camera panned back to Cathy Joice, she was standing next to a young man in civilian clothes. He wore old Levi's and a plaid shirt, and dark glasses made him look older than he was.

"This is Lieutenant Matthew Nelson Blue the fourth," she said. "He is the Lieutenant who commanded that patrol. Corporal Strosher was his man. He died at this Lieutenant's feet. Lieutenant Blue, can you tell us, in your own words, what happened that night? How did Corporal Strosher get killed by another American firing at him from only one hundred feet away?"

"Strosher got hit standing up, right here," said the Lieutenant. He took a step to his left and turned to face the grassy landing strip where, only a few weeks before, he and Strosher and the rest of his men had watched the DC-3 full of heroin lift off into the black sky, heading God knows where.

"He followed me from the treeline, and he stood right there and he died the way so many men have died in this war. He died bravely . . . and . . . and . . . he died for the same reason so many guys like him died before him and after . . ."

He looked away, running his hands through his short hair, then he looked back at the ground where Strosher had lain.

"I don't know whether I should be saying this on television. I mean, his folks might see this. I wrote them about Strosher and the way he died, but I didn't tell them everything."

"Go ahead. Say it. I'm sure they know he died with courage."

"Yeah, they know that much," said the Lieutenant. He paused to regain his composure.

"We came up on this plane, and ten, maybe a dozen American guys were loading the plane with something. We didn't know what it was. We didn't know what they were doing here. So I took my binoculars and satisfied myself that they were in fact Americans. Then I stepped from the woodline, and my men followed me, and I called out to them."

"Then what happened?"

"One of the American guys wearing jeans and a camouflage T-shirt shot him through the stomach, and Strosher fell right here."

The camera panned from the Lieutenant's face to the grass at his feet.

The camera panned back to Cathy Joice. She was standing with three men now: the Lieutenant, the Colonel, and the General.

"We have three generations of Blues here today," Cathy Joice said, facing the camera. "General Blue is a veteran of World War II, having commanded a division, a corps, and an army in North Africa, Italy, and the Battle of the Bulge. Colonel Blue is a veteran of Korea, having commanded both a platoon and a company in that conflict. He also served in Vietnam, commanding a battalion in the Delta. Lieutenant Blue was weapons platoon leader for the Second of the 22nd Infantry, in the 25th Infantry Division."

She turned to the three men.

"A lot of people back home are going to wonder how this incident in the jungles of Laos—how the court-martial of Lieutenant Blue— has changed things between you. You represent three generations of this nation's military history. Among you, you have fought in three wars. Did you ever think it would come to this?"

The General nodded to his son, the Colonel.

The Colonel cleared his throat.

"In the Army I grew up in, you were expected to do what you were told to do. But things are different now."

"What is different, Colonel Blue?"

"This war has changed things," said the Colonel. "I never saw anything like this happen in Korea. It used to be, when a man made a mistake, he admitted it and he moved on. But not in this

Army. Not today. They ordered my son to destroy his after-action report about the killing of Corporal Strosher. When he refused, they ordered him out on a night patrol, and they ordered him to call in fire on his own position. There was no reason for the mortar fire they ordered. No one in the battalion perimeter was in jeopardy that night. The fire that the Battalion was receiving was harassing fire from small arms and a 60-mm mortar. No one in that Battalion got killed. No one got wounded. Still, when they ordered my son to fire his mortars and he saw that the fire mission would have wiped out his own patrol and he refused the order, they court-martialed him for desertion in the face of the enemy. It is incredible to me. A part of me still doesn't believe that it could happen."

"And the other part of you?" Cathy Joice asked.

"The other part of me knows differently. Something happened out here that no one wanted to see come to light, and my son saw it, and he suffered for having seen it. The verdict of that court-martial confirms this. It's a sad day. A damn sad day for our Army, and it's a damn sad day for our country and what we're supposed to be doing here."

"General Blue, what is your reaction to what has happened?"

"I feel the same way my son feels. It's a damn sad day for this Army and this country. If this nation of ours has to become involved in the illicit traffic in narcotics in order to fight this war, then we're fighting on the wrong goddamned side. If they're sending our boys out on operations like Iron Fist One to protect this narcotics trade, then we don't deserve to win this war. This war is destroying our credibility in the world, and it's destroying our Army. What happened in this field of grass was criminal. This war is being fought as a criminal enterprise. And when my grandson was court-martialed, the truth about it came out. We have seen the truth told in the courtroom, but I wonder if we've learned enough to save ourselves, to end this war before it ends us."

"Lieutenant Blue, what is your reaction to what your father and your grandfather have said?"

The camera found the Lieutenant's face. He was still looking at the ground.

"One of our guys killed another one of our guys right here," said the Lieutenant. "Nothing will change that. Not ending the war. Nothing. Strosher died for no good reason at all."

He looked up at Cathy Joice, and the sadness on his face was visible even behind the dark glasses.

"Ever since I was a little boy, I wanted to be an officer in the Army like my father and my grandfather. When I was growing up, my father and my grandfather were who I wanted to be. Their friends were my ideals. I wanted to be just like them."

"And now?"

"Now I don't know if it's possible anymore. After what happened . . ." His voice trailed off, and he looked down at the ground.

"After what happened here, I just don't know. I mean, I stood up and called out to them and they turned and shot Strosher dead, right at my feet. Who would have thought? Americans smuggling drugs to fight this war? Americans killing other Americans? Jesus. They just killed him, then they tried to cover it up. It's too much."

He shuffled his feet in the grass and looked away and took a few steps and then spoke again, quietly, off camera.

"He's dead. Strosher's dead for no good reason at all. That's what's happened to the Army. And that's all I know. Every day they send guys out here. Every day, guys are dying out here. And it should never happen again."

Cathy Joice turned to her cameraman and said, "Cut." He dropped the 16mm camera to his side. She watched as Lieutenant Blue and Colonel Blue and General Blue walked together across the grassy clearing in Laos, heading toward the woodline where the Lieutenant had hidden with his men that night.

"What's going to happen now, Dad?" the Lieutenant asked.

"I don't know, son. I just don't know." He wrapped his arm around his son's shoulders and hugged him to his side as they walked.

"I did the right thing, didn't I? I mean, what else could I have done?" The Lieutenant stopped and looked at his father and his grandfather imploringly.

"You did the right thing, son," said the Colonel.

"You're goddamned right you did the right thing, boy," said the

General. "And you don't need the verdict of that goddamned court-martial to certify your actions as honorable."

"Then why did it have to turn out this way? Why did Strosher have to die? Why did they have to court-martial me? Why, Dad? Why?"

His father stopped walking and turned to look across the grassy strip of Laotian wilderness. Then he turned and looked at his son and his father.

"Some men might say, and you might hear, that what happened in this field was the fortunes of war, that in a war zone the rules are different, that men behave differently in combat from the way they do in life. But that's wrong. The rules are the same. A man's a man, no matter where he is. A soldier's a soldier, in peacetime or in war. You can't forget that, son. We've forgotten that here in Vietnam. That's why we've lost this war. We've told so many lies for so many years, to ourselves and to each other, that it took a general from the enemy to march into the room in order for the court-martial to hear the truth."

The Colonel paused for a moment, then he turned to his father and said, "How about you, Dad? What do you think?"

The General spat in the dirt at his feet and squinted into the distance, into the sun. Then he looked at the Colonel and the Lieutenant.

"What I think is, I'm pretty goddamned lucky to have the son and the grandson I have. Pretty damn lucky, and just proud as hell. A man couldn't ask for better troops than those I see standing here in this field right now. You wonder what's going to happen? Well, you don't have a worry in the world, boy. You stood up for what you knew was right. You're a Blue, goddammit. And you're a soldier. That's all you'll ever need."

Date Due

OCT 4 1989			
NOV 27 1989			
MAR 5 1990			
FEB 23 1994			